www.MinotaurBooks.com

The premier website
for the best in crime fiction.

Log on and learn more about:

The Labyrinth: Sign up for this monthly news-
letter and get your crime fiction fix. Commentary, author
Q&A, hot new titles, and giveaways.

MomentsInCrime: It's no mystery what our
authors are thinking. Each week, a new author blogs about
their upcoming projects, special events, and more. Log on
today to talk to your favorite authors.

www.MomentsInCrime.com

GetCozy: The ultimate cozy connection. Find your
favorite cozy mystery, grab a reading group guide, sign
up for monthly giveaways, and more.

www.GetCozyOnline.com

MINOTAUR
BOOKS

**Critical acclaim for James D. Doss
and his Charlie Moon mysteries**

SNAKE DREAMS

"Outstanding… The narrator clearly is having fun as he unveils his tale, liberally laced with Native American lore, character idiosyncrasies, comedic asides, and a plot that weaves and twists like a highway in the Rockies."

—*Library Journal* (starred review)

"*Snake Dreams* is the thirteenth novel in this series, and since it's a very good one—funny, smart, and totally different—it's a great place for readers to discover Moon."

—Toronto *Globe and Mail*

THREE SISTERS

"One of his best yet!" —*Booklist*

"Wild, authentic…and highly satisfying."

—*Detroit Free Press*

"A finely cut gem." —*Publishers Weekly* (starred review)

"James D. Doss' novels about Charlie Moon…feel as if the author is sitting around a campfire, spinning a tall tale that engulfs a circle of listeners…Doss' tale is evocative of the area and of Indian lore, and his chatty, down-home style shines in *Three Sisters*." —*Florida Sun-Sentinel*

"Doss' trademark humor keeps Charlie and Scott wise-cracking as the plot spins smartly along to an unpredictable ending…Moon mysteries still charm us with Western voices and ways." —*Rocky Mountain News*

MORE…

STONE BUTTERFLY

"The Moon series deftly blends traditional mystery elements with Native American mythology—a surefire read-alike for Hillerman fans."
—Booklist

"Droll, crafty, upper-echelon reading."
—Kirkus Reviews (starred review)

"Style, pathos, enthusiasm, and humor to spare."
—Mystery Scene

"A clever plot...will keep readers turning the pages."
—Publishers Weekly

SHADOW MAN

"Doss likes to toss a little Native American spiritualism and a lot of local color into his mysteries. Fans of the series will be well pleased."
—Booklist

"Fans of Daisy Perika, the 80-something shaman who brings much of the charm and supernatural thrill to James D. Doss' mystery series, should like *Shadow Man*...nice reading."
—Rocky Mountain News

THE WITCH'S TONGUE

"With all the skill and timing of a master magician, Doss unfolds a meticulous plot laced with a delicious sense of humor and set against a vivid southern Colorado."
—Publishers Weekly

"Doss' ear for Western voices is remarkable, his tone whimsical.... If you don't have time for the seven-hour drive from Denver to Pagosa, try *Witch's Tongue* for a taste of southern Colorado."

—Rocky Mountain News

"A classy bit of storytelling that combines myth, dreams, and plot complications so wily they'll rattle your synapses and tweak your sense of humor." —*Kirkus Reviews*

DEAD SOUL
"Hillerman gets the most press, but Doss mixes an equally potent brew of crime and Native American spirituality."
—*Booklist*

"Lyrical and he gets the sardonic, macho patter between men down cold. The finale is heartfelt and unexpected, and a final confrontation stuns with its violent and confessional precision." —*Providence Journal-Bulletin*

THE SHAMAN LAUGHS
"Harrowing...suspenseful."
—*The New York Times Book Review*

"A mystery that combines the ancient and the modern, the sacred and the profane, with grace and suspense."
—*Publishers Weekly*

THE SHAMAN SINGS
"Stunning." —*Publishers Weekly* (Starred Review; named Best Book of the Year)

"Magical and tantalizing."
—*The New York Times Book Review*

"Gripping...Doss successfully blends the cutting edge of modern physics with centuries-old mysticism."

—*Rocky Mountain News*

ALSO BY JAMES D. DOSS

The Widow's Revenge

JAMES D. DOSS

St. Martin's Paperbacks

This is a work of fiction. All of the characters, organizations, and events portrayed in this novel are either products of the author's imagination or are used fictitiously.

THE WIDOW'S REVENGE

Copyright © 2009 by James D. Doss.
Excerpt from *A Dead Man's Tale* copyright © 2010 by James D. Doss.

Cover photo of redrock landscape © Pete Turner at Getty Images.
Cover photo of porch © Veer Images. Cover design and illustration by Danielle Fiorella.

For information address St. Martin's Press, 175 Fifth Avenue, New York, NY 10010.

Library of Congress Catalog Card Number: 2009016660

ISBN: 978-0-312-53247-5

Printed in the United States of America

Minotaur hardcover edition / November 2009
St. Martin's Paperbacks edition / November 2010

St. Martin's Paperbacks are published by St. Martin's Press, 175 Fifth Avenue, New York, NY 10010.

10 9 8 7 6 5 4 3 2 1

For
Bob Cady—Los Alamos, New Mexico
Don and Margaret Hagerman—Highlands Ranch, Colorado
and
George and Mary Tubb—Tyler, Texas

CHAPTER ONE

LA PLATA COUNTY, COLORADO

The Widow Montoya's Farm

Suspended high in the southern sky, the silvery satellite pulls a diaphanous cloud veil over her naked, pockmarked face. Is this a matter of modesty—does the pale lady prefer not to be seen? Or might it be the other way around—is there something on the widow's property that White Shell Woman prefers *not to see*?

THE SLEEPER

As a youth, Loyola sought adventure, wealth, and pleasure. In her wiser, twilight years, she treasures peace above all earthly delights; a good night's rest is a gift beyond price and the soothing lullaby of rippling waters a powerful soporific. This is one of the reasons the widow has clung to her isolated farm, which is bordered by Ignacio Creek.

The other is that the stubborn old soul is determined to die in the house where she entered the world screaming bloody murder.

Only a few moaning groans and irregular heartbeats ago, when Mrs. Montoya settled her brittle bones and creaky joints into the brass four-poster and pulled a quilt over her old gray head, the widow believed herself to be alone in her isolated home. And she was, if beady-eyed mice, clickety-critching crickets, dozing blackflies, venomous red wasps, bulbous black widow spiders, and other pestilential residents were not included in the census.

Which was why, when she was awakened suddenly from a deep and blessedly dreamless sleep, the elderly woman was startled to hear the sound of voices. *Oh my goodness, somebody's broke into my house!* Sitting up in bed, she realized that this was not so. But outside, somewhere beyond the restful hush of the rushing waters, she could detect low murmurings. Malicious mutterings. But were these unsettling articulations actually *voices*? The lady cocked her ear.

It's them damned witches again—they've come back!

As she had on previous occasions, Loyola strained vainly to make out the words.

Those jibber-jabbering brujos *sound like they're under the water.*

The weary woman knew she wouldn't get another minute of sleep. *I wish my grandson was here; I'd send Wallace out to tell his nasty friends to be quiet.* But the great oaf had been gone for . . . how long—only a day or two? Or had it been a week? Loyola could not remember. Not that Wallace's unexplained absence surprised his grandmother. Her long and mostly unhappy experience with members of the other gender had led her to some firm conclusions.

Whenever you need a man, he'll be somewhere else.

Where? *Either with some of his idiot men friends in a stinking saloon—or with some slut of a woman.*

And when the rascal is at home, he'll lay around watching TV, expecting a good woman to fix his meals, mend and wash his filthy clothes, and take care of him like he was a snotty-nosed five-year-old.

Even so . . .

The lonely woman sighed. Tears filled her eyes.

It would be nice to have a man around the house. A man

who has a gun and knows how to use it. It occurred to her to call the police.

A pair of salty drops rolled down her leathery cheeks.

A lot of good that'd do. After all the times I've had them out here for one strange thing and another they couldn't find any trace of, they figure me for an old crank. Cops ain't worth the dirt under their fingernails.

Loyola recalled the single exception. *Charlie Moon came out every time I called, and he never made sport of me when I told him about that big, hairy monster that looked like an ape or that thirty-foot-long purple snake with black whiskers and horns like a billy goat.* Sadly, Daisy Perika's nephew had quit his job with the Southern Ute police and moved up north years ago to a big cattle ranch. *And I ain't laid eyes on him since.* But wasn't that always the way with people: the good ones go away, the no-accounts are always underfoot.

Pushing away the hand-stitched quilt, she grunted her way out of bed. *Like always, I'll just have to take care of things myself.*

Loyola stepped into a pair of tattered house slippers and shuffled over to the closet, where she selected a pea-green government-issue woolen overcoat that her late husband had brought back from the war in Europe. Pulling it on, she made up her mind. *Tonight, I'm going to go find out where they are and tell them either be quiet or I'll get the pistol out of the closet and shoot the lot of 'em!*

A reckless old soul. But courageous. Also dangerous.

By the time she opened the back-porch door, the voices had fallen silent. This was, one would imagine, fortunate. But for whom? Loyola Montoya—or those folk whose confounded mutters and murmurs had disturbed her slumbers?

It is too early to say.

But after retiring to her parlor rocking chair, the elderly lady intended to stay wide awake until that cold, gray hour that would precede a wan, yellowish dawn.

During that interval, she dozed intermittently. And fitfully.

In Loyola's fretful dreams, malevolent witches peered through her windows.

Turned knobs on her locked doors.

Whispered obscene curses.

In her dreams.

If dreams they were.

CHAPTER TWO

GRANITE CREEK, COLORADO

As Loyola dozes in her rocker, another sleeper is about to experience some difficulty. The character of immediate interest is Scott Parris, who happens to be a sworn officer of the law—but not one of those policemen Loyola Montoya has called for help. Parris and Loyola have, in point of fact, never met. When the harried old lady has a problem, she generally calls the Ignacio town cops or the Southern Ute tribal police. This is the proper thing to do, because Mrs. Montoya lives in a jurisdiction that is quite some distance to the south of Granite Creek, in which fair city Mr. Parris is chief of police, for all the good that does him, which isn't that much on his best day, what with dealing with a quarter-wit DA (Bill "Pug" Bullet), a police force that would rate a tad better than run-of-the-mill were it not for a couple of cops (Eddie "Rocks" Knox and E. C. "Piggy" Slocum) who cause the boss no end of heartburn. Not that Scott Parris's life is all bad.

He has the singular good fortune to have Charlie Moon for a friend, and the Southern Ute tribal investigator owns the Columbine Ranch, which is semifamous for its purebred Hereford stock and (of more interest to Parris) features maybe the finest alpine lake in the whole state—and Lake Jesse is unsurpassed for trout fishing. Also on the plus side is Parris's current sweetheart (Willow Skye), who is a little more than half his age and endowed with a staggering IQ. Regarding his main squeeze, Willow is kind to animals, perpetually cheerful, also quite an eyeful from her spun-honey curls to those dainty little toes with rose-painted nails. But do not leap to conclusions. Though some members of their tribe might deny the following assertion: no woman is perfect; this young lady's single shortcoming is a serious if not fatal flaw—Dr. Willow Skye (PhD in abnormal psychology) is determined to *improve* her boyfriend. Not that Mr. Parris does not have acres of room for upgrading and then some, but he is happy just the way he is. But enough about couples and other plurals. Let us return to the subject of sleep.

Scott Parris has had a long and tiring day.

After a healthy belch relieves the pressure of his bedtime snack, the widower turns off the TV, stomps off to the darkened bedroom, switches the window air conditioner on, slips between navy-blue sheets, and drifts off to sleep.

And to dream. All night.

About what? Oh, this and that.

Mostly subjects of no great interest, so we shall skip over the preliminaries and get right to the *main event*, which occurred just before a blushing sun peeped over the mountains to see whether yesterday's world was still here. The middle-aged cop's dream was to be the first installment in a series of—

No.

Mr. Parris was *not* to be afflicted by a series of those annoying recurrent dreams one so often hears about, where the unfortunate sleeper is afflicted over and over with the same tedious night-vision, such as when he is obliged against all common sense to trudge down a long, dark corridor—always getting closer to the closed door, but never quite arriving to discover what nameless horror lurks behind it, ready to *pounce*.

No doubt because he had a certain gift for originality and was an enthusiastic viewer of television, Scott Parris was about to be treated to the first installment of an educational melodrama—each episode of which would form a distinct segment of a compelling plot. And, no doubt because the GCPD chief of police was an ardent fan of Western lore, his episodic dream series would begin—and end—*way back when*.

Aha! It is about to commence.

As the curtain rises, watch his brow furrow.

EPISODE ONE

Granite Creek, Colorado, 1877

Scott Parris finds himself in a makeshift courtroom that is provided with filthy brass spittoons, a pair of shifty-eyed lawyers, a surly-looking Judge "Pug" Bullet, arresting officers Sheriff Ed "Peg-Leg" Knox and his sidekick deputy "Pig" Slocum, and a jury of twelve solemn men (all with ample growths of whiskers on their chins), who have just returned with a verdict for the tough-looking prisoner. Among the audience are a half-dozen newspaper reporters scribbling copious notes, a crowd of curious townsfolk who have come to gawk at the proceedings, and, in the back of the room—a slender, seven-foot-tall man dressed in fringed buckskin, beaded moccasins, and a wide-brimmed black Stetson festooned with an eagle plume.

The Indian—a hard-eyed Ute who goes by the name of Charlie Moon—is Marshal Parris's closest friend.

This is a typical scene in the life of a lawman of the period, but even with his Ute comrade present, Parris is ill at ease.

What makes the lawman edgy? The identity of the center of attraction—i.e., the prisoner who is waiting to hear what the jury of his twelve so-called peers have to say about the charge.

Who is the prisoner?

No, not a member of the marshal's family.

One of his good friends?

A wasted guess—Charlie Moon is Parris's only friend.

The man who had been charged with a capital crime is known by friend and foe alike as—U.S. Marshal Scott Parris.

How did the reputable lawman get himself into such a scandalous fix? Well, it's a sad story, but an instructive one for those sensible souls who prefer to stay clear of serious trouble. It happened like this, on the second day of May, when a certain bad hombre and his gang of cutthroats hit town and began to throw their weight around—

Hold on. Something important is about to happen.

The judge bellows, "We ain't got all day, Hobart—tell us one way or another. Is the accused criminal guilty as charged, or is the jury a bunch a idiots?"

The foreman of the jury gets to his feet.

The crowd falls silent.

How silent?

The judge taps his black imported Kentucky Black-Leaf cigar on the edge of his bench. The warm, gray tobacco ash breaks off.

Falls

Falls . . .

Sssssshhhhh . . .

That's the sound of the ash hitting the oak floor.

Judge Pug Bullet aims his cigar at the foreman. "Well, don't just stand there looking like a addlebrained jackass, Hobart—has the jury reached the correct and just decision, or will I be obliged to lock the whole lot of you up in the horse stable till you get it right?"

"We have, Pug—uh, Your Honor." Hobart Watkins clears his throat and aims a liquid projectile at the nearest spittoon. "We find the accused guilty of all charges."

"Guilty?" Marshal Parris gets to his feet, raises his manacled hands to make fists. "Guilty of what?"

Judge Pug yanks out his .44 Colt and bangs the pistol handle on a two-by-ten pine plank supported by a pair of whisky barrels, which serves as his bench. "Siddown, you no-good piece a dirt—and shut your trap!"

"I'll be damned if I will!" Scott Parris glares at the

homely man in the shabby black cloak. "This ain't nothin' but a kangaroo court of half-wits and misfits!"

If the Law is to retain any semblance of dignity, such outrageous outbursts must be dealt with, and promptly. The judge nods to the rough-and-ready lawmen, who will be more than happy to do the dealing-with. Promptly.

Sheriff Knox balls his gloved mitt into a knotty fist and gives Parris a healthy box on the ear.

Roaring like a wounded griz, the prisoner loops his manacle chain around Knox's neck, tightens it until the sheriff's eyes bulge and threaten to pop out of their sockets.

Coming to the rescue, Deputy Slocum gives the marshal an enthusiastic punch in the abdomen. Lower abdomen. Below Parris's silver belt buckle. But not low enough to cripple him.

Returning the friendly gesture, Parris knees Slocum in the crotch.

As it is apt to do in such situations, pandemonium breaks out.

Strangers begin throwing punches left and right.

Ladies begin to swoon right and left.

Awakened by the ruckus, an aged redbone hound scowls at the hysterical bipeds, gets up, and walks out of the place without so much as a by-your-leave.

Demanding order in the court, the judge fires his pistol into the ceiling. Three times. Which, considering the fact that there are ten rent-by-the-hour rooms upstairs for ladies and their gentlemen guests, is more than a little reckless. But the gunshots get the job done.

As if by magic, the saloon begins to fall quiet again. Male members of the audience cease to brawl. A few even apologize to one another. Fainted ladies promptly regain consciousness, and began to fan themselves.

After giving the downed deputy a healthy kick in the ribs, the prisoner disentangles his manacle chains from the sheriff's neck.

Glaring at the accused, His Honor proceeds to do his duty. "The prisoner shall be hung by his neck until—" The *chief officer of the court pauses to press his thumb against his nose, blow said prominent snout, and wipe it on his sleeve before he commences to deliver the tail end of the weighty sentence: "Until he's dead as a fossil!"*

Fade to black.

Scott Parris turned over and groaned. *Well, that was one helluva nightmare.* He opened his eyes and blinked at a window. *It's still dark outside.* Knowing he wouldn't be getting any more sleep, the chief of police snatched up the bedside telephone and punched in the familiar number.

Charlie Moon was on the ranch headquarters east porch with a mug of coffee, waiting for the dawn. After checking the caller ID on his cell phone, the full-time Ute rancher, part-time bluegrass musician, and sometimes tribal investigator greeted his friend in the following manner: "Columbine Ranch. It's five-ten A.M., the temperature is Just Right, and our Motto of the Day is the same as it was yesterday—Eat More Beef."

"H'lo, Charlie." Parris grinned at his Indian friend. "You sound like you're already up and at 'em."

Charlie Moon grinned back. "I'm always busy, pardner—there's no flies on me. But if you're having a slow week over at the cop shop, and hinting around about how it's been way too long since we went fishing, just say the word."

Parris wanted to say the word. "Thanks anyway. I've got way too much work to do."

"Sorry to hear it." The rancher waited to hear what the call was about.

"Charlie, this'll seem strange, but d'you recall that time a few years back, when you got your skull cracked. . . ." Parris felt his face blushing, "and you had that weird near-death experience?"

"That'd be a hard thing to forget, pard."

"D'you mind I ask you something about it?"

The Ute smiled at his unseen friend. "Would it do any good for me to say, 'Yes I do'?"

"No it wouldn't." The town cop cleared his throat. "If I remember correctly, you told me you were happy over yonder on the . . . the *other side.*"

"Your memory's working fine."

Scott Parris inhaled deeply. "Then why'd you come back?"

Starlight sparkled in Charlie Moon's eyes. "To look after you."

CHAPTER THREE

CHARLIE MOON'S AUNT

Daisy Perika has a tendency to forget how blessed she is to spend her twilight years in the snug, sturdy house Charlie Moon and his ranch hands built for her in the eastern wilderness of the reservation. Not only is the crabby old soul miles from her nearest human neighbor—a circumstance greatly to the advantage of all concerned—but Daisy's home is situated on a site that can best be described as picturesque. Imagine living at the yawning mouth of *Cañón del Espíritu* and in the late-afternoon shadow of Three Sisters Mesa, whose stony siblings serve as sentries to warn the tribal elder of those booming storms that so often roll down from the San Juan Mountains to spit white-hot fire and boast thunderously of their destructive power.

How sad that, as Daisy carried a basket of foodstuffs to seventeen-year-old Sarah Frank's red pickup truck, she cast not a glance at the Sisters' dark profiles, or at the cloud of warships floating by in majestic parade.

Neither was she aware of the approach of a neighbor.

THE DANCING DWARF

The *what*?

This sounds very much like a put-on, but events that would be eyebrow raisers even in Crestone, Colorado, or

Sedona, Arizona, are reportedly commonplace in the vicinity of Spirit Canyon. Moreover, it is whispered that Daisy Perika attracts strange company. And speaking of which (company), one is reminded of how those whom we least look forward to see approaching our front door have the aggravating habit of dropping by at the most inopportune times.

If the Ute woman, currently preoccupied with preparations for a visit to her nephew's vast high-country cattle ranch, had known who (what) was trudging up the dusty pathway from *Cañón del Espíritu*, she would no doubt have groaned, set her remaining teeth on edge, and said something like, "Isn't it always the way. You plan a nice day and something is bound to happen that'll mess it up." Daisy would have recoiled at any suggestion that she was a pessimist, but she believed in an oft-quoted version of Murphy's First Law:

> *If Something Can Go Wrong, It Will.*

This was (according to the tribal elder) a knockoff of an archaic Ute proverb, from which is derived Professor Perika's Eleventh Contention, i.e.:

> *Just About the Time You Get Ready to Leave the House, the Little Varmint Will Show up Wanting Something or Other.*

Though the rural environs wherein Daisy's home is situated supports dozens of life forms that she would designate as *varmints*, the specific pest referred to in the aforesaid proverb is neither insect, arachnid, canine, feline, reptile, rodent, nor a member of any other group you might care to mention. Being one of the few of his kind that survives from the olden times, this varmint is not only a rare and endangered species—he is a singular creature indeed. So much so as to be almost unheard of outside the boundaries of the Southern Ute reservation, and even on the res, only a dozen or so traditional Utes have accurate knowledge of such creatures, and those experts tend to disagree with one another on minor details.

But enough of the preamble. He is about to appear *in the flesh*.

IT'S SHOWTIME!

Daisy was lugging a small cardboard box of homemade jams and jellies to Sarah Frank's F-150 when she spotted the unwelcome, self-invited guest. He was peeking from behind a piñon trunk. The shaman pretended not to see the little man, which should have been easy, seeing as how the creature was apparently attempting to hide from her. This was merely a ploy to set up his Big Entrance.

The *pitukupf* danced directly into Daisy's path.

No, we do not refer to a lighthearted gait, or to an effeminate, mincing step. *Danced* is to be taken literally.

Despite his considerable age, which was rumored to be several hundreds of years—probably in excess of a thousand—the little fellow was an agile and enthusiastic dancer. Picture a stunted, twisted, evil version of Fred Astaire. As he danced, the knee-high performer also tipped his floppy-brimmed hat and flashed a possum smile that exposed a set of tiny, yellowish, pointy teeth. While standing in place, he tapped out a captivating rhythm with his moccasined feet.

The tribal elder had seen such shenanigans before and was not impressed. Daisy knew that the *pitukupf* could be likable—even charming—when he wanted something.

Something like a jar of strawberry-rhubarb jam from the Ute elder's cardboard box.

Nasty little scamp! She resisted a temptation to return his toothy smile. "Whatta you stomping around on my property for?" *As if I didn't know.* It was always the same with this one-dimensional personality. He rarely asked for an outright handout; the dwarf preferred to cheat his nearest neighbor and only friend. Barter was the name of his crooked game. The little gossip would propose a trade—his valuable knowledge about something or other for a few tidbits from Daisy's pantry. On occasion, he might express an interest in an inexpensive trinket such as a pocketknife, mirror, or an old-fashioned dollar pocket watch that tickety-tocked his lonely hours away.

The diminutive entrepreneur doffed the scruffy lid and responded to the shaman's query in a direct fashion. And though he spoke modern Ute, Spanish, and English with enviable fluency, he preferred to converse in an archaic version of the Ute language that was difficult even for Daisy to understand.

What it all boiled down to was that the dwarf had picked up some information that would be useful to his neighbor. He preferred to tell her *right up front*, but all the sprightly dancing had weakened him. His blood sugar was low. Could she spare a jar or two or three or four of the sweet, fruity confections she carried?

Daisy replied that she could not. These jams and jellies had been prepared for Charlie Moon, who was her closest living relative. The shaman took this opportunity to remind the *pitukupf* of those several occasions when he had acted in bad faith. She wanted no more dealings with him. With that, she took a stride directly at her neighbor, who, when he was not wearing his tiny hat, hung it in his abandoned-badger-hole home in *Cañón del Espíritu.*

With a quick side step, the agile little man got out of her way. He watched in dismay as Daisy placed the box of preserves on the floorboard of the pickup and slammed the door shut. He suggested that she reconsider.

She did. "Okay, here's the deal." Daisy picked up a dead juniper limb and shook the sturdy club at him. "If you're not out of sight in five seconds flat, I'll whack you all the way into the middle of next week."

The little man hung his head. Exhaled a long, melancholy sigh. Looked as if he might cry.

Daisy wasn't fooled for a second. *Silly little booger.* But he did look so *sad.* And hungry. "Oh, all right. I've got some Kroger's strawberry jam in the pantry."

The homely little face brightened perceptibly.

"And I got half a store-bought cherry pie in the bread box."

The famished visitor licked his thin, gray lips.

"And I guess I could give you Sarah's old plastic compact." She grinned wickedly at the dwarf. "The mirror's cracked, but so are you."

Overjoyed, he commenced the energetic two-step.

Daisy put her hands on her hips, a stern look on her wrinkled face. "But first, tell me what you know that I don't."

Predictably, her cunning little neighbor suggested a compromise. Half a story for half a pie. The balance upon payment of strawberry jam and mirror.

"Forget it."

This old woman was a hard sell. The expert bargainer proposed an up-front hint.

"Let's hear it, Shorty."

He took off his hat and dropped it. (No. Not that hat. The hint.) Which was to the general effect that someone Daisy knew was about to get into serious trouble.

She sneered. "Who?"

The sly little fellow shook his shriveled head, which was about the size and texture of an apricot that had suffered through the scorching heat of a long, dry summer. A hint was a hint, his expression said. If she wanted to know more, deliver the goods!

Daisy advised her visitor that she would go inside and get the strawberry jam and the half pie. But if her half-pint neighbor made the least attempt to get into the pickup and mess with Charlie Moon's goodie box, she would use her sharp butcher knife to slit him from gullet to—

No. Repeating what she said would only encourage the vulgar old woman to worse excesses.

CHAPTER FOUR

THE SHAMAN'S BRAINSTORM

Not one of those cloaked by night's dark shroud, that sneaks in silently and waits until it is directly overhead before commencing to *ka-boom!* slumbering souls wide awake and wide-eyed. Daisy Perika's mental storm began more like a whiff of fragrant sage-scented moisture, the low rumble of a distant cloud rolling slowly over the San Juan Mountains' round shoulders.

On the way to get the preserves and pie, as the old folks used to say, Daisy "got to thinking" about the situation. Opening her front door: *Two or three times every year, I end up doing a deal with the* pitukupf. *And more often than not, I get the short end of the stick and end up looking like a silly old fool.* Padding silently across the parlor carpet: *And even when I get a teensy smidgen of useful information, that slippery little runt always holds something back on me.* Into her kitchen: *But it's my own fault for having anything to do with the dwarf.* Click-clicking her heels across the linoleum: *Father Raes Delfino warned me for years to have nothing to do with the scoundrel.*

At the propane range, Daisy put her fingers on the enameled surface above the pilot lights, determined from the warmth that they had not been blown out by a draft. She shook her head. It wasn't fair. *The scrawny* pitukupf *must be ten times as old as I am, but he prances and dances around like a teenager, and I can barely walk.* What it all boiled down

to was—*I'm too tired to fool around with the likes of him.*
She squinted at the clock on the stove, watched the slender
black hand steal away precious seconds. *My time is running
out and I need to spend what little I've got left like an old
miser with nothing in her purse but a few thin dimes.*

First order of business: *What I have to do is stop having
any dealings with the* pitukupf.

Like so many well-meant resolutions, this one was easier
said than done.

I hardly ever go to see him in Cañón del Espíritu *anymore. But what can I do when the nasty little imp comes to
visit me?* Today's encounter had demonstrated the difficulty
of her dilemma. *And he don't just come to my house; the
cheeky rascal is likely to show up practically anywhere.* She
recalled that embarrassing Sunday morning years ago when
the brazen creature had shown up in church during Holy
Mass—and had practically sat in her lap! Daisy had a sneaking suspicion that Father Raes had caught a glimpse of the
dwarf, who was supposedly invisible to whites. *And only
last year* (or was it the year before that?) *the* pitukupf *visited
me at Charlie Moon's ranch.*

*Somehow, I've got to figure out some way to keep clear
of him.*

The problem was well defined. But what was the remedy?

Daisy sighed. What made it so hard was that, like all his
kind, the little man was a recluse. *I'm the only friend he's
got. He don't talk to anybody else. I wish there was somebody he'd rather pester than me.*

But who? Hardly any of the young people in the tribe
believed in the Little People, and those few who did were
terrified of meeting one of the dwarfish clan, much less doing business with them. Oh, what to do!

But Daisy was no quitter. *There must be someone—*

"Aunt Daisy?"

"Ahhh!" It would be an unwarranted exaggeration to report that the old woman practically jumped out of her skin,
but she was startled by the sudden appearance of Sarah
Frank at her elbow. She feigned a slap at the girl. "Don't do

that—you scared me out of a year's growth!" She scowled at the young woman. "I thought you was in your bedroom, putting stuff into your suitcase."

"I was; then I came into the kitchen."

Daisy snorted. These young people had a snappy answer for everything. *Why, in my day—* The tribal elder paused. Cocked her head as if she heard something coming. Narrowed her eyes as if to catch a glimpse of it.

The barometer plunged precipitously.

Gale winds shrieked and bent trees to the ground.

The rain was horizontal, drops whizzed by like bullets.

Fortunately, these were merely metaphorical barometers, winds, and rain.

The *brainstorm* had hit full force.

Her notion was radical. And a long way from being a sure thing. More like what Daisy's poker-playing nephew would call "a real long shot." Never mind. The Ute elder was willing to give it a try. *The girl is only half Ute, but that might be enough.* The wily old woman turned a warm gaze on the innocent. "Sarah, I'd like you to do a little favor for me."

"Okay. What?" The Ute-Papago orphan—not a relation of the tribal elder—was always doing something for "Aunt" Daisy.

Daisy told Sarah *what.*

This struck Sarah Frank as a strange request, even coming from the unpredictable old woman. Which was why she repeated what she thought she'd heard, practically word for word. "You want me to get the jar of Kroger strawberry preserves and that stale half a cherry pie *and* my old plastic compact—and take them outside and set them on the cedar stump?"

Daisy nodded.

Sarah shrugged. "Okay."

Most teenagers would want to know why. The old woman smiled. *What a sweet child.*

CHAPTER FIVE

THE CRUCIAL EXPERIMENT

Sarah placed each item on the stump, then backed off to inspect the arrangement with a critical eye. "Is that okay?"

The shaman nodded. "It'll do just fine." Daisy turned to glare at the *pitukupf*, who was loitering a few paces away, directly across the stump from Sarah. The little man seemed rather older than a few minutes ago, when he hadn't looked a day over nine hundred years. *Hah! Little Mr. Silverheels doesn't look like he's in the mood for kicking up a jig now.* She studied her smallish adversary's uneasy expression. *I think he's afraid of the girl.* Which might be a good thing. The critical issue was, did Sarah have enough Ute blood flowing in her veins to enable her to perceive the presence of the *pitukupf*? It was not necessary that the girl see him right away—that might scare her half to death. *If she just has the* feeling *that he's here, that'd be enough for now.*

Daisy recalled her first encounter with the *pitukupf*, when she was about eight years old. She had been able to see only the little man's footprints in the sandy bottom of *Cañon del Espíritu*, and a faint impression of his shadow on a bloodberry bush. The aged woman leaned on her oak staff and addressed the sullen-looking dwarf. "Well, there it is—everything you asked for. Start talking."

The *pitukupf* did not utter a word. Neither did he move. He might have been carved from knotty pine, his thin gray lips sealed with piñon sap.

Sarah stared at the peculiar old woman. "Aunt Daisy—can I ask you something?"

"Sure."

"Who are you talking to?"

"The little man."

"Oh." The girl felt her skin prickle. Her eyes darted right and left. "Uh—where is he?"

Daisy pointed her walking stick. "Right there."

Sarah stared intently at the spot. *There's nothing there. Well, not that I can see. Maybe Aunt Daisy is teasing me.* The determined youth tried harder. She engaged all her senses and powers. *I still can't see anything.* Except . . . *Except for something like smoke.* No, *smoke* did not quite describe it. *It's more like a haze.* But not like the thick gray fog that sometimes spilled out of *Cañón del Espíritu's* mouth. *It's more like when the morning sun shines on a roof that's still wet with last night's dew.* And the wisp of smoke-fog-haze was about the right size to be the dwarf that Daisy had described on so many dark winter nights while they sat close to the flames crackling in the fireplace. And Sarah could almost make out a leering little face. This was beginning to be scary. *There's probably nothing there. It's just my imagination. And even if I do see something, I'm not sure I really want to.*

Neither the young woman nor the old one was aware of the fact that Mr. Zig-Zag had appeared on the scene. Sarah's black-and-white spotted cat was sitting by his mistress's left ankle, staring directly across the stump at the space where the dwarf was supposedly present. This did not necessarily mean that the cat saw the little man. It was more likely that an intelligent and observant feline like Mr. Z-Z, having perceived where the human beings were looking, was merely exhibiting a cat's natural curiosity about an empty spot in space.

If the apparition looked back at the toothy mammal with some apprehension, that was probably because those of his ilk detested members of the feline clan.

When Daisy turned to fix her gaze on Sarah, she noticed

the cat. *You see him, don't you?* The shaman's beady little brown eyes fairly glinted with expectation as she spoke to the girl. "Well?"

The youth drew in a breath of fresh air. "I may see just a little *something*."

"Tell me about it."

Like thoughtful spaniels do, Sarah cocked her head. "It's nothing much."

Daisy chuckled. *Neither's he.*

"Sort of like a shady spot." She strained to expand on this. "It's like something was soaking up the light."

Daisy smiled. *She sees the little booger all right.* But the development of any useful skill takes time. With a little bit of luck, the more the girl looked, and the more she *wanted* to see—the clearer the *pitukupf*'s image would be. "Anything else?"

There was. But, being a polite young lady, Sarah hesitated to mention the distinct olfactory sensation.

The tribal elder pressed. "Well—what is it?"

Sarah hoped that the little man (if he was really there) was not a sensitive sort. "Well, I think I can *smell* something."

Daisy chuckled at the *pitukupf*'s outraged expression. "Something like three-day-old roadkill?"

"Oh, no." The girl shook her head so hard that her long black locks whipped across her face. "Nothing like that!" *More like something sour.* Spoiled milk? She strained to think of a suitable euphemism. "The scent is . . . well . . . kind of *tart*." She smiled reassuringly at the hazy image. "But not at all unpleasant." Since she was four years old, this was as close as Sarah had come to outright lying.

The dwarf smirked at the Ute elder.

"Hah." This was all Daisy could come up with. Fun was fun, but enough dillydallying around. Sarah had done better than expected; now it was time to work the other side of the potential match. Daisy shook her walking stick at the dwarf. "Okay, come and get the stuff this nice little girl brought out here for you."

The nice little girl froze, clasped her hands over her face.

She also peeked between her fingers at the stump. *Oh, if somebody I can't see picks up the jam or the pie, I'll just die!*

Not to worry. Death was not an option. Not today.

The dwarf evidently had no intention of demonstrating his presence by so bold a demonstration of levitation. In a hoarse whisper, the Ute leprechaun advised the shaman that he would collect the jam, pie, and mirror after she and the half-breed child had departed.

The old woman sneered at her neighbor. "There won't be anything on the stump unless you tell me everything you know, and I mean *right now*." Daisy shook her formidable walking stick at the dwarf. "And it'd better be good and none of it made up." She stamped her foot. "And don't you think for a minute I won't know the difference."

The *pitukupf* was insulted by this rude display. Even chagrined. For a moment, it seemed as if he might simply turn and walk away. But Daisy wouldn't budge, so in the end, he gave in. What he had to say concerned one of the few Apaches that the Southern Ute tribal elder counted as a friend.

As Daisy listened to the little man's stunning narrative, she considered the dire implications of this report. *If what he says about Loyola is true, there's not much I can do . . . not by myself.* A hopeful thought occurred to her: *I could tell Charlie Moon about it.* This notion came with a counternotion attached: *But he'd never believe me.* This was a knotty problem that would likely take some time to unravel. And time was a commodity that the busy woman had no surplus of. *After me and Sarah get to the Columbine, I'll telephone Loyola and get her side of the story.* The shaman had not dismissed the possibility that the dwarf was either outright lying or, at the very least—painting over the truth with a thick coat of *pitukupf* varnish. *Soon as I know the facts of the matter, I'll figure out what to do about it.*

With an almost painful intensity, Sarah strained her ears in an attempt to hear the dwarf's words. The shaman's apprentice heard nothing. Well, almost nothing. There was that odd, whispering twitter, like a dry breeze rattling dead cottonwood leaves.

CHAPTER SIX

THE JOURNEY NORTH

After a final check inside her house to make sure the propane water heater was set to Pilot and all the electric lights were turned off and the circuit breaker that powered the well pump was likewise de-energized, Daisy locked the front door and made her way slowly across the yard. The tired old woman steadied herself with her sturdy oak walking stick as she grunted and groaned herself into the passenger side of the pickup.

About four miles and twenty minutes down the rutted lane, as they intersected Fosset Gulch Road, Sarah made a significant announcement: "I'm going to have a talk with him."

The shaman smiled at the woman-child. "The dwarf?"

Sarah shot her a shocked look. "No, with *him*."

Realizing now what this meant, the old woman did not respond.

After they crossed over the Piedra bridge and onto the steaming blacktop of Route 151, the girl pointed her pickup more or less northwest, and added, "We've got to get things straightened out."

Still, the aged passenger held her tongue.

Silence reigned as they passed the entrance to Chimney Rock Archaeological Site, where the Twin War Gods loomed ominously in the sky, gazing toward the Three Stone Sisters, whose lengthening shadows would soon darken the windows of Daisy's home.

Not a word was said when Lake Capote appeared on the right side of the highway, or when Sarah turned west on Route 160.

But not too many minutes later, when they entered Bayfield, the seventeen-year-old's brow furrowed into a thoughtful frown. Having carefully considered all aspects of the situation, Sarah summed up with this irrefutable assertion: "Either Charlie Moon wants to marry me—or he doesn't."

"He doesn't," Daisy Perika snapped. "Now stop yammering so much before you give me a splitting headache!"

Did this cruel retort hurt Sarah Frank's feelings? Hard to say. But all the way to the Columbine Ranch, the girl uttered not another word.

CHAPTER SEVEN

ESCALATION

One Minute after Midnight

That was when Loyola Montoya heard it.

This was not one of those creepy night sounds that prickles the skin and sets the heart to thumping—such as the sinister creaking of footsteps across squeaky old floors, blood-curdling gurgles commonly attributed to antique plumbing, or a rude bump-in-the-night *something* that delights in disturbing the sleep of honest citizens. Not a bit. This was quite unlike any creaking-gurgling-bumping phenomenon that Loyola had ever experienced.

It sounded like somebody whimpering.

A more or less sensible soul, Loyola was aware that she sometimes awakened hearing leftover sounds from a lingering dream. The sleepy woman raised her head from the pillow and listened intently. *It seems quiet enough now, so I'll just lay down and close my eyes and—* No. *There it goes again.* But now the sound was not so much a whimpering as a plaintive *bleating.* Of the kind that will not cease until attended to.

Like a hungry baby or Nancy the nanny goat. The animal was a sound sleeper, who rarely stirred in the middle of the night unless threatened by a hungry coyote. Or bear. Or mountain lion.

Damnation—if it ain't one thing, it's something worse!

Loyola got out of bed and padded into her darkened kitchen, where she heard the pitiful summons for a third time. *Maybe the poor thing's scared of the witches, and wants to come inside.*

The lady of the house picked up a butcher knife with her right hand, used her left one to unlock the back door. She opened it.

What did she find?

Not a coyote or a bear or a mountain lion.

But her dear old nanny goat was, in a manner of speaking, on the back porch. The poor creature, throat slit, was hanging upside down from a two-by-six rafter. Nancy's blood dripped onto the porch floor. As the Apache elder cut the goat down, tears rolled down her leathery cheeks. She said a few comforting words before putting the animal out of its misery.

Loyola felt rather than saw several pairs of eyes watching her from their dark concealment. The sly night breeze whispered in her ear: *You'd better get out of here . . . find someplace to hide.* Triggered by a signal from somewhere deep in her visceral region, the elderly lady's adrenaline pump turned on to prepare her for flight or fight. The former choice was not an option. Cold fury invariably vanquishes fear—along with any residue of common sense.

Loyola set her jaw. *This time, those witches have gone too far. There's going to be nine kinds of hell to pay!* The outraged old woman addressed her unseen tormenters aloud with a cold, hard calmness. "You've done it now, you mean sons of bitches." She raised the butcher knife over her head like a banner. "This means *war*!"

This was no idle threat.

The furious old warrior entered her house without bothering to lock the door behind her. She stomped across the kitchen floor, marched into her bedroom, and opened the corner closet. Loyola yanked her dead husband's World War II .45 caliber automatic pistol out of a scruffy old duffel bag. She ejected the magazine, counted seven fat cartridges, popped the magazine back into the slot, and expertly loaded one into the barrel.

Loyola returned to her darkened kitchen, the .45 in her hand. By now, the angry, dangerous lady was aching for revenge. Out of nowhere, a question occurred to her: *What would Geronimo or General George Patton do in a situation like this?* The answer was obvious.

Attack.

Despite her shortcomings in making sound judgments, the elderly woman was not such a fool as to make a frontal assault that was bound to end in disaster. She sat down at the kitchen table to rest, and to consider the situation. *All of those witches are young and strong, and I'm outnumbered by at least a dozen to one.* The widow had a few modest aspirations, chief of which was to live to be 101 years old.

She realized that successful assaults, particularly those made by the flinty-faced Apache chieftain and the daring World War II general, invariably followed carefully laid-out plans. But most important of all, those military strategists were known for making swift, bold moves that the enemy *did not expect.* Loyola had one significant advantage over her enemies: *They expect me to cower all night here in my house like a frightened old woman who's scared of her shadow.* Her course of action was obvious: *I'll surprise the murderous rascals!*

But how? And to what end?

Job One was to determine the enemy's precise location, strength, and intentions. The aged lady, who was missing several teeth, hung a gapped Cheshire grin in the darkness. *First off, I'll go spy on 'em.* This daring plan was both gratifying and invigorating. And might lead to unexpected opportunities. Such as—*If I can draw a bead on one of those snakes, I might just take a potshot at him before I slip away.* A healthy kick of adrenaline reinforced her morale. *With a little luck, I might kill two or three of 'em.* The mere thought of spilling blood made her heart race. *Hah! That'd make 'em think twice before they murder another old woman's goat!*

Chief-General Montoya pressed the automatic pistol's cold steel against her thin chest. *I'll show that collection of riffraff who's boss around here.*

CHAPTER EIGHT

RECONNOITERING THE ENEMY ENCAMPMENT

Loyola pulled on a pair of comfortable leather moccasins and a navy-blue woolen coat—and packed the .45 automatic into a black canvas shopping bag. A few owl-hoots after 3 A.M., she left her house by the front door, locked it behind her with the key she kept on a string around her neck, and made her way oh-so-quietly along the weed-choked lane toward the paved road. At that junction, the latter-day warrior turned her face south to begin a long, roundabout hike to an old, little-known footbridge across Ignacio Creek.

Along the way, Mrs. Montoya began to have a few misgivings. Such as: *This is probably the dumbest thing I've ever done in my life.* And: *Those witches'll probably string me up to a tree limb and slit my throat, just like they did my poor old nanny goat.* But after she had crossed the rotting pine bridge to the opposite bank, there could be no thought of turning back.

Like her Apache ancestors, she crept silently through the willowy underbrush along the stream bank. The trek was more difficult and the going slower than she had expected. Loyola worried that dawn might break before she reached her destination. After ever so many scratches, stumbles, and rips in her cotton stockings, she stopped abruptly. Squinted. *Is that what I think it is?*

It was.

A flicker of light from a small campfire.

Loyola dropped to her knees and began to crawl. Now so near her objective, skulking was such great fun! She was reminded of those old black-and-white picture shows where stealthy red Indians delighted in sneaking up on unwary cowboys who slept close to the coals of a campfire. She imagined herself taking a scalp with such delicate skill that the victim wouldn't know what'd happened until after he'd had breakfast and decided to comb the lice out of his hair. *I wish I'd brought a razor-sharp hunting knife, so I could clench it between my teeth.*

As she crawled along, dragging the canvas bag that contained her heavy artillery, the fun gradually diminished. During this ordeal Loyola scuffed her knees, tore her skirt half off, and muttered unladylike curses in her native tongue.

When she was close enough to hear the poppity-crackle of the campfire and the muffled sounds of voices, the wild-eyed old woman crouched behind a prickly huckleberry bush. After a pause to catch her breath and say a prayer, Loyola raised her white-haired head just enough to take a quick look. What she saw did not appear to be a sinister gathering of Satanists.

This seemed to be nothing more than a bunch of ordinary folks camping out and having a good time. A tall, skinny fellow was telling off-color jokes. Several were chugging beer from longneck bottles. There was a sizable carcass on a spit over the fire, and one of their number was ladling a thick, fragrant sauce onto the roasting meat.

Loyola sniffed the mouthwatering aromas. *That barbecue sauce smells too good to be store bought.* She sniffed again. *And the meat smells like roasted pork.* But (she thought) you could bet your Social Security check that those goat-murdering bastards didn't buy their meat like upright citizens. *They must've killed one of Lonnie Ross's pigs.* Wouldn't bother *them* that Lonnie's wife was sickly and that the young couple had four hungry children to feed and Lonnie hadn't worked since he got laid off last Christmas. When Loyola heard someone laugh, angry tears welled in her eyes. *First they murder my sweet little nanny goat, now they're pic-nicking on one of my dirt-poor neighbor's pigs.*

It was apparent that someone had to do something about this outrage. Loyola knew very well who that *someone* was, and also what that *something* was—and she was more-than-ever determined to draw warm blood.

But not before she'd learned everything she could about this devilish bunch.

Straining to hear, the aged spy cocked her ear. As she'd hoped, snatches of conversation did reveal something about their malevolent plans. Quite a lot, in fact. She tried very hard to commit every bit of it to memory. After Loyola had absorbed as much as she could without becoming completely befuddled, she gave up the tedious intelligence-gathering game.

The time had come to get down to serious business.

THE WIDOW'S REVENGE

Loyola Montoya raised the heavy pistol in both hands, closed her left eye, took careful aim at the back of the near-est and biggest witch, and whispered, "With a little luck, I'll drill the son of a bitch right through his black heart." Stiff-ening her back and setting her teeth in anticipation of the roar of the .45 and its jarring recoil, she hissed through her teeth, "This is for Nancy." The expectant marksman pulled the trigger.

Nothing.

The weapon in her hands might as well have been a use-less lump of pot metal. Accustomed to conversing with herself when puzzled, Loyola commenced her whispering. "What went wrong?" She glared at the pistol. "I must've left the safety on." (She had.) But the shootist knew how to rem-edy that error. And she tried. Ever so hard. But though her thumb searched ever so diligently for the smallish latch, it could not find the contrary thing. *Oh, what an old fool I am.* Humiliated and deflated, she muttered, "Damn!"

Whispers and hisses are one thing (or two?); a mutter, quite another.

Two or three someones had heard Loyola's heartfelt "Damn!"

One was the man whose broad back had been her intended target. He shushed his comrades to silence with a subtle gesture, then turned to stare directly at the spot where the Apache elder was concealed behind the huckleberry bush.

The other members of the coven followed his gaze.

Thirteen evil stares are a formidable force to be reckoned with.

Loyola froze. But not entirely. The thumb on her right hand was (unbeknownst to the dangerous lady) still searching for the safety.

The big man made another barely perceptible gesture. Four other *brujos* separated from the circle to join him. The five, striding-purposefully about two yards apart, approached the old lady's hiding place.

The Apache warrior's determined thumb found what it had been looking for, and her trusty trigger finger reacted—

Boom-boom-boom! (They are not called *automatic* pistols without good reason.)

"Yi-yi-yikes!" (With each thunderous report, the startled shooter yelped.)

Simultaneously with the *booms!* and Loyola's yelps, devil worshipers were falling to prone positions with arms outstretched. No, they were not calling on their Father Below for deliverance. The prudent supplicants were hitting the dirt so as to present the smallest possible targets. Sad to say (one cannot help but side with the sniper), the tactic was effective. Not one of the hated thirteen was struck by the zipping lumps of lead.

The sole casualties were a gnarly branch on a twisted piñon, a quarter-million-year-old chunk of brownish red sandstone, and a left front tire mounted on one of the unhappy campers' stolen motor vehicles. We are not talking shabby, off-brand retread. The fatally wounded tire was a brand-spanking-new Goodyear whitewall.

One hesitates to moralize, but this helpful advice simply *aches* to be offered: It is unwise to shoot a hole through a man's automobile tire. Particularly when his religious persuasion encourages him to all manner of violent excesses.

FLIGHT

That single word pretty much sums it up. Loyola made a hasty retreat, and, like a flushed partridge—anything but a silent one. The venerable pistol still smoking in her right hand, she splashed across the shallow creek, fairly trotted through the sickly orchard, mounted her back porch two steps at a time, unlocked the door, slipped inside, and latched it behind her.

An impressive performance for one of her years. Perhaps her last before the final curtain falls?

The exhausted woman stumbled across the kitchen, tripped over her feet, and tumbled to the floor. She lay as still as a discarded rag doll, staring unseeing at the dark ceiling, gasping for breath. Poor old soul. Morbid thoughts flitted about in her mind like black moths trapped under an iron pot. *Well, I guess this is it.* Death's cold hand pressed hard against her chest. *I wish I could've killed some of those witches while I still had the strength.* Alas, she felt her life force fading away. *I always figured dying would hurt more than this.* Her tired old heart thumped slower and slower, then began skipping beats. Feeling terribly alone, Loyola remembered her grandson. *I wonder if Wallace will find my body. And where the half-wit will bury me. Probably in some weedy cemetery next to a landfill.* Her hands and feet had gone from prickly-chilly to completely numb. *I hope one of my lady friends will tell the mortician to put that nice, black silk dress on my corpse. And my black slippers.* Loyola's vision had narrowed. She was looking down a long, dark tunnel. *Well, what in the world is this?* She could see a hint of light at the far end. *That looks like a candle flame a thousand miles away. But I seem to be getting there pretty quick!*

For a soul who had no great hankering to be husked from her earthly shell just yet, this was an ominous development. And one whose outcome must remain shrouded in mystery. There are strict rules about who can approach that boundary, so we have no choice but to leave the Apache elder's spirit as it continues swiftly on the one-way journey toward—

Wait a minute. What is this?

The whole business is very unseemly, but the supposed corpse is twitching.

Moreover, the aged heart has thumped. There—it thumps again.

And look at that—her wrinkled face smiles.

One can only conclude that the stubborn woman has *refused to die.*

Why—because she is determined to live and fight another day?

No doubt. Evidently, the old warrior still has plenty of fire in her belly.

But there may be another, more revitalizing reason for her tenacious hold on life. Though her terrifying adventure into the witches' lair was absolutely exhilarating, Loyola's appetite for revenge has not yet been sated.

But with every faint heartbeat, things were returning to normal.

After lying on the floor for what seemed an eternity, the old woman gradually realized where she was and remembered where she had been. She also recalled bits and pieces of what she had heard in the witches' encampment. Some of it had to do with Granite Creek, a town miles to the north. Which was not far from where Daisy Perika's nephew owned a big cattle ranch.

Loyola was exceedingly fond of Charlie Moon. She could not count how many times when (back when he was a uniformed Ute cop) the amiable man had responded to her calls. Not only had Charlie invariably taken care of the problem—*he never made fun of me.* And there was another thing: *That skinny Ute ain't afraid of nothing.* Recalling the fact that Charlie did not believe in witches, Loyola wondered whether such an apparent shortcoming might not turn out to be an advantage. Surely, she reasoned, the witches would be put on edge—perhaps even seriously off-kilter—if confronted by a gritty nonbeliever. Why, Charlie Moon would spit in their eyes, break their arms and legs, yank their heads off—and, after these preliminaries, get really mean-and-dirty tough.

That settled the matter.

I'll call Charlie.

But realizing that it was still dark outside, the weary woman decided that she could use an hour or two of serious shut-eye. *I'll phone him after the sun comes up.* Flat on her back on the cracked kitchen linoleum, the automatic pistol gripped tightly in her hand, the plucky old soul yawned. And drifted off to a dreamless sleep.

CHAPTER NINE

THE DAWNING OF A NEW DAY

As Sarah Frank helped Charlie Moon wash the breakfast dishes, she was trying to think of a way to approach and then broach the delicate subject. Her budding female intuition suggested that the first order of business was to maneuver the Object of Her Affections into a pleasant, quiet spot where they could be alone. Preferably under a blue sky, in a field of fragrant wildflowers where butterflies fluttered by and honeybees hummed sweetly and so on and so forth. After considering several suitable locations on the Columbine, she selected that gently rolling high prairie that was bejeweled by an alpine lake. *Okay.* She inhaled and held her breath. *Here goes.* This was going to be difficult, but the thing had to be done. Straightening her back, the young lady got right to it. Handing her prospective husband a freshly washed saucer, Sarah said—with only the slightest quaver in her voice, "After that big breakfast, I think it'd be nice to go for a walk."

Moon nodded approvingly as he dried the saucer. "It'd do you good."

The teenager's face burned. "What I meant was . . . I thought maybe you'd like to go for a walk too."

"Well, that sounds like a fine idea but—" The fellow generally completed everything he started, including sentences. But Moon had heard the urgent warble of the telephone.

Sarah sighed, rolled her big, brown eyes, and departed for the parlor.

After drying his hands on the dish towel, Moon picked up the telephone. "Columbine Ranch."

A familiar voice crackled in his ear. "Charlie Moon— why, that *is* your voice. I'd know it anywhere. I expect you remember me; this is Loyola."

"Good morning, Mrs. Montoya." He smiled at his memory of the eccentric Apache elder. "I hope you're doing well—"

"Well I'm *not*, and I don't have time for silly chitchat, so you listen close to what I've got to say."

"Yes ma'am." *She's a lot like Aunt Daisy.*

"I've got a serious problem. You remember my grandson Wallace?"

"Yes I do. His father was a friend of—"

"Don't mention my son to me, Charlie. He was a no-account who didn't have a friend in the world except for vermin like himself. And Wallace's momma was one of that horse-stealing, egg-sucking bunch of Anglos from over by Trinidad and you know well as I do that not a one of those yahoos was worth the powder it'd take to blow 'im to hell. And even with some good Apache blood pulsing through his veins, Wallace didn't turn out much better. When he should be here looking after me, he's gone—and you can bet your last greenback dollar that he's hanging around with a bad crowd." She paused long enough to get a breath. "A while back, Wallace started hanging around with them damned witches that've been plaguing me every night for a week. Or maybe it's been for a month. Nowadays, I tend to lose track of time. Back when I was young, I didn't have any need for a calendar or a clock, but ever since my eighty-eighth birthday it's been all downhill. Wallace is probably shacked up with some slut—"

"Excuse me, Mrs. Montoya, did you say *witches*?"

"Charlie, if you keep interrupting me, I'll lose track of what . . . Now what *was* I talking about?"

"Something about a plague of witches."

"Oh, right. Witches. And I want 'em off my property right now! So strap that big pistol onto your skinny hip and pin a big, shiny policeman badge onto your shirt and streak your face with war paint and saddle up Old Biscuit and gallop down here right now and—"

"I'm not an SUPD officer anymore, Loyola."

"I know that. But from what I hear, you're some kinda big-shot tribal investigator. If that ain't so, just tell me."

Charlie Moon was distracted again, this time by a glimpse of someone hovering in the shadowy hallway. One of Aunt Daisy's few pleasures was eavesdropping. Charlie pretended to be unaware of her presence.

"Charlie?" Concerned that she had been disconnected, Loyola shouted in Moon's ear, "Charlie Moon—are you there? If you've hung up on me, I'll just call back."

"I'm here."

"Good. So tell me—do you big-shot Ute tribal cops wear uniforms?"

"Sure we do."

"What color?"

"Gray."

She snorted. "Sounds to me like a damned Johnny Reb outfit."

He managed a wan smile. "Why do you think they call us the *Southern* Utes?"

"Ha-ha!" Pause. "What was I talking about before you started yappin' about uniforms?"

"You were telling me how you preferred a well-dressed state police officer to a shabby SUPD cop."

"Oh, no I wasn't—and don't you be smart-mouthing me, Charlie Moon, or I'll tell your aunt Daisy on you, and she'll give you a whack on the bean with that big stick she leans on." Pause. "Oh, now I remember. It was about them nasty witches. You strap that big pistol onto your hip, and pin your shiny policeman badge onto your shirt, and get down here soon as you can and *kill every last one of them sons of bitches!*"

"You really think that's necessary?"

"Well of course I do! You know what they say: 'The only good witch is a dead one.' I want every last one of 'em planted under six feet of dirt!"

Moon tilted his head to gaze at the beamed ceiling. "I'm not allowed to shoot anybody before you fill out the appropriate form."

"Form? What *are* you babbling about?"

"Official Complaint Form number 595, which is for requesting a legal killing. Line One is where you print your full name and Social Security number. On Line Two, the complainee—that's you—specifies exactly what ordinances and/or tribal laws the alleged malefactors have broken that calls for summary capital punishment."

"Well that's the silliest damn thing I ever heard of."

"Maybe so, but rules are rules, Loyola. I can't go shooting a U.S. citizen dead right on the spot unless they've committed a serious offense. Like spitting on the sidewalk without a signed permit or jaywalking in front of a yellow school bus or—"

"These witches kill innocent animals."

"What kind of animals?"

She shouted in his ear, "They murdered my sweet little nanny goat!"

Moon sighed. Whenever one of Loyola's animals died, she refused to accept the misfortune as a natural event. The Apache elder evidently felt compelled to place blame on a tangible something or someone. The culprit might be a suspiciously sinuous coil of smoke curling up from a neighbor's chimney, an unspecified toxin that she supposed was seeping from the earth to pollute Ignacio Creek, lethal radiation from electric power lines, or, that most convenient scapegoat of all—a *witch*. "You absolutely sure that somebody killed your goat?"

"Oh, no—I guess it's just as likely that poor Nancy tied her hind legs to the back-porch rafter, then slit her own gullet with that straight razor she carries in her hip pocket!"

Somebody strung up her goat and cut its throat? Moon

didn't know what to make of this, and any response that might have been forming in his mind was interrupted by Loyola, who had just inhaled a fresh breath of air.

The words fairly spilled from her mouth: "And now they've killed and roasted a big pig. Wasn't *my* pig, though—poor old Dora died years ago."

"Dora?"

"Sure. You remember my old sow. The witches must've stolen their roasting pig from my neighbors. But slaughtering other folks' livestock is just the start—these witches kill *people* too."

"That's a pretty serious charge."

"Well it's the truth. Just last night, I heard 'em talk about it with my own ears." She paused to snicker a gleeful "hee-hee" before continuing. "I snuck out of the house and creeped up to their camp." Loyola was sorely tempted to tell Moon how she'd fired several .45 slugs at the trespassers, but thought it best to skip over a violent detail that might detract from her credibility. It seemed more prudent to emphasize the intelligence-gathering aspect of her adventure. "I listened to what they was jibber-jabbering about. And guess what—that bunch of snakes was planning their next sacrifice!"

Moon arched an eyebrow. "Sacrifice?"

"Sure. That's what witches do." *For a grown man, Charlie Moon sure don't know much.* "From what I was able to pick up, this particular bunch kills somebody about every twenty-nine days, and always right at the time when . . . when . . . what's-her-name . . . oh, you know who I mean."

"Afraid I don't."

"Oh, I remember now. White Bead Girl—that's who I was trying to think of." She added, in a snappish tone, "Just to be contrary, you Utes call her White Shell Woman."

Moon smiled at the Apache elder's reference to the moon.

"These witches sacrifice a human being when White Shell Woman has smeared her whole face with black mud."

"The Dark of the Moon?" *That must be coming up pretty soon.*

"That's right. And those devils plan to murder somebody up north, close to where you live." She hummed a few bars of "Dig a Hole in the Meadow." "What *is* the name of that little jerkwater one-horse town?"

"The only town within forty miles of the Columbine is Granite Creek."

"Yeah. That's the burg all right."

He laughed. "I expect it's grown some since you were here."

"Well I won't dispute that." The ninety-six-year-old snorted. "They invented TV and went to the moon since I've been twenty miles from my farm. But Granite Creek is where the witches' next sacrifice will happen."

Humoring the cantankerous old soul seemed the wisest course of action. "You'd better tell me all about it."

Longer pause.

"Loyola?" Moon pressed the phone hard against his ear. "You okay?"

"Shhh—don't disturb me. I'm trying to remember." Her exasperated sigh seemed to breathe in his ear. "What's that president's name? The one I always admired so much."

"Well I don't know, Loyola." Moon enjoyed a grin. "Us Southern Utes tend to favor Jefferson Davis."

"Oh—that's his name all right, but the other way around." Charlie heard Loyola stamp her foot. "Oh, you know the one I mean—the president with his face on the nickel."

"Mr. Tom Jefferson?"

"That's the one. What them witches plan will happen at Jefferson's General Store—no, wait a minute. That's not right." Loyola groaned. "Oh, my mind gets all tangled up and I can't remember what to *call* things." Talking to herself, the aged woman muttered, "Alphabet soup . . . hammers and nails . . . buckets and pails . . . puppy dogs' tails . . . sugar and spice and everything nice . . ."

Poor old woman. Maybe I should send a social worker

out to see her. Moon heard a tick-tick-tick. Wondered what it was. *Sounds like she's clicking her false teeth.*

Loyola Montoya rarely wore her dentures. She was tapping a yellow, No. 2 lead pencil on her kitchen table. "I got mixed up, Charlie. What was we talking about?"

The sad man sighed. Closed his eyes. "What the witches are planning to do in Granite Creek."

"Oh, right. And it's a regular coven—I counted about a dozen. And some of them—maybe the whole bunch—are right out of the funny papers, at least they *pretend* to be."

"Is that a fact?"

"Sure as crab apples are sour. What I mean is, their *names* are from the funny papers. But you can put a stop to this nasty business before it commences, Charlie Moon. Oh, look at the time! I can't talk all day—how soon can you get here?"

"Tomorrow afternoon."

"I could be stone cold dead by then—strung up like poor Nancy, with my throat slit ear to ear!"

"Tomorrow morning, then." The tribal investigator smiled at memories of his visits as a uniformed SUPD officer. "But I don't work for nothing. I'll be expecting a sugary snack and something cold and nutritious to wash it down with."

"You don't need to remind me." Loyola Montoya cackled a crackly old-woman laugh. "I never saw a grown man eat as many cookies and drink as much milk as you do, Charlie Moon—and without ever putting on a pound of fat. Just bring your six-shooter and thirteen bullets and—" A sharp intake of breath. "I just heard something rustling around on my back porch."

"Probably a raccoon."

"Either that, or it's my stupid grandson who's finally come home from his drinking and whoring, or it's one of them damned witches come to spy on me through the window. Sometimes I think they prowl around my house when I'm away. I wish I had better locks and latches on my doors. A blind man with only two fingers on his hand could open the back door with a bent tenpenny nail. These long-distance calls cost an arm and a leg—I can't talk to you anymore." This terse announcement was followed by a sharp click. Loyola had hung up. Moon returned the telephone to its cradle.

From her twilight sanctum in the short hallway between the dining room and the kitchen, Daisy Perika had heard enough to conclude that Charlie Moon was talking to Loyola Montoya. Evidently, the *pitukupf*'s report was not a fabrication—the strange old Apache woman was in some sort of trouble. Daisy was pleased to know that her nephew was going to look into the matter. She chose this moment for her entrance. "I was wondering if you might like to have a fresh cup of— Oh!" She raised both palms in an expression of embarrassed surprise. "I didn't know you was talking on the telephone." Daisy headed to the cookstove. "You want me to get you some coffee?"

"Thank you." Moon patted her bent back. "I don't mind if you do."

Still smarting from her failed attempt to get Charlie Moon alone, Sarah Frank returned to the kitchen. The young lady also had a cup of coffee. Black and sweetened with Tule Creek honey, which was how Charlie had his.

CHAPTER TEN

A RECIPE FOR HEARTBURN

After her early-morning conversation with Charlie Moon, Loyola Montoya had enjoyed several quiet, peaceful hours. Shortly after the sun had slipped away to ready itself for another day, a sprinkling of stars sparkled above her ten acres of brush, weeds, and sickly apple trees. Loyola turned off the kitchen lights and listened by the screen door. *I don't hear anything.* In the distance, a dog barked. *Which don't mean they're not out there.*

After perhaps twenty seconds, which passed like as many minutes, the widow began to entertain the hope that the witches had departed to set up camp elsewhere.

She pulled on a tattered black sweater, picked up the .45 caliber pistol off the table, made sure the safety was *off*, and slipped out the back door. Her eyes had adjusted to the dark kitchen and could see reasonably well in the patchy splashes of moonlight.

It was a balmy, pleasant night. Here and there in the orchard, cheerful crickets chirped. From behind the willows, the burbling murmur of the stream soothed her weary ear. The old woman took a deep breath of night's calming fragrance, exhaled it with a satisfied sigh. *Those nasty witches must be gone.*

Accepting this hopeful assertion as fact, Loyola concluded that she had put a big scare into them last night when she'd fired the pistol. *They don't know what I might do next, and they've decided not to hang around and find out.* She could not resist a spiteful "heh-heh." The old-fashioned soul was bolstered by the thought that her gun-toting adventure proved how well things could work out when a woman didn't wait for other folks to solve her problems. It was like her grandmother's favorite old saying: *If you want your garden to grow, do the planting and hoeing yourself.*

It occurred to Loyola that with the *brujos'* retreat, the Ute tribal investigator would be making a long trip for nothing. *And I'll look like a fool when Charlie Moon shows up and witches are as scarce around here as pink giraffes.* She playfully aimed her pistol at an inoffensive fence post. *I suppose I ought to call the ranch and tell him they've packed up and left for a safer hiding place—there's no need for him to drive all the way down here.* On the other hand . . . *Witches or not, it'd be nice to see my young friend again.* She took a last look at the starry night sky. *I might as well go back inside and bake some cookies; Charlie Moon really likes my oatmeal-walnut-cherry recipe.* Which presented a problem. While Loyola had an ample supply of Quaker Oatmeal, she was all out of walnuts, shelled or otherwise, and there was not a cherry in the house—fresh, canned, or dried. But challenges were the spice of life, and she was always able to improvise. The lack of walnuts was dispensed with forthwith: *I've got that little sack of piñon nuts I gathered last year.* But what could a person substitute for cherries? As she mulled over what she had in the pantry, Loyola could not come up with a respectable solution, so she settled on deceit. *If I just stir something red into the batter, I bet Charlie won't even notice the difference.* Like famished dogs, hungry men tended to gulp and swallow their food without appreciating the more subtle nuances of flavor. *I could blend in some red pepper chips.* She smiled. *Or some chopped pimentos.* But what would it be, peppers or pimentos? Having no time to dillydally over small decisions, the firm-jawed cookie maker decided to use both. *And if the recipe turns out to be tip-top, I'll enter a batch of oatmeal, piñon-nut, red chili pepper, and pimento cookies in the La Plata County Fair next year.*

Surfacing from her culinary musings, Loyola noticed that the night-sounds were no longer soothing to her soul. The crickets had ceased their chirping; the stream's happy gurgling had shifted to a malicious, gossipy whisper. A chill, dry breeze rustling crispy elm leaves produced a raspy, gasping sound—a drowning soul's final breath.

Despite an involuntary shudder, Loyola reassured herself that the witches were long gone. Nevertheless, the prudent woman retreated into her house and closed the porch door behind her. Even in the familiar comfort of her kitchen, she did not feel entirely safe. What if one or two of those brutal goat slayers had remained behind with the intention of evening the score? *I've got my pistol, but I can't stay awake till Charlie Moon gets here. And while I'm sleeping, one of them rascals could slip into my bedroom and slit my throat!*

She recalled that her grandmother had warded off the devil's disciples by hanging a string of garlic cloves over every possible entrance to her home, including the fireplace. (Witches are notorious for slipping down chimneys.) Loyola searched her dusty pantry, but found only two cloves hanging from a rusty nail—not enough to prevent a witch from coming through even one door or window. But there was a more efficient way to use the stink: *And it ought to keep those murderous rascals away from me.*

Did she string the pair of pungent roots around her thin neck?

Certainly not.

Loyola Montoya ate both garlic cloves *right on the spot*.

Tough old lady.

CHAPTER ELEVEN

EXCELLENT FRINGE BENEFITS

After a brief but deep and restful sleep, Charlie Moon enjoyed a mug of honeyed coffee on the headquarters porch. The rancher was serenaded by the song of an uproariously happy river splashing its way over a glistening cobblestoned highway to the faraway western sea. Yonder on a rocky ridge, a wily old canine raised her nose to commune with an unseen waning moon and managed a passable imitation of cowboy singer Don Edwards mimicking a yip-yipping coyote—and thus was the circle of mutual admiration closed. Pretty good stuff, and you'd think a man would be satisfied, but this was not enough for Mr. Moon. Never one to deny himself a lawful pleasure, he topped off the treat by filling his eyes with the eastern sky, which was aglow over the Buckhorns with a silvery-white phosphorescence. Exclusively for his benefit, the silver radiance melted into liquid gold, followed this with shimmering streaks of pink, then swirls of deep purple. Good things have a way of passing away too quickly, and this sterling performance was completed within a dozen heartbeats.

The tribal investigator drained his mug, went inside and strode across the parlor and into the hallway, where he stopped in front of a mirror mounted on a closet door. Knowing that Loyola would expect him to look his very best, Moon had dressed in his gray Sunday-go-to-meeting suit, matching gray bull-hide cowboy boots, and a dove-gray John B. Stetson.

The tall man straightened his black string tie and checked the sharp-as-an-ax creases in his custom-made slacks. As a final touch, he pinned the gold Southern Ute tribal investigator shield onto the left pocket of his white shirt.

He evaluated the resultant image with a critic's flinty gaze. Pronounced it *not bad.*

In a final adjustment to the *strictly business* portion of his outfit, Moon checked the .357 Magnum six-inch-barrel pistol holstered on his hip. No problem there. Loaded for bear. On a social call such as this, the sidearm was merely ornamental, but appearance was (by Moon's careful reckoning) about 92 percent of getting a lawman's job done, and Loyola expected a visiting cop to be suitably armed.

What a fine morning this was.

What an extraordinary day it would be.

LOYOLA'S TEN ACRES

The sun was hanging nine diameters high in a pale blue sky when Charlie Moon turned off the paved road and onto the rutted dirt lane that wound its serpentine way through a quarter mile of sage, piñon, and juniper before finally terminating at the farmhouse that Loyola Montoya had called home since the deepest, darkest years of the Great Depression.

Moon parked the Columbine Expedition in the scant shade of a sickly elm. A pair of inquisitive yellow jackets landed on the windshield and peered at the new arrival. Ignoring the winged, stinging insects, the tall, thin, gray-clad man got out of his automobile. He strode across the weed-choked yard toward the slightly awry front porch of a weather-beaten frame house, which had not felt the touch of a paintbrush since Loyola's husband had died almost thirty years ago. Hopeful cottonwoods had sprouted here and there. Also sage and prickly pear. The invited visitor stepped onto the porch, hoped his bull-hide boots wouldn't break through one of the rotted pine boards. He tapped on the front door, which opened under the pressure of his knuckle to exhale a musky scent of staleness. Moon took hold of the door, tapped harder.

Nothing.

"Hello inside—anybody home?"

He could hear the tinny tick-ticking of a small wind-up clock.

This did not feel *right*.

The lawman called out louder, "Mrs. Montoya—it's Charlie Moon."

A warm breeze rattled dry cottonwood leaves.

The lawman stepped inside. He stood in the gloomy parlor, waiting for his pupils to dilate. Little by little, the familiar interior of the widow's home materialized. The small brick fireplace that featured a fancy wrought-iron grate. A sagging old sofa that reminded him of a swayback mule his grandfather had ridden to Ignacio every Saturday morning. A recliner flanked by a Walmart lamp with a plastic shade and a handmade maple magazine rack. Though sensing that the effort would prove futile, Moon called again for the lady of the house. He was rewarded with the expected nonresponse.

Over the stale scents that inhabit any old, lived-in house, the Ute's nostrils picked up something that commanded his attention. Or was it two somethings? No, three. He raised his nose, sniffed in a larger sample. The strongest of the scents was both familiar and oddly sweet. Roasted meat?

Yes. Pork, he guessed.

I bet she's cooked up a big breakfast for me, then wandered off somewhere. Moon recalled that there was a root cellar under the kitchen. *She's probably gone down there to get a jar of preserves.* The second, more stringent aroma, was kerosene. No surprise. Loyola cooked her meals on an eighty-year-old kerosene stove.

But what was that underlying, peculiar odor? He took another sniff. *That smells a lot like . . . burned hair.*

The lawman drew his sidearm and took five long strides across the living room, a shorter one into the kitchen's twilight. The firearm hung heavy in his hand.

What he found there shall not be described in any detail.

Suffice it to say that the aged woman, whose body was on the floor, had expired in a localized fire. That the blaze had apparently started when a kerosene lamp had been knocked off the kitchen table. That Loyola's gray hair was mostly burned off.

That her roasted flesh smelled *sweet*.

Feeling himself about to retch, Charlie Moon sprinted out the back door, off the porch, and into the edge of the apple orchard. He tried vainly to fight off an attack of dry heaves, and the nightmarish image and scent.

Sufficient for the day was this horror. Sufficient for a lifetime.

His lungs needed a breath of fresh air—his face, beams of heavenly sunshine.

Which blessings were promptly granted.

Within thirty minutes of the tribal investigator's terse cell-phone call, three Ignacio PD units and a La Plata County sheriff's pickup had arrived. The four official motor vehicles delivered a total of seven uniformed cops.

While Moon was telling the town cops and the sheriff about the grisly scene in the old woman's kitchen, they were joined by SUPD Officer Danny Bignight, who had gotten the word, as the Utes say—from the *talking drums*. Barely a minute later, a state policeman pulled up, with La Plata County ME Wilson Schmidt's gray van trailing so closely behind that it might have been towed by the trooper's low-slung Chevrolet sedan.

After a preliminary examination of the corpse and its immediate surroundings, the medical examiner's tentative finding was that Mrs. Loyola Montoya had probably suffered a stroke or heart failure and collapsed. In the process of falling, the elderly woman had knocked a lighted kerosene lamp off her kitchen table, which had started the blaze. An autopsy would be performed on the blackened body and a detailed, official investigation made into the cause of the fire, but it was unlikely that these routine procedures would shed any new light on the widow's final misfortune.

The tribal investigator reported Loyola's complaint about "witches" and what he had discovered upon arriving at her home. While waiting for those with jurisdiction to show up, Moon had waded the creek and found evidence of a recently abandoned encampment. Judging from a quick examination of tire tracks and footprints, he estimated that four vehicles and at least ten persons had been camping on land owned by the Blue Diamond Natural Gas Company. An effort would be made to track down those trespassers who had hounded the unfortunate woman, but most of the lawmen were in agreement with the ME's preliminary opinion—that Mrs. Montoya had died of natural causes.

The two Indians saw the matter from somewhat different perspectives.

SUPD Officer Danny Bignight had considerable respect for modern forensic science and didn't doubt for a moment that the Apache elder had died more or less as the medical examiner theorized. The Taos Pueblo Indian didn't know how they'd done it, but he figured that one way or another, the band of *brujos* Loyola had complained to Moon about were responsible for her death.

Charlie Moon also accepted the ME's tentative finding of accidental death, but, like his friend Danny Bignight, the tribal investigator suspected that there was more to the fatality than met the medical examiner's eye—contributing factors. Some bad guys had trespassed on Blue Diamond land and gotten crosswise of Loyola. One insult and threat had led to another until . . . *Just for meanness, they killed Loyola's goat and strung it up on her back porch.* The stress of the angry encounter had probably led to Loyola's stroke or heart attack. *If that's really how she died.* He flexed long, lean fingers that could straighten an iron horseshoe, then fold it back into a U. *I'd like to get my hands on whoever it was.* Such a gratifying opportunity seemed highly unlikely—the thuggish half-wits would be far away by now, probably in another state. It bothered Moon that they would probably never pay for what they had done. *Not in this world.* What troubled him even more was an overdose of regret that was settling sourly into his gut. *If I'd driven down here yesterday, right after I hung up the phone from talking to Loyola, she'd probably still be alive.* And not only that . . . *There's a good chance I could have dealt with those so-called witches.* He raised a sorrowful gaze to the pale blue sky. *But I put off the trip.* Why? *Because I'm just a part-time lawman. And not a very good one at that.*

The time had come for some serious soul-searching.

CHAPTER TWELVE

RETURN TO THE COLUMBINE

After he finished his lunch, Foreman Pete Bushman bit off a big chaw of Red Man Tobacco and went to sit on his front porch and chew. While awaiting the boss's return, he entertained himself by spitting at blackflies. By and by, he heard the Ute's automobile. He got up from his straight-back chair and ambled slowly across the yard to flag Charlie Moon down as the rancher slowed for a clattering crossing of Too Late Creek bridge. The scruffy-bearded stockman had not heard about Loyola Montoya's grisly death down in La Plata County, much less the discovery of the charred corpse. As the tribal investigator lowered the passenger-side window, Bushman leaned on the door and grinned at the owner of the outfit. "Glad to see you, Charlie. There's some things I need to talk to you about, mainly—"

"Not now, Pete." Moon turned away from the foreman's intense, beady-eyed gaze. "Whatever it is can wait till later."

"No it can't." Bushman jerked his chin to indicate his residence. "Dolly's down in her back again and—"

"I'm sorry, Pete." Moon steeled himself for a conversation he preferred to avoid. "Does she feel well enough to go into Granite Creek and see a doctor?"

"Oh, sure. Fact is, we just got back from town. Doc Martin prescribed some little red pills, said Dolly should take it easy for a week or two. Maybe a month."

"I hope that'll do the trick. Make sure your wife gets all the rest she needs."

"Oh, I'll do that all right." Bushman turned his head and spat at a fuzzy brown caterpillar. "But I've got an awful lot to do, so I'd like to hire somebody to help look after my ol' lady till she's feeling some better. Kind of like a lady's companion."

Moon nodded. "See to it, then."

Pleased by this easy victory, the foreman figured this was an opportune time to press a related issue. "And then there's the new horse barn that needs to be roofed before winter sets in, and you know how that can happen here in September. But we're shorthanded, Charlie, and—"

"Hire whoever you need, Pete."

This was too easy. The cranky foreman glared at the boss. "Well I generally do, but only after you give me your okay."

"Consider it given." Moon nodded curtly, drove away.

Pete Bushman watched him go. *Well don't that beat all.* He took off his tattered straw hat and scratched at his perpetually itchy scalp. Of all the people he knew, Charlie Moon was the most amiable. *I wonder what's gnawing on his leg.*

Moon stalked into the ranch headquarters parlor, mumbled an incoherent greeting to Sarah and Daisy, and headed upstairs—as his aunt would later say, "stomping snakes all the way."

The women stared at the empty space in his wake, flinched at the slam of his office door.

Sarah's unwrinkled brow came very near furrowing. *I've never seen Charlie so upset. Well, except for that time Aunt Daisy got him so mad about . . .* But such unhappy incidents were best forgotten.

Daisy Perika glared. *I bet one of his precious cows fell over and died.* But she knew how remarkably resilient her nephew was, and what a potent cure delicious food could be for a man who was out of sorts. *When we sit down to try that green chili pork posole that me and Sarah cooked up, he'll feel lots better and tell us all about his troubles.*

Charlie Moon was not in the mood for pork.

But, as it happened, the meaty issue was academic. He would not come downstairs on that Saturday evening. Not even for supper.

CHAPTER THIRTEEN

ACUTE INSOMNIA

Which is what Charlie Moon was suffering from. Also . . .
guilt.

About two hours before dawn, the restless man finally
gave up, rolled out of bed, and dressed from his heels to the
crown of his head. He stepped quietly out of his upstairs
bedroom and onto the hardwood-floored hallway, made his
way just as softly down the carpeted stairway, and eased
himself out the front door without (he hoped) disturbing the
ladies whom (he believed) were fast asleep in their downstairs bedrooms.

Both were wide awake, worrying about the most important man in their lives.

Tired of lying on her back, Daisy turned onto her right
side. *I've never seen Charlie so down in the mouth that he
went into hiding and wouldn't even come out for supper. And
now he's sneaked out of his own house.* The old woman turned
onto her left side and sighed. *One of his friends must've
died.* But who? And then it came to her: *Maybe something
bad happened to Loyola.*

Sarah Frank stared at the beamed ceiling. *I wonder
where he's off to?* Salty tears filled her eyes. *If Charlie loved
me even a little bit, he'd tell me about his troubles.*

Outside in the chilly night, Moon was trolling the depths
of his dismal thoughts. *I should've realized right away that
Loyola was in serious trouble.* He fixed his gaze on a thin

sliver of silvery moon. *Once upon a time, I was a halfway decent cop.* His dark face was set like flint. *But those days are gone.* The tribal investigator's fingers found the gold shield that was still pinned to his white shirt. *I don't deserve to wear this.* He knew what he had to do. *I'll drive down to Ignacio tomorrow and toss this badge on the tribal chairman's desk.* But wait a minute. *This* is *tomorrow.* It wouldn't be long before morning would dawn over the highlands. The chairman wouldn't be in his office today. . . . *But I'll find Oscar Sweetwater, wherever he is—and turn in my badge.*

He slipped into his Expedition, shut the door with as little noise as possible, and eased the Columbine flagship over the Too Late Creek bridge slowly so that the rattling of redwood planks would not disturb anyone's slumbers. An ailing Dolly Bushman especially needed her rest, and the foreman's residence was just on the other side of the bridge.

The drive south to the reservation would take the Ute through Granite Creek, where most of the population would still be asleep. It would also take him through one of the finest stretches of God's creation, which was just what he needed. Breakfast would also be good for what ailed him and steaming-hot coffee would sure hit the spot, but a stone-quiet early-morning drive with blue-gray granite mountains soaring heavenward at every direction is a tonic that tends to clear a man's head of musty cobwebs and other debris. Mile by mile, the troublesome stirrings in Moon's mind gradually subsided. Halfway to town, he began to feel tolerably better. *What I need is some useful work to do.* Like getting a line on Loyola's grandson. *If I could track Wallace Montoya down, he might be able to tell us something about those so-called witches.*

By the time Moon passed the Granite Creek city-limits sign, first light was beginning to glow over the mountains and the lean fellow who had skipped supper last night was beginning to feel a dim glimmering of appetite. *I'll stop at Chicky's Daylight Bakery for coffee and doughnuts.* But it has been said, and truly, that men do not live by bread alone; Moon needed nourishment for his soul. Feeling the deep ache of that hunger, the Ute realized that this was the dawn of a Sunday morning. After refreshment at Chicky's, the lifelong Catholic would attend early-morning Mass at St. Anthony's, which was about six blocks from the doughnut dispensary.

Chief of Police Scott Parris was also feeling a deep ache, but this one was of a purely physiological nature. A dull throb in his left arm was troubling his sleep. As if reeled in by the persistent pain, the ardent angler drifted ever so slowly upward from the muck of a deep, murky river. Just above his buoyant spirit, warm sunlight glistened invitingly on a rippled surface. There, the dreamer would be freed from dark fantasies to encounter a new day.

He almost made it.

Poor fellow apparently got snagged on something or other. The sinister, irresistible undertow pulled him away toward one of those epochs labeled "Way Back When."

The summer of 1877.

But where? In this instance, a location where justice was dispensed with a lusty vengeance. Granite Creek, Colorado.

EPISODE TWO

The Holiday

It was his dream, and U.S. Marshal Scott Parris was the center of attention again. But even for a man with more than a fair share of ego, being center stage was not particularly gratifying. Local citizens who had never seen a lawman hanged had arrived in a great swarm, like greenflies that had picked up the scent of dead flesh.

Almost three hundred curious spectators had arrived on foot, half again as many on horseback, and several dozen had shown up in heavy mule-drawn wagons or fine carriages hitched to high-stepping horses.

The crowd had gathered in front of the courthouse to witness his execution at the Hanging Tree—a hideously deformed old cottonwood. To facilitate the day's big event, a stout lower branch had been sawed off to a sturdy six-foot projection, which the hangman had notched with a hatchet to receive the rope.

The fact that he was seated backward on a white, pink-eyed mule, with his hands tied behind his back, made it difficult for the prisoner to retain even a semblance of dignity. But Scott Parris did his level best. The cold-eyed U.S. marshal sneered at the offer of a last cigarette. Ditto for a stiff shot of rye whiskey. If the hanging judge had been within range, Parris would have spat in his eye.

As the hangman mounted a shaky stepladder to slip a noose around Parris's neck, a Methodist parson approached with the Good Book in his hand. "Marshal, do you have anything you wish to say before sentence is carried out?"

Parris glared at the kindly man. "Damn right I do!" he bellowed at those citizens who had gathered to watch the show. "What was it I did?"

There was no response from the suddenly hushed congregation.

The hangman, who had another appointment in Leadville, tightened the noose.

The condemned man had another question, which he dared not utter for fear of what the answer might be: Where's my buddy—where's ol' Charlie Moon?

Judge "Pug" Bullet nodded at the hangman, who gave the albino mule a good slap on the flank.

Off went the startled creature, scattering the holiday crowd.

His body dangling heavily from the hemp rope, Scott Parris gasped. Choked. Was still for a few final heartbeats, then—

As if attempting a macabre ballet, his muscular torso twisted. Twitched.

The dancer's swollen, grape-purple face gaped blindly at his entranced audience.

One last spine-wrenching twist. A final spasmodic twitch.

Somewhere in the audience, an appreciative viewer applauded.

A wasted effort.

There would be—could be—no encore.

The performance was over.

The actor's corpse hung silent, still . . . turned slowly on the corded hemp.

Hovering above the thinning congregation of flesh-and-blood gawkers, Marshal Parris's disembodied self scowled at his hideous corpse. He murmured to no one in particular, "I'm sure glad my sainted mother never lived to see her little Scotty end up as a damned . . ." He choked on the western expression for hanged outlaws, then spat it out—"A damned cottonwood blossom!" The heavy weight of anger and humiliation was almost too much for a spirit to bear.

Mercifully—or so it seemed—the undertow of Sleep's dark stream released Parris's soul to the embrace of a wet, gray dawn, which in itself was not a bad thing; rain is a great blessing in the arid high country west of the Front Range. The pesky fly fouling this cloudy pie-in-the-sky? Only this: When *actual* horrors come to call, they must be confronted face-to-face. Waking up is not an option.

The Granite Creek chief of police rolled onto his back, gasped, hacked a painful series of strangling coughs. *Oooohh . . . my throat hurts like hell.*

Rubbing his eyes, he recalled something about a big crowd and a soft-spoken man with a Bible in his hand. *Must've had a weird dream.* Most of the unlikely melodrama had already slipped away, and by the time Scott Parris's feet were on the floor, the morbid spectators and kindly minister had concealed themselves in some dark closet of his memory.

CHAPTER FOURTEEN

HIS SOUL'S REFRESHMENT

Counting Charlie Moon, there were twelve worshipers at the early-morning mass, which—as it began—was not noticeably different from thousands of others that the lifelong Catholic had attended.

The priest's deep voice reverberated off the beamed ceiling and paneled walls: "In the name of the Father—" all present crossed themselves, "and of the Son, and of the Holy Spirit."

The hushed *amens* might have been the wings of a dozen unseen doves fluttering about in the twilight heights of the sanctuary.

The celebrant continued, "The grace of our Lord Jesus Christ and the love of God and the fellowship of the Holy Spirit be with you all."

Unheard beneath the other voices, Moon responded in a whisper, "And also with you."

"As we prepare to celebrate the mystery of Christ's love, let us acknowledge our failures and ask the Lord for pardon and strength."

The congregation joined with the priest: "I confess to almighty God, and to you, my brothers and sisters, that I have sinned through my own fault in my thoughts, and in my words, in what I have done, and in what I have failed to do. . . ."

Stung by the painful reminder of what he *had failed to do*, Charlie Moon was suddenly struck deaf and dumb. The familiar words caught in his throat; the priest's voice was drowned out by a heavy silence that seemed bent on suffocating his soul. For some time—precisely how long he could not tell—he might have been at the bottom of a deep well. And then he heard—or *thought* he heard—a distant murmuring.

Oh, I'm dead now—dead, dead, dead!

Her voice was instantly recognizable.

But don't blame yourself, Charlie Moon.

The old woman was coming closer. *Don't give it a thought.* She appended an addle-brained cackle. *Oh, no—it's not* your *fault.* The Apache crone seemed to be sitting in the pew beside him. *There's no way you could've got there in time to help me.* A pause for sighing. *It happened not long after dark.*

From the corner of his eye, Moon thought he could see a wispy image of the dead woman. He could definitely smell the pungent scent of kerosene, the horrific odor of burned hair and roasted flesh. And then . . . and then—

The whatever-it-was reached out with an icy hand—*touched his face.*

Charlie Moon could not move. Like a sleeper stranded between a nightmare and wakefulness, he was paralyzed.

He felt her clammy breath, and caught a whiff of garlic as Loyola Montoya whispered in his ear, *Alphabet soup. White Shell Woman smears mud on her face. Hammers and nails. Buckets and pails. Puppy dogs' tails. Sugar and spice and everything nice. When White Shell Woman smears mud on her face. Hammers and nails . . .*

Over and over she repeated the string of nonsense, then added, *Remember what I told you . . . Jefferson's General Store . . . something terrible!*

Moon closed his eyes. *Please, God . . . make it stop.*

For too many racing heartbeats, the urgent prayer went unanswered.

Then—intermittently, as if from a dream—he could hear the voices of the priest and the small congregation. The words drifted in from some faraway place.

"Glory to God in the highest, and peace to his people on earth . . . we worship you, we give you thanks . . ."

Over it all, Loyola prattled on: *Hammers and nails. Buckets and pails. Puppy dogs' tails . . .*

Though he could not make a sound, Charlie Moon managed to move his lips. *You take away the sin of the world . . . have mercy on me.*

Such a plea cannot be ignored.

The agonizing spell was broken by the voices from flesh and blood:

> ". . . *For you alone are the Holy One*
> *You alone are the Lord*
> *You alone are the Most High*
> *Jesus Christ,*
> *with the Holy Spirit,*
> *in the Glory of God the Father."*

"Amen!" the stricken man said, mildly alarming the small congregation, causing even the decorous priest to arch an eyebrow.

Moon was too relieved, too happy to be concerned about committing a churchly misdemeanor. Though a fading hint of the telltale scents remained, whatever had been haunting him had fallen silent. The *presence* was gone.

Aunt Daisy, who had experienced more ghostly encounters than (as she liked to say) "Bayer has aspirins," would have insisted that her nephew had been visited by Loyola Montoya's wandering spirit. Without a doubt, the dead woman wanted to tell Charlie something. When he had the time (and inclination) to mull over this unsettling experience, Charlie Moon would conclude that he had been visited by a guilty conscience.

The Gospel reading was from the third chapter of

Matthew, where St. John the Baptist describes how the Lord—winnowing fork in his hand—will clear his threshing floor to gather the wheat into his barn—and burn the chaff with unquenchable fire.

Pretty strong stuff.

The homily was on the same subject.

Though Charlie Moon tried hard to concentrate on the message, he remained distracted by the memory of the *visitation.*

After receiving Holy Communion, he left the century-old brick church and pushed his comfortable black Stetson down to his ears. He was making long strides across the parking lot when a flash of lightning illuminated that jagged row of dark peaks that looms over Granite Creek.

As he approached his parked car, Charlie Moon remembered the razor-thin crescent that had hung like a scythe over last evening's sunset. White Shell Woman had already muddied up most of her face. If Loyola had heard the "witches" discussing their intent to commit a "sacrifice," the planned crime might have been committed last night. *Or it could happen tonight. Or for that matter . . . right now.*

At that very instant, as he was reaching for the car door, a long tongue of lightning took a good lick at an old, diseased, precariously leaning elm tree across the street. A withered branch splintered and burst into flames that illuminated the gray morning. Simultaneously, as if an inner flash of light had brightened a dim corner of his mind, the tribal investigator experienced a remarkable epiphany.

The priest's homily contained the key that would unlock the mystery of Loyola's seemingly meaningless phrases. It was all a matter of separating the wheat from the chaff, the true from the false. Easier said than done, of course. Charlie Moon went with intuition.

And perhaps, just a touch of inspiration.

I'll toss out puppy dogs' tails. Ditto for sugar and spice and everything nice.

The chaff was discarded. Now, *pay close attention to what's left.*

Loyola had been unambiguous about one critical point: the witches would strike in Granite Creek. Moon barely heard a heavy rumble of thunder. *But where in our fair city?*

Again, the absent apparition nattered at him, *Hammers and nails.*

The Ute felt rain pelt his face. *A carpentry shop? Or maybe a general contractor?*

The haunt seemed to be frustrated: *Hammers and nails. Buckets and pails.*

A hardware store? Maybe. *But which one?* There were four establishments in Granite Creek that dispensed hammers, nails, buckets, and pails.

The dead woman would not shut up. *Alphabet soup . . . Alphabet.*

Alphabet. A-B-Cs. ABC Hardware?

It fit.

But Granite Creek was also home to ABC Auto Supply, ABC Dry Cleaners, and ABC Auto Repair. And . . . Alpha-Pet Veterinary Hospital. *Puppy dogs' tails.* But that had been discarded as chaff.

Moon felt his face flush. *This is getting downright silly.*

But wait a minute . . . The intended victim was someone whose name reminded Loyola of President Jefferson. That wasn't much help. Counting first and last names, there were probably four dozen Jeffersons in the county. On the other hand, Loyola had said, *That's not quite right.* Maybe the name she'd heard had only *sounded* like the president's surname. But what sounds like Jefferson? The man who'd been awake all night could not think of a single example. Except . . .

Jeppson.

Jeppson's ABC Hardware.

Moon stared through his automobile window without seeing the other worshipers, several under brightly colored umbrellas, emerging from the church.

What he did see, writ large:

Mrs. Montoya was a widow.
      Mrs. Jeppson is a widow.
Mrs. Montoya lived alone.
      Mrs. Jeppson lives alone.
Mrs. Montoya was murdered.
      Mrs. Jeppson . . .

Barely two minutes later, after greatly exceeding the posted speed limit, the Southern Ute tribal investigator arrived at the oldest hardware store in Granite Creek.

CHAPTER FIFTEEN

ABC HARDWARE

Located on the corner of seventh street and Roosevelt Avenue, Jeppson's ABC Hardware was the successor to a general store that once had been the centerpiece of a thriving business district. Alas, the Red Horse Saloon, Floyd's Barber Shop, the First Miner's Bank of Granite Creek, the Purina Feed Store, and several more—all had long ago closed their doors. The widow Jeppson lived in a 1940s-era two-story brick home that was situated about two blocks from her hardware store, that struggling enterprise now a faded and somewhat seedy anachronism in a neatly trimmed residential neighborhood. The venerable purveyor of *hammers and nails, buckets and pails* was surrounded by thirty acres of modern homes and a scattering of three-story apartment complexes that resembled those motels that cluster around interstate exits. As Charlie Moon turned in at ABC Hardware, a light rain salted with sleet began to sift through a vaporous gray mist. Turning on the windshield wipers, he noted that there was only one other vehicle in the parking lot—a twenty-year-old Ford Econoline van with California plates. Its rusted-out, sooty-black body appeared to have been brush painted by an amateur who was in a big hurry. Not much there to elevate the experienced lawman's eyebrow. Aside from the fact that the van was puffing exhaust.

Which minor extravagance raised a few questions in Moon's mind.

Such as: *With the only business on this side of the street closed, why's somebody in an old clunker burning gasoline?* One query so often leads to another. *And why, with a hundred spaces to pick from, did he back into a handicapped parking space at the front entrance?* Questions posed in the absence of clear answers are such a vexation—and also a challenge to the imagination.

Moon eyed the driver's dim form. *He could be a lookout for some bad guys who're already inside.* The poker player rolled that long shot over in his mind. *It's a lot more likely that he's an out-of-towner who's waiting to meet someone.* The Ute checked his dashboard clock. It was almost 9 A.M. *He might be a customer who hopes the hardware store will open in a few minutes.* The experienced lawman considered other innocent possibilities. Calculated probabilities.

Came to a decision.

He pulled out of the parking lot, headed in the general direction of that fine place where he hung his hat, and more than that—tended strictly to his own business. The pull of warm hearth and peaceful home was almost irresistible, but before Mr. Moon could enjoy those domestic pleasures, he had a detour to take and an unpleasant task to attend to. One that was likely to ruin someone's day. *Mine, most likely.*

Aside from the man in the van, only one other person had witnessed Charlie Moon's transient coming and going. Across the street from the hardware store, seated alone at a table for two in the Caffeine High Coffee Shop, this singular individual sipped a cup of black Honduran coffee spiced with genuine Louisiana cane sugar and pure Mexican ginger, and from time to time penciled notes on a small spiral pad. The most recent entry was:

> *Dk blue Exp CO Pltes entrd ABC pkng lot apprx 8:56 AM*
> *Flwr logo on drv's dr & sign: COLUMBINE something BRANCH? RANCH? (Rem—Chck Yel Pges)*
> *Exp Dprtd apprx 8:57 AM*

In a potential emergency, such as the high probability of an imminent encounter with an armed officer of the law, the coffee sipper known as Trout was prepared to either (a) set fire to or (b) eat the incriminating pages, and had done so on three previous occasions (two quick burns, one hurried ingestion that led to acute indigestion). Trout was not particularly concerned about the cowboy-hatted man in the big SUV, who was gone now and very nearly forgotten.

Barely three blocks from the hardware store, Moon turned right at a stoplight, then drove another two blocks before turning right again on a shady residential street. The tribal investigator parked the Expedition in front of a Home for Sale sign, opened the tailgate window, and removed an essential tool of his trade from under a blanket. He strapped the weighty assembly around his waist.

SENTRY NUMBER ONE

The young man behind the wheel of the Ford van had an inexpensive walkie-talkie in his left hand, a stainless steel, snub-nosed, ivory-gripped .44 Magnum revolver in his right. He laid the heavy weapon on the seat beside him, thumbed the Talk button on the radio-frequency-communications device. "Skeezix?"

"I'm here, Dag."

"That Expedition I told you about that came and went—it hasn't circled back or anything."

"Glad to hear it." The raspy voice in his ear added, "But don't get careless. Keep your eyes on the street."

Which was just what the subservient sentry did.

Indeed, Dag—who had his gaze fixed on the parking lot and street out front—paid no attention whatever to either of the van's door-mounted rearview mirrors. Not that it would have helped if he had. The tribal investigator (so those who know him say) had a way of slipping up on you that made him invisible in bright daylight. Surely an exaggeration. But this was a murky morning, and, despite his considerable height, Charlie Moon did have a talent for quasi-invisibility. The Ute was helped along when the heavens opened to spray a hard, slanting rain that turned murky morning into semi-night and suddenly concealed Moon's dark form.

Add all these factors up and you have the reason why, barely six minutes later, Dag was unaware of the shadowy figure cloaked in a black raincoat who was at work behind the van.

Why did the driver not hear the soft, hissing sounds?

The van windows were rolled up to keep out the chill. Also because the engine was running. Ditto, the defroster fan.

Why was he unaware of the gradual shifting in the vehicle's stance?

Hard to say.

But Dag's faculties were not entirely faulty. Indeed, he absolutely lurched at the sound of a big knuckle rapping on his window, went slack-jawed at the sight of the grinning face on the wet side of the glass, felt his heart race as the voice said, "I believe these belong to you."

The driver dropped the walkie-talkie into his shirt pocket, put his hand on the pistol resting by his right thigh, and lowered the window by half an inch. "What's that?"

The stranger with rainwater dripping from his hat brim displayed the delicate items between finger and thumb. "A couple of spring-loaded valves." Moon jerked his head to indicate the back side of the van. "They should be in your rear tires. Inside the valve stems."

Our scholar (a fine-arts major) had a hard time assimilating complex technical information. "What?"

Moon explained: "When the valve stems aren't in place, the air comes out."

At the moment, Dag was also a man of few words. Two of them were "Uh . . ." and "Uh . . ."

The very soul of Patience, the Ute mechanic explained: "Somebody unscrewed these valve stems. That let all the air out. Both of your rear tires are flat as pancakes."

Dag found a few more words: "Hellfire and damnation!"

As an unconscious gesture, he raised the wicked-looking pistol just high enough for the tribal investigator to see it. "Who'd do a mean thing like that?"

A reasonable question. The answer was instantaneous.

Moon jerked the van door open and unhinged the young man's jaw with a hard right hook that just about took Dag's head off.

The storm that had pulled a curtain over the hardware store parking lot was only mildly frustrating to the observer across the street, who had no way of knowing that Dagwood had been assaulted by a local citizen.

The second person present in the Caffeine High Coffee Shop was a sleepy-eyed Salvadoran whose name tag identified him as an assistant manager; the versatile fellow also served as cook, dishwasher, janitor, and waiter. In that latter capacity, he sidled up to the only occupied table. "You be wantin' anythin' else?"

"A double espresso." The customer amended the order: "No, make that a triple. With sugar and spice."

The assistant manager grinned. "And everythin' nice?"

"What?"

"You say 'sugar an' spice,' so I say 'and everythin' nice.'"

"Oh." *Did I really say that?* "Sorry. A slip of the tongue." Trout smiled. "I meant to say 'sugar and nutmeg.'"

CHAPTER SIXTEEN

SENTRY NUMBER TWO

The rear-guard lookout was posted at ABC Hardware's alley entrance, just inside a narrow steel door on the loading dock. The quasi-intellectual member of the team had developed a tendency to while away his time pondering life's many pernicious perplexities and vertiginous vicissitudes, but only after he had looked up all three words in an unabridged dictionary. At this moment, Dilbert was pursuing his hobby whilst leaning against a small forklift. The malcontent was musing about how unfair the setup was. *While Skeezix and Snuffy are up front having fun with the dopey old woman, what am I doing?* Rubbing the snub-nosed barrel of a stainless steel, ivory-gripped .44 Magnum revolver thoughtfully against his chin, the young man responded to this question: *I'm standing here in the dark, contemplating my navel.* A long, self-pitying sigh. *I am so totally bored.* He tapped the pistol against his fleshy nose. *I wish something would happen. Anything.* After making this foolhardy wish, he employed his wonderfully fertile imagination in an attempt to envision himself in some faraway, exotic place. A medieval dungeon crawling with rabid rats and ravenous body lice. A dark, stinking chamber where an insane sorcerer brewed up—

Dilbert cocked his ear. *What was that?*

A rapping on the door? Yes, but very subtle. More like a tapping.

He leaned forward, strained to hear.

Who was that rapping-tapping on his chamber door?

No kind of bird that he would care to meet.

The sentry got a firm grip on his sidearm.

Another rap-rap.

It might be Dag, come around back to tell me something. But if it is, why don't he just use the walkie-talkie? Maybe the instrument had crapped out. *Or maybe Skeezix signaled for radio silence.* The sentry whispered, "Who's there?"

No response.

Guess I'd better go outside and have a look.

Guess again.

Every nerve fiber in his unwashed body, every pulsing neuron and synaptic junction in his addled brain—all screamed in unison, *Don't open the door!*

Did he pay the least attention to this sensible multitude of nerve fibers, pulsing neurons, and synaptic junctions? Of course not. Curiosity trumped them all.

Dilbert's left hand reached out. His pale, clammy fingers grasped the brass knob and turned it. He pushed the loading-dock door open just enough to stick his head out into the inclement weather.

Aside from rain and sleet on his face, what did Mr. D. get for his trouble?

Sudden, total darkness.

Nothing more.

MRS. JEPPSON

The widow was in her office, tied to a chair. Terrified by what was happening, she could not remember what day of the week it was, much less the combination to the antique Mosler safe. Several stinging slaps across the face had not helped her memory.

A big, burly, black-bearded bear of a man stood over the helpless victim. Laying his stainless steel, snub-nosed, ivory-gripped .44 Magnum revolver on the proprietor's desk, Skeezix pulled a razor-sharp Buck hunting knife from a sheath at the small of his back. What sort of man was this? Let it merely be said that he *enjoyed* pressing the cold blade against Mrs. Jeppson's trembling upper lip. "Now listen close, you old bag a bones. Here's the deal—either you cough up the combination or I slice off your nose."

"Go ahead, Skeez—cut her damn nose off and make her *eat* it!" (This encouragement came from Snuffy, a pale, slender sadist with a blond buzz cut, who had his stainless steel, snub-nosed, ivory-gripped .44 Magnum revolver stuffed under his belt.)

The befuddled old woman whimpered. "Please . . . I just can't remem—"

"Ah—excuse me."

The startled thugs turned to see a tall, dark, thin man in a black raincoat standing in the office doorway.

Oh, thank you, God! Mrs. Jeppson used this heaven-sent distraction to stretch her leg. Yes, just one leg. No, the leg did not need stretching. The point was to get her toe onto an alarm button under her desk and press it. Her late husband had informed her about the security system's several helpful features, but all the widow recalled was that if she pushed on the big button, the police would come. She did not remember Mr. Jeppson's remarks about the security camera, which was concealed in a wall clock whose face was the very picture of innocence. Sad to say, the alarm button was a long way away, and her leg was inconveniently short.

Skeezix was the first to find his voice. "Who'n hell are *you*?"

"The name's Moon." As if apologetic for barging in on a private party, the uninvited guest was holding his gray, Sunday-go-meeting John B. Stetson hat in both hands. The right side of Moon's raincoat had been pushed back to expose the long-barreled .357 Magnum holstered on a belt studded with ammunition. The Southern Ute tribal investigator's gold shield glistened on his shirt pocket. "It is my intention to arrest you. But before I do, it is my duty to advise you that anything you say may be used as evidence against you."

The elderly lady stretched her leg ever so hard. *Oh, dear—I hope my hip joint don't pop loose.*

Skeezix's brow furrowed into a perplexed frown. "Did Trout send you to see what we'd do?" He cocked his fuzzy head. "You part a the game—like extra points?"

Mrs. Jeppson got her toe on the button. Pressed it.

"I'm here on behalf of Loyola Montoya." Moon saw Skeezix's eyes go flat at the mention the dead woman's name. "But if you tough guys figure this is a game, either fold your hands—or make your play."

The tough guys thought it over. Pushing old women around was one thing. This fellow—who was either stone crazy or deadly dangerous—was quite another. Fear gnawed at their innards. But (and their adversary was counting on this) even the lowest sort of vermin will fight when cornered. The fingers on their gun hands flexed, edged ever so slowly toward their stainless steel .44 Magnum revolvers until . . . their fingertips touched the ivory grips.

The shake of the tribal investigator's head was barely perceptible. Moon's tone was soft as a summer rain falling on moss. "That'd be a serious mistake."

Both hands froze.

Skeezix's lip curled into an ugly sneer. "There's *no way* you can draw that big horse pistol before we blow you away."

Sidekick Snuffy echoed his agreement: "No way!"

"Boys, I won't argue the point." Still grasping the brim of his gray Stetson with both thumbs, Moon made no move for his sidearm. Smiling like a kindly uncle, he addressed his blustering adversaries oh so softly—barely above a whisper: "But you'd be well advised to place both hands behind your necks, fingers interlocked."

Skeezix snickered.

Snuffy snorted.

Snicker and Snort snatched their pistols.

The snub-nosed .44 Magnums spoke simultaneously: *bam-bam!*

And that was that.

Count two big holes drilled through Charlie Moon's fine cowboy hat.

CHAPTER SEVENTEEN

THE CAFFEINE HIGH COFFEE SHOP

The lonely employee of the small establishment was standing at the window, watching sleet peck at the rain-streaked glass, when over the grumbling of the thunderstorm he heard two very distinct sounds. "Hey—didn't that sound like gunshots?" Getting no response from his customer, the assistant manager turned to repeat the question.

The smallish table for two was deserted, the triple espresso unfinished.

These Americanos are always in a big hurry. The easygoing Salvadoran ambled over to the table, picked up a twenty-dollar bill, and rubbed it between thumb and finger as he calculated the total plus tax and how much would be left over for his tip. Nothing to write home about, but every dollar counted. He sighed and returned to the window. Almost immediately, he heard a faraway wailing sound.

Sirens.

Damn! Somebody must've gotten shot across the street. He chewed on his lower lip. *The police will come around looking for witnesses, asking all kinds of personal questions.* Such as: "We'll need your name, address, and a telephone number." *And if you don't look and talk just right, they're liable to ask for papers.* The undocumented worker hurried away from the window to switch off the lights and

hang a Closed sign in the front entrance. After pulling on a
hooded raincoat, he evacuated the premises by the alley exit.

RESPONDING TO THE ALARM

GCPD officers Eddie "Rocks" Knox and his partner, E. C.
"Piggy" Slocum, were first on the scene, to be followed
quickly by a Colorado State Police officer and GCPD Officer
Alicia Martin, who escorted Mrs. Jeppson upstairs to a small
apartment formerly used by the elderly woman and her husband.

In these familiar surroundings, the spunky widow prepared herself a steaming pot of rooibos tea and opened an
imported tin of yogurt-coated cherries, which treats she
shared with Ms. Martin. Thus calmed and fortified, the
owner of the hardware store proceeded to make her statement to the uniformed lady.

A RUDE AWAKENING

Scott Parris had been sleeping in on this rainy Sunday
morning. After his Old West nightmare of being lynched by
the Law, the chief of police was enjoying a pleasant dream
wherein he relived a 1998 antelope hunt on the wide-open
plains south of Raton, New Mexico. He had the crosshairs on
a pronghorn when something jangled loudly in his left ear.
Parris awakened with a grunt, grabbed the bedside telephone, and was advised by dispatcher Clara Tavishuts that
Knox and Slocum had responded to a security-company
alert that had turned out to be an armed robbery at ABC
Hardware. The officers had arrived at the site and called in
to report two men shot dead, two others seriously injured.

"Thanks, Clara, I'm on my way." The chief of police
slipped into a pair of faded jeans and a red felt shirt, pulled
on his scuffed Roper boots, and donned the venerable felt
hat his daddy had worn in the 1940s. As he sprinted through

the front door, the cop stuffed most of his shirttail into his britches. He scooted into the aged Volvo, kicked up a spray of driveway gravel, and skidded sideways onto the street. He showed up at Jeppson's ABC Hardware just in time to see Doc Simpson's team arrive.

Almost an hour later, after two ambulances had hauled the injured off to Snyder Memorial Hospital, and the medical examiner had taken charge of the hardware-store office where the shooting had occurred, the chief of police took the Ute tribal investigator into a storage space in the rear of Mrs. Jeppson's store. Scott Parris seated himself on a wooden well-pump crate and pointed his finger at a nail keg.

Charlie Moon sat on the small wooden barrel, leaned back against a stack of plywood, stretched his long legs.

"Okay," Parris said. "Let me see if I've got this straight." He held up a meaty hand, glared at his palm, turned down the little finger. "You show up here shortly before nine this morning and spot a suspicious character in a Ford van parked by ABC Hardware's front entrance."

Moon nodded.

The chief of police turned down Finger Number Two. "After making him as the driver for some bad guys inside the hardware store, you drive a few blocks away and park your wheels. You strap on your pistol, walk back, let the air outta the van's rear tires. And after you show the driver the valve stems, you break his jaw, and—"

"I didn't have much choice. He had a bad-looking pistol in his hand."

"Please don't interrupt me, Charlie."

The Ute shrugged.

Parris turned down Finger Number Three. "After you take the van driver's .44 Magnum revolver, you go around back of the store, punch the daylights out of another guy who sticks his head outta a rear door—and you also take his .44 Mag, which is identical to the van driver's pistol."

Moon was wearing his poker face.

"Then," Parris growled, "you march into Mrs. Jeppson's office, where she's being threatened by two more bad guys—

also armed with .44 Mag revolvers—and you shoot both of
'em dead!"

Moon shook his head.

The chief of police arched both of his bushy red eyebrows. "What?"

"You forgot something."

"What?"

The Indian pointed at the white man's hand.

Big smart Aleck. His face glowing pink, Parris pressed
the fourth finger down. "And then . . . and then." *Dammit,
Charlie made me forget where I was.* He took a deep breath,
exhaled slowly. "You've been a law-enforcement officer for
a long time, Charlie. Long enough to know how the game is
played."

The accused showed no sign that he disagreed with that
statement.

"This ain't the Southern Ute res, Charlie."

By a faint nod, the tribal investigator allowed as how this
was so.

Not sure where he was going with all this, Parris went for
the ad-lib. "And you don't have a half ounce of jurisdiction
in Granite Creek."

Moon begged to disagree. "Actually, pard—about two
years ago, during that nasty business over at the Yellow Pines
Ranch, you swore me in as your deputy. And even though I
wouldn't want to embarrass you by mentioning that I'm still
waiting for about nine hundred and ninety-eight dollars of
back pay, I'm bound to tell you that I don't recall that you
ever unswore me. So, unless I'm disremembering, I'm still a
sworn deputy to the chief of police of Granite Creek."

Parris's face deepened to beet red. Veins in his thick neck
started to throb. "I don't care if you're a U.S. deputy marshal
and your territory is every square foot of Colorado this side
of the Front Range!" He unfolded all four digits and wagged
his pointing finger at Moon. "Point is, you should've put in a
911 call. If you had, my officers would've come out here and
took care of business. But no, you had to do the job all by
yourself." He paused before hitting his friend below the belt:

"It ain't enough that you shoot these guys with the pistols you took off their buddies. No—you had to go for head shots—and *through your hat*." Parris's thin grin was sharp as a knife. "Some folks might figure you wanted to play the hot-shot, shoot-'em-up, two-gun movie-star cowboy."

That hurt enough to make Charlie Moon flinch. The groundless charge also set his teeth on edge. "Maybe I should've waited for your uniformed cops to get here." The tribal investigator's follow-up was icy. "But if I had, Mrs. Jeppson might be dead now."

Parris glared at the cheeky Ute.

Charlie Moon stared back.

Finally, the chief of police averted his gaze to his boots. "I guess it was lucky that you showed up just in time to prevent a killing." *Too damn lucky.* "But tell me just one thing." He cleared his throat. "Strictly off the record." Parris looked up at his friend. "How'd you happen to be in this particular neighborhood on a rainy Sunday morning? I mean—what brought you here?"

The Indian had seen this arrow coming. "I came to check on Mrs. Jeppson. Wanted to make sure she was okay."

Parris was goggled-eyed with surprise. "You had a reason to believe she was in danger?"

"Mmm-hmm." Moon eased his lanky frame up from the uncomfortable nail keg. "When you check out these bad guys, you'll find out they're connected to the death of Mrs. Loyola Montoya."

Parris cocked his head. "That Apache woman down in La Plata County?" *I thought that was some kind of accident.* "Didn't she knock over a coal-oil lamp and set herself on fire?"

"That's what the medical examiner believes."

"But you don't?"

Moon shook his head.

"So how'd you come to expect these boys would hold up ABC Hardware—and on this particular morning?"

"I wasn't sure of the exact day, much less the hour."

"Okay." Parris got up with a grunt. "So tell me something you was sure of."

"When I talked to Loyola on the phone—that was on the day before she died—the poor old soul told me she'd heard these 'witches' planning something nasty. But not in La Plata County—it'd happen here in Granite Creek."

Parris's normally expressive face went dangerously blank. He responded in a monotone, "And you didn't bother to tell me?"

Moon shook his head. "I hate to admit it, but I didn't believe a word she said." Without any allusion to his peculiar experience during Holy Mass, the tribal investigator explained how some of the things from the elderly lady's disjointed testimony had "kind of come together in my mind" right after he'd left St. Anthony's that morning.

The chief of police listened to every word, without interrupting.

Buckets and nails equals hardware store.

Alphabet soup suggested ABC.

Jefferson sounds like Jeppson.

Scott Parris thought that made sense. Sort of. He even bought the part about White Shell Woman rubbing her face with mud, suggesting a new moon as the time for the crime. But the white cop had a hunch that his Ute friend was holding something back.

CHAPTER EIGHTEEN

SUPPERTIME AT THE COLUMBINE

Which is a mighty fine time to be there with Charlie Moon and his family and friends—which on this evening includes the Ute's aunt Daisy, his ardent admirer Sarah Frank, and the tribal investigator's closest friend—Chief of Police Scott Parris. Not to mention Sidewinder, the official Columbine hound dog, and Mr. Zig-Zag, Sarah's aging cat, who are at present curled up on the west porch, watching the nearest star settle into a rosy slumber. All very comfy and cozy. But are these furry creatures as happy as the human beings inside the ranch headquarters, who are anticipating a sumptuous feast? It is hard to say with certainty, but both canine and feline nostrils are finely attuned to those scents that hint of meaty beef bones from locally grown Hereford stock, and thinly sliced ham imported from Virginia.

Mr. Moon is in the headquarters kitchen, preparing the meal.

While watching Charlie work, Scott Parris offers helpful advice.

Little Miss Sarah is setting the dining-room table with bowls, cups, plates, and stainless flatware. It is also her privilege to light the tall, yellow tallow candles. All six of them.

Tribal Elder Daisy Perika is in the headquarters parlor, fiddling with her nephew's rarely used television. What manner of cultural enlightenment does the inscrutable old woman search for? *Wheel of Fortune*. Will she find her favorite game show? Stay tuned.

Happily, within the confines of Charlie Moon's little slice of Rocky Mountain paradise, about nine evenings out of ten turn out to be this good, and the tenth is likely to be even better. Every once in a while, there is an exception.

The chief of police was helping himself to a pre-supper cookie when the phone in his shirt pocket vibrated. He pressed the instrument to his ear and barked, "Parris here." The lawman listened to a report from the GCPD dispatcher until it was time to say, "Thanks, Clara." The smug cop returned the phone to his pocket and grinned at his best friend. "You're gonna love this, Charlie."

The Ute was stirring an extra dash of black pepper into a gallon pot of pinto beans. "Whenever you say that, I don't."

"Oh no, this is great! Get this—while you were facing the last two bad guys down, Mrs. Jeppson switched on the automated alarm that forwards an alert to SUPD, and—"

"I already heard about that."

"Well if you'd let me slip a word in edgewise, you'd find out what you *didn't* hear—activating the ABC Hardware silent alarm also turns on a closed-circuit TV. The security company has a black-and-white video of the shoot-out. With a sound track."

Ceasing his stirring, Moon frowned at the beans.

"Hey, don't worry about seeing yourself on the tube." Parris assumed the reassuring tone he used when advising worried wives that a husband who'd been missing for a week would turn up sooner or later. "That recording is evidence in a crime. It won't be shown except in a court of law, when the two bad guys you beat up go to trial."

"Yeah. I guess you're right." Moon added a half dash of turmeric, just a tad of garlic salt, and commenced stirring the pinto beans.

What neither the tribal investigator nor Granite Creek's top cop realized was that only minutes after the robbery, a part-time employee of the security firm had downloaded the lurid video onto a five-hundred-gigabyte flash memory stick, which he promptly concealed in his vest pocket. The young man had complained of a brain-splitting migraine and left for the day. Within forty-five minutes, he had sold the video file to a Denver broadcasting conglomerate that was affiliated with a major network. Honoring his verbal agreement, the thief would wait until one minute after midnight (Mountain Time) before posting the video on the Internet for the whole world to see. In the meantime, the network would broadcast the hot property across the lower forty-eight and every province in Canada.

At about this time, Sarah showed up in the kitchen.

Oblivious to how his life was about to be turned upside down, Moon advised his teenage helper that it was time to summon the diners. It mattered not that all except one were present to hear this news. Ask anyone who knows and they will tell you that traditions are essential to the civilized life. Just as Sarah Frank was about to apply the thin steel rod to the hundred-plus-year-old Columbine triangular dinner gong, Daisy Perika, who was in the parlor, seated within a yard of the television, let out a shout loud enough to be heard all over the house: "Hey, everybody—come get a look at this!"

Sarah (rod and triangle still in hand) showed up first to gape at the TV screen, where a handsome talking head in a Los Angeles studio was informing his millions of viewers that a certain Colorado rancher who also served as a tribal investigator for the Southern Utes had foiled an armed robbery this morning in a small-town hardware store, severely injuring two of the suspects and killing two others outright in an Old West–style gunfight.

Scott Parris appeared in the dining-room doorway to cock his balding head at the anchorman. The story was bound to be on the news tonight, but *Charlie won't like it.* Little did Parris realize how much Moon would not like it—or that the story would be *fleshed out* with an illegally procured video of the event. Moon's best friend turned his impishly grinning face toward the kitchen. "Hey, Chucky—some yahoo on the TV is talking about you."

Their host, who had been busy removing a savory, twelve-pound beef roast from the oven, came to see what the matter was. The timing could not have been more fortuitous. Or, from Moon's perspective, more *inopportunitous,* because just as he entered the parlor, the network news anchor was about to give the Ute's chain a severe rattling. The face smiled at the tribal investigator as if Moon were the sole member of his audience, and made this enticing announcement: "Be forewarned, the video clip we're about to run—which was captured on the hardware store's security camera—contains some extremely violent scenes."

Parris muttered a mouth-filling oath under his breath.

Moon steeled himself.

The TV chameleon instantly exchanged his Mr. Smiley Face mask for a Solemn as a Mortician expression. "We particularly advise parents with small children to take this explicit violence into consideration."

Tens of thousands of small children leaned closer to their TV sets. Twice as many innocent eyes goggled in anticipation, tender little shell-like ears cupped ever so slightly forward.

As the snip of black-and-white closed-circuit TV filled the television screen, the scene looked for all the world like fiction. The camera had caught the bad guys more or less from the back, but the tall, slim fellow with the cowboy hat in his hands was—in a phrase—center stage.

The flesh-and-blood Charlie Moon froze. *Oh, no.*

THE REPLAY

The digitized Ute might have been Cool Hand Luke.

"I'm here on behalf of Loyola Montoya. But if you tough guys figure this is a game, either fold your hands—or make your play."

Viewers from Key West to Vancouver watched the bad guys' hands move ever so slowly toward their pistols.

Thousands of hearts skipped a beat when the tribal investigator shook his head. "That'd be a serious mistake."

The dead men's hands froze.

Because of the camera angle, not a living soul could see
Skeezix's lip curl into a sneer. "There's *no way* you can draw
that big horse pistol before we blow you away."

Even the dullest ear could hear Snuffy echo his agreement: "No way!"

"Boys, I won't argue the point." Charlie Moon's voice
was soft, barely above a whisper. "But you'd be well advised
to place both hands behind your necks, fingers interlocked."

Rapt viewers from San Diego to Kennebunkport heard
Skeezix snicker, and Snuffy snort.

Snicker and Snort went for their pistols, the .44 Magnums concealed under Moon's John B. Stetson hat spoke as
if with one voice: *bam-bam!*

Count two holes through drilled Charlie Moon's black
cowboy hat.

But that was *not* that.

There was more.

A gaping crater appeared in the back of Skeezix's skull.
A gusher of sooty-black blood sprayed out.

Snuffy's fuzzy head exploded as if the oaf had swallowed
a live grenade. Bits of enamel-white bone shrapnel went
zinging this way and that, bits of brain splattered hither and
yon—including a tiny globule of cerebellum that splatted
fatly on the security-camera lens and (under the force of gravity) began slowly crawling down the polished optics. Yes,
crawling.

For about six heartbeats, the Columbine headquarters
was dead silent. Then—

"My *God* in heaven!" No, that was Scott Parris, the hardened cop who believed he'd seen every grisly thing that
could happen to a human being.

Sarah was shocked dumb and numb.

Even Daisy Perika did not utter a word.

A mortified Charlie Moon closed his eyes, shook his head.

How did the rest of the huge television audience react?
The Nielsen Reports will not be in for hours. In the meantime, let us consider a nonrandom Sample of One. While this
will not be representative in a mathematical sense, it may

prove more interesting than mountainous compilations of statistics.

OUR SELECT AUDIENCE

At the very instant that Moon closed his eyes and shook his head, another dismayed viewer switched off the TV set, threw the remote control at the blackened screen, and uttered that serviceable expletive that so often succinctly sums up a situation: "Damn!"

This hardware-store foul-up was nothing short of a disaster. The Family would be extremely upset, with the young Turks calling for instant, bloody revenge and the older and cooler heads advising a pulling back—a licking of wounds—and taking time to think things over. The resulting tension could split the clan asunder. *So what do I do to make things right?* A measured, pragmatic response was called for—a course of action that would please both factions. Blood must be spilled, and additional members of the Family put in harm's way. This being the case, the potential payoff must justify the risks taken. Which demanded a carefully worked-out plan.

A thoughtful drumming of fingers on the coffee table.

A series of long, wistful sighs.

Fond recollections of days gone by when carefully conceived burglaries, bold robberies, audacious car thefts, and cold-blooded assassinations at twenty-five thousand dollars a pop had gone off slick as boiled okra. These activities had kept the Family prosperous, even during hard times. Then, there were those more or less incidental murders along the way that provided essential training and inexpensive entertainment.

During all this finger drumming, wistful sighing, and bittersweet nostalgia, a variety of possible reactions to the Hardware Store Catastrophe presented themselves. After eliminating the least-attractive options, those few that remained were intriguing. So much so that it seemed a shame to discard even one. Indeed, combining these ingenious elements into a single, grand-slam strategy produced a highly appealing plan.

And so it was that Trout made the fateful decision.

WE RETURN TO THE COLUMBINE

Only moments after the distressed Head of the Family tossed the remote control at the perfectly innocent made-in-China television set, Charlie Moon's telephone began to ring. The first caller was the perky little lady who owned and managed Harriet's Rare Books in Granite Creek.

"Hi, Charlie—it's me."

He recognized the voice of one of his favorite local characters. "Hi yourself, Harriet. What's up?" *Like I don't know.*

"I was just watching the boob tube and caught the latest news."

"I hope you don't believe everything you see on the TV."

"Don't be so doggoned modest, Charlie. I'm glad you shot those two no-goods—the only complaint I got is that you didn't kill the other two!"

"Well—"

"Oh, don't go explaining how you was only doin' your duty and all that 'I'm just a simple-cowboy' malarkey. You're my favorite fella, you big galoot! There, I've said what I had to say. G'night, Straight-shooter."

"Good night, Harriet." Moon was talking to a dead line.

Over the next several days, the tribal investigator would receive dozens of calls. Most were congratulations from gun-toting locals who wished they'd had a piece of the action. Moon also listened patiently to stern lectures from well-meaning citizens who were convinced that the tribal investigator was a gun-happy fanatic who had deliberately violated the sacred civil rights of the *alleged hardware-store robbers.* Unique among the calls was a 3 A.M. death threat from a San Francisco vegetarian who had no interest in the shootings; she hated anyone who produced meat for human consumption. The most persistent were journalists who wanted an exclusive story on the shoot-out. Moon's solution was to give the telephone to Aunt Daisy, who would demand a million dollars up front for "my version of what really happened." Finally, there were four proposals of marriage—the most charming of these from an adoring eight-year-old in Torrington, Wyoming, who thought Mr. Moon was "way cool!" He suggested that the ardent young lady call him back in about thirty years.

Such experiences can make a man wonder whether having a modern telecommunications device installed in his home is such a great notion. Oftentimes, in the evenings, Charlie Moon would disconnect the descendant of Mr. Bell's remarkable invention.

CHAPTER NINETEEN

EPISODE THREE

The Lawman's Funeral

As the guest of honor, recently deceased U.S. Marshal Scott Parris was prepared to enjoy his send-off. Poor fellow. Less than a dozen mourners showed up—and not one of them bothered to grieve, lament, or bewail his passing in any way whatsoever. The Methodist preacher did say a few comforting words over the cold-as-a-carp corpse, which was laid out on an unpainted pine door supported by a pair of straight-back chairs courtesy of the Tennessee Saloon, which was where the funeral was held.

Sheriff Eddie "Rocks" Knox showed up to snort at the pale cadaver before tap-tapping his oak peg leg over to the bar, where the owner of the establishment was complaining that he'd had more customers back in '77, during that big spring blizzard that had heaped up eight-foot drifts on Copper Street.

Deputy "Pig" Slocum passed by to smirk at the dead man, then joined the sheriff at the bar, where he tucked away a half-dozen boiled eggs while drinking two mugs of beer.

Worst of all, Parris's sweetheart showed up.

Why was this so unpleasant?

Because Miss Willow Skye, who had been the local

schoolmarm right up to the day of the hanging, had turned over a new leaf or two.

First, the prim little lady had abandoned her noble avocation to pursue a new career. No, she had no aspiration to become president of the Ladies Temperance League. Her new title was Bar Room Floozy, and Miss Skye had (with her usual enthusiasm for new projects) gone for the whole nine yards. Loud, bawdy speech. Garish, low-cut dress. More makeup than would adorn a respectable circus clown's face. She was pushing watered-down whiskey across Copper Street at the Kentucky Saloon. Willow's byline was, "Hi, cowboy—new in town?"

Her second leaf?

Willow showed up with her new boyfriend—Judge "Pug" Bullet.

It was almost too much for the corpse to bear. It wouldn't have taken much more for Parris's remains to get up and walk right out of there.

The dead man was greatly relieved when Charlie Moon arrived. Parris's Ute friend wrapped his cold body in a red-and-black Indian trade blanket and tied it on the back of a fine, frisky pinto pony, which he led away toward the Columbine Ranch. On the way, Moon's cell phone jangled.

No. That is absurd. There were no such instruments in 1877, and the dreamer is a stickler for historical accuracy and fictional authenticity. There must be a plausible explanation for the anomaly. . . . Hold on—stand by for a timely correction.

Here it is: the thing responsible for the infernal jangling was the cordless telephone by Scott Parris's bed.

The chief of police rolled over, grabbed the instrument, and pressed it to the side of his head. "H'lo?"

The voice was very faint and faraway and Parris was getting danged tired of being awakened by the telephone.

"Speak up—I can't hear a damned thing you're saying!"

When the caller shouted for *him* to talk louder, the bleary-eyed man realized that she was yelling *into his mouth*. He turned the phone around and spoke in that manner which is widely described as *sheepish*. "Who's calling?"

She told him.

Before the bedside clock could say *tick-tock*, the chief of police was wide awake and had his big, bare feet on the floor. He nodded at the invisible person. "Sure. I can do that."

After hanging up, Parris proceeded with the usual rituals of shaving, showering, and coffee. And planning the next several hours. A commendable, if futile effort—as if a man could see what lay in wait for him. As it happened, this would be the third-worst day of his life. Moreover, things would not get better right away. His second-worst day would begin with tomorrow's dawn.

The worst day of them all?

That was years ago. When Scott Parris lost his wife.

CHAPTER TWENTY

MR. MOON RECEIVES
AN UNEXPECTED INVITATION

It was midmorning when the cell phone in Charlie Moon's jacket pocket vibrated. The rancher, who had been inspecting progress of construction at the Columbine's new horse barn, checked the caller ID to make sure this was someone he wanted to talk to. It was. "Good morning, pardner."

"G'morning Charlie. How're you doing?"

"Tolerable and then some." Scott Parris's voice, which normally boomed in his ear, was subdued. Artificially so, Moon thought. *Something's up.* "What's on your so-called mind?"

Even the white man's edgy chuckle betrayed an inner tension. "Oh, nothing much." The chief of police licked his lips. "I was wondering if you had time for an early lunch."

The Ute consulted a burnished-gold sun that was hanging at about ten o'clock high in the mists over the Buckhorn Range. "How early?"

"Oh, say about eleven thirty?"

"I might be able to fit that into my busy schedule. But I'm particular about where I eat my beans and biscuits. Where'll we be chowing down—some greasy spoon?"

"Not this time. I've got a private dining room reserved at the Silver Mountain Hotel—the small one they call the Mayflower."

What's this all about? Moon grinned at his invisible comrade. "That's a mighty pricey place—you buying?"

Relaxed by this conversation with his friend, the town cop reverted to his boisterous voice. "Don't fret about parting with any precious greenbacks—I got the tab covered right down to the eighteen-percent gratuity." Parris inhaled a deep breath that swelled his barrel chest. "So can I look forward to the highly overrated pleasure of your company?"

The Ute's laugh thundered in his ear. "Hard as I try, I can't recall the last time I refused a free meal."

Almost an hour later, Charlie Moon pushed through the heavy door at the Silver Mountain Hotel. The rancher had barely gotten inside when his progress was impeded by a motley collection of retired businessmen, has-been politicians, and other old-timers who inhabited the lobby to sip free hotel coffee and swap outrageous lies. These enthusiastic natives insisted on shaking the local hero's hand and congratulating Moon on the service he had provided the community by his summary execution of that pair of outlaws who were holding Mrs. Jeppson at gunpoint. Only one among them had the poor taste to bring up the subject of the *survivors* of the ABC Hardware robbery, and the hard-eyed water-well driller did so with a frank expression of dismay that Moon had not ". . . finished the job you'd got started."

This combination of heartfelt compliments and stern upbraiding was painfully embarrassing. Regretting that he'd not had the foresight to enter the hotel by the service entrance on Burro Alley, Moon mumbled something about having an appointment and hurried down a paneled hallway to the hotel's cluster of private dining rooms. *I'm glad to have that behind me.*

His ordeal was not quite over. The tribal investigator was recognized by one of several dozen hotel guests who had seen his performance replayed on television. Despite Moon's effort to bypass another humiliating encounter, a smallish woman in a purple velour pantsuit blocked his path with the stubborn expression of a lady who is used to getting her way.

Unsure of what to do, he stared at this obstacle.

She returned his stare with her right eye. Her left orb appeared to be looking over his shoulder. "Well—this is certainly a fortuitous encounter." The cross-eyed woman reached out to grab Moon's hand. "It is *such* an honor to meet the local gunslinger!" She worked the rancher's hand like a pitcher-pump handle. "I'm Daphne Donner."

"Pleased to meet you, ma'am." Moon tipped the Stetson with his free hand. "But at the moment I'm on my way to—"

"This is a special treat for me, I can tell you that." Her cherry-tinted lips curled into an impish smile. "It'll be something special to tell my friends back in Alder Creek about how on my vacation, I actually met the famous Indian gunfighter *in the flesh*. Not that you've got all that much meat on your bones!" After cackling at her little joke, she released the man's hand. "I am just *so* thrilled—would you mind too awfully much if I asked for your autograph?" Apparently interpreting Moon's embarrassed silence as an assent, she reached into her voluminous purse, presumably for a pen and something to write on.

Just when there seemed to be no escape, the potential victim was saved by the appearance of a crusty old rancher, who bellowed out, "Hey, that's either a seven-foot cedar fence post with a hat on, or it's ol' Charlie Moon." This pithy witticism was punctuated with a braying "haw-haw." "Howdy, you cold-blooded man-killer!"

Glancing over his shoulder at the grinning stockman, Moon returned Hobart Watkins's howdy, then addressed Mrs. Purple Pantsuit. "I need to get to a meeting right now and—"

"Oh, shoo—away with you then!" Dismissing the shy fellow with a flick of her wrist, the snappish little woman snapped her purse shut. "But if I'm lucky enough to see you again, I will absolutely *insist* that you inscribe your name in my little book."

Making his escape from tourist and neighbor alike, Moon heard the lady calling out behind him, "I've got lots of famous people's autographs, like Woody Allen and President Nixon and Dolly Parton and . . ."

Her shrill voice faded as he turned a corner.

MR. MOON IS ASTONISHED

No, that is insufficient. When the tribal investigator opened the door to enter the Mayflower Room, which Scott Parris had (so he'd said) reserved for a private luncheon, Charlie Moon was more like flabbergasted. Also stunned. Stupefied. And quite taken aback.

This was not so much because the single occupant of the bijou dining room bore not the slightest resemblance to the Granite Creek chief of police, nor even because she was a strikingly handsome woman who (even on her days off) carried a concealed automatic pistol. The reason for Moon's astonishment was that FBI Special Agent Lila Mae McTeague was an old flame, of sorts. Of the sort that had dumped him about a year ago, and whose lovely hide and hair he'd never expected to _____ in. Which was no doubt why his brain could not pro_____ any words for him to say.

Not a problem.

Having a reliable _____ on how to react to unexpected situations, Moon's ri___ ___ reached up and removed his brand-new John B. St_____ "Well—hello."

"Hello yourself, Ch___ e tall, slender woman smiled at the befuddled man___ ched out—and this _really_ hurt—to _shake his hand._

He used the hand hol___ vide-brimmed hat to point at the door, which had cl___ ___s wake. "I was expecting Scott." Moon's face burne___ _n with his mouth stapled shut could've come up with something better than that._

The attractive lady smiled. "I hope you're not too terribly disappointed."

The tongue-tied fellow managed a weak grin. "If I am, ma'am—I expect I'll get over it."

"The chief of police will return in a few minutes." Lila Mae pulled her hand from his firm grip. "Please sit down."

The man allowed as how he preferred to stand.

In that case, so did the former sweetheart.

Moon placed his Stetson on the cherry dining table and waited to see what the woman had to say.

Lila Mae fixed her gaze on his black hat and frowned, as if she were attempting to extract the cube root of 17,576 without aid of pencil, paper, abacus, or electronic calculating machine. What she was actually contemplating was how best to clear the atmosphere of the murky history hanging between them. Before forging ahead, she cleared her throat. "I wish there was time to talk about other things, Charlie." *That sounded rather lame.* "But . . ."

"But you're a very busy lady."

Whether it was real or imagined, Lila Mae detected a hint of flint in his tone. "As a matter of fact, I am." She looked Moon straight in the eye. "This is strictly business." She added, with an edge that cut right to the bone, "Official business."

"Works for me." Hearing the hotel's hundred-year-old hall floorboards squeak under his hefty friend's weight, Moon called over his shoulder, "It's okay, Scott—you can come in now."

After a tense interlude wherein the embarrassed friend's blood pressure climbed by about twenty points, the antique porcelain knob rotated. There was a creak of brass hinges as the blushing face of GCPD's top cop appeared in the doorway. "You two about ready for some lunch?"

Lila Mae McTeague addressed the county's highest-ranking law-enforcement official as if he were a junior waiter: "I'll have a small fruit salad."

Moon had lost his appetite. "I'll pass."

"You sure?" Parris frowned at the Ute. "The Prospector's Sourdough Ham Sandwich is on special today."

Moon assured his friend that he'd get a bite to eat when he was hungry.

"All right then. I'll go place the order." By the time the dining-room door closed behind him, the heavy clomp-clomp of Scott Parris's scuffed Roper boots was—as some of the old-timer cowboys still say—"a fur piece away."

CHAPTER TWENTY-ONE

LILA MAE GOES FISHING

The FBI employee seated herself at one end of the polished table for eight and began to pick at an array of grapes, strawberries, melon, and pineapple that was tastefully arranged on a crystal plate.

Selecting a spot at her left, Scott Parris got right to work on a hot ham sandwich and potato chips.

The tall tribal investigator towered over the diners like a lone pine.

McTeague used a silver fork to spear a red-ripe strawberry. "You're making me nervous, Charlie." She pointed her fork at the chair at her right elbow. "Please sit." She popped the strawberry between crimson lips.

Moon preferred to stand, was of half a mind to leave—but it is hard to resist a lady's request, and her "sit" had been preceded by "please." He seated himself across from his best friend, who promptly offered the Ute half of his ham sandwich and a fair share of the potato chips.

"Thanks, I'll pass." Mr. Moon gave neither sandwich nor chip the merest glance; his gaze was fixed on Lila Mae's face. *Every time I see her, she's prettier than the last time.*

Without looking up from her plate, she said, "Please don't stare at me, Charlie."

"Makes you uncomfortable?"

"Very much so."

"Sorry." The discarded boyfriend stared harder. "Can't help myself."

The attractive lady struggled to conceal a smile. "You are absolutely incorrigible."

"If I knew what *incorrigible* meant, I might take offense."

"I trust that you will consult a dictionary at the first opportunity." She dabbed at her mouth with a napkin. "In the meantime, would you mind telling me about your experience at the hardware store?"

"No." He jutted his chin. "And yes."

She arched an eyebrow. "This response does not illuminate."

"No, I won't consult Mr. Webster. And yes, I would mind."

Her expressive brow arched an additional millimeter. "As to the 'yes,' I request the courtesy of an explanation."

"Well, since you put it that way—" Moon leaned back in the straight-back chair and cocked his head a tad to the left, which was his habit when preparing to explain something. "That business at ABC Hardware was an unpleasant experience. If I was to start talking about it, I'd likely get to feeling sorrowful. And whenever I feel sorrowful, I tend to spoil any kind of social occasion you might want to mention—like this one."

"Oh, please don't concern yourself on my account." She flashed a pearly smile. "You have my permission to feel as sorrowful as you want. I promise not to care in the least."

Moon's mouth opened; he snapped it shut before it said something he would regret. The tribal investigator countered with a question of his own: "Has the Bureau got a line yet on Mrs. Montoya's grandson?"

"We are pursuing that issue with due diligence, but so far all the leads on Wallace Montoya's whereabouts have been dead ends. Never mind; sooner or later, we'll find him." Special Agent McTeague glanced at her wristwatch. "The Denver Field Office is expecting a call from me in nine minutes flat. Certain persons there will be anxious to hear my verbal report on our conversation." She raised her gaze to mesh it with Moon's. "So please tell me about your unpleasant experience at the hardware store."

Moon decided to get this business over with. "There's nothing much to tell, Agent McTeague." He watched her eyes glaze at the deliberately impersonal reference. "I spotted the beat-up old Ford van, thought it looked suspicious. I checked things out, ran into some trouble, dealt with it best as I could."

She stared at the remarkable man. *And he's not playing the modest "aw shucks ma'am it warn't nothin" grade-B movie cowboy. That's really the way Charlie Moon sees life. You encounter a problem, you fix it. Simple as that.* The woman felt an odd tingle along her spine. *Leaving him may turn out to be the worst mistake I ever made.* Hoary old metaphors of *spilled milk* and *water under the bridge* did little to console the lady. "Please tell me about the encounter with each of the four men. Starting with the one in the van."

"The driver had a pistol in his hand. I had to take it away from him, and I couldn't very well do that without hurting him." Feeling a sudden hunger pang, Moon glanced at the untouched half sandwich on Parris's platter. "The lookout at the rear entrance was armed, so it was necessary to deal with that situation too. Bad guys Three and Four were threatening to murder Mrs. Jeppson and they pointed revolvers at me . . . so I had to shoot both of 'em."

Lila Mae presented an enigmatic smile that *Mona Lisa* would have envied. "You shot each of them in the *head*."

He heard himself mumble, "I wanted 'em *dead*."

"And under the circumstances, quite rightly so." She helped herself to another strawberry. "I understand that you accomplished the task with confiscated sidearms—and shot them *through your cowboy hat*."

"I had the pistols I took from Bad Guys One and Two under my hat." *And cocked.* "When Three and Four threw down on me, I barely had time to pull the triggers." Moon was pained by the bitter memory of the ruined John B. Stetson, which had been his favorite and most expensive lid.

"This is very important, Charlie." Lila Mae leaned forward, so close that he felt the warmth of her fruit-scented breath on his face. "Do you recall either of the armed robbers mentioning the others by name?"

"Sure." Moon nodded to indicate Scott Parris. "It's all in the official police report. There was a Dag. And a Skeezix."

"I've studied the report carefully. Were there any other names?"

When she touched the tips of her fingers to the back of his hand, the gesture was sufficient to strike Moon dumb. But only for about three rapid heartbeats, when a detail was jarred loose from the depths of his memory. "One of the guys that was bullying Mrs. Jeppson—I think he mentioned somebody."

"Good. Can you remember the name?" She squeezed his hand; the effect was electric.

"Well . . ." The overvoltage, it seemed, had wiped his memory clean. "Uh, no—I don't." *But it was right on the tip of my tongue.*

"Please try, Charlie."

He did. *Nada.*

"Can you recall the context in which the name was used?"

He closed his eyes to concentrate. "Yeah. Under the circumstances, it was a peculiar question. One of the thugs asked did so-and-so send me."

"So-and-so?"

"Sorry. That's the best I can do."

"No it's not." She banged his hand on the table. "This is *extremely* important. Try harder."

He tried ever so hard. Came up empty. "Maybe it'll come to me later."

"It will—and when it does, call me that very instant." She released his hand. "You have my mobile phone number."

"Yes I do." *But after you left town last year, you stopped taking my calls.*

Reading the bitter remembrance in Moon's eyes, Mc-Teague averted her gaze. "These hardware-store robbers are members of a well-organized criminal gang that has a history of assault, robbery, and . . ." *Some rather bizarre practices that I'd rather not mention.* "Bureau Intel has been gathering data on them for almost six years. Evidence, though admittedly scant, suggests that we are dealing with a group of closely knit associates. A few are probably old friends, but it is considered very likely that the majority of them are related."

At this reference to kinship, Scott Parris's antenna went up. "Like brothers and cousins and whatnot?"

"Yes." Having almost forgotten the cop's presence at the table, McTeague turned a blank gaze on Parris. "For that reason, we refer to them as the Family." Her conscience cringed at this half-truth. But it was vital to observe the Bureau's need-to-know policy. "They are rarely active between October and May, but tend to organize their 'summer vacations' around various felonious activities."

Parris rolled this over in his mind. "Sounds like a bunch of happy campers."

"Yes, don't they?" McTeague suddenly beamed on the chief of police. "You might expect them to visit the seashore or Disneyland—or, as in this instance, the Rocky Mountains. One can just picture them swimming, playing softball, eating indigestible hot dogs, drinking cheap beer and fizzy soda pop. And we believe that they do." Lila Mae turned to flash the big eyelashes at Charlie Moon. "After the usual festivities are concluded, the Family turns its attention to other, more serious activities." The playfulness was absent from her voice. "Under a single person's leadership—an individual whom I shall refer to as the Supervisor—they plan and execute a variety of felonies." Again, she leaned toward Moon. "Such as stealing motor vehicles in Topeka, Kansas. And burglarizing a gun store in Lordsburg, New Mexico— where approximately three weeks ago they walked off with ten handguns and four rifles, not to mention three thousand, five hundred and twenty-three dollars in hard cash. After which, they evidently crossed the border into Colorado and selected a remote campsite in the vicinity of Mrs. Loyola Montoya's home." She crossed her long legs, allowed a slim black slipper to hang on the tip of her largest toe, which could not be appropriately described as *big*.

The lawmen waited for the shoe to drop.

It would. With a significant *plop*.

The narrator was gratified by their rapt attention. "Presumably because Mrs. Montoya made some protest about their presence, Family members bashed in the old lady's skull and set her home afire." She paused to appreciate the expressions on the lawmen's faces, which ranged from *startled* (Chief of Police Parris) to *flinty* (the tribal investigator). "Ah—I deduce that you two have not yet been informed about the La Plata County ME's final report on the autopsy of Mrs. Montoya's battered and burned body, which was issued—" another glance at her six-thousand-dollar platinum wristwatch, "not quite two hours ago." Special Agent Lila Mae McTeague was having entirely too much fun. "A few days after disposing of Mrs. Montoya, the Family employed the stolen vehicles and firearms in an armed robbery at Jeppson's ABC Hardware here in Granite Creek—only to have their carefully planned attempt foiled by one Mr. Charles Moon, who just happened to happen by early on a Sunday morning, while on his way home from St. Anthony's." She effected another, more-thoughtful pause. "Which is somewhat peculiar, as Mr. Moon's home on the range and the ABC Hardware store are in opposite directions from the Catholic church." Special Agent McTeague waited for a nibble.

Moon ignored the bait.

Scott Parris enjoyed his role as bystander.

This small, increasingly tense drama was interrupted by a discreet tap on the dining-room door.

"C'mon in!" Parris bellowed.

A slender waiter opened the door to inquire whether the guests of the Silver Mountain Hotel required any further food or beverages.

Charlie Moon asked for an eight-cup pot of bubbling-hot New Mexico Piñon coffee and a pint jar of honey.

The waiter nodded as if this request was perfectly ordinary.

Which, for Mr. Moon, it was. The rancher's preference for sweetening his high-caffeine brew with Tule Creek honey was well known in these parts.

The *nine minutes flat* had passed.

Using a secure mobile telephone, Special Agent Lila Mae McTeague made her call to the Denver FBI Field Office. On the Granite Creek end of the conversation, most of what Moon and Parris heard was limited to terse remarks such as: "Mr. Moon recalled a reference to someone who might have been the Supervisor, but he cannot remember the name." And: "Yes, I agree. There's no doubt that it's an interstate case involving multiple felonies." Plus the big finale, which gave Chief of Police Scott Parris a nasty surge of heartburn: "Very well. I will advise the local police department." She listened and nodded. "Of course. Your office is best prepared to deal with the state police."

After saying goodbye, she turned her attention to the lawman with acid in his throat and blood in his eyes. "The Bureau will officially take charge of the case at eight A.M. tomorrow, when our team will arrive at Snyder Memorial Hospital to transfer the surviving suspects in the hardware-store robbery to a federal medical facility."

Parris was not surprised. The FBI was infamous for taking charge of headline-grabbing cases. He put on his best poker face, which was considered only fair to good by his card-playing buddies. "Why wait all night—why not strap the bad guys to gurneys and wheel 'em away right now?"

McTeague, who was a bit slow when it came to half-witticisms rampant on a field of sarcasm, cocked her head at the local cop. "Because it will take several hours to generate the necessary documents, and to prepare the Bureau's public statement for the morning newscasts."

"Oh, right." To his credit, Parris did not bat an eyelash. "I should've thought about all that government paperwork—and how long it takes to put together an effective PR operation."

Yes, you should have. But McTeague was not a malicious sort; she felt only pity for the country-hick cop. She was somewhat startled by Charlie Moon's deep voice.

"This Supervisor character—why didn't I see him at the hardware store?"

"Because that particular individual is the planner. And, though I detest the expression—the *brains* of the Family."

"Sounds like he don't like to get his hands dirty."

Her response was about ten degrees below zero. "If I may say so, Charlie—your tendency to assume that anyone with intelligence and status must be a male is . . . well . . . somewhat *off-putting*."

"I don't assume any such thing." It was his turn to lean close to the lady. "When I talk about thugs, saying 'he' and 'him' is just a habit. Over the years, most of the bad guys I've banged heads with were men." Moon should not have grinned. "But I have to admit that from time to time, I've run into some tough-as-nails women."

Over the top. The Indian cop had gone a woman too far.

The tough-as-nails fed made no effort to conceal her displeasure. "Oh you have, have you?"

"Mmm-hmm." His sly smile was tinged with a teasing hint of suspicion. "I hope you're not keeping some big Bureau secret from me and Scott."

The lady—who was not sharing everything she knew—blushed.

He should have stopped right there. But, sensing that he had pricked a nerve, Moon could not resist persisting. "If there's hard evidence that this Supervisor is a brainy woman of status who plans criminal activities for this so-called Family, I'd say me and Scott have got a right to know."

Scott Parris enjoyed a hearty chuckle.

Special Agent McTeague glared at the tribal investigator. *He can be so infuriating!*

CHAPTER TWENTY-TWO

A SHORT STORY

In the hope of enjoying a few hours of restful peace, Mrs. Jeppson had unplugged her telephone. But, for perhaps the ninth time since dawn, her doorbell said, *Brrrinnng!*

"Oh, that annoying thing!" *All these newspaper and TV reporters are such an awful bother.* The widow groaned herself up from her favorite chair and approached the door warily to press her left eye (the good one) to the peephole. The harried woman had intended (as on the eight previous occasions) to pretend that she was not at home, but this stranger was, in some manner that she sensed but would have had difficulty explaining . . . *different.* Her eye twinkled in the peephole. *And such a nice, friendly face. And, as everyone knows, the countenance is the mirror of the soul. Didn't some clever person say something like that?*

Before she knew she was going to, the lady of the house called out, "What do you want?"

"Got some business to take care of." The nice, friendly face smiled. "I won't take a minute of your time, Mrs. J."

"Oh!" She covered the unpredictable mouth with her hand. *I can't remember anyone but my dear husband ever calling me that. Perhaps this is one of his friends, and no telling where from.* The late Mr. Jeppson had a great many friends, scattered from one end of the country to the other. But, as recent events had demonstrated, one could not be too careful.

Oh, I don't know what to do! She shouted again, "Are you a friend of my husband?"

"Oh, that and more, ma'am." The caller's disarming smile flashed like a stray ray of sunlight. "I'm a friend of the family."

Well. Curiosity got the better of her.

Mrs. Jeppson opened the door and invited the stranger into her home.

Now, whether the claim to being "a friend of the family" was strictly true, and in the sense that the widow was led to believe, this much must be said in defense of the visitor's integrity: a promise made was a promise kept.

The business to be conducted was completed in *less than a minute*. The caller was in and out in forty-four seconds flat.

How about that.

CHAPTER TWENTY-THREE

GOOD HELP IS HARD TO FIND

The intensive care unit on the second floor of Snyder Memorial Hospital is comprised of three hallways, joined at the ends to form a U. The nurses' station, located at the bottom center of that twenty-first letter of the alphabet, has a daytime staff of eight nurses and as many aides, but from midnight until 8 A.M. the ICU is managed by two RNs and an LPN. On this particular night, the junior member of the team had failed to show up. This absence did not annoy her coworkers so much as the fact that, as one of them had put it, "The lazy bitch didn't even bother to call in so Personnel could arrange for a replacement."

As is so often the case, this complaint was both uncharitable and unjustified.

At twenty minutes past midnight, an energetic, no-nonsense RN showed up with papers from the employment agency. The replacement apologized for being late, and was provided with a briefing that included an introduction to the state-police officer who was night guard for the two patients in adjoining end-of-the hall rooms. The policeman explained that the pair had been arrested in connection with the notorious ABC Hardware Store robbery. John Doe Number 1, aka "Dagwood," was lightly sedated and had his broken jaw wired shut. John Doe Number 2 ("Dilbert") was fully conscious and able to speak, but had little to say aside from: "I don't know anything about any robbery. Don't even know why I'm here. Can't remember a solitary thing—not even my name."

After exchanging pleasantries with the uniformed cop, the nurse got to work on such essential tasks as waking patients from restful slumbers to dispense prescribed sleep medications. The stand-in also managed to calm the injured truck driver in room 208, who complained that the powerful opiate being dispensed via his IV ". . . isn't doin' a damn thing about this awful pain in my left foot." After reminding the drugged-to-the-gills accident victim that his left leg had been amputated at the knee, the nurse explained the curious phenomenon of phantom pain and assured the man that the dull ache could be alleviated by a cold compress on his forehead, which it did. The medical profession has barely begun to plumb the remarkable efficacy of the placebo effect.

2:10 A.M.

State Police Officer Henry Joyce, who had been reading a tattered copy of Christopher Morley's *The Haunted Bookshop*, had not heard the almost soundless approach of the rubber-soled footsteps. He was mildly surprised to look up from a yellowed page to see the efficient practitioner of practical medicine carrying a stainless steel tray that was partially covered by a white cotton towel. The cop yawned. "What've you got—a tasty little late-night snack for my bad guys?"

The substitute nurse smiled back. "Afraid not. What I'm dispensing won't be so pleasant as cookies and milk."

"Great big hypodermic, huh?"

Great big smile. "Something like that."

"Well, I hope you stick 'em deep and make it hurt." Joyce laid his book on another chair. "I'll have to check out the tray before you go into their rooms. Sorry, rules and all that."

No objection was made to this understandable requirement. On the contrary, the nurse had intended all along to *demonstrate* the procedure that was (allegedly) about to be carried out on the survivors of the botched ABC Hardware

Store robbery. Whether or not the cop's curiosity was completely satisfied remains open to speculation, but this much can be said with certainty—Officer Joyce made no effort to prevent the nurse from entering either room.

CHAPTER TWENTY-FOUR

PANIC

Wherever that three-digit number is dialed—be it New York City, Houston, Los Angeles, or Granite Creek, Colorado—the response is reasonably predictable.

In that serene tone that suggests that in the *big picture* all is right with the world, the voice says something more or less like, "Police. What is the nature of your emergency?"

About nine times out of ten, the trouble reported by the citizen represents no more than a mere flicker in the space-time continuum. The dime her two-year-old swallowed will pass through his digestive tract without ill effect. An officer will be dispatched to deal with the drunken party next door. The smoke you smell is not evidence that your apartment building is going up in flames; it has drifted in from a wild-fire in an adjacent state. And then there is call number ten. But even if your husband is choking to death on a chicken bone or some wild-eyed lunatic wielding a carving knife has broken into your home in the middle of the night, never fear—the legally constituted authorities are more than able to deal with the situation. It was in this confident manner that the GCPD dispatcher took the 911 call at 3:05 A.M. "Granite Creek Police. What is the nature of your emergency?"

For a moment, the only sound on the line was that of someone inhaling a breath. Holding it. Sucking it in again. Then, a raspy woman's voice: "The nature of my emergency? Hey, I don't know *what* the hell's going on."

"What?"

"Are you deaf as a stone? I said—" the caller was jittering right on the edge of hysteria, "that I don't know what the hell's going on!"

"Yes, I heard you." *She's scared out of her gourd.* A few simple questions usually did the trick. "Please give me your name."

"Peggy." A cough. "Uh, Peggy Rosenthal."

"Okay, that's good. Now tell me where you're calling from."

"The hospital. Snyder Memorial."

That tallied with the caller ID on the computer monitor. "Are you employed at the hospital, or are you a patient?" Snyder Memorial had a psychiatric ward.

"I'm a nurse in ER, but right now I'm in ICU." A pitiful whimpering. "I came to find out why nobody up here was answering the phone."

Now we're getting somewhere. "So what's the problem?"

Silence.

"Peggy—are you there?"

"Yeah. I'm here." A moan. "All by myself."

Either she's nuts or something really bad has gone down. "Tell me what's wrong."

Another indrawn breath, which was exhaled as a sigh. "They're dead."

The dispatcher frowned at her computer monitor. "Who's dead?"

"All of them." The sound of a fist banging on something, over and over. "Oh, God—maybe this isn't *real*. Maybe it's an awful nightmare—maybe I'm asleep." The caller began to weep. Between wrenching sobs: "Or maybe I'm going stone crazy!"

"Peggy—are you all right?"

"No, you bone-headed idiot, I'm not all right! How could I be—there are dead people all around me!" The nurse made a choking-gurgling sound, then managed to compose herself. "I'm sorry. I'm just overwhelmed by all this . . . this . . ."

"That's all right, dear. Now tell me who's dead."

"They're *all* dead!"

"Yes. I understand. But could you give me some names?"

The caller was no longer listening. "I don't have any idea who killed them—or why—or even how!" The ER nurse's voice dropped to a suspicious whisper. "There's not a mark on the bodies—not a *mark*." Five seconds of dead silence. "You want my professional opinion, I'll give it to you—I believe every one of them was *poisoned*!"

"Please don't hang up, Peggy. I'll dispatch officers right away."

CHAPTER TWENTY-FIVE

SUSPICION

It was late morning when Sarah Frank heard the approaching vehicle. Visitors of any stripe were a welcome novelty during her long, quiet days on the Columbine. Most of the time. Precisely how such premonitions occur remains an impenetrable mystery, but from somewhere deep within Sarah's budding feminine intuition, warnings began to bubble up. They were to the point, and terse. *Unwanted company. Intruder.* And worse still . . . *Competitor.*

Thus alerted, the slender wisp of a girl hurried to a Columbine headquarters parlor window. She pulled the curtains aside just in time to see a shiny new automobile rumbling over the Too Late Creek bridge. The gray sedan was unknown to the Ute-Papago orphan, but not the tall, statuesque brunette who got out of it, slammed the door, and headed to the west porch. *She's come to see Charlie.* And would soon be knocking on the front door.

Unnerved by the sudden appearance of this world-class rival for the affections of Mr. Moon, the seventeen-year-old girl ran headlong across the parlor, down the dark hallway, and into the dining room, where she quickly concealed herself in the shadowy coolness.

No sooner was Sarah hidden than she heard the sound of the determined lady's knuckles rapping against the three-inch-thick 1870s-era oak door that could stop a flint-tipped Arapaho arrow or a .44 caliber pistol bullet.

Feeling like a fool, the girl closed her eyes. *This is totally stupid—I can't just stand here in the dark.*

McTeague knocked again.

I'll have to go let her in. Sarah clenched her fists. *But what'll I say—"Hello, Miss McTeague, it's so nice to see you"?* No, that wouldn't do. How about: *"Oh, you must be looking for Charlie. I'm so sorry, he's gone for a few days. Where? Oh, to Wyoming, I think it was—or maybe Montana."* No, that was another string of lies, even worse than *"it's so nice to see you."* And God expected a person to stick strictly to the truth.

Steeling herself for a confrontation with this archenemy, Sarah had already abandoned her place of concealment when she heard Charlie Moon's cowboy boots clomping down the stairway. She watched him stride across the parlor to open the door.

Half expecting a visit from Scott Parris, the smile Moon wore for greeting his best friend slipped away when he saw Lila Mae. Her face was chalky gray. *Something's wrong.*

Something was. The FBI agent was about to tell him about it when she noticed the slim girl hovering at the far end of the parlor like a shy ghost. As Sarah withdrew soundlessly into the hallway, the fed said, "We have to talk, Charlie. Someplace private." McTeague's strained voice suggested a bone-dry, bent-double cottonwood branch that was about to snap. "I have something to tell you."

"Let's go upstairs." He led the way. *I've got something to tell you.*

Sarah, who was peeking around the corner as they ascended the stairs, stared in stunned disbelief. Charlie's bedroom was on the second floor. *He never takes women up there.* As far as she knew. *Well, he never takes me up there.* On the other hand . . . *I guess I should mind my own business.* But wait a danged minute—Charlie Moon *was* her business, and Job One was to make sure the competition didn't muscle in and take over!

Action was called for.

Almost before she knew it, Sarah was sneak-creeping up

the stairs. What would she do when she got there? *If they see me, I'll just say, "Would you like some coffee? I'll be glad to make a fresh pot and bring you some."* At the instant her eyes were even with the upstairs hallway floor, Sarah heard Charlie Moon close his office door. *Rats!* But there was this consolation: *At least Charlie didn't take her into his bedroom.* Not yet. But with a woman like *that*, they might end up there in a few minutes. She continued the sneak-creeping. This time, along the upstairs hallway. Inch by inch, she went. Ever closer to the closed office door. Sarah couldn't hear a word they said. There was the tempting keyhole, fairly *begging* to be peeked through. Not that she would ever stoop to such a petty misdeed.

Moon invited his guest to sit on an old, scruffy-looking, delightfully comfortable leather couch. "What's up?"

Special Agent McTeague plopped herself down. "I hardly know where to begin." She had opened her mouth to give it a try, when—

What was this? Aha—another rumble on the Too Lake Creek bridge.

"That will probably be Scott Parris," McTeague said. "Let's wait until he gets here before I tell you what's happened."

"Fine with me." Moon remained standing. "In the meantime, I've got something to tell you."

"About what?"

"The name I heard mentioned in the hardware store."

Oh, please, God! The FBI agent held her breath. Prayed that he would say—

"Trout. That's what the bad guy asked me—'Did Trout send you?'"

"Yes!" McTeague vaulted off the couch and raised her fists in a victorious gesture. "Trout is the top dog in the Family—the one who plans the jobs and calls the shots. Good work, Charlie!"

"You sound just like my first-grade schoolteacher." Moon grinned. "Do I get a shiny gold star on my forehead?"

Better than that. *Just as Sarah Frank put her eye to the keyhole*, the lady grabbed the long, lanky cowboy by the neck and pasted a big, enthusiastic kiss—square on his lips!

Charlie Moon stood there and took it like a man.

The keyhole peeker gasped; her heart *stopped*. And started up again.

Releasing the startled man from her embrace, the FBI agent placed a call to the Denver FBI Field Office. The SAC's digital recorder advised the caller to leave a brief message. "This is Special Agent McTeague. Mr. Moon has tied Trout to the hardware-store robbery. More later."

Scott Parris parked his sleek black-and-white Chevrolet patrol car beside McTeague's rental car and went stomping across the headquarters yard.

Tears streaming down her face, Sarah Frank was barely aware of her leaden feet descending the stairway when Parris banged his big fist on the door and boomed out, "Hey—lemme in!"

After hurriedly wiping her eyes, Sarah opened the front door.

His face about as cheerful as warmed-over oatmeal, Parris tipped his hat at the sad-faced girl. "Where are those two?"

The Ute-Papago girl pointed at the ceiling.

The chief of police looked up. Seeing no one hanging from the chandelier, he picked up right away on the meaning of her gesture. The quick-witted fellow muttered a perfunctory "thanks" before bounding up the stairway three steps at a stride.

As was her habit at such emotion-charged moments, Daisy Perika appeared, leaning against her walking stick. "What in the world's going on?"

Sarah mumbled that she did not know. *And I don't care.*

But she did, poor kid. And sooner or later, caring too much would prove to be—

But we must not anticipate.

CHAPTER TWENTY-SIX

WORSE THAN BAD NEWS

Scott Parris clomped his big boots along the upstairs hall-way, jerked Moon's office door open, and barged into the rancher's private sanctum like a man looking for a knock-down, drag-out brawl with anyone who crossed his path. Without so much as a "hello," the chief of police tossed his old-fashioned felt fedora onto Moon's desk and fell heavily onto the leather couch. "What a day," he growled. "I don't know how things could get worse." But the gloomy cop harbored a suspicion that one way or another, things would.

Moon frowned at his friend, who seemed to have aged a decade since yesterday. "What's happened?"

The fed seated herself beside the chief of police and shot a glance at him. "You want me to tell him?"

The cop rubbed a stubby thumbnail over the couch arm, making a deep crease in the soft leather. "No, I'll do it." He looked up at Charlie Moon. "You'd better sit down for this."

"Bad as all that?"

"Worse." Parris crossed the crease to make an X. "If this business was only 'bad,' I'd be tickled half to death."

Moon pulled up an armchair to face his guests. As he eased himself into it, his knees brushed McTeague's, and he caught a hint of a scent of expensive perfume. It was enough to make a man dizzy.

Oblivious to such hormonal distractions, Parris thumbed a lopsided circle around the X. "Last night, a person or persons unknown entered the ICU at Snyder Memorial and killed everybody on the floor."

Moon's eyes narrowed to slits. *"Everybody?"*

"Every living soul." The lawman inspected the circled X with a critic's hard eye, then rubbed it out. "Except for the two survivors of the hardware-story robbery." Parris was experiencing a peculiar sense of detachment from reality; even his spoken words seemed to be coming from somewhere outside himself. When a sharp pain surged in his chest, he took a deep breath and gritted his teeth until it passed. "Those bastards are gone with the wind." He gave McTeague a sideways glance. "They were snatched by that gang of low-life murderers the FBI calls 'the Family.'"

The tribal investigator was also feeling pain, but of the psychic kind. "How many dead altogether?"

"Sixteen." A burning sensation seared Parris's left arm. *Go ahead. Kill me. I don't give a hot damn!* "Two night nurses. A state cop—some new guy I didn't know. They tell me he had a wife and twin baby girls." For the longest time, the lawman was unable to speak. He tried vainly to swallow the lump in his throat. Coughed. Swallowed again. Finally, he croaked, "And thirteen patients."

"That's an awful lot of killing," Moon whispered.

Parris opened his mouth. Shut it. He put his hands over his eyes and wept silently while his massive shoulders shook.

Lila Mae McTeague wanted to hug the big man. Tell him not to worry. By and by, everything would be all right. She resisted the motherly urge.

Moon tried to think of some comforting words. Came up empty.

At a loss for what to say or do, the FBI agent and the tribal investigator stared at the floor.

After making a peculiar choking sound, the hard-boiled lawman got up, stalked into the hallway, and shut the door behind himself. Softly.

A crotchety old clock on the office wall tickety-tocked precious seconds away, perhaps to be deposited in some hidden cache of time that would be recycled one fine day.

The Ute addressed his former girlfriend. "Anybody see the killers?"

Fighting off the urge to snap, *Only the dead,* McTeague shook her black mane. "So far, we haven't located a witness who saw anyone."

"Somebody must've heard something." Moon glared at the closed office door. "Screams in the night. Somebody putting up a fight."

"Yes, one would think so." The woman's tone was even, almost *detached*—as if they were discussing the likelihood of rain tomorrow or how best to skin a channel catfish. "Evidently, the thing was done very quietly."

"So how'd these people die?"

The lady admired the expertly lacquered fingernails on her left hand. "The medical examiner's preliminary findings—and this was based upon the four corpses that had been examined when I received the oral report—is that the victims' brains were penetrated by a slender, pointed instrument." Apparently satisfied with her expensive manicure, the federal cop licked her tastefully tinted lips to savor the bittersweet flavor of a lipstick called Raspberry Sunset. She had left a slight trace of this concoction on Moon's mouth. "The working portion of the weapon was no less than eight centimeters long and approximately four millimeters in diameter." She cocked her head, as if to mull this data over. "A common ice pick, I should think." Anticipating Moon's next question, Lila Mae McTeague touched a pointy crimson fingernail to a cultured pearl on her earlobe. "The wound entry point was in the victim's left ear canal."

Charlie Moon experienced a sudden earache. Absurdly, this sympathetic response was followed instantly by recollection of the phrase *better than a sharp stick in the eye.*

The office was suddenly uncomfortably warm. Oppressively stuffy.

At a rumble of distant thunder over the Misery Range, the rancher got up to open a window.

Wearing a sheepish smile, Scott Parris opened the door, thereby providing a path for a pleasant draft. The fresh breeze lifted a pair of gauzy window curtains that a long-dead occupant of the Columbine had crocheted more than eighty years ago. Parris explained his absence in this manner: "I asked Sarah to make us a pot of coffee."

"Good idea." Moon was unable to return his friend's strained smile. "We're going to need it."

McTeague, who seemed to require no audience, might have been talking to herself. "The working hypothesis is that a person posing as a qualified nurse gained access to the ICU." Before Moon could ask why, she explained. "The LPN who was scheduled to work the graveyard shift didn't show up, but a substitute apparently did. We found an unintelligible scrawl on the night-duty log that is evidently the sub's signature. After performing some routine duties and gaining the confidence of the state-police officer who was guarding the hospitalized felons, the phony stand-in probably murdered the officer first, then ice-picked the two nurses. The next step would have been to unlock the ground-floor door below the ICU and let in the Family members who would assist their hospitalized comrades in their escape. While that was happening, the counterfeit nurse would have had sufficient time to murder all of the ICU's thirteen other patients."

Moon tried without success to avoid visualizing the cold-blooded massacre. His mind's eye watched a wild-eyed, white-frocked nurse dash from room to room, stabbing a bloody ice pick deep into the brains of terrified sick folk who were too weak to defend themselves. "Have you located the nurse who didn't show up for work?"

Already the color of slate, Parris's face faded a shade grayer. He had forgotten to add that grisly statistic, which raised the body count to seventeen.

"I regret to say—yes." McTeague had fixed her gaze on a Cattleman's Bank calendar on the office wall, which featured an oil painting of a purebred Hereford bull. "Just before dawn, the victim's corpse was discovered in the trunk of her 1992 Mercury sedan, which was parked behind the hospital."

Parris groaned. "Killing a cop who's guarding their

buddies, even murdering the nurses—that's bad enough." He balled his right hand into a big fist that he wanted to *hit something with*. "But only a criminal lunatic would kill all those sick people *just for the hell of it*."

Despite her cool exterior, McTeague was beginning to feel the strain. "The hospital murders were not committed by a lunatic, or 'just for the hell of it.'" As she turned her head to glare at Parris, the fed's tone was icy. "The helpless victims were killed with definite and practical goals in mind— the most obvious being to eliminate any possibility of leaving a witness behind. Even a seemingly comatose survivor might have seen or heard something that would help us identify one or more members of the Family." She eyed the disheveled town cop with distaste, like an epicure who has discovered a dung beetle in her cream-of-mushroom soup. "And there was a secondary objective to the mass murder, which was at least as important as rescuing two of their injured comrades."

Parris set his formidable jaw bulldog-fashion. "And what might that be?"

He is almost cute. "The members of the Family consider themselves to be a pretty tough bunch of hombres. And like all of their ilk, they have their pride."

Mr. Bulldog goggled at the woman. "Pride?"

"Well of course." Explaining the obvious to dimwits was so very tedious. "Try to view the situation from their perspective. When a local cowboy just happens to wander by the hardware store and manhandles their team of four"—she shot a sharp look at Moon—"they end up looking like a bunch of bumbling amateurs. And in addition to suffering acute embarrassment, the Family ends up with two men stone cold dead, and two more seriously injured." McTeague enjoyed provoking the angry chief of police. "I am firmly convinced that the hospital massacre was a sort of in-your-face method of making a point." She waited for the hoped-for response.

Parris did not disappoint. "Point?"

"Certainly."

"With who?"

"The local chief of police, of course."

He jabbed his chest with a thumb. "Me?"

"Who else?" McTeague plunged her verbal dagger deep into his ego. "Until the Bureau assumed jurisdiction, you represented the legally constituted authority." She twisted it. "And while being interviewed by the news media, you referred to the Family as 'a bunch of cowardly bums, who like to beat up on old women.'"

Oblivious to this attack, Parris didn't blink. "Well, they are—cowardly murderous bums, who ought to be strung up on the nearest cottonwood and their bodies left to rot in the sun!"

Left with no other weapon, the fed resorted to a disdainful sniff. "A very evocative picture, and you are entitled to your point of view."

Evocative, indeed. The picture of hanging bodies rotting in the sun reminded Scott Parris of something. An execution he could not quite call to mind; a death sentence carried out a long time ago. *Must've been an old photograph I saw in one of my Western-lore magazines.* But it felt more like a scene from a nightmarish dream.

McTeague's reply was icy. "The point the Family made was simply this—that despite your best efforts, they are still in business."

"Not for long," Parris said.

This was McTeague's setup for the cheap shot. "I agree. Now that the Bureau has jurisdiction, with almost a hundred agents on the case."

The local cop rolled his eyes, barely contained a derisive snort.

The FBI agent turned her head to regard the craggy-faced Indian. A romantic of sorts, she imagined Charlie Moon living in those days before the Shining Mountains were overrun by mountain men, explorers, prospectors, soldiers, ranchers, cowboys, various categories of land-grabbers, and finally farmers, merchants, and poor families desperate for a home nearer to that far horizon where the sun went down. *Charlie is quite civilized. But a hundred and fifty years ago, he'd have been a*

*bloodthirsty savage wearing scalps on his belt and commit-
ting unspeakable atrocities against the settlers.* Miss Mc-
Teague had the benefit of a fine liberal education with three
degrees from two of the finest Ivy League universities—but
history was not her strong suit.

The object of her lurid imagery was lost in Lila Mae Mc-
Teague's enormous eyes.

He's so sweet. Somewhere deep inside, the lady sighed.
Perhaps I should consider rekindling our relationship. She
recalled what had happened last year. *No. I could never forgive
him for that. Not even if he was innocent.* Like the members of
the Family, Lila Mae also had her pride. "Well, Charlie, you
always manage to find trouble."

Mr. So Sweet felt warmed by his old flame. "I don't go
looking for it." *Trouble seems to have a way of finding me.*
Just like Aunt Daisy. *Maybe it's in our blood.*

As it happened, the aforesaid aunt was approaching.

Bam! (This was Daisy kicking the office door.)

"Open up!" (Also Moon's irascible auntie.)

Why did she not merely rap a knuckle lightly on the door
and ask politely whether her nephew and his guests would
mind being disturbed for a moment? Because Daisy did not
have a free hand. Her sturdy oak staff was grasped in one, a
hot pot of coffee in the other. Nevertheless, with the assistance of her walking stick, the tribal elder could stand briefly
on one foot, which left the other appendage free to kick
with.

Now, the matter of her snappish command. The old war-
horse was winded from climbing the Columbine headquarters stairs and in no mood for wasting precious breath on
superfluous words.

When Charlie Moon opened the door, his nearest living
relative pushed the stainless steel percolator at him. Spot-
ting a hint of crimson on her nephew's mouth, Daisy aimed
a beady-eyed stare at McTeague. "That's pretty lipstick,
Toots—I hope you don't use it all up before you leave." With
this parting shot, the crotchety woman turned and plodded
away.

Scott Parris frowned at the empty space where Daisy had been. *What was that all about?*

Lila Mae, who understood Daisy's implication, smiled at Charlie, who didn't.

Having long since given up any attempt to make sense of his peculiar aunt's behavior, Mr. Moon responded with a slight shrug, closed the door, and put the coffeepot on his desk. "I'll go down later and get us some cups."

As it happened, that errand would not be necessary.

CHAPTER TWENTY-SEVEN

SHE DELIVERS A MESSAGE

Lightly: *tap-tap*.

Pause.

Softly: "Excuse me—may I come in?"

For the second time in two minutes, Charlie Moon opened his office door.

The seventeen-year-old had washed the tearstains from her face, brushed her jet-black hair until it glistened, and smeared enough $3.98 per stick Pink Passion on her lips to startle the object of her ardent affections. She offered a bemused Moon a heavy Nambe Ware tray bearing two man-size mugs and a dainty flowered China cup for the lady. Also three stainless steel spoons, a miniature brown crockery pitcher of half-and-half, and a silver bowl filled with snow-white sugar.

Without a glance at Miss McTeague or Mr. Parris, Sarah turned and walked away.

But—and this detail is significant—there was *no honey* on the tray.

This deliberate omission of the obligatory bee nectar for sweetening his coffee was Sarah's message to Moon. Strong stuff. Possibly even overkill. But the cavalier fellow who (so she thought) went around kissing every woman in sight (excepting herself) needed to be taught a stern lesson.

Moon glanced at the tray. *She forgot the Tule Creek honey.*

SPECIAL AGENT MCTEAGUE'S
AFTERTHOUGHT

After Charlie Moon had poured coffee for his guests, Miss McTeague took a sip. Whilst sipping, a thought occurred to m'lady, which led her to query the chief of police thusly: "How many GCPD officers have you assigned to guard Mrs. Jeppson?"

Parris's highly expressive frown asked what she meant by that. And why she thought the operation of his department was any of the $&%$# FBI's %#$&$ business.

Assuming that this man of late middle age was merely confused by her question, the federal cop explained. "I refer, of course, to the potential threat to Mrs. Jeppson."

What threat? "What threat?"

"You didn't read the fax?"

"What fax?"

She rolled her big, pretty eyes. "The urgent memorandum the Bureau forwarded to your office yesterday."

"I spent practically all of yesterday with you." A blue vein worming its way across his temple started to throb. "During the past thirty-six hours, I've been in my office for maybe ten minutes."

McTeague's haughtily lifted chin suggested that this was no excuse for not keeping up with official correspondence. Also that Scott Parris was a stereotypical incompetent yokel cop who probably got his tin star out of a box of Sugar Pops. "Then let me brief you on the essential facts contained in the facsimile message. Three years ago almost to the day, the Family staged their annual summer-vacation crime spree in Arkansas." Though it would be an act of flagrant hyperbole to declare that the fed spat out the words like an automatic pistol belching hot bullets, there was a measured intensity in her delivery that commanded attention. "When a Little Rock pawnshop owner responded to an attempted armed robbery by firing five loads of buckshot into two of their members, the Family ended up with one man dead on the spot and another mortally wounded. They carried both of their fallen comrades away." She inhaled an aromatic breath of Columbine air that was lightly scented with old leather and wet sage, and exhaled it with these words: "Nine days later, the Family had their revenge on the operator of the small business, who had wreaked havoc with his Browning automatic shotgun. They made him watch while they slit his twelve-year-old son's throat and crushed his eight-year-old daughter's skull with a crowbar."

Did she have their undivided attention? Yea, verily. The chief of police and the tribal investigator were like men made of stone.

And McTeague was just getting up to steam. "After committing these atrocities, a member of the Family placed one of Trout's custom-made improvised explosive devices on a kitchen chair. The father of the slain children was forced to sit on it."

Parris found his tongue. "You're gonna tell us they watched the poor guy get blown to smithereens?"

"Nothing so vulgar." She arched her left eyebrow. "Trout has designed a particularly insidious IED that incorporates a common aluminum pie pan. It is used to terrify the Family's victims." Special Agent McTeague went to the open window, lifted her gaze to admire an azure sky. "When the pie-pan assembly is compressed, a pressure switch closes to arm the detonator. If and when the victim's weight is removed from the explosive device, the detonator fires." She turned to her audience, the balmy breeze playing with her dark locks. "The explosive charge is not sufficient to kill instantly. The purpose is to mangle the victim, who will either bleed to a painful death within a few minutes or survive with hideous injuries. A member of the Family explained this to the bereaved father, after which they left him to endure his horrific predicament. They undoubtedly expected the pawnshop owner to panic and make an attempt to leap off the chair, but Mr. Shotgun was a tough cookie. He sat in the booby-trapped chair for almost six hours—staring at the corpses of his murdered children. He was determined to survive so that he could hunt the gang down and kill every last one of them. Eventually a neighbor showed up to borrow something or other, and called the local police, who called the state police, who contacted the Bureau, which immediately dispatched a team of explosive experts, who extricated the pawnshop owner from his precarious situation." She paused to catch her breath.

So that's how those bastards play the game. Parris stared at the attractive FBI agent without seeing her. *Eye for eye, tooth for tooth.*

McTeague felt uncomfortable under the cop's hard gaze. "In light of the Family's history of returning to avenge themselves, the Bureau's concern is that they might send someone to murder Mrs. Jeppson, who had the audacity to activate the silent alarm in her hardware store. If you don't have sufficient personnel to protect this local citizen until we arrest this group of killers, the Bureau would be happy to provide some help."

"Thanks anyway."

I knew that's what you'd say. "Very well, then. But if you should change your mind, the offer stands."

The chief of police got up and snatched a Granite Creek County telephone directory off Moon's desk. He searched under the *J*s until he found Jeppson, then called the widow's home. With every ring, Parris's pulse rate increased. *Damn!* He put in a call to GCPD and barked at the dispatcher before she had time to answer, "Clara, patch me through to Unit 242 or 246—whoever's closest to the Jeppson residence at—" he checked the phone directory, "at 3260 Juniper Loop."

"Yes sir." She did.

As luck would have it, Officer Martin and her partner Boyd Keever, on routine patrol in Unit 246, were barely four blocks from the Jeppson residence.

Parris issued his orders to Alicia Martin, advising his favorite officer to put the pedal to the metal. The chief of police also informed Martin that he would remain on the telephone until she checked things out at Mrs. Jeppson's home.

Twenty-eight seconds passed like the worst twenty-eight hours of Parris's life.

With brief respites for essential oxygen, Charlie Moon and Lila Mae McTeague held their respective breaths until the chief of police shouted into his miniature telephone, "Well if she don't answer, then break the damn door down!"

He heard an enthusiastic grunt as Officer Keever, a former Kansas State fullback, made splinters of the door.

The silence that followed was of that sort that knots the gut.

Parris yelled loud enough to be heard several yards from the officer's portable radio, "Hey—talk to me!"

Officer Keever picked up, advised the chief of police that the elderly lady was on her living-room floor, apparently unconscious. Dispatch was sending an ambulance. Officer Martin was applying mouth-to-mouth and Keever (when he was not being interrupted with demands for information) was doing his best to keep up with chest compressions.

"Okay, Boyd—good work. But please keep me posted."

"Yes sir. I'll do that."

Additional unbearable silence.

Parris was startled when Keever's gruff voice spoke into his ear with an update. More specifically, a correction. The widow Jeppson was dead. "You sure?"

"Yes sir. And for quite some time—the body's cold." He added, unnecessarily, that no further attempt at resuscitation was called for.

Parris closed his eyes. "How'd the old lady die?"

It was to be the Loyola Montoya diagnosis all over again.

Most likely a heart attack, Keever opined. Or maybe a stroke. But it might've been an aneurysm, which (he informed the boss), "is what happens when one of your arteries swells up like a balloon and pops, and that's lights-out. End of story." The officer confided that he had a second cousin who'd died of an aneurysm. "And I was there on the spot to see it happen. Right in the middle of laughing at a joke about a monkey who brings a pet parrot into a bar for a lime daiquiri, Cousin Floyd keeled over like a felled tree— dead before he hit the floor. Damnedest thing I ever did see."

Parris had gritted his teeth through this fascinating family anecdote. "About Mrs. Jeppson—you're sure there's no sign of violence?"

"No sir. Well . . . nothing we can see."

The chief of police caught a look from Special Agent McTeague. "Take a look at her ears."

"Sir?"

"Her *ears*, Keever. You'll find one on both sides of her head." Parris paused to gulp in a breath. "I'm sorry. This has been a tough day. Just tell me whether you see anything—"

"Hey, Chief—there's a drop of blood on her left ear. Wow! How'd you know—"

Officer Boyd Keever was talking to a dead line.

Parris had disconnected without the courtesy of a good-bye. The grim-faced cop turned to Charlie Moon, looked the Ute directly in the eyes. "Charlie—the mean sons of bitches who did this shouldn't be arrested, indicted, tried, convicted, and provided with free room and board for the rest of their unnatural lives. Oh no." He wagged a big finger at the tribal investigator. "Whoever gets the chance should do *exactly* what you did in the hardware store. Pull the trigger—shoot 'em dead." He turned on his boot heel and was gone.

Charlie Moon and Special Agent McTeague stared at the office door Scott Parris had slammed. Listened to the big man stomp his way down the hallway, then the stairs.

The fed summed up the situation succinctly: "He's stressed out."

CHAPTER TWENTY-EIGHT

THAT EVENING

Though he had been in bed for almost an hour, Scott Parris was not quite asleep. neither was he entirely awake. The weary man was caught in that gray in-between world.

But wait.

His breathing has become regular; the weary man is slipping off into a welcome slumber.

EPISODE FOUR

A Final Resting Place

The journey from the funeral in Granite Creek's Tennessee Saloon had taken a full two days, and though the corpse did not mind the jarring ride on the back of the Indian's piebald pony, the spirit, who was still more or less attached to its fleshly husk, did.

Which was why U.S. Marshal Scott Parris was pleased when Charlie Moon, mounted on a fine black stallion, finally crossed the river and led the tethered pony to the lonely, windswept crest of Pine Knob, where it was rumored that several of the Ute's close friends and careless enemies were buried. Before he got down to the serious business of the evening, Moon built a small campfire and laid a rustler's branding iron in the middle of the dancing flames.

Apparently in no great hurry to dispose of his best friend's remains, the Indian prepared himself a supper of roasted rabbit and coffee.

Twilight gradually darkened into night, exposing a thin crescent of silver moon above the jagged Misery Mountains.

Somewhere off to the south, the obligatory coyote yip-yipped.

At this poignant signal, Mr. Moon rolled up his sleeves.

Parris watched with considerable satisfaction as the Ute used a short-handled miner's pick and a square-bladed spade to dig the grave. This was not a morbid interest in being buried—it is always a pleasure to watch another fellow do backbreaking work.

When the task was completed, Charlie Moon got to work on the grave marker, which was a weathered plank.

Parris watched with rapt fascination as his friend removed the red-hot iron from a heap of glowing embers. The lawman's spirit wondered: What'll he put on the marker?

Charlie Moon burned a name onto the smoking wood.

SCOT PARIS

Dammit, Charlie, that's not how you spell it. Any dope knows Scott has two ts. And you ought to know my last name has two rs.

Oblivious to these nitpicking complaints, Moon burned the deceased's title.

U.S. MARSHAL

The dead man smiled. That's nice. And he spelled it right. Under that, the Ute etched in these numbers:

1822–1877

Well, at least he got this year right. The spirit rolled its spirit-eyes. But I was born in 1823.

"Hmmm," the Indian said.

Parris watched with fascination as his buddy puzzled over the epitaph.

Charlie Moon thought.

Thought some more.

Aha!

As the Ute applied the hot iron to the moldering plank again, the U.S. marshal's spirit leaned close to see what tribute his pardner would leave for posterity to marvel over. *Maybe something about how I never took a dime of graft, or never backed down from a fight, or how I drilled "Lightning" Bull Bates between the eyes before his Navy Colt ever cleared leather.*

Sad to say, Parris was not able to see what words of fond remembrance his pal had inscribed on the wood. As so often happens when we are just on the verge of finding out—a dark cloud slipped across the crescent moon. In an instant, Pine Knob was black as the inside of (this was the dreamer's metaphor) a buzzard's gizzard.

It was bad enough to be deprived of enjoying one's epitaph. Worse still was the unanswered question that nagged at U.S. Marshal Scott Parris.

What did them black-hearted bastards hang me for?

CHAPTER TWENTY-NINE

THE FOLLOWING DAY

Charlie Moon would never have thought of mentioning the Family's cold-blooded murders to Daisy or Sarah, particularly during their evening meal. His supper talk was limited to observations such as how welcome the recent rain had been, and that the moisture would help green up the bone-dry six sections north of Pine Knob. Happy tidings were gratifying to talk about; bad news could wait.

But, as it happened, not for as long as Moon had hoped.

Only two hours earlier, with Sarah at her elbow, the tribal elder had tuned in to the afternoon news on her semiantique tabletop vacuum-tube radio, which had been an anniversary gift from her third husband, whom Daisy praised as being "not nearly as bad as the first two." They had been informed about the "Snyder Memorial Hospital Massacre," right down to gory details of how the FBI was searching the grounds for a bloody ice pick, and that the no-show night nurse had been strangled with a piece of copper wire and stuffed into the trunk of her car. Daisy and Sarah were also informed about the tragic Widow Jeppson homicide. Now, the Ute tribal elder and the Ute-Papago orphan realized why Charlie Moon, Scott Parris, and the strikingly pretty FBI agent had held a private conference in Moon's office the day before.

Under the trying circumstances, the old woman and the young one agreed not to bring up the subject. If the most important man in their lives eventually decided to say something about the killings, it would be something along the lines of, *It's a bad businesses, but it's not ours.* Charlie Moon would remind them that with hungry predators pulling cattle down, drunken Columbine cowboys starting fights in town, and expensive equipment breaking down left and right, there was more than enough trouble to deal with on the ranch without worrying about what went on in town. He would assure the ladies that Granite Creek PD, the state police, and the FBI were on top of it. Next time you turn on the radio news, the bad guys will be behind bars. Or, better yet, dead.

AFTER SUPPER

While a thin, gray twilight was settling in on the high plains between the blue-gray Buckhorn Range and the shimmering, mystery-shrouded Misery Mountains, the major characters at the Columbine headquarters had settled down, each to attend to his or her particular business.

Partly to keep his mind off the mounting murder count, but mainly because he was determined to take a hot shower before bedtime, Charlie Moon was inside installing a new thermocouple in the propane water heater, where the pesky pilot light kept going out.

A dark blue woolen shawl pulled snugly around her stooped shoulders, Daisy Perika was perched on the west-porch swing. Despite the fact that Mrs. P. was singing the few phrases she could remember from "Now the Day Is Over" with an expression of childlike innocence befitting a medieval saint, one cannot entirely dismiss the possibility that the enigmatic old soul was figuring out some new and interesting way to create troubles for her nephew.

Seated nearby in a form-fitting wicker chair, Sarah Frank was figuring out several new ways to make herself attractive to Mr. Moon. No. She shook her head. Attractive was not aiming high enough. The thin little slip of a girl smiled. *Irresistible.* That was what she would shoot for.

Napping in Sarah's lap, Mr. Zig-Zag pursued his own fantasies, but that information is not available. Whatever spotted tomcats may dream about, they keep it strictly to themselves.

Sidewinder was stretched out on the plank porch between the hymn-crooning old woman and the hopeful young lady. His long muzzle rested between a pair of paws so large as to give him a comical appearance, but the sad-faced dog was a deeply serious personality who never went for laughs. And, unlike felines, those of the doggish persuasion are not at all reticent in sharing even their most intimate experiences. (At the moment, Sidewinder is enjoying a siesta fantasy where he stalks the most outrageously huge jackrabbit any canine has ever imagined. Big as a full-grown buck elk.)

As his happy dream of sufficient rabbit flesh for a nine-month winter began to deteriorate into something less pleasant, the hound commenced to snort. Groan as if suffering sharp pains. Shudder like a wolfish ancestor caught in a late-spring blizzard.

With the exception of a hungry coyote who had once aspired to have her cat for supper, Sarah adored all of God's furry creatures. She observed the old dog with girlish compassion. "I wonder what's the matter with him."

The tribal elder, who had a ready answer for every question, snapped, "Indigestion." *That dumb dog'll eat anything that can't outrun him, from banana peels to watermelon rinds.*

THE DOG'S EYES

Though tightly shut at the moment, they are known to be large, brown, and marvelously expressive. The anxious beast awakened abruptly to peel the lids off his eyeballs and stare intently toward an old-growth grove of giant cotton-woods. Like a company of furloughed old soldiers who refused to muster out after the war was declared lost, the woody brigade occupied a low ridge between the headquarters building and Too Late Creek. The hound got to his feet, lowered his head, and muttered a low, guttural growl. Hair bristled on the back of Sidewinder's neck.

Sarah's gaze followed the dog's. *He sees something.* The girl saw nothing but shadows under the cottonwoods.

Then, the hound did the *oddest* thing. Without taking his gaze off the whatever-it-was, he sidled over to the old woman, pressed himself hard against Daisy's leg—and *whimpered* like a frightened puppy. For a valiant animal who had never backed down from a confrontation, be the enemy a snarling cougar, diamondback rattlesnake, or grizzly bear, this was a peculiarly pitiful performance. Perhaps strangest of all, he was seeking comfort from a bad-tempered old woman who was not the sort of bosom buddy that a four-legged canine person would be inclined to share a meaty ham bone with.

Daisy scowled at the dog. *Now what's gotten into him?*

A fair question.

And Sidewinder's eccentric performance had only just begun. Just as Charlie Moon stepped onto the porch, the creature raised his head in wolflike fashion to let out one of those long, mournful howls that make neck hairs stand up and skin prickle.

Daisy's neck hairs.

Sarah's skin.

It took a lot more than a dog's howl to spook Charlie Moon. Seating himself on a redwood bench, the man patted the dog's head. "What's the matter, old boy?"

Daisy answered for the animal. "He's scared of something."

As if to validate this assertion, the hound responded with another yowling howl, which was even eerier than the previous complaint.

Moon remained unmoved. "Sidewinder's not scared of anything alive." As it happened, this assertion was not only true—it was a highly relevant observation.

Daisy squinted at the cluster of cottonwoods. *I can just about make out a fuzzy something or other out there. But only if I look to one side of it.* It was, she thought, like trying to see a dim star. If the tribal elder looked directly at it, the fuzzy something vanished. As if it had a will of its own, Daisy's right hand moved toward the hound's bristled neck.

When her fingers touched the animal, it was as if an electric current tingled its circuitous path through her hand, along her arm, up her neck, into her brain, and then—zipped along the optical nerves to her *eyes.*

Whether or not this was literally true, the shaman instantly *knew* that she was seeing what the hound saw—in what might be described in the current technical vernacular as "high-resolution black-and-white." And at the instant she realized this, it seemed as if the *thing* knew it too, because it began to drift. But not away.

No such luck.

Daisy held her breath. *Here it comes, across the yard, directly toward the porch!*

Perhaps assured by the aged woman's touch, Sidewinder did not flinch. He bared a set of formidable teeth, uttered a barely audible growl that *Daisy felt rumbling in her own belly and throat.* Seemingly sharing the dog's sensations, the shaman had a sense of smell keener than she could have imagined. Be it the pungent scent of pine needles, oddly sour human body odors, the wildly fragrant perfume of a distant rainstorm—her olfactory experiences were almost overpowering.

Unnerved by the hound's unseemly behavior, Sarah hugged herself and murmured to no one in particular, "This is scary."

"There's nothing to be scared of." Moon's assertion did little to comfort the girl. "I expect it's just a hungry old cougar skulking about." But, try as he might, the Ute's keen eyes could find nothing amiss in the twilight, which was slowly thickening into night. Moon picked up Daisy's sturdy walking stick and ambled out into the yard for a better look.

Appalled at this display of imprudence, Sarah went into the parlor to find a rifle.

Daisy Perika was barely aware of their departures; what the shaman saw froze her old bones to the *very marrow.* Coming ever closer was something that appeared to be the residue of a human being—the *leftovers.* A strand of rusty barbed wire

was twisted around its neck, the eyes were goggled as if
about to pop, and a swollen tongue protruded rudely from its
mouth. That should have been sufficient, but no—the naked,
flayed corpse was slathered in a mixture of clay and something oozy that smelled oddly sweet. And (Daisy thought)
vinegarish.

This was more than enough to ruin an elderly lady's peaceful evening, but what unnerved her most of all was—the
hideous apparition was floating *upside down*, its head about
a yard above the ground.

The shaman's long, doggish ear flicked when someone
whispered into it, *That's Wallace—my stupid grandson.*

Daisy: *Loyola—is that you?*

Sure. A cackle of laughter. *Who'd you expect, Cleopatra?*

Daisy (sternly): *What's this all about?*

Well what do you think? The spirit breathed a sigh. *It's
about murder—mine and my grandson's. I warned Wallace
to stay away from those nasty* brujos, *but did he listen? Oh,
no, he wanted to buddy around with that devilish lot—and
look what he got for his trouble!*

Though Daisy could not speak aloud—the shaman was
limited to barks and growls—she *thought* the question:
Where's his body?

The dead woman's familiar voice crackled in her ear: *Go
through the willows, wade across the creek, and follow the
stink and you'll find Wallace. That's where those witches
left him, to rot like a—*

She had intended to say *like a butchered pig!* but the
Apache ghost's narrative was interrupted by the following:

Uurrrgle . . .

What was that?

It can best be described as a gurgling sound.

Aarrkle . . . ooble . . .

There it goes again.

The source of this unseemly disruption?

The upside-down corpse. Loath to be left out of the conversation, it floats ever closer to the porch where Daisy and
the hound commune with Loyola. The bruised lips twist as

the mouth attempts to speak around the swollen tongue. *Orrrk . . . urrble . . . waaarrk!*

Warning growls rattle in Daisy-Sidewinder's throats.

The upside-down horror pauses. Jitters uncertainly this way and that. Edges a tongue's length closer to the porch.

The shaman-hound amalgamation bares both sets of teeth; two pairs of hindquarters tense for attack. It looks like there's going to be a great big brouhaha until—

The Daisy half of the duo hears Loyola say, *Oh, go away, Wallace—you're stinking the place up!*

Hideous, odorous apparitions are not bereft of feelings. The rudely dismissed specter withdrew toward the cotton-wood grove, presumably to sulk therein. Considering what occurred on the way, perhaps the shadowy presence was not looking where it was going. Or, the collision may have been deliberate.

As Sarah Frank appeared on the headquarters porch with a loaded and cocked Winchester carbine tucked under her arm, Daisy-Sidewinder were watching the retreating residue of Wallace Montoya pass directly *through* Charlie Moon.

As would be expected, the sensible rancher caught neither sight nor scent of such an unlikely phenomenon. And if Mr. Moon did experience a sudden clammy coldness in his bones during the unseemly intersection, that sensation was undoubtedly due to a slight breeze stirring the chill of night.

CHAPTER THIRTY

PRELUDE TO BIG TROUBLE
(IN D MINOR)

After her unsettling encounter with the invisible Loyola Montoya and the all-too-visible corpse of the Apache crone's strangled grandson, it is hardly surprising that Daisy Perika did not sleep well. But the hardy Ute elder was up with the sun to help prepare a hearty Columbine breakfast. While tending to a dozen pork sausage patties sizzling in a sooty-black Tennessee Forge iron skillet, she said to her nephew, "I need to make a quick trip down to my house today."

"I'll be glad to drive you down to the res." Charlie Moon was breaking brown-shelled eggs over a twin to the sausage skillet. "We can leave right after we eat."

"Oh, you don't need to do that." She patted his arm in motherly fashion. "You being so busy nowadays, I wouldn't want to bother you." Even *pretending* to be nice rankled, so she dropped the pretense. "Seeing as how you're a big shot who kills robbers in hardware stores and has his face on every TV screen in the country—you're bound to have better things to do than drive an old woman someplace."

He took the low blow with a grin. "That's mighty thoughtful of you."

"No matter how much I might need help from somebody, I always try to take the other person's problems into account." She smiled benignly at the third member of the breakfast club. "Sarah can drive me in her red pickup."

The teenager, who was filling coffee mugs from a blue enameled percolator, responded with a cheerful, "Okay."

Daisy gave her nephew a sly sideways glance. "I only need to pick up a few things, like that leather beadwork I've been working on for Myra Cornstone's new baby." *How many kids has Myra got now? I guess I stopped counting at six.* "We'll be back before the sun goes down."

Sarah stirred the first of two teaspoons of honey into Moon's coffee. "I'll take Mr. Zig-Zag with me."

This was just the cue Daisy needed. "That'll be nice." As an apparent afterthought, she added, "We'll take that flop-eared dog along too—so your cat will have some company." The counterfeit Lover of All Creatures Great and Small sighed with feigned compassion. "That sad-eyed old hound never gets to go anywhere. A little trip down to my house will do him good."

Busy scrambling eggs, Moon seemed not to hear.

Which pleased Daisy. *Charlie's got a lot on his mind and lots of things to do.*

He did.

Immediately after breakfast, the rancher's busy day began when Foreman Pete Bushman dropped by for a south-porch conference. At the top of Bushman's list was letting the boss know that he'd hired a nice young woman to "help me look after Dolly."

Moon expressed his pleasure at this news, but he had to be getting along now to take care of some other business.

Bushman was not finished. "And I hired some men to give us a hand while we're raising the new horse barn. What with the hard times and so many folks out of work, there's a better crop to pick from than most years." The foreman spat tobacco juice through his beard and hit his target—a startled horsefly who had stopped to rest awhile on the porch step. "None of 'em are actual stockmen, but one of 'em worked for a year on a dairy farm and the other three are jackleg carpenters—or so they say."

"Well, I expect they'll be worth their pay." Green Columbine hands drew low wages, slept on the hardest cots in the bunkhouse, and helped themselves to all the high-calorie food and strong black coffee a hardworking man could get down his gullet.

Bushman watched the assaulted horsefly buzz away in search of a friendlier neighborhood. "If they don't tow the line, I'll send 'em packin'." Looking vainly for another live target, the aggressive tobacco chewer aimed his surplus spittle at a lime-green cottonwood leaf that had just floated down from a lofty branch. Ready. *Splat! Shoot—I missed the dad-blamed thing by a good inch.*

During the foreman's misfire, Moon had managed to slip away.

About a minute after that, Daisy and Sarah—the latter carrying her cat—appeared on the front porch, which faces west. The tribal elder paused to nudge the somnolent hound with her walking stick.

Without raising his muzzle from the porch, Sidewinder opened his eyes halfway. He glared at the old woman as if to say, *Don't bug me, Granny.*

Exposing most of the peglike teeth she had left, Daisy presented the dog with the kind of smile that sends terrified little children screaming into their mothers' clutches. "G'morning, pooch. You want to go for a nice little ride?"

The hound yawned, closed his eyes.

Sarah eyed the lazy dog. "I guess he'd rather stay here."

"No he don't, the old tick-mattress is just playing coy. Wants me to sweet-talk him." Daisy pointed her walking stick at the red pickup. "Go on out there and lower that tailgate. Me'n Lassie's ugly cousin will be along directly."

Though doubtful of the predicted outcome, the girl did as she was bid.

As soon as Sarah had turned her back, Daisy nudged the hound more urgently. The precise location of her prodding was that tender orifice under the base of his tail.

Getting the point, the canine lurched to his feet. He turned to bare his teeth at the rude aggressor.

Pleased by this display of spirit, Daisy cackled a wicked laugh. "I like dogs with spunk, but don't mess with me, you mangy old fleabag, or I'll lay your skull wide open!" To demonstrate how that task would be accomplished, she raised her oak staff like the club it was. "Now go get your butt in that truck before I lose my temper."

Sidewinder kept his hindquarters where they were.

Blood in her eye, the tribal elder raised the oak staff a tad higher.

For a few strained heartbeats, the determined descendants of wolf and Eve stood toe-to-toe. Eyeball-to-eyeball.

Daisy (ready to strike!) did not blink.

The hound (prepared to bite!) did not budge.

This gut-wrenching standoff might have gone on for ever so long, except—

Thunk!

This was the sound of Sarah lowering the F-150 tailgate. The girl turned, gaped at Daisy. *She's going to hit him!* To prevent such a dastardly deed, the teenager clapped her hands and called to the dog, "C'mon, Sidewinder—let's go for a ride."

The beast raised his nose to make a disdainful sniff at the old woman. Following this cutting insult, the hound turned, departed for the truck in a deliberate gait, and loped into the bed of the F-150. Before the girl had raised and latched the tailgate, Sidewinder had laid himself down again.

Daisy ground her teeth at the annoying animal and glared at the upstart teenager. *There was no need for that. Another few seconds, I would've had that dog on a dead run for the pickup—with his tail tucked between his legs.*

CHAPTER THIRTY-ONE

DAISY'S BIG DAY

The pickup-truck ride southward from the Columbine was mighty fine for humans, also for canine and feline creatures. It could hardly have been otherwise: this was one of those delightful summer days when feathery cloud skiffs skim effortlessly over glassy-smooth turquoise seas and sweet heavenly breezes refresh the world-weary soul. Moreover, ecstatic little bluebirds flittered about their joyful business, and carefree butterflies fluttered hither and yon amongst wildflowers so lovely that even the most jaded eyes would have ached at the vision.

No wonder Sarah Frank was happy. Until—

Until, when they approached a familiar crossroads, which the youthful driver intended to pass directly through, and her aged passenger barked an order: "Make a left."

"But that's not the way to your—"

"We'll go to my house later." Daisy whacked her walking stick on the dashboard. "Turn here!"

Sarah did, and after Daisy commenced to yell and wave her arms, she made a hurried U-turn. When the unnerved driver was certain that she had the F-150 headed in the direction Daisy wanted to go, she posed that deep question that philosophers and sages have pondered through the ages: "What are we doing here?" And another, almost as profound: "Where are we going?"

Her surly passenger did not care to be interrogated by impertinent young whippersnappers. "You'll find out when we get there."

Some twenty-two minutes later, Sarah nosed the pickup into a weed-choked driveway very near the middle of Nowhere, Colorado. "That rickety old house with all the black-and-yellow tape wrapped around it—is that where the elderly woman died in the fire in her kitchen?"

Having arrived at her intended destination, Daisy was in a jovial mood. "This is where Loyola Montoya lived before she died."

Sarah cut the ignition to a heavy silence. "I don't think we should be here."

As Daisy eased her aged frame out of the pickup, the spotted cat slipped past her heels. Once on the ground, she leaned on her oak walking stick and turned to instruct the driver. "Go around back and let that dog out of the truck."

Sarah raised the door on the fiberglass camper shell and lowered the tailgate in the expectation that the Columbine hound would come bounding joyfully out, eager to explore this virgin territory.

It was not to be.

Sidewinder approached the tailgate, but, apparently having taken a liking to the amenities of the pickup bed (which included straw and a tattered old quilt), he showed no sign that he intended to disembark. Not that he was lacking the normal canine interest in unexplored real estate. The dog raised his nose to sniff the fragrant scent of moist sage, the tempting aromas of a variety of succulent rodent species, and . . . *something else.* He stared suspiciously at the older of the human beings.

Shaking her wooden staff at the hesitant creature, Daisy barked, "Get out of there, you lazy old son of a bitch!"

The object of this insult might have taken offense at being labeled "lazy" by Daisy. Or perhaps something else was on Sidewinder's mind. For whatever reason, the animal refused to budge.

Which situation called for direct action. The Ute woman reached for Sidewinder's black leather collar and gave it a healthy jerk.

Caught off guard by this unwarranted act of aggression on his person, the four-legged creature had little choice but to disembark.

But as soon as the hound hit the ground, he attempted to hide himself under the pickup. And no doubt would have if the old woman had not grabbed him again, this time by the tail. At Daisy's touch, the animal froze. Once again, the shaman smelled through his nose, saw through his eyes—spoke to him through his mind. *We ain't leaving this place till you go and find that dead man—so get to work before I tie a knot in your tail!*

We vertebrates who are not endowed with tails cannot imagine the horror of having such an appendage *tied into a knot.*

The dog capitulated.

Within a few heartbeats, Sidewinder was slowly circling Loyola Montoya's dreary old barn of a house. After completing two revolutions, the canine satellite zigged and zagged a couple of times before following his nose into the sad little apple orchard where the dry husks of last year's crop had rotted on the ground.

Pleased, Daisy hobbled off after the dog. *That's right. Head for the stream.*

Sarah did not like the looks of this. "Where are you going?"

Daisy called over her shoulder, "You want to find out, come along."

The girl followed her cat, who followed the Ute elder, who followed the hound.

This odd quartet passed through the dismal orchard and down a narrow path that went under a wasp-infested grape arbor to an outdoor privy. The dog veered off the privy path to follow a lesser branch through tick-infested weeds. This latter thoroughfare terminated abruptly at the bank of Ignacio Creek. Sidewinder paused to look back at the Ute elder.

Daisy pointed her stick at the gurgling water. "Keep going."

After a moment's hesitation, the hound loped across the stream to the opposite bank, where he disappeared into a thick cluster of willows.

The old woman braced herself, then stepped into the rippling waters. *Ohhh, that's cold!* She slipped on an unseen stone, almost lost her balance, but just in the nick of time—

Sarah appeared at Daisy's side to provide a helping hand.

With the aid of her walking stick and the girl's support, the old reprobate made it across the stream (which was knee-deep at the center) and cursed her way up the opposite bank.

They pressed on to the far side of the willows and found themselves in a large field with a huge cottonwood at its center. The rest of the more or less open space was dotted with piñon, juniper, and land-mined with vicious clusters of prickly-pear cactus. At the edge of this open space, and standing so directly in front of them that it appeared to have been placed on those coordinates for the express purpose of excluding a cranky old Ute woman, a skinny Ute-Papago orphan, a spotted cat, and a long-nosed hound—was a neatly lettered sign.

Property Line
Blue Diamond Natural Gas Company
NO TRESPASSING

Grateful for this unambiguous instruction, Sarah picked up her tomcat and hugged him to her chest. "We'd better go back to the pickup."

Daisy Perika snorted, mumbled a vile curse in the Ute tongue, spat on the sign, and—as an example to the timid girl—walked past it.

Sarah stayed put.

Which was okay with Daisy. But the intrepid hiker was displeased when she realized that she was entirely alone. She turned to shout at the dog, "What're you waiting for, a yellow taxicab?"

It may be that Sidewinder simply had no burning interest in further exploration, and it is even possible that the noble creature had scruples about infringing upon the gas company's private property—but given their remote location, it seems improbable that he was waiting for some form of motorized transport. Whatever his reasons, the dog had reverted to form: he would not budge.

Further angry shouts, energetic walking-stick shaking, even dire threats involving disembowelment—none of this altered the animal's view. Her quiver almost empty, Daisy was at a loss about which poison arrow to fire next, when, as it sometimes does, something unexpected occurred.

The stubborn hound, who had been inspecting a line of black ants marching across the sandy soil, suddenly jerked his neck and focused his brown eyes on something above the earth.

Expecting to see something of interest, such as a low-flying raven or red-tailed hawk, Daisy looked up.

As did Sarah

And the cat.

But search the sky as they might, there was nothing unusual to be seen.

Never mind. The dog's interest was riveted by this unseen nothing.

And the old shaman had a pretty good notion of what the animal was looking at.

As if tugged by an invisible leash, Sidewinder was pulled forward, his gaze ever upward. The lanky, four-legged creature passed Daisy, who followed him for about fifty yards—until the dog stopped beneath the towering cottonwood. Looking down, the hound whined, hesitated . . . reached out with his left front paw and began to scratch at the earth.

Immobile as the trunk of the old tree, Daisy held her breath.

CHAPTER THIRTY-TWO

CALLING MR. MOON

Sarah Frank had not advanced from her position behind the gas company's Do Not Trespass sign.

But even from a distance, she was keeping a close eye on Daisy Perika. Sarah had seen the mischievous old woman in action on several previous occasions, and she did not like the looks of things. *Daisy's up to something and she'll get all of us into trouble.* ("Us" included her cat and Charlie Moon's dog.) *But what can I do?*

Call the Man, that's what.

The girl put Mr. Zig-Zag down and dialed a number on her cell phone. After seven rings, Charlie Moon's recorded voice spoke into her ear: "This is the Columbine Ranch. You can leave a message after the tone." After the machine provided the aforesaid tone, which was more like a chirrupy *beep*, Sarah spoke softly, so Daisy would not hear. (The sound of a human voice carries a long way in places remote from the incessant drone and hum of our mechanized civilization.) "Charlie, this is Sarah. Me and Daisy are at the place where that old Apache woman was killed. Well, not actually in her house, or even on her property. We waded a little stream and now we're on some land that belongs to a gas company and they have a No Trespassing sign and Daisy and Sidewinder are way out in a big field and Sidewinder's digging a hole in the dirt and I thought you ought to know and—"

"I know all about it."

Charlie's voice is so loud and clear. "You sound like you're right here." *Like you could reach out and touch me.* Thrilled at the thought of his touch, Sarah felt a big hand on her shoulder, shrieked a terrified "eeeeeek!" flung the cell phone into the air, and turned to see Charlie Moon's laughing face. After a stunned moment of gaping at the solid-looking apparition, she stamped the ground. "You *scared* me!"

Picking up her cell phone, he laughed louder.

Sarah tried ever so hard to frown, but the effort made her face ache. Charlie's sudden appearance bordered on the magical. "How did you get here?" She stared at his dusty-dry cowboy boots. "Did you cross the creek?"

"Sure." Moon managed to swallow the grin as he put the cell phone into her hand. "These new high-tech boots are coated with Teflon—they shed water like freshly oiled goose feathers." He had walked on a fallen log across the stream.

This lighthearted exchange was interrupted by Daisy's yell: "Charlie Moon, get yourself over here and have a look at what me'n this hound have found." She raised her stick in a gesture to bar the girl's path. "Sarah, you stay right where you are."

Having had quite enough of being ordered around for one day, Sarah pointedly ignored the old woman's command, and though she had to make two strides to Moon's one, she stayed beside *her man.* This turned out to be a mistake. Big one. What the Ute-Papago girl saw when she got to the spot would haunt her dreams until the day she died.

Ignoring the imprudent girl and pretending not to mind that her sneaky nephew had followed them all the way from the Columbine, Daisy pointed her walking stick at Sidewinder's shallow excavation.

Protruding absurdly from the soil were the soles of a pair of bare feet. Blackened, stinking bare feet with the toes all curled underneath. Like (Sarah thought) *when you have cramps in the middle of the night.*

Moon put his hand on Sarah's shoulder again. Gently this time.

She looked up at the love of her life.

He gazed down at the winsome seventeen-year-old.

She raised a hand to shade her dark eyes from the midday sun. "You want me to leave."

The tribal investigator nodded and pointed. "Wait over there where you were—yonder by the stream. And don't say a word to anyone about what you've seen."

She nodded.

After watching Sarah Frank walk away, Moon squatted and blinked at the blackened feet.

Daisy's gravelly voice crackled behind him, "That'll be Loyola's grandson Wallace."

He turned his head to frown at his aunt. "You sound pretty sure of that."

"Sure enough to bet you a twenty-dollar bill." Daisy vainly attempted to straighten a back that was bent with age. "And you want to know something else?" She interpreted his silence as an affirmative reply. "After them witches strangled Wallace with—"

"Strangled?"

"That's what I said. And don't be interrupting me! They did it with a hank of barbed wire. And after they choked the life out of him, they roasted him over an open fire."

Moon stared at the inscrutable woman.

"Well, don't just stare at me like I've been eating loco-weed stew—say something!"

"Okay. Why would they do that?"

"Why would they roast him?"

Moon nodded.

"Well that's a dumb question—for the same reason they soaked his body in barbecue sauce!"

The tribal investigator frowned. "What in the world makes you think—"

"Because I *smelled* it." Her beady-eyed stare dared him to argue the point.

Knowing that look too well, Moon shrugged. "Well, if you're right, your nose is a lot better than mine."

"Hah!" *If you knew whose nose I smelled that barbecue through, you'd think I was ready for the funny farm.* Daisy shook her walking stick at the annoying nephew. "We're not dealing with your run-of-the-mill witches, Charlie—this is a bunch of damned cannibals!" Daisy had unwittingly uttered the descriptor that Special Agent McTeague had deliberately omitted during her conversations with Parris and Moon. The FBI's full designation for the criminal group was—the *Cannibal Family.*

"Whatever you say." The tribal investigator got to his feet and looped his long arm around the eccentric relative. "Now here's the deal. This situation has got to be reported. But I'd rather you and Sarah weren't around when the cops show up."

"And why not?" Daisy banged her walking stick within a half inch of the pointy toe of his boot. "It was me and Sidewinder that found Wallace's body."

"That's the very reason I don't want you here."

As her nephew proceeded to explain about the inevitable publicity, Daisy Perika listened with a burning intensity. She didn't mind talking to newspaper reporters or being interviewed on radio or TV. Not a bit. But when her concerned relative explained that it might be extremely dangerous to become known to the "witches" as an upstanding citizen who had discovered critical evidence that could be used against them in a court of law, the tribal elder began to have second thoughts. *These witches didn't just kill Loyola and her grandson; they murdered Mrs. Jeppson and all of those nurses and sick people over at the hospital.* And third thoughts. *Doing away with one more old woman wouldn't be nothing to them—it'd be like stepping on a bug.* "All right, then." Deep martyr's sigh. "Have it your way. I'll go back to the ranch with Sarah and act like I'm just a useless old woman who never does nothing that anybody appreciates."

Despite the grim situation, Moon managed a wan smile. "I appreciate that. And remind Sarah to keep quiet. I don't want anyone to know that either of you have even been here."

"Whatever you say." Off she went.

After his aunt had departed with the girl and her cat and left nothing behind but a lot of quiet, Charlie Moon began to wish he had somebody to talk to. Being alone except for the corpse (an unseemly partner for conversation) and the Columbine hound (who was regarding Moon with an inquisitive look), the choice was easy. "Well, it's just you and me now, pardner." Fixing his gaze on the dead man's feet, the tribal investigator explained to the dog how important it was that this discovery be kept as quiet as possible. The less this bloody-handed band of murderers knew about what the Law was up to, the better. Which raised the issue of how much Law to summon to the crime scene. The answer was obvious: the fewer the better. After pondering his options, the lawman knew what he had to do—though it went against the grain.

Charlie Moon dialed the programmed number on his cell phone.

When she saw the caller ID, Special Agent McTeague answered immediately. "What's up, Charlie?"

"I'd rather not say on an open line."

"Bad news?"

"Mmm-hmm."

"Tell me where and when and what to bring."

"The widow's farm. Try to get here before dark. You'll need a full forensics team. AC generators. Lights. A tent. The works."

"Got it."

A half hour before the sun set, the first of two Bureau helicopters settled onto the Blue Diamond Natural Gas Company's property to deliver Special Agent McTeague. Charlie Moon told his ex-girlfriend everything he knew about Daisy and Sidewinder's fortuitous discovery of the corpse. Which wasn't the whole story, of course. Which was just as well.

Grateful for his decision to limit knowledge of this big break in the Cannibal Family case, Lila Mae agreed to treat the connection to Daisy Perika, Sarah Frank, and Charlie Moon as Bureau Confidential. Even as she made this promise, McTeague advised the tribal investigator that the FBI would make the discovery of the corpse public. A news conference would probably be scheduled for tomorrow morning. Moon was about to suggest that the feds might want to consider holding off for at least a few days, but his words were drowned out by the *whump-whump* of Chopper Number Two, which disgorged the regional FBI forensics team. With barely a glance at McTeague and Moon, they set up their equipment and got down to business right on the spot.

Charlie Moon stayed to watch.

A shiny black polyethylene tent was assembled over the makeshift grave. Inside, an array of battery-operated flood-lights and two high-resolution digital cameras were placed on tripods. The team began by vacuuming sand and grit away from the blackened feet. They proceeded with pointed little trowels, toothbrushes, and dental picks. It would take virtu-ally all night for the dedicated, hardworking specialists to expose the remains.

About an hour before sunrise, the inverted corpse of a middle-aged male was removed from the burial site. Prelimi-nary imprints and photographs of incisors, cuspids, and bi-cuspids were uplinked to a communications satellite and forwarded to D.C., where specialists were waiting to compare the corpse's teeth to prison dental records of Loyola Mon-toya's grandson.

The remains were positively ID'd as one Wallace M. Montoya.

Score one for the tribal elder.

There was more.

Though not yet ready to sign her name on the dotted line, the FBI forensics-team leader (who had earned her MD and PhD at Johns Hopkins) stated her professional opinion that Mr. Montoya had expired after suffering numerous superfi-cial bruises and lacerations. All this, in addition to the item placed so cruelly around his neck.

The barbed wire.

Score two for the tribal elder. Which is somewhat gener-ous, because, as it happened, strangulation was *not* the cause of death. While still alive and wearing the barbed-wire necklace, Mr. Montoya had been, in technical parlance,

". . . exposed to excessive temperatures." The unfortunate fellow had been—slowly and with considerable skill— *roasted*.

Score three for Miss Daisy.

Charlie Moon shook his head and wondered, *How could Aunt Daisy have known so much about this nasty business?* Not that he would ask her. *She might tell me.*

Oh. One more thing.

After being cooked, Wallace's corpse had been expertly butchered. An estimated thirty pounds of flesh had been deftly sliced from his buttocks and limbs. Moreover—and this would be Daisy's score number four—the body had been slathered with sauce.

Very tasty, homemade stuff, the Bureau forensics-team leader opined.

And though a detailed analysis would have to wait until the remains arrived at the FBI Forensics Laboratory, the enthusiastic young scientist was willing to stick her neck out and assert that the recipe called for plenty of corn syrup, a smallish proportion of sorghum molasses, white vinegar, tomato sauce, and—just a pinch of paprika.

CHAPTER THIRTY-THREE

HARRIET'S RARE BOOKS

Topping out at four feet eight inches, weighing in at maybe eighty-five pounds when she was wearing her knee-high gum boots and heavy wool overcoat, the bookseller was not an imposing figure. Except when Harriet had her .38 caliber, double-action Colt pistol in her hand, which she was likely to in short order if a customer offended her.

Harriet's minor eccentricities, along with the lack of demand for musty, yellowed old volumes that cost an arm and a leg, were the reasons why her business was not exactly booming. Though there was no shortage of tough customers hereabouts, the townsfolk tend to steer clear of those entrepreneurs whom they deemed to be certifiably insane. Thankfully for Harriet, there were a few locals who were pleased to frequent her bookstore, and "Little Butch" Cassidy topped this short list. The proprietor had taken quite a liking to this customer, who was barely a head taller than herself and absolutely filled to the brim with book learning. Butch was also a cash customer who never departed without four or five books tucked under his arm.

Which was why, when the bell above the door announced his entrance with a tinny "ding-a-ling," the wild-eyed little woman grinned and shouted, "Hey, Shorty—long time no see!"

The Columbine cowboy tipped his wide-brimmed hat and began to poke around in a box of books the proprietor had recently purchased from an estate sale, and was about to inquire whether she had acquired any G. K. Chesterton or George McDonald first editions, when the magic of the moment was interrupted by a second person entering the premises.

From the newcomer's unkempt appearance and wily-coyote expression, the proprietor rightly deduced that this was not a potential customer. On the contrary . . . *That shifty-eyed jackass is a shoplifter if I ever laid eyes on one.* Instant assessment was her specialty, meting out just punishment her bounden duty. Harriet's eyes hardened, and her hand vanished into the deep pocket on her denim apron, where her grubby little fingers were pleased to feel the comforting chill of blued steel.

The suspect patron was *this close* to having a bad shopping experience.

Fortunately for all concerned, the object of Harriet's suspicions broke the spell by introducing himself.

MR. SMITH

The broad-shouldered six-footer removed his sweat-stained straw hat, sidled up to Butch, and said, "You're one of them cowboys that works for that big-shot Indian, ain't you?"

Butch thought he knew where this was going. *Poor fella's looking for a handout. Well, I guess I can spare a dollar or two.* The easy mark allowed as how he was a Columbine employee.

"I figured you was." The stranger pointed at the street. "I saw you get out of that old F-150 that has COLUMBINE RANCH painted on the door. I'm Smith. *Bill* Smith." He delivered this introduction in the manner of that distinguished actor whom he considered to be the best James Bond of them all.

"Pleased to meet you." The shorter man pumped Smith's hairy paw. "I'm Cassidy. *Butch* Cassidy." Suffice it to say that Cassidy outdid Smith with the most wonderfully precise intonation, and an ear-pleasing British accent.

Caught off guard by this snappy comeback, the stranger cast a doubtful glance at Harriet, whose face suggested a shriveled crab apple with oily ball bearings for eyes. He also took note of the fact that the woman's hand was in her apron pocket. Along with another bulge, which looked suspiciously like a pistol. Nothing is so scary as a tetchy old woman with a deadly weapon. Smith whispered to Butch, "I got something to tell you. Maybe we oughta go outside."

Which they did.

Butch Cassidy had the guy figured for just another derelict with a sad tale to tell about how he'd once had a fine job in a Fortune 500 company corner office, a ten-room house in Aspen, and an eight-figure bank account. His luck had gone sour with the stock-market crash, and all he needed now was a modest loan so he could purchase a bus ticket back to his daddy's little turnip farm near Stumptown, West Virginia.

After he heard what Bill Smith actually had to say, the Columbine cowboy was more than a little surprised. Charlie Moon's employee wondered how much of the glib-tongued drifter's account was on the up-and-up. *Maybe the whole wagonload?* Butch's sunburned brow furrowed. *More likely, not a solitary word.*

Either way . . . *The boss will have to hear about this.*

CHAPTER THIRTY-FOUR

THE CALL

Charlie Moon was standing by the river, helping himself to a stiff dose of crisp, high-country air. Hour by hour, day by day, the tribal investigator was increasingly enjoying the peace that filled this wide valley between the smoky-blue granite mountain ranges. It was a pleasure to be home again, where no ill wind carried the scent of roasted man-flesh to a man's nostrils, and criminally insane misfits did not rush around helter-skelter, wreaking havoc among elderly widows and their errant nephews, not to mention the infirm and those selfless souls who do their utmost to nurse them back to health. In this little corner of paradise, a discouraging word could not be heard over the breeze rattling cottonwood leaves, the river roaring happily as you please and from time to time rolling a small boulder along on the submerged pathway.

When the telephone in Moon's jacket pocket vibrated, he strode a couple of steps from the riverbank before taking the call from Mr. Cassidy. After hearing about every third word of what Butch had to say, he withdrew five long strides farther from the noisy river. "Sorry, all I got was that you're in Harriet's shop, checking out some books—could you start from page one?"

"It's probably this old cell phone, boss—ever since I dropped it in the horse trough the danged battery won't hold a charge."

"Bring it by the headquarters and I'll issue you a brand-new one." Moon grabbed on to his black hat to prevent a gust of dusty wind from taking it to Kansas and yelled at his miles-away employee, "So what's up?"

Butch Cassidy gave his employer the executive summary: "I run into this fella who's a buddy of that poor guy the FBI found buried upside down. I think you might want to talk to him."

Moon still got two or three calls a day from someone who wanted an interview with the Indian who'd shot those mad-dog killers at ABC Hardware. The Ute, who preferred to remain out of the public eye, had never forgotten his third-grade teacher's favorite proverb.

FOOLS' NAMES AND FOOLS' FACES
ARE OFTEN SEEN IN PUBLIC PLACES

"This fella who claims to be a pal of Loyola Montoya's grandson—any chance he's sniffing around for a story about the recent crime spree?"

"This guy a journalist?" Butch brayed a donkey laugh in the boss's ear. "No way."

"So what do you take him for? Butcher, baker—Indian chief?"

"He's nothing special—just another dime-a-dozen drifter who looks for work when he can't find any loose change in his pocket for booze." Recalling the fact that his boss was a recovering alcoholic, Cassidy blushed. "What I mean is, he smells like a beer keg and looks like . . . well . . . let's put it like this, boss—this guy would have to dress up some to pass for a bum."

Moon grinned. "That bad, huh?"

"I'd guess he found his wardrobe in a Dumpster." A pause while Cassidy cast a wary glance at the subject of discussion. "But just in case he's on the level, I think you ought to talk to him."

"Okay. Put him on."

"Yes sir."

Moon heard snatches of a muffled conversation between Cassidy and the stranger, then an unfamiliar voice in his ear. "Uh, hi."

"Hello, Mr. Smith."

"Look, I don't want to waste a minute of your time—all I wanted to do was say *good for you*. I mean for shooting two of those rotten bastards that killed poor ol' Wally—and his grandma. I learned all about it on the TV. Too bad the two you banged up was busted outta the hospital and got away. But if there's any justice left in this sorry old world, they'll be picked up, tried, and fried in the hot seat. Well, that's about all I gotta say." A raspy cough. "Sorry, I smoke way too many coffin nails. But I can quit anytime I want to. Stopped three times already, just this week. Ha-ha!"

Moon smiled at the archaic joke. "Sounds like you and Wallace Montoya were pretty close."

"Well, I'll say this much—we shared what we had. Beans, tortillas, beer—and enough hard time for a dozen lifetimes. Ever since I heard that that bunch of crazy hoot owls had murdered Wally, I've been just aching to get even. But I don't suppose I'll ever see any of 'em again."

"You've actually *seen* these bad guys?"

"Oh, sure—just like I told Mr. Cassidy." Smith cleared his throat. "Well, not every single one of 'em, I don't suppose. But that afternoon when I dropped by Wally's granny's house . . . when was it? I guess about a week or so before the old woman was murdered. Anyway, Wally was down by that little stream, shootin' the breeze with these four guys—or maybe it was five." A sigh. "My memory ain't what it used to be. Anyway, there was these guys—oh, and a couple of women who I guess was traveling with 'em. One was a sure-enough looker. Anyhow, when I showed up, the guys sort of drifted off into the underbrush. Not one of 'em said a word to me—but that good-looking girl, she did take a long, hard look at me. After they was gone, Wally and me headed into town to toss back a few brews and jaw some about old times, but he wouldn't say all that much about the people that was camped out by his granny's property—except that they was serious bad actors. Oh, there was some other big talk that I didn't pay much attention to at the time—like how Wally was going to join up with their gang and get rich quick. Me, I figured that bunch for a scummy gang of dope pushers."

Moon had been holding his breath. "The chief of police in Granite Creek is a friend of mine. I'm sure he'd like to hear what you've got to say about—"

"Not a chance!" Three heartbeats. "Uh, sorry. Didn't mean to yell in your ear like that, Mr. Moon." Deep intake of breath. "Here's the thing—Smith's not my real name. I've done some hard time and when I finally got paroled down in Texas, I got a job in a pecan orchard, but that didn't last a week. Hell, I don't even remember exactly what happened except that I got into a case of beer with some thirsty wetbacks and before you know it I'd broke into somebody's house trailer and stole an old TV set that wasn't worth twenty bucks—can you beat that?"

Moon could, but he had no desire to remember all the follies and misadventures he'd suffered while under the influence. "So John Law's looking for you?"

Smith chuckled. "Well, not like I was Jesse James, but they're lookin' all right. And once those badge toters in the Lone Star State get on your trail, they don't ever let up." Another cough. "Look, I know you're a busy man, what with all them cattle and whatnot to look after, so why don't I just give the phone back to Mr. Cassidy and—"

"Where did you do time in Texas?"

A hesitation. "Rolling Plains. That's where I met Wally."

"I know the place."

"Don't tell me you did time there too."

"No, but a few fellas I ran into have." *Including a pair of car thieves I arrested that got extradited back to Texas on manslaughter charges.* "Mr. Smith—or whatever your name is—you might as well know right up front that I used to work for the Southern Ute Police Department as a uniformed cop. Right now I'm a tribal investigator. And on top of that, I'm a part-time deputy to the Granite Creek chief of police."

The felon muttered a colorful curse the Ute had never heard before. "If your cowboy had told me that, I'd never of said a single word to you."

Moon watched cottonwood and willow branches bending in the wind. "If all the Texas authorities want you for is stealing an old TV set, you'll have no problem from me." Sometime in their lives at least half of the Columbine cowboys had been in trouble with the law. "Are you looking for work?"

"To tell you the honest truth, I'd rather go lookin' for trouble. But I'm flat broke and could use a job until I make enough doe-ray-me to buy me a bus ticket back home to Tennessee."

"If you'd like to apply for a job, tell Butch and he'll bring you to the ranch."

"As easy as that?"

"There's nothing easy about working on the Columbine. You put in an honest day's work for a day's pay. And you have to stay sober while you're on the job."

"Oh, I guess I could do that. For maybe a week or two." Dead silence. "D'you expect me to tell you everything I know about those outlaws that murdered Wally?"

"That's not a condition of employment." Moon closed his eyes as the wind tossed dust and grit in his face. "Put Mr. Cassidy back on the line."

After moving out of Smith's hearing, Butch asked the pertinent question: "So what do you think?"

"Chances are, Smith never heard of Wallace Montoya before he saw the news on TV—my guess is he's conning us for a job. But just on the off chance he's legit, we won't lean on him. If Smith decides to stay in town, that's fine—but see if you can find out where he's hanging his hat."

"Okay, boss."

"But if he's interested in a job at the Columbine, bring him along and introduce him to Mr. Bushman. I'll keep clear of Smith till he's ready to talk to me." Moon had an afterthought: "Soon as you get back to the ranch, bring me your sick cell phone."

"Right."

After breaking the connection with Butch Cassidy, the Ute Catholic's lips moved in a silent, urgent supplication. *Please, God—we need this witness.*

Having spoken to the deity, the rancher checked in with his foreman. Charlie Moon told Pete Bushman what to do if Butch brought a Mr. Smith to see him.

Two hours later, the self-proclaimed ex-con alcoholic was hired on at the Columbine.

CHAPTER THIRTY-FIVE

BAD NEWS FOR BREAKFAST

Which tends to spoil even the keenest manly appetite, which was why when Charlie Moon was informed by Foreman Pete Bushman that another steer had been killed by a predator—this one over yonder where Dry Creek meets up with Sunrise Arroyo—the owner of the outfit left half his morning meal on the platter, gulped down a half cup of honeyed coffee, and marched out of the dining room and into the parlor, where he opened the gun cabinet and selected a suitable rifle.

As a grim-faced Moon exited the headquarters, Bushman had to sprint to stay at the tall man's heels. "The cowboy that found the carcass figgers it was a bear that done it. Probably a big black, maybe even a griz." Perversely enjoying this opportunity to ruin the boss's day, Bushman was determined to have his say. "If you'd a listened to me four or five years ago, and started killin' off all these beef-eatin' bears and cougars, we wouldn't still be losing two or three prime beeves every month."

Following a good night's sleep, Daisy Perika was enjoying one of those rare mornings when she fairly bubbled with excess energy. She displayed this happy state by cleaning off the dining-room table, all the while singing in a crackly voice, "You're not behind the plow, Joe—you're in the Navy now, Joe." Though there were no fixed rules about such matters, the table-cleaning chore was normally attended to by Sarah Frank, who was absent from the dining room. Where was the Ute-Papago teenager?

She was positioned at a parlor window, watching Charlie Moon's back as the object of her passionate affections (rifle in hand) made yard-long strides toward the seventy-year-old horse barn, which would soon be replaced with a new one. *I wish Charlie would ask me to go with him sometimes.* From her narrow perspective, which was focused on a single objective, this was an eminently reasonable aspiration. *When we're married, I'll need to know everything I can about running a big cattle ranch.* She punctuated this wishful thinking with a wistful sigh, and continued to reason her way toward becoming Mrs. Moon. *I can already ride a horse as good as most of these cowboys.* And not only that . . . *I can shoot a rifle and hit a soup can at fifty yards.* A worried frown squenched her coal-black eyebrows. *I hope the bear or mountain lion or whatever's out there don't hurt him.* Sarah closed her eyes and prayed for her future husband's protection.

Bless her sweet, innocent heart.

CHARLIE MOON RIDES

And at a brisk, frisky trot. But not on his favorite mount.

Trusty old Paducah was in his stall—lame and awaiting a visit from the veterinarian. What was so special about this particular member of the equine clan? For one thing, Paducah did not shy at rattlesnakes coiled in his path or bolt at thunderous bolts of lightning, and Moon could fire a .50 caliber rifle from the saddle without the stolid animal as much as *flicking an ear.* Which behavior some folks might say (and some cowboys did) was clear evidence that the animal was "deef as a stone" and lacking the least measure of common horse sense. Didn't matter.

On that subject, Charlie Moon had the only opinion that counted, and he appreciated having an even-tempered, unflappable horse tucked between his knees. Whatever his al-

leged shortcomings, Paducah was a steady-as-you-go sort of
mount who would always bring a rider home again, dead or
alive. That said, the rancher was satisfied to be astraddle Midnight, a spirited, shiny black gelding whose muscles rippled
in the slant of the morning sun. It took a tight rein to prevent
the energetic animal from breaking into a headlong run toward the junction of Dry Creek and Sunrise Arroyo, which
was where the forested lower slopes of the Buckhorns
blended into the boulder-dotted glacial plain known on the
Columbine as the East Range. The rider was in no hurry.
Moon had much to think about, and he figured that being in
the saddle for a while would help him sort a few things out.

Such as:

*College is awfully expensive. I hope Sarah'll be satisfied
with an in-state school.* Fort Lewis College in Durango was
tuition-free for Indians. *That'd be a good place for the girl
to find herself a fine young man. One with good prospects.*
Moon thought maybe he would take Sarah on a tour of the
campus, which happened to be his alma mater.

And:

*Pete Bushman is getting too old for running a place the
size of the Columbine. I need a younger man who knows
about stuff like modern ranch-management techniques and
computers and whatnot.* The Wyoming Kyd was the obvious candidate. But Bushman was one of those stubborn,
old-fashioned stockmen who would work until Death laid a
cold hand on his shoulder. *Maybe I can ease him into some
easier job.* A possible solution came to mind: *I could move
Pete and Dolly into the headquarters on the Big Hat spread,
and move a few head of cattle over there for him to look
after.* Congratulating himself for coming up with this dev-
ilishly clever notion, Moon resolved to speak to the foreman's
sensible wife about a move to the Big Hat.

And most of all:

I need me a wife. The lonely bachelor considered a few
possibilities and was startled to find the singing librarian
right there at the top of his short list. *Patsy is about as pretty
as a woman can get without making a man's eyes pop right*

out of their sockets. And she's sweet as honey in the comb. He could imagine the delight of spending all his days with this outstanding lady as his wife. He tried hard to think of a negative. Came up with nothing worth mentioning. Tried harder. There was this one thing—Patsy was a town girl. *I wonder if she'd take to ranch life?*

Which brought him down a notch to consider Possibility Number Two.

Beatrice Spencer is plenty smart, and good-looking. And she owns the Yellow Pines Ranch. Which was not a working spread, but nine sections of Yellow Pines joined the Big Hat, which bordered the Columbine, and wouldn't that make a world-class operation. Bea, of course, was a headstrong woman who was likely to be bossy, and would be more like a general partner than a loving wife. He tried to find a bright side and did: The cleverest of the three Spencer sisters was capable of running a big ranch all by herself. *That would come in real handy if I broke a leg. Or got stomped to death by a crazed horse or shot between the eyes by a drunken cowboy or chewed up by a—*Whoa!

As Midnight topped a low, rocky ridge, Moon reined the horse to an abrupt halt.

He had spotted the carcass.

CHAPTER THIRTY-SIX

TROUBLE

When someone tapped lightly on the headquarters west-porch door, Sarah Frank was sitting by the parlor fireplace, watching the flames and mooning over you-know-who. When she opened the door, Annie Rose's pretty face smiled at her.

"Good morning." The slender woman who had been hired to act as Dolly Bushman's companion looked hopefully over Sarah's left shoulder. "May I speak to Mr. Moon?"

Though Sarah tried ever so hard to smile back, her thin little lips would not cooperate. "He's not here."

As if she doubted this report, Annie cocked her head to glance over the girl's *right* shoulder. "Oh—he's gone so early in the morning?"

Sarah's head bobbed in a nod. "He went to look at a dead cow." She appended an explanation for the presumably city-bred woman: "Ranch work starts really early."

Annie's smile morphed from *friendly* to *amused. So does competition for desirable men.* "When do you expect his return?"

"Hard to say." The seventeen-year-old shrugged. "Charlie could be gone all day." She made an effort to be polite: "I could give him a message when he gets back."

"That's very kind of you." The mature young woman cocked her head. "You may tell Mr. Moon that I called."

"Uh . . . what for?"

The poor little thing is so charming. And so deeply in

love. Annie responded to a wicked impulse. "Tell him that he can take me to dinner tomorrow evening."

Both of Sarah's eyebrows arched—like drawn bows. "Dinner?"

Annie's dark eyes sparkled. "At the Silver Mountain Hotel." With this parting shot, she turned and crossed the thick-planked porch.

Sarah's mouth gaped guppy-fashion. *Tell him yourself, you sneaky man-hunter—I won't set up your dates for you!*

Down the steps Annie Rose went, and across the yard. Her mischievous suggestion had been one of those spur-of-the-moment inspirations that—in hindsight—might look more like a stroke of genius. *I wonder if he might take me up on it?* As she considered the advantages that might be gained from an evening out with Mr. Moon, the clever lady felt rather proud of her impromptu performance. Sufficiently so that she was inspired to begin whistling "Oh, What a Beautiful Mornin'."

Sarah fumed. *Oh—just look at how she walks, all twisty-twisty like her hips are out of joint.* Some of these older women were without a trace of shame. A thoughtful expression furrowed the girl's smooth forehead. *If I wanted to, I bet I could learn to walk like that.*

Not that she ever would.

MORE TROUBLE

Annie was barely out of sight and Sarah was about to close the west-porch door when a white Toyota pickup rattled across the Too Late Creek bridge. Down the graveled lane it came, tugging a small cloud of brownish yellow dust. The familiar motor vehicle belonged to the Columbine Grass's pretty girl singer, who was also a librarian. An unmarried librarian. An astonishingly pretty unmarried librarian.

The pickup charged into the headquarters yard and parked with a lurching jerk under a tall cottonwood.

Right *between* Charlie Moon's Expedition and Sarah's red F-150 pickup.

Well.

Patsy Poynter, who was about nine times better-looking than Annie Rose, got out with all the pent-up energy of an excited teenager, which Sarah thought inappropriate in a woman who must be pushing thirty.

The blue-eyed blonde was carrying a canvas grocery bag. As she hurried across the yard, Patsy used her free hand to wave at the shy Indian girl. "Hey, sweetie!"

This enthusiasm, at the same time infectious and magnetic, pulled Sarah through the door and onto the west porch. Waving back, she murmured a tepid "Hi."

The bluegrass band's girl singer looked this way and that. "Where's Charlie?"

First that kissy-kissy FBI lady, then twisty Annie Rose, now pretty-face Patsy—why don't they just move in with him? Sarah resisted the temptation to roll her eyes and heave a heavy sigh. "He's not here."

Because this information did not precisely respond to her question, Patsy rephrased and repeated it: "Well where *is* he?"

Sarah jutted her chin to indicate an easterly direction. "Over at Sunrise Arroyo." *She won't know where that is.*

The innocent librarian stared toward the Buckhorns. "Where's that at?"

"Near the foot of the mountains."

"Well what's he doing over there?"

"Looking at a dead cow."

Patsy P. cringed. "Ick."

Sarah could not help smiling. Anticipating the lady's next question, she provided the answer: "Charlie probably won't be back for hours and hours. Maybe not till after dark."

"Oh." Disappointment fairly dripped from Patsy's doll-like face.

Which pleased Sarah immensely. "Would you like to come inside and wait?"

"That's not an option, honey. I've got to get back to town." She frowned. "But I'd like to get together with Charlie sometime soon, so we can practice some songs."

Now the seventeen-year-old rolled her eyes and sighed. But it was a slight roll and a light sigh—not so much that Patsy would notice. "I'll tell Charlie when he gets back." She inquired whether Miss Poynter had a particular day and time in mind.

"I'm not working tomorrow evening, so if he's available—"

"I don't think he can make it then."

Patsy's wide eyes said: *Oh? And why not?*

This highly expressive query called for a response.

"I think," Sarah said, "that he may have a date."

A date? The pretty face drooped. "Well then . . . Oh, I almost forgot what I came for." She offered the canvas bag to Sarah. "I brought him this."

As the girl accepted the offering, a delicious aroma wafted up to her nostrils. "What is it—cookies?"

Patsy Poynter shook her head and the Goldilocks mop. "Brownies. I made 'em myself, and they're almost still warm."

"They smell really good."

"Help yourself to some, sweetie."

"Well, thank you. I'll tell Charlie—"

This exchange was interrupted by another arrival. A big, brown, boxy UPS truck. The driver parked in the yard and hopped out with two armloads of parcels, which she—

Yes, still another she. But not another cover girl.

The hardworking UPS employee unloaded her burden on the Columbine headquarters porch, pointed at a long, slender parcel. "That one's for Charlie Moon."

"Oh," Patsy shrieked, "he'll be so happy!"

The strictly business driver was already headed back to her van.

Sarah squinted suspiciously at the package. "What is it?"

"A banjo Charlie ordered two or three weeks ago."

"Charlie bought himself a new banjo?"

"It's not exactly what you'd call *new*, honey. That five-stringer is a real old-timer, and very expensive—probably cost Charlie two arms and a leg." She clapped her hands. "Hey—why don't we saddle up a couple of horses and take the banjo to Charlie and surprise him?" Patsy's big, sky-blue eyes glowed and seemed to grow even larger as she expanded upon the plan. "We could take the brownies and some coffee—and have a nice little picnic."

"Charlie's miles away and we might not be able to find him." Sarah picked up the parcel in both arms, cradled it close to her chest like a precious baby. "But soon as he gets back, I'll tell him about the banjo. And the nice brownies you brought."

And that was precisely what she intended to do.

But the dust behind Patsy Poynter's departing Toyota pickup had barely settled when Sarah decided that the stunning blonde's notion was worth considering. Why wait until Charlie returned to present him with the treasured musical instrument? With every beat of her youthful heart, the plan (no doubt enhanced by the conspicuous absence of its pretty author) became increasingly appealing.

Off to the stables Sarah went with Patsy's brownies and the mail-order banjo. In less time than it takes to eat a tasty chocolate pastry and pick a few licks of "Muleskinner Blues," the seventeen-year-old had saddled up her pinto pony and was off *like the wind*.

CHAPTER THIRTY-SEVEN

CHARLIE MOON'S ERROR

Correction—make that plural.

And not merely two errors. What the rancher's folly added up to was a trio of mistakes—those sorts of blunders that even an experienced stockman makes when his blood runs hot about slaughtered purebred stock and he's in too big a hurry to stop and think about the hungry creature he's dealing with, and how those bloody teeth and slashing claws are liable to end up ripping *his* flesh.

It was not as if the fellow had galloped off half-cocked, without a sensible thought in his head. Before mounting up, Moon had checked his Winchester rifle and made sure a round was in the cylinder. Now, as horse and rider approached the mangled steer, both the human and the equine eyes scanned the sparse, boulder-strewn forest for any sign of a predator.

The keen-eyed man saw nothing.

Neither did the horse, but the mount's muscles were as tense as twisted coils of tempered steel, his nostrils flared for a danger scent, and his ears flicked this way and that. The animal might have bolted at the sudden jump of a grasshopper.

Within a few yards of the kill, Moon dismounted and looped the reins loosely around a spindly little aspen.

Error Number One: *Loosely*.

Number Two was leaving his rifle in the fringed leather scabbard on his mount.

Blunder Number Three? Not strapping on his .357 Magnum sidearm before leaving the Columbine headquarters.

Though a warning simmered somewhere in the depths of his mind, and there was a cold tingling rippling up (and down) his spine, 99 percent of the rancher's attention was focused on the dead animal. The Hereford had been pulled down at the edge of the East Range pasture, on the fringes of a forest of white-trunk aspens and blackish-blue spruce.

From time to time, a sizable black bear would attack a young or sickly animal that had wandered away from the herd, and a griz would kill anything on four legs—or two, for that matter. This looked more like a mountain lion's work. But before giving the crack shots among his cowboys permission to hunt down the likely suspect, the rancher had to be certain. Moon circled the carcass. There were several deep bite marks on the unfortunate bovine's neck. Its belly had been ripped open and one of the hindquarters shredded. He paused to take a long look at two barely discernible pad prints. *This wasn't done by a bear. Sure as I'm standing here, this was—*

Moon's nervous horse bolted and hit the breeze like a pack of red-eyed timber wolves were nipping at his knees. No, a grasshopper was not to blame. Put it down to that bloodcurdling sound from the aspens—the female feline's throaty growl.

The stranded man had no option but to stand his ground.

How dangerous was this predator? Of all the large cats, the cougar is the only one that purrs like the kitty nestled in your lap. Yes, *purrs*. Isn't that sweet? Not when you're about to become dead meat.

To go along with her purr, m'lady also had big, sharp teeth, and an array of pointy vesicles on her tongue. So does your ordinary tabby cat, which is what makes her delicate little tongue feel like sandpaper when she licks your hand. Why mention this detail? Because the equivalent apparatus on the larger relative's tongue enables the mountain lion to *lick the flesh off your bones.*

Or, in the case at hand, off Charlie Moon's bones.
The situation was serious.

CLIPPITY-CLOP, CLIPPITY-CLOP

This is not a radio-studio sound effect—rather the audible result produced by an actual pinto pony's hooves saying "Goodbye, dirt!" to those meters, rods, and furlongs slipping rapidly behind. Sarah Frank is mounted on the spotted equine; mount and rider are headed toward that location where Mr. Moon hopes to face down a fearfully dangerous predator. The girl could not have imagined the drama that she and her pony were clippity-clopping into, which is not to suggest that Sarah had been shortchanged when imagination was being doled out. The teenager had her fair share, and more. Which was a good thing. Most of the time. An unbridled ability to imagine fantasy into reality can prove to be hazardous, especially to a seventeen-year-old girl who is passionately in love with a Brown-Eyed-Handsome-Man. Particularly when said BEHM, for whatever reason, does not respond in like manner. Even more so when he seems to be an irresistible magnet for the seventeen-year-old's competition. It does not help that these mature women are endowed with superficial good looks and know how to walk in such a way as to make men lust after them. Which more or less sums up what was nagging at Sarah as her pinto galloped its merry way across the high plains.

But, by and by, it occurred to her that not *all* her heartburn could be charged to the likes of Lila Mae McTeague, Annie Rose, and Patsy Poynter. Charlie Moon was partly to blame. After a few dozen more clippity-clops of bouncing along in the saddle (which may have been affecting her brain), make that *largely* to blame. *Why can't Charlie be smart enough to see what's going on?*

Why, indeed. But this is one of those ageless and imponderable questions that is quite beyond the cognitive powers of us common folk. Such matters shall be left to the domain of brainy philosophers, eminent psychologists, talk-show hosts, and other erudite scholars.

But Sarah had the bit in her mouth and would not let go.

The farther she rode toward Sunrise Arroyo, the madder she got. Urging her pony into a faster trot, the girl ground her teeth. *Charlie treats all those hussies like they were something special. And he treats me like a kid!* She hated that three-letter word. Loathed and detested it. *If he ever calls me kid again, I'll . . . I'll . . .*

The passionate young lady did not complete the thought, but the fact that she was about to fantasize some unspeakable mayhem is relevant to what happened when she came over the same ridge Charlie Moon had topped, and spotted him standing by a steer's carcass, staring into the trees. *Oh, he makes me so mad!* She dug her heels into her mount's flanks. The pinto broke into a full gallop.

Like Charlie Moon and his recently departed mount, neither Sarah nor her pony spotted the cougar that was partially concealed in a thickish cluster of youthful aspen shoots. Neither did the fact register in her overheated brain that Moon's black horse was not among those present and accounted for.

The full-grown mountain lion did see the angry girl (longish parcel clutched tightly under her left arm) charging like a Mongol warrior on a crazed pony. The sizable cat was moderately unnerved by this novel sight, and, being of a prudent disposition, Ms. Cougar turned tail and melted silently into the shadowy forest.

The cavalry, it seemed, had arrived in the nick of time.

Charlie Moon turned to determine who his rescuer might be. He would not have been surprised to see Butch Cassidy, the Wyoming Kyd, his crusty old foreman, or even one of the new hires. When he saw Sarah coming on like John Wayne in *True Grit*, he imagined her with the reins clenched between her teeth, and laughed out loud. What a girl!

Sarah might have gotten past the laugh, which she interpreted as follows: *So. He thinks I look comical.*

Moon waved a big hello and shouted, "Hi, kid!"

Oh! Sarah's eyes narrowed. Her scowl turned into a hateful frown.

When it looked like the spotted pony was out of control and might run him down, Moon sidestepped, with the intent of grabbing the wild-eyed animal by whatever he could get hold of, or yanking the girl out of the saddle. Whatever opportunity presented itself.

At the instant before a collision, Sarah reined her pony in. The pinto made a wide circle around the steer carcass before coming to a dead stop.

She sure seems excited. Moon assumed his characteristic grin, and repeated the unforgivable sin: "Well, kid—I'm sure glad to see you."

"Oh you are, are you?" Out of breath, she took time to inhale a helping. "I guess you should be—I brought something for you."

Moon eyed the UPS box. "What's that?"

"Your damned old *banjo*, that's what!"

The man who had never heard so much as a *darn* or *dang* pass between the prim little girl's lips could hardly believe what he'd heard. "What?"

She repeated it. Verbatim. And louder this time.

Well. "I appreciate you bringing it." He pointed his chin at the parcel. "But that's a genuine Stelling's Golden Cross that cost me about three head of prime beef, so please be careful and don't drop it."

Sarah had no intention of dropping anything. She raised the parcel over her head, flung it in his general direction. Yes, *flung* it. Hard as she could.

More by luck than skill, Moon made a catch that any receiver in the history of the National Football League would have admired.

Being busy removing something from a saddlebag, the young lady did not fully appreciate this manly display of athletic prowess. "And here's your stupid brownies!" She tossed the canvas bag at Moon's head. The missile went well over its intended target, but the alert receiver managed to snatch her wild pass—without dropping the boxed banjo.

Sarah whirled her mount and was gone in a cloud of dust.

Not so very far away, she raised a defiant chin. *I guess I showed him!* From somewhere in that small fraction of her mind that retained a degree of rationality, a pertinent question was posed: *Showed him what?* Well, that was a no-brainer. *I showed Charlie that I'm not some dumb kid.*

After a few bumpity clippity-clops, her throbbing heart had settled down to about ninety thuds per minute. The rider eased off some on her hard-pressed pony, which settled down to a leisurely trot. Ever so gradually, a measure of sanity returned. As it did, the girl's face contorted into a painful grimace. *I showed him that I'm an idiot.*

Presumably to emphasize his agreement, her mount snorted.

Sarah Frank's eyes overflowed with tears.

Bemused and bewildered, Charlie Moon watched the enigmatic creature ride away. *Poor kid. Something must be bothering her.* But even if he'd had a knack for understanding what motivated this particular member of the tender gender, there was not a lot he could do about it at the moment. So the full-time rancher, part-time tribal investigator, sometimes banjo picker did what any man who hadn't finished his breakfast would do.

He seated himself on a black basalt boulder and helped himself to a chewy brownie. *That sure does hit the spot.* After enjoying a half dozen more of Patsy Poynter's delicious pastries, Moon opened the long, narrow box. What he found inside pleased him very much indeed.

In practically no time at all, the bluegrass musician had tuned the dandy instrument and within a heartbeat or two after that he was picking "Turkey in the Straw," which sounded worlds better than it ever had on his fair-to-middling banjo. Despite the fact that he was stranded in this remote place with neither horse, rifle, nor sidearm, Moon seemed blissfully unaware of the mortal danger that still lurked in the fringes of the mountain forest.

Not so.

Despite his ignorance of that sex that remains mysterious to 97 percent of men (the other 3 percent are engaged in self-deception), Moon knew his cougars.

Little by little, and ever so cautiously, the mountain lion crept closer. She cupped her ears to a sound that had been never heard in this neck of the woods.

Charlie Moon cocked his head to glance at the glowing feline eyes. "See how you like this." He served up a lively rendition of "Old Joe Clark" that might indeed have the power to soothe the savage beast.

Or not.

The jury was still out.

Though the outcome remained uncertain, the cougar reclined on a grassy mat under the aspens and listened with a terrible intensity.

By and by, after drifting into a selection of old standards made famous by such luminaries as Bill Monroe and the Bluegrass Boys, Flat and Scruggs, and the like (for this was evidently what Moon's singular audience preferred), the musician terminated the impromptu gig and got up from the boulder. As he placed the venerable banjo back into the box, the performer addressed the predator in this manner: "Much as I would like to stay and pick a few more tunes for you, it's time for me to get on down the road toward home."

Apparently dissatisfied with this announcement, the big cat growled.

The rancher eyed the hungry creature who shared his liking for beef, though Moon preferred his steaks on a plate and not so rare. "Now here's the deal. I'm going to leave, but I don't intend to take my eye off you till I'm over the ridge." He tucked the banjo box under his arm. "I expect you'll come and help yourself to a supper of prime Hereford, and I won't begrudge you that. But hear this, big cat—if and when you and me meet again, I'll have something with me besides a five-string banjo." (Think .44 caliber Winchester.) "So from now on, you'd better feed yourself on elk or deer. You kill another purebred steer, I'll send a half-dozen crack shots with rifles out here to track you down and send you straight to the Happy Hunting Ground."

Was he serious? You can bet your boots and saddle.

Did Moon really believe the mountain lion understood English? Not for a second. But the Ute was convinced that animals have a facility for picking up the gist of a threat.

Having finished his speech, Moon made his retreat.

As he had expected, the cougar matched him step for step.

But this predator who could lick the flesh from his bones stopped at the steer's carcass, where the sweet scent of raw flesh was fragrant to her nostrils.

True to his word, Charlie Moon didn't mind the famished animal enjoying this particular meal. In the cattle rancher's hardscrabble occupation, an occasional cougar kill was part of the cost of doing business. The key word here is *occasional*.

CHAPTER THIRTY-EIGHT

THE LONG WALK

The distance from the junction of dry creek and sunset Arroyo to the ranch headquarters was only nine miles and change, but that's a serious hike for a man shod in cowboy boots, especially when he's been humiliated by losing both his horse and rifle, and come face-to-face with a couple of angry female creatures who gave every indication of wanting to bite his head off (actually in one instance, metaphorically in the other). On top of all that, Charlie Moon was obliged to tote his classic banjo, which managed to get heavier with every step.

But the walk wasn't all bad. There were pluses.

Like the last of the brownies, which tasted just as good as the first one.

Also, since he'd signed his name on the dotted line and taken title to the Columbine, this was one of the few times Charlie Moon had ample time to admire the east-pasture landscape, and he liked what he saw very much and then some. The land's fine attributes included the reddish tint of the soil, knee-high buffalo grass that carpeted the prairie between boulders of basalt and granite that ranged from the size of basketballs to pickup trucks. Most of these lumpy specimens were streaked with veins of white, yellow, or pink quartz—a few with all three.

And there was much more to admire.

Here and there a pink-barked ponderosa or a lonely, cone-shaped spruce provided a perch for a gawking crow that croaked at the rancher, or an irate pygmy owl that scowled down her hooked beak at this impertinent human biped who was trespassing into the exclusive domain of wild things.

In this delightful environment, Moon also had plenty of time to think. And to wonder about various and sundry issues. He indulged himself in both activities.

I wonder what Lila Mae's up to right about now. He smiled as a jackrabbit sprang from behind a boulder to go racing across the prairie, big ears flopping in comical fashion. *I bet she's in the Hoover Building, meeting with a dozen other uptight feds that're all duded up in suits and vests and shiny shoes.* His smile broadened. *Special Agent L. M. McTeague will be letting 'em know who's the boss and telling 'em what's what.*

Some twenty miles to the west, just over the bluish gray Misery peaks, a storm cloud's mottled belly growled and grumbled.

Sarah Frank heard the thunder shortly before Moon's eardrums were vibrated by the low rumbling. She was in her bedroom at the headquarters, stuffing a scruffy gray dress into a scuffed suitcase. The seventeen-year-old's eyes were dry now, her course firmly set in her mind. *I'll leave a note for Aunt Daisy, telling her that I've left in my pickup.* . . . The pickup Charlie had given her on her sixteenth birthday. A lump materialized in her throat. *He's been so good to me.* Truer words were never spoken. *And I've treated him like dirt!* She fought back a fresh deluge of tears. But, after making such a fool of herself, there could be no turning back. *I'll tell Aunt Daisy that I'm going to Tonopah Flats in Utah.* Sarah's plan was to stay with Marilee Attatochee (her *real* aunt) until she could earn enough money to rent her own room. *Maybe I can get a job as a waitress at the Cowboy Restaurant.* She sighed. *I'd rather work at that nice little newsstand next door, but they probably don't need anybody, and besides, nobody tips girls who sell newspapers and magazines and paperback books.* The prospective waitperson began the hopeful process of estimating how much she'd make working seven days a week, ten or twelve hours a day. *In three or four months I'll be able to afford a nice little apartment.* As Sarah finished her packing, the hopeful girl-woman furnished all three of the imaginary rooms with inexpensive but tasteful furnishings from the Tonopah Flats Goodwill store.

Finally, Sarah snapped the sad little suitcase shut and frowned at the shabby piece of luggage. She considered writing a note to the man she had wronged. *No.* That would be the easy way out. Also the coward's solution. *I can't leave before I apologize face-to-face to Charlie Moon.*

Another, seemingly irrelevant thought percolated to the surface: *I wonder where Charlie's horse was when I threw the banjo and brownies at him?* Her brow furrowed. *Probably tied up in the aspens, where I couldn't see it.*

The Footsore object of Sarah's thoughts was about halfway home when he saw a distant puff of dust. *That's a horse and rider.* Moon squinted. No, make that two horses. Only one rider. *Well thank you, God. Midnight had enough horse sense to head back to the barn, and some cowboy with more than an ounce of brains between his ears is bringing my mount back to me.* He smiled when a variation on this theme occurred to him: *It might be Sarah, bringing a pair of horses to run me down with.*

As Moon's rescuer came closer, he could clearly hear the sound of eight hooves pounding the ground, and he got a better look at the rider—who was definitely not a she. This was a big, broad-shouldered fellow. Could be any one of a dozen hands.

It was the alcoholic ex-con who called himself Bill Smith.

Moon was pleased to see that Bushman had provided the new hire with decent clothes, all the way from a weather-beaten but serviceable wide-brimmed hat down to footwear that looked familiar. *Those boots belonged to Texas Joe, who got knifed last year at that bar fight over in Pueblo.*

The Columbine's superstitious cowboys would go barefoot before they'd wear a dead man's boots, and Moon figured Smith would probably shed them once he found out.

The man who claimed to be Wallace Montoya's buddy reined his mount in and eyed the Ute with a wide grin. "We ain't actually met face-to-face, Mr. Moon—I'm Bill Smith."

"I know who you are."

"Yes, I s'pose you do." Smith's eyes twinkled. "I've seen you a couple of times too."

"I'm sure glad to see you right now." Moon took hold of his mount's reins.

Smith laughed. "Didn't know if I'd find you dead from a broke neck or maybe with nothin' more than a busted leg and some cracked ribs. But here you are, forked-end down just like you never got throwed."

"I didn't get throwed," Moon grumped. "But thanks for bringing me my mount." He aimed an accusing stare at the big black.

As if aware of having committed a serious infraction, the animal looked away.

Moon mounted the still-skittish horse. "How'd you know where to come looking for me?"

"That fuzzy-faced old foreman came down to the bunkhouse right after you rode out and said you'd gone to check on the dead steer, and he told us where it'd got killed." Bill Smith used his sleeve to wipe sweat from his forehead. "And Mr. Bushman said, 'When that Indian says he's goin' to take care of somethin' by hisself, it's best to leave him be till he gets the job done. So all a you boys just keep your distance." He gazed at the UPS parcel with more than casual interest. "I hope you don't mind me asking—whatcha got in that box?"

"A five-string banjo."

"Well, that's nice." Smith seemed bemused. "You always tote a banjo when you check out dead livestock?"

Moon nodded. "A serious musician is never without his instrument."

"Well I guess it's a lucky thing you didn't take up the piano."

The banjo picker grinned. "So tell me how you're getting along on the Columbine."

"Oh, all right I guess." Smith shrugged. "I never did work so hard, though." His eyes sparkled with merriment. "And the pay ain't exactly something to brag about."

"You do a good job, and maybe in a year or two I'll see that you get a raise. Say two percent."

"That's mighty generous of you, Mr. Moon."

"It's mighty kind of you to say so. How're the other new hires doing?"

"*Other* new hires?"

"Sorry. I guess being the last cowboy taken on this month, you wouldn't know who the others were."

"I would if you told me."

Moon frowned. "To tell you the truth, I don't even know their names yet." With a notable exception. "Well, except for Miss Annie Rose—the young lady who's been tending to Dolly Bushman."

"Oh, I've heard about *her*. Never managed to get a close-up look." Smith turned his head to grin at the boss. "But the boys who've got a gander at that gal say she's a dandy piece of eye candy."

There were two good reasons that Charlie Moon did not respond to this remark. First and foremost, the owner of the outfit was burdened with the duty of setting a good example for his uncouth cowhands; even a nod or smile might encourage a coarse fellow like Smith to make an unseemly observation about the lady. Second, the Ute had not yet met the *dandy piece of eye candy* so referred to, which omission raised a relevant issue. Any boss worth his salt made it his business to know everything worth knowing about his employees. Mr. Moon was not one to shirk his obligations. *First thing tomorrow morning, I'll drop by the foreman's residence to see how Dolly's getting along. And if I don't forget, I'll ask Dolly to introduce me to her nurse.*

All the way back to the ranch headquarters, Moon and Smith gabbed about this and that, but not once did the subject of Wallace Montoya come up.

The tribal investigator was the very soul of patience. *When Smith's ready to talk to me, he will.*

CHAPTER THIRTY-NINE

MOON'S AFTERNOON

Following his lively morning, Charlie Moon had every right to expect the P.M. hours to be relatively quiet. Even peaceful. To ensure this happy outcome, the footsore man treated himself to a hot shower. This blessing was enhanced by a long soak in a tub of even hotter water, which he enjoyed while pondering a particular Greek who had spent a lot of his time pondering one thing and another. Archimedes, so the story went, had experienced a significant eureka! moment while submerged in his bath. Something to do with how the displacement of a liquid by any object that a student of natural philosophy cared to immerse in it (no matter how complex the shape) would instantly reveal said object's volume.

Mr. Moon had no such epiphany, or for that matter any thought worth reporting. His muscles and mind were completely relaxed as the sensible man napped in his bath.

And after he had awakened, scrubbed himself briskly with a coarse towel, put on clean everything, and gone outside to sit on the porch—the rancher was convinced that on his best day, any big-brained Greek fellow you could name had never felt any better than he did right this minute.

After easing himself into the light embrace of a cushioned redwood chair, he closed his eyes and sighed. *Now, if everybody will just let me be . . .*

His ears picked up the patter of petite feminine slippers inside the parlor.

The creak of the screen-door hinges.

Those same slippers pat-pattering across the porch floor.

I'll make like I'm asleep. He let his chin fall closer to his chest, allowed his lips to part just enough for a phony snore to pass between them.

Good try, Charlie.

A throat cleared. A voice whispered, "Charlie—are you asleep?"

Despite his best efforts, Moon's lips grinned. *Dang!* He opened one eye. "Yes I am."

Sarah Frank, who had put on her prettiest blue dress for this difficult occasion, could not meet his gaze. She looked down at the redwood planks, also at her shiny black slippers. "I just wanted to say that . . . I mean . . ." Her voice cracked. "I'm so *awfully* sorry—"

Moon's long arm reached out to pat the repentant girl on the back. "I don't know of anything you've got to be sorry for."

Oh, he's so sweet! This undeserved kindness caused tears to flow down her burning cheeks.

His grin widened to expose some of the finest teeth Sarah had ever seen in a man's mouth. "Except that you came all the way out here and didn't bring me a cup of coffee."

"Oh, I'll go make a fresh pot right now. And soon as it's done, I'll bring you a big mug." She added (sweetly), "With honey, just the way you like it."

"That's mighty nice of you, but there's no hurry." Moon took a closer look at the girl's face, which looked much older than her seventeen years. *Poor kid—she seems awfully tense and worried.* "Before you run off to perk a pot of coffee, set yourself down and relax for a while." Moon shook his head. "No, not way over there on the swing." He pointed his chin at a nearby chair and watched her slip into it. *What she needs is a few hours away from here.* "Tell you what. How about we take a drive into town."

Her mouth gaped. *Just us two?* "You mean . . . me and you?"

"That's what I had in mind." He assumed a deadly serious expression. "Unless you'd like to invite Aunt Daisy along."

The poor girl's face sagged. "Well . . . I guess I could ask her."

"I hope you won't." Moon laughed. "Now do you want to go to town or not?"

"Well, yes." She primly smoothed her skirt "That would be very nice." This response was more ladylike than whooping out big wa-hoos! whilst doing cartwheels from one end of the porch to the other. Realizing that her tearstained face could use a touch-up, Sarah jumped up from the chair. "I'll go in and get ready."

"Take your time."

"Oh, I'll be done in a minute or two."

He smiled at the young lady's rash promise. *That'll be the day.*

After the screen door closed behind her, Moon closed his eyes again. *Well, there goes my restful afternoon.* But it would be good to spend a few hours with the girl. *I'll take her to that old-fashioned drugstore on Copper Street and buy us a couple of ice cream sundaes. After that, maybe there's a G-rated Disney movie we could see at that new seven-screen picture show.* He figured that while she was getting ready, he would have time for a genuine nap. Within a minute, or perhaps it was two—the fellow was just beginning to drift off to dreamland—the screen door slammed and a seventeen-year-old girl's voice said, "Okay, let's go!"

And so they did. And had a fine afternoon and evening, which was spiced with ice cream, interesting conversation, happy laughter, a so-so movie, and a slow, pleasant drive back to the Columbine.

The girl went to bed happier than she had been in years. Wait. We have a correction directly from the source: *Oh— I'm happier than I've ever been in my whole life!*

Charlie Moon's long day was not over.

At around about that time of night when the hours drop from the dozen mark to zero and get started all over again, the rancher (who had been sitting in his upstairs bedroom rereading his favorite Will James novel) decided to go outside and enjoy another spell of sitting on the porch. But not to nap. Mr. Moon was wide awake, and hankering for an hour or so in the swing.

Setting his sixty-eight-year-old copy of *My Life as a Cowboy* aside, he switched off the lamp, stepped softly along the hallway, down the stairway, across the parlor, and onto the west porch, where the swing waited in the moonlight.

But, as so often happens, there was an obstacle between the man and his destination.

He murmured to the animal, "What're you doin' up so late?"

The hound did not respond.

Zigging right, Moon made a move to pass the dog.

Sidewinder zigged left to block his path.

What's wrong with him? He attempted to get around the hound's left side.

Sidewinder sidestepped right.

This was just the sort of nonsense that takes all the fun out of a man's plan to enjoy some downtime on his porch swing. Moon aimed his pointing finger at the dog's head. "I'm not in the mood for playing games. You get outta my way or I'll—"

Sidewinder bared an impressive set of pointy teeth. Muttered a low growl.

Sensing something elemental in this display, the Ute froze. *What the hell has got into this peculiar animal?* He spoke softly. "What's wrong, ol' fella?"

The descendant of wolves turned his head to stare at the comfortable seat that was suspended from the porch roof by a pair of rusty iron chains.

He's telling me to stay away from the swing. That could signify almost anything, including an old dog that was mentally unbalanced, but the descendant of a tribe who had survived by paying attention to intuitions, omens, and other anomalies considered the implications of the situation.

There could be a rattlesnake underneath it, coiled and ready to fang my ankle. He squatted and had a look under the swing. All clear. No snake there.

Possibility Number Two: *Maybe the chain is ready to break.* Moon didn't strain his brain trying to figure out how a dog could possibly know a thing like that. *Sometimes they just do.*

Then, there was Possibility Number Three. There might be something under the folded blanket that Aunt Daisy had draped over the wooden swing to protect herself and Sarah from splinters. These two ladies in his life liked to sit there together and chat about this and that. *This* was Charlie Moon; so was *that.*

He patted the old dog's head. "Thanks, fella. I understand there's some reason you don't want me to sit on the swing, so I won't."

Sidewinder relaxed.

"But I need to find out what it is. So instead of blocking my path, why don't you help me."

The eccentric dog sidled up to the porch swing, pushed his nose against the blanket, then turned to gaze at the human being.

"Okay, pardner—I get the message loud and clear. Let's have a look." Moon picked up a broom that Daisy used to sweep the porch. He pushed the broom handle under the blanket, lifted it—gawked at what he saw.

Well what the hell is that?

Almost as soon as the question had formed in his mind, Moon knew the answer. He also recalled how, just a few hours ago, Sarah had come *this close* to sitting on the swing.

The lean Indian stood as still as the long-dead ponderosa on top of Pine Knob. He remained immobile while the satellite that shared his name moved three diameters across a silky-black sky. It took that long for him to consider the implications of his discovery. And decide what to do about it.

And once he did, his mind was made up. Now, anyone who knows him will tell you that the owner of the Columbine is not a mean-spirited man, and he has never been one to hold a grudge. But the Ute was determined that somebody was going to be sorry for this.

Damned sorry.

While Charlie Moon was making his unsettling discovery on the Columbine headquarters west porch, Scott Parris was in his king-size bed, enjoying the benefits of a deep, restful sleep. Until the GCPD chief of police began to slip backward in imaginary time . . .

EPISODE FIVE

Pine Knob—Six Feet Under

The thick quilt of a cloud that covered the silver moon sliver had grown even darker, and U.S. Marshal Scott Parris was still unable to read the epitaph that Charlie Moon had burned on his wooden grave marker. This did not dampen the freed spirit of the recently deceased lawman; the wraith watched with satisfaction as the Ute Indian wrapped and tied a heavy cotton cord around the blanket that covered his corpse. That's the way, Charlie—make it good and snug so I won't get overly chilled when winter comes.

His parcel ready for depositing in the earthy vault, Moon straddled the narrow pit and lowered the white man's body into its final resting place.

Parris leaned over the grave to observe these solemn proceedings with a critical eye. Easy does it, now. Don't drop me. I wouldn't want to get any bones broken—

Zzzsssst!

That was the sound the spirit heard as it was pulled into the corpse.

Aaaghhh!

*This was Parris's muffled scream as he found himself
inside the blanket.*

*Trussed up like a mummy. Unable to move. Facedown.
Suffocating!*

The dreamer awakened, flailing his arms, gasping for
breath—to find his face buried in a fluffy pillow. Parris
rolled over, tossed the offending pillow across his bedroom,
where it knocked a framed photograph of his mother off the
wall. He lay flat on this back, stared at the ceiling, and inhaled several lungfuls of fresh air. *Wow. That was a bum-
mer of a nightmare.*

There was this consolation: *When you're dead and buried, that's The End.* This nightmare was the final installment of the episodic dreams. Or so he thought.

IN THE COLUMBINE ATTIC

At about the time Scott Parris was awakening from his horrific dream, Charlie Moon was wide awake and entirely focused on the task of placing two extremely dangerous items
into his massive attic safe. When the job was done, he closed
the door and twirled the dial.

There. That'll do for now. This was not a perfect storage
place, but he couldn't think of a better one for the short run.
*I'm the only one who knows the combination. In a few hours
I'll have Daisy and Sarah out of the house, and I'll make
sure these things are disposed of before they get back.* He
frowned. *But if something goes sour and I'm not around
day after tomorrow, somebody could eventually get hurt.*
How might such a calamity come to pass? A half-dozen
hair-raising scenarios occurred to him. The most likely of
these: *A locksmith with a court order might open the safe
door so lawyers could go through my personal effects.*

A man's responsibilities do not end with his death.

Charlie Moon searched several cardboard storage boxes
until he found a yellow pad and a roll of masking tape. He

printed instructions on a sheet of paper and taped it onto the safe door.

DANGER!
DON'T OPEN THIS SAFE
Call Special Agent McTeague
She'll know what to do
C Moon

CHAPTER FORTY

START WITHOUT ME

During a long night of sitting on the shadowy front porch with a heavy pistol strapped to his hip and a Winchester carbine in his lap, Charlie Moon mulled over his problem. Ignoring the perfect illusion that planets and stars were passing ever so slowly overhead, he considered a number of potential solutions, each with flaws that could prove disastrous. Moon was acutely aware that he wasn't holding any face cards or aces, but life was a chancy game at best, and any course of action was better than waiting for the black-hearted villain across the table to make his play and ruin your day.

The tribal investigator's sole advantage was that he knew he was in deep trouble, and—*they don't know I know.* The issue was how best to use that edge. Moon was leaning toward a strategy that would force the other player to show his hand before he'd intended to. Which called for a tactic that would unnerve the enemy; do something that he could not possibly anticipate. But whatever the plan, it was essential to protect Daisy, Sarah, and all those hardworking folks on the Columbine who depended on the boss to make the right decisions. *One way or another, I'll have to isolate the bad guys. Separate the goats from the sheep.*

A cold white glow of first light just was beginning to show over the Buckhorns when the man finally settled on a plan. The first step was to have a little powwow with Jerome

Kydmann. *I can always depend on the Kyd to do what needs doing. And he never asks a lot of questions—just gets the job done.*

His decision made, Charlie Moon began to feel tolerably better. Not all that short of optimistic. Perhaps having *something to do* was just the medicine he needed.

The morning had dawned bright and cloudless, but with a lingering redness in the west and also in Moon's eyes, when (at breakfast) he announced his intention to Daisy and Sarah. The elder and the younger lady were equally surprised, but did not question his instructions. Daisy had noticed that no-nonsense glint in her nephew's eyes that made it clear that neither queries nor complaints would be tolerated. Sarah did not sense that anything was amiss.

Immediately after the morning meal, Daisy and Sarah, accompanied by Mr. Zig-Zag and the official Columbine hound, departed in the girl's pickup. Sarah's Ford truck was followed by the Wyoming Kyd and a pair of cowhands in another, less spiffy-looking F-150. All three of these sharp-eyed Columbine employees were armed and—presumably in light of the recent crime wave—advised to keep a close eye on the womenfolk.

The Kyd and his companions figured something more was up than Moon had let on, but, aside from the foreman, nobody on the Columbine was in the habit of questioning the boss. When Mr. Moon had that grim, flinty look, you just tipped your hat, said, "Yes, sir," and did what the man said.

When foreman Pete Bushman heard the small caravan rumbling over the Too Late Creek bridge, he hurried over to a living-room window and watched as they passed by his residence. *Now what is this all about?* Preferring face-to-face exchanges to telephone conversations, he headed to the headquarters to find out.

Charlie Moon informed his crusty straw boss that Mr. Kydmann and the assigned cowboys were accompanying

Daisy and Sarah over to the Big Hat. And that all labor on the Columbine would cease by noon.

Stunned by this unanticipated news, Bushman barely got the "Why?" past his lips and through his unkempt beard.

"Because an hour after noon is one o'clock," Moon explained. "Which is when the big shebang at the Big Hat begins to commence."

Pete Bushman stared blankly at the inscrutable Ute. "What'n hell big shebang are you talking about?"

Moon managed to look surprised at this shameless display of ignorance. "You haven't heard?"

Bushman allowed as how he had not heard a single, solitary word.

"Then you're probably the only soul on the Columbine that doesn't know about the big Breaking in the New Banjo celebration." Moon picked up his Stelling's Golden Cross and expertly claw-hammered a sprightly little introduction to "Soldier's Joy" before continuing his narrative: "At one o'clock there'll be a light lunch of beef burgers, home-fried potatoes, and baked beans. The horseshoe pitch is scheduled for two o'clock, an old-fashioned square dance at three—at which you'll be doing the calling and fiddling—and at four o'clock there'll be a quarter-mile horse race where wagering with cash money will not be discouraged. From five o'clock sharp to sundown is suppertime, and soon as folks have had their fill—why, that's when the big hoedown kicks in."

Bushman eyed the Columbine Grass's lead musician. *That sounds just dumb enough to be true.* "And like always, your foreman is the last person you bother to tell what's going on."

Moon assured his highest-ranking employee that the omission was a mere oversight. "Now you and Dolly better head for the Big Hat." He added, with a twang from the highest-pitched string, "And don't forget to take your granddaddy's fine old Bavarian fiddle."

The grizzled old white man—who might have been crouched under a covered wagon, aiming his .50 caliber buffalo rifle at a war-painted redskin astride an unshod pony—eyed the sly Indian through slitted lids. "Charlie, I ain't got no time for foolishness. Is this another one a your jokes?"

The Ute assured him that he was as serious as *a plague of giant range worms come to dine on prime Columbine pasture.* Having had his say, Moon picked up again on "Soldier's Joy."

This time, he's got the brain fever for sure. Not that it mattered. Once the boss had made up his mind, there was nothing for a long-suffering foreman to do but go along—no matter that he had forgotten more about running a cattle operation than this upstart Indian would ever learn if he lived for a thousand years, which wasn't likely. But that didn't mean a fellow had to give in without a fight. Over the merry banjo picking, Pete Bushman (who's arthritic right knee was aching) gloomily predicted that there would be a rip-roaring storm not long after sundown. The self-appointed forecaster advised Moon to plan for two or three inches of rain on any outdoor picnic he had in mind and to make sure the Big Hat headquarters was rigged to handle not only the eats—but the music and dancing too.

The boss stilled his fingers long enough to direct his hairy-faced subordinate to *make it so.* Almost as an afterthought, the owner of the outfit mentioned that he would be running a little late on account of ". . . some last-minute business that can't wait till tomorrow. But don't wait for me. I want everybody to have a grand old time, and I'll get there soon as I can."

Bushman, who knew his men pretty well, thought the boss's smile looked a little strained.

By the time he got back to the foreman's residence, Dolly was busy filling a bushel basket with three loaves of baked-last-week sourdough bread, two sugar-cured hams, and the pies and cobblers she always kept on hand for such emergencies. The foreman's wife, who was feeling better than she had in a month, didn't look up from her therapeutic work. "Don't forget to bring along all four of the hand-crank ice cream freezers, Pete. And plenty of ice and rock salt."

"Okay." Hoping to recruit some help, Pete looked around. "Where's what's-her-name?"

"Annie's in her bedroom—getting ready for the party, I expect." Eyeing the pantry, Dolly decided she would take along an extra pound of coffee beans.

As was so often the case, Pete Bushman's weather forecast would prove to be right on the mark. Shortly after sundown, there would be a gully-washing rain the likes of which had not been seen in these parts for a coon's age, nor would be for some years to come.

Accompanying the deluge, lusty gusts of wind would lay tall pines on the ground and earthshaking thunder would play rhythm for long, spindly legs of lightning that danced insanely across the granite peaks.

A splendid display, for so few human observers to appreciate.

Not that the Columbine would be entirely lacking in human souls.

Charlie Moon would be present.

A few others would also remain behind. Why?

Each had his (or her) reason.

A case in point—

DOLLY BUSHMAN'S NURSE

As it happened, Charlie Moon was not the only workaholic on the ranch.

Whether by coincidence or deliberate plan, it turned out that Annie Rose also had "some last-minute business" that could not be put off. She convinced Pete and Dolly Bushman to leave for the Big Hat party without her. Dolly's nurse-companion promised to show up after her work was done.

The Bushmans were barely out of sight when Ms. Rose legged it from the foreman's residence to the ranch head-quarters, practically danced up the porch steps, and banged her delicate fist on the west-facing door until Charlie Moon opened it to get an eyeful of this new hire for the first time.

Well. *She is good-looking.* Making no secret of the fact that he was not pleased to see her attractive face at this particular time and place, the boss responded to Miss Rose's cheerful "Hello" with: "You ought to be headed for the Big Hat, with Dolly."

Now, pretty women know they're pretty, and this was not exactly the reception that Annie Rose had hoped for. Talking faster than was her habit and all in one breath, the lady explained that Dolly was doing just fine now and didn't need much looking-after and she had some urgent things to get done that would take at least all afternoon and probably into the evening and it had occurred to her that she'd never been to the Big Hat before and she simply *hated* to drive after dark in unfamiliar places almost as much as she *detested* the thought of wasting expensive gasoline. "So can I ride with you to the party?"

The Ute admired a woman who spoke her mind, even when it took so many words to get the job done. "I'll be running late. And you can't miss the turnoff to the Big Hat." As if it would help, he pointed east. "Take the first left after you leave the Columbine gate, which is only about fifteen miles down the highway. You can't miss it—there's a big sign shaped like a cowboy hat." Sensing that he was not convincing the attractive lady, Moon managed a genial smile. "Why don't you let your work wait till tomorrow, and head on over there with the others and have a good time."

She cocked her head. "Why don't you?"

It was one thing to admire a woman who spoke her mind, but Moon figured he wouldn't care to spend overly much time with one. "Tell you what—if you're on the foreman's front porch when I pass by, I'll slow down enough so you can open the door and jump in."

"Such a charming offer—I am absolutely bowled over." With this, Annie Rose turned on her heel and departed.

Moon watched her cross the headquarters yard, then the

Too Late bridge. He didn't stop watching until the shapely little lady had turned into the Bushmans' front yard. *Now that's a remarkable woman.*

And she was.

TWILIGHT

For perhaps the hundredth time since she had returned to the foreman's residence, Annie Rose began with Step One of the Procedure. Watching the sixty-watt bulbs in the copper chandelier, she flicked the light switch up. Then down. As on the previous occasions, they winked on, then off.

Following this electrifying response, she proceeded to Step Two, which involved picking up the Bushmans' telephone as if to make a call. Annie didn't dial. All she did was listen, expecting to hear the usual drone—

But this time—*no dial tone.*

Aha! The game was afoot.

THE SIGNAL

Annie Rose walked through the Bushmans' kitchen and stepped onto the back porch, where she placed a satellite-telephone call that would be relayed to several colleagues. Her message was brief, and cryptic.

"This is Orphan with confirmation. It is Showtime. I say again—Showtime."

CHAPTER FORTY-ONE

TIDYING UP

As Charlie Moon seated himself behind his desk and switched on the gooseneck lamp, he remembered how his attorney had been nagging him for years to get this unpleasant task behind him. The rancher could almost hear the lawyer's stern voice—"If you keep putting this off, some fine day you'll wake up and find out it's too late." A bitter smile creased the tribal investigator's face. *Some fine day* had come, and he might not see the sun rise on another one.

He took a single sheet of white paper from a drawer, selected an old-fashioned fountain pen from an assortment of writing instruments in a black-on-white Chaco cup, and got to work. When he was finished, he read the document carefully to make sure he had not omitted anything of importance.

CHARLES MOON LAST WILL AND TESTAMENT

I wish I had time to do this right, but things seem to be coming to a head. If anything happens to me, like I end up dead, this is what I want done with what money is in the Columbine account and whatever can be raised by selling off stock and equipment—

> *1. All my debts should be paid off, with my employ-*
> *ees getting their pay first. After that's done, who-*
> *ever else I owe can fight over what's left.*

2. *Any income from the round house I own down by Ignacio, which is leased to the schoolteacher—I can't remember her name right now—all of that should go to my aunt Daisy Perika, and after she dies it should go to my best friend, Scott Parris. Scott also gets all of my guns and fishing gear. And my Expedition if he wants it.*

3. *All of my so-called real property, including the Columbine and the Big Hat spreads, is for Sarah Frank, who's the daughter of my other best friend, the late Provo Frank. Provo and his wife died years ago. That's all I can think of, but if I've forgotten anything important, I expect my attorney Mr. Wilbur Price will take care of it. Sorry, Wilber—I should've done this a long time ago, like you said.*

4. *Almost slipped my mind. Scott Parris gets the four sections that include Lake Jesse and the priest's log cabin. Sarah inherits that property when Scott dies.*

The author shook his head. *That walks like a three-legged dog, but it's the best I can do right now.* After signing and dating the document, he slipped it into an envelope, upon which he printed this instruction:

TO BE OPENED IN THE EVENT OF MY DEATH
C MOON

C Moon put his will into a desk drawer.

CHAPTER FORTY-TWO

DAISY STEPS INTO DARKNESS

What with heart-stopping, neck-and-neck horse races where weeks of hard-earned wages changed hands, not to mention lively bluegrass music that had set maybe sixty pairs of cowboy boots a-stomping, and enough tasty food to feed the entire population of Fishtail, Montana, for a month, everybody at the Big Hat Breaking in the New Banjo party was having a fine and dandy time. With one notable exception. It was not that the Ute elder didn't enjoy the occasional festive gathering. Daisy Perika had been known (as recently as the previous year) to kick up her heels at a dance and let out a lusty whoop or two.

Not tonight. Daisy felt distinctly uneasy. Something she could not quite put a name to was *pulling on her.*

When the Ute woman slipped outside, her stealthy departure onto the back porch went unnoticed except by the Columbine hound, who had settled down into a comfortable spot he'd found between a rusty old hand pump and a leaky horse trough. Unaware of the canine spy, Daisy leaned on her walking stick for quite some time. She entertained herself by watching a motley collection of puffed-up clouds gather over the craggy mountain range that served as a formidable boundary between the Big Hat and the Columbine. She also listened to a few faraway rumbles of thunder, and sniffed a faint hint of rain in the air. Her senses thus fortified, she decided to remove herself farther from the boisterous crowd.

Being unfamiliar with her nephew's smaller ranch, Daisy had no particular destination in mind. Fine adventures and deplorable follies often begin in just such circumstances.

Whether to protect the Ute woman or because he also hankered for a dose of solitude, Sidewinder tagged along behind. As Daisy plodded ever so slowly, her four-legged companion zigzagged this way and that in doggish fashion, sniffing at such fascinating items as sprigs of dry buffalo grass, wickedly armored prickly-pear cactus, and, best of all—prairie-dog holes where prudent sentries darted into subterranean chambers to warn their rodent relatives of impudent trespassers passing by overhead.

After some more or less aimless meandering, the odd couple found themselves in a lonely spot where the heavy silence created a convincing illusion that the barely audible, almost dreamlike sounds from the cowboy festivities were unreal—an ethereal echo from some long-ago hoedown where no one could have dreamed of such marvels as automobiles, electric lights, and telephones. This solitary spot, barely a half mile from the Big Hat headquarters, was situated on the twisted spine of a long, rocky ridge.

Here, Daisy and Sidewinder were dwarfed by earth and sky, and everything worth singing or dreaming about—pale moon and dark mountains, sparkling stars and streams—had been named by dozens of wanderers from centuries past, whose ghostly presences the shaman sensed gathering about her. It was as if these lonely souls had risen from their graves for the privilege of witnessing some dramatic event.

The spell of Place can be immensely powerful.

Whether it was the soul-stirring isolation, the unexpected pressure of the hound suddenly leaning against her leg like a frightened puppy, or the lady's fertile imagination—Daisy Perika experienced a dreadful premonition that her world was about to be shaken. She turned her wrinkled face toward the east, where night was rolling in like a vast, relentless tide. Not a problem. That happened every evening about this time. What prickled the skin on her neck was the certainty that—*something is coming.*

Something was.

Far away down the ridge, the old woman caught a glimpse of it. Something small, and bright—a tiny point of light? She squinted. No. *Three* tiny points of light, which were getting bigger, brighter with each of her thumping heartbeats. Daisy believed she knew what was coming. She had expected this encounter for almost twenty years.

The weary old soul was more than ready.

She was eager.

As the apparition got close enough to identify, she raised her staff in welcome salute to the three ponies that ran shoulder-to-shoulder. Though the muscular animals were running about waist-high on an invisible path *above* the ridge, the shaman could hear their unshod hooves striking flinty stones, kicking red-hot sparks into empty space. Flanked by two pintos, the snow-white horse in the center had no rider. *That'll be for me.* A pair of handsome, bronzed figures rode the spotted ponies. Their dark locks whipped in the wind. *Those must be my angels.*

"Here I am," Daisy whispered. She raised her oak staff higher and shouted in a voice that cracked with age, "Swing low, sweet chariot!" *And slow down—so I can get on and ride all the way home.* She couldn't wait to go.

Alas, there was to be no Swinging Low.

No slowing.

No going home.

Seeing the joyful wildness in the horses' eyes and smelling their sour sweat, Daisy realized her error. Plumed and painted for war, these mounts and riders had not come for her. Moreover, the phantom animals seemed to be bent on running the Ute elder down.

Daisy stood her ground.

Clippity-clop.

Nostrils flared, teeth bared—eyes afire!

Clippity-clop.

The tribal elder closed her eyes. *God help me!*

The apparition passed directly *through* the terrified woman, chilling her to the very marrow.

Daisy did not bother to turn her face to the west, where the departing horses and riders had been swallowed up by night. It was as if they had never been; the vision had ended.

Seemingly paralyzed by this unparalleled experience, the hound regained his mobility—and his voice. Sidewinder's bony old frame rattled in a sudden, uncontrollable shudder; the traumatized creature began to whimper and whine.

Daisy patted the dog's head and offered a few consoling words. "Shut up, you old bucket of [expletive deleted], or I'll yank your tongue out by the roots." Following this act of charity, the kindly old soul commenced to consider the ghastly sight that had visited her on this night. Not many heartbeats thumpity-thumped before she reached a few preliminary conclusions.

This business didn't have nothing to do with my *death.*

On the contrary, the omen pointed to some *other* person who was destined to make that final ride. The visionary knew from long experience that such dramatic premonitions were rarely about distant relatives or casual acquaintances. *It'll be somebody close to me.*

But who?

Charlie Moon's aunt thought she knew.

If the war pony's *missing rider* was not already dead, his spirit would certainly be cleaved from flesh before the sun came up again. Daisy Perika hoped (and prayed) that it wasn't already too late to prevent a dreadful calamity. Barely aware of the nervous dog who was staying so close by her side, the worried woman set her face toward the bright lights and lively music.

CHAPTER FORTY-THREE

COMMUNICATIONS DIFFICULTIES

Jabbing her walking stick at the hard earth like a mad-woman bent on slaying invisible fire ants and imaginary scorpions, Daisy Perika returned to the Big Hat headquarters in half the time it had taken her to make the journey to the lonely ridge above Piddlin' Creek. Bypassing the partying on the front porch and in the parlor, the agitated woman entered the kitchen by the back door, where she found a battered old telephone mounted on the knotty-pine wall.

Daisy's hands shook as she punched in the number for the Columbine landline. After trying three times to connect and suffering through the same computer-voice response ("We are sorry, but the number you are calling is either disconnected or temporarily out of service . . ."), she dialed 911. The instant she heard the Granite Creek Police Department dispatcher's familiar voice, Daisy demanded to speak to Scott Parris. Being acquainted with Charlie Moon's irritable relative, Clara Tavishuts knew better than to ask, "What about?" She promptly patched the call through to the chief of police's black-and-white.

Forewarned that Charlie Moon's irascible old auntie was on the line and apparently angry about something or other, GCPD's top cop steeled himself and grinned. "What's up, Daisy?"

"My temper, that's what—and I ain't got no time for any stupid small talk. The Columbine phone ain't working."

Parris blinked at the dark ribbon of road that was slipping under his automobile at a mile a minute. *So who am I, the telephone company?*

Daisy might have read his mind. "Something's wrong with Charlie and you're the police, so don't even think about passing the buck—do something about it!"

"I'm on the way to the ranch now." Parris rolled his eyes at the night sky. "I'll check things out and call you when I know something worth telling. Are you back at your home on the res?"

"No I'm not. Me and Sarah are at the Big Hat."

Scott Parris frowned. "The Big Hat?"

"What am I talking to—a cop or an echo chamber?"

"Well, it just surprised me that you two would be all the way over there—"

"That's where we are, all right—and we've got plenty of company. The Bushmans are here and the Wyoming Kyd and the one they call Butch, and Six-Toes, and the big blacksmith whose name I can't remember—and all the rest of those half-wit ranch cowboys—the whole kit and caboodle." A pause while she sucked in a breath. "Everybody's here but Charlie."

That doesn't make any sense. "Everybody?"

"Well, except that sweet little nurse who's been taking care of Dolly. And maybe a few more. I don't know every last soul that works for my nephew and I don't reckon I'd want to."

"What're so many of the Columbine crew doing over at the Big Hat?"

"Having a big party, that's what." She barked in his ear, "And after this bunch of cow-pie kickers fills their bellies with food, they'll get back to playing more of that silly hillbilly music and kicking up their heels way into the night— just like everything was all right."

My buddy's having a party and he didn't invite me? "Why isn't Charlie there with you?"

"Well if I knew *that*, I'd know what's going on— wouldn't I?"

She gets more peculiar by the year. And meaner. "I expect Charlie's probably got the Columbine phone disconnected because of all those annoying calls he's been getting from TV and newspaper people. Have you tried his cell phone?"

"No. I've got the number on a little piece of paper, but I can't find it in my purse."

"Tell you what, Daisy—you relax and have a good time at the party. I'll get in touch with Charlie and make sure everything's okeydokey."

"You promise?"

"Cross my heart and hope to . . ." A sharp pain twisted like a corkscrew in his chest.

"Hey—did you cut me off?"

"Uh—no, Daisy. But I've got another call coming in on my radio. Talk to you later." *If I'm not dead.* Parris folded and pocketed his miniature telephone and picked up the microphone. "What is it, Clara?"

"I've got a call for you, sir—FBI."

"Patch 'em through."

"Just a sec."

Parris listened to his dispatcher's side of the conversation, which consisted mainly of a string of *yes sir*s and *I understand*s.

Clara Tavishuts's voice rattled in the dashboard speaker. "The special agent would rather not conduct a conversation on our radio system. He'll place a call on your mobile phone. I gave him your number."

"Right." He was hanging the microphone on the hook when his cell phone buzzed. "Hello. Chief of Police Parris here." He listened to the news. "Is that a fact?" Listened again. "You have, huh?" Frowned. "Got it." Nodded. "Sure. I'll let Charlie Moon know." *But not this instant.* The tribal investigator would have to wait for a couple of minutes.

Immediately after disconnecting from the fed, Parris called his dispatcher. Without explaining why, he directed Clara to call in every GCPD officer—no excuses would be accepted. She was also instructed to request assistance from the state police. Every cop available within fifty miles was to converge on the Columbine.

Clara reminded the boss that three officers were on vacation, two more were sick, and the state police were already spread thin. "I'll do what I can, but don't hold your breath."

Parris broke the connection, mumbled an appropriate expletive, which was instantly followed by a second chest pain. *Must be indigestion.* The frustrated cop fumbled around in several pockets until he found a package of Tums. He popped a pair of antacid tablets into his mouth and crunched them like chalky candy while he dialed the programmed number for Moon's cell phone.

The Ute rancher answered immediately. "Hello, pardner."

"Hiya, Chuck. Say, I just had a call from the Bureau about that item you gave me. They lifted three decent fingerprints off it."

"So tell me who they belong to— Hold on a minute."

"What is it?"

"Electric power just went off." Pause. "But the diesel generator kicked in."

Parris scowled at a few fat pelts of rain that were beginning to splatter on his windshield. "Has your telephone landline crapped out too?"

"Yeah. A big storm's rolled in, and we've been having some pretty fair gusts of wind."

Parris was stabbed by another searing pain, this one accompanied by an icy premonition. "Your phone and electric-power problems may not have anything to do with the storm. The guy from the FBI told me those prints match some they lifted from a crime scene in Arkansas. What the Bureau would like to know is how the prints of a high-profile Family member ended up on something that belongs to the Columbine. And so would I."

"We'll get into that when I have time, pard. But from what the feds told you, it looks like I've got a member of the Family here with me."

"Listen, Charlie, those wolves don't hunt alone—they

run in *packs*. And if they're planning something for tonight, there's probably at least of four of 'em on the Columbine—a full team."

Moon drew in a long breath. "That's what I figure."

"So why didn't you call me?"

"I thought about it, but didn't want to tip my hand. I shut down the ranch today and sent everybody over to the Big Hat."

"Why'd you do that?"

"For a party."

"That's not what I meant and you know it."

"If the bad guys are here, I figured it was best to force their hand—tempt them into making a move they hadn't planned." Moon waited a few heartbeats. "And I needed a plausible excuse to get Daisy and Sarah off the ranch. And Dolly Bushman."

"And seeing how you manhandled those thugs in the hardware store, you figured you could do it again. All by yourself."

"I know the territory, pard. And I've got another advantage—those rascals don't know that I know they're on the Columbine." *At least I hope they don't.*

Parris scowled at his invisible friend. "Do you realize the spot you're in?"

"Sure. I figure I've got Trout cornered here on the Columbine." *And most likely, a team of his top guns.*

"That ain't funny, Charlie. And just to keep the record straight, the special agent I just talked with didn't say the prints belonged to Trout—he just said they belonged to a—"

"I heard you. A 'high-profile member of the Family.' "

"Hang on, buddy—don't go and do something stupid. I'll be there in nothing flat. And I've already called in some extra troops."

"I appreciate it. But I can deal with this."

"The hell you can—you'll get yourself killed! Now just hole up where they can't find you till I show up. Oh, and another thing—and this is important. It's about Dolly Bushman's nurse. She's—"

All Charlie Moon heard after that was a dead-cold, bottom-of-the-well silence. Coincident with Parris's chopped-off sentence, the rancher had seen a bright flash through his office window. For a second or two, it had lit up the crest of Black Frog Butte, which was where the telephone company's microwave antennas were located.

They've dynamited the phone tower.

Despite the fix he was in, Moon could not help admiring the Family's thorough approach to doing business.

Parris shouted, "Charlie. Are you there?" His big, meaty hand tried to *squeeze* Moon's voice out of the mobile phone. "Talk to me, Charlie." *Please talk to me.*

It was not to be.

Charlie Moon waited. *Anytime now, they'll take down the diesel backup.*

Before the thought had faded from the rancher's mind, the bulb in his gooseneck lamp dimmed to yellow, brightened, dimmed again, then—went black.

OVER YONDER

Just across the Buckhorn Range, at the smaller ranch that Foreman Pete Bushman liked to call the Baja Columbine, folks were having a fine old time. Well, *most* folks. Charlie Moon's aunt Daisy was not in a mood to enjoy the raucous hand-clapping music and rowdy boot stomping that passed for dancing.

Nevertheless, it was sure-enough Party Time, and Sarah Frank was feeling mighty fine in her pretty blue dress when the Wyoming Kyd made his way across the crowded Big Hat headquarters parlor. Now, it is an indisputable fact that the Kyd has the biggest, brightest smile in all of Granite Creek County, and don't you know he was flashing all his pearlies at the shy seventeen-year-old. Sarah felt a surge of pleasure at this unexpected attention; also, a sharp elbow jab her in the ribs. She turned to blink at Daisy Perika's leathery face.

The tribal elder, who had appeared as if from nowhere, croaked in Sarah's ear, "Something's wrong over at Charlie's place."

The girl's eyes widened. "What?"

Daisy told her what. "When I call his phone, Charlie don't answer." There was much more to it than that, of course, but it wouldn't help matters to tell the Ute-Papago orphan that she had seen three spirit-ponies trotting along in the thin, dry air above the rocky ridge.

The Kyd, who had arrived just in time to hear Daisy's remark, had a ready explanation: "The boss is prob'ly on his way over here."

Daisy, who didn't appreciate Mr. Silly Grin butting in, shook her head. "I don't think so."

Prompted by the sound of distant thunder, the handsome young man added, "Or maybe the storm's knocked the phone service out. Wind prob'ly blew a tree onto the line. Happens all the time." He turned his smile back on Sarah. "Young lady, you are looking *entirely* too pretty tonight."

"Oh . . ." Her face burned under his appreciative gaze.

Not one to let up when he figured he was making some progress, the Kyd tipped his snow-white, four-hundred-dollar Stetson. "If Charlie don't show up by the time the music starts, can I count on the first dance?"

"Well—I don't know. . . ."

Daisy glared at this young *matukach* upstart. "I think somebody ought to go back to the Columbine and check on Charlie." The old woman had a strange feeling that Scott Parris would *never get there*.

Jerome Kydmann laughed. "Oh, the boss don't need any checking on. Charlie Moon can take care of himself." He jerked a thumb at his cowhide vest. "I'm the fella that needs some attention." He reached out to take Sarah's hand. "Now how about it. Do I get that first dance—or don't I?"

The girl glanced at the cranky old woman, who seemed determined to spoil her fun—then at the good-looking young cowboy. *It might teach Charlie Moon a lesson if I danced with Mr. Kydmann.* She reflected the Kyd's smile back at him. *Maybe even make him a little bit jealous.*

Well. What was a romantic, impressionable young lady to do?

Being who and what she was, Sarah made a decision.

CHAPTER FORTY-FOUR

ACCOUNTING FOR THE MAJOR PLAYERS

On the Columbine
The Deadly Quartet

The four new employees, who had hardly exchanged a word among themselves since being hired on by Pete Bushman, were huddled together in a thick stand of willows. They muttered and murmured about this and that. A passerby (had there been one) would have concluded that they were old friends, perhaps members of a close-knit *family*. The hypothetical passerby would have been correct on both counts, and most likely dead before he had time to entertain a second thought.

Three of the hardcases were armed with .44 Magnum revolvers and brand-spanking-new Winchester 94 carbines. The fourth, who had the distinction of being the team leader, also had a .44 Magnum revolver hanging heavily on his hip, but instead of a carbine he carried a propane weed torch whose searing flame could be activated by the press of a button. The instrument had been modified to produce a ten-foot tongue of fire that could lick the skin right off a man.

The trio of riflemen watched the ranch headquarters for some sign of the long, lanky Indian.

The flamethrower-toting team leader was waiting for the

go-ahead signal from a predator who was a step higher up the food chain than himself.

DOLLY'S NURSE

Annie Rose was on the Bushmans' front porch, making a second call on her satellite telephone. "This is Orphan. Scramble. I repeat: *Scramble*!" This being the final signal, she stashed the communications device in her purse, where a well-oiled 9-mm automatic pistol would keep it company.

THE EX-CON

Alone in the bunkhouse and enjoying the rumbling of thunder, Bill Smith neither fretted about the gathering storm nor cursed the inky darkness. The cheerful, big-shouldered man got up from his cot to touch a forty-nine-cent cigarette lighter to a six-inch tallow candle. He twisted the wax cylinder into a ketchup bottle and placed the makeshift lamp in a window. Admiring the tiny flame, he threw back his head and crooned, "O-oooh . . . Let my little light shine!"

THE TRIBAL INVESTIGATOR

After checking the pistol strapped to his belt, Charlie Moon stepped softly down the darkened stairway and into the cavernous headquarters parlor.

ON THE ROAD

Rolling like a cannonball on steroids toward the Columbine, Charlie Moon's best friend prayed that he would not be too late.

Someone is bound to ask: "How fast does the chief of police roll in his supercharged black-and-white GCPD unit?"

Whilst soaring sickeningly over undulating ridges and dipping perilously into shallow hollows, Scott Parris proceeds at 115 miles per hour.

Faster on level straightaways.

CHAPTER FORTY-FIVE

WE TAKE SO MUCH FOR GRANTED

Such as light, which is so precious—even the feeble illumination from distant stars, luminescent clock dials, gas pilot lights, and the like. Those faintish glows enable us to maneuver at night without bumping into such hazards as sooty coal scuttles, sappy cedar fence posts, and dozing snapping turtles.

Smothered under mile-thick clouds, the Columbine might as well have been buried within the twisted innards of a West Virginia coal mine. Aside from an occasional flash of lightning that was almost blinding, the darkness was total.

As the man who had just penned his last will and testament groped his way toward the kitchen, he had some time to think. *Unless I'm wrong—and I'm not—this'll end up being at least four against one.* A sobering thought for a man who did not harbor suicidal tendencies. And not only that . . . *I don't know where these guys are holed up and ready to draw a bead on me.* Plus (and this was a big minus)—*They're bound to know that I'm here in the headquarters.* The poker player frowned at the long odds. *They also know that I'm likely to go out to the machine-shop shed and try to restart the diesel generator.* A dicey situation. *There must be some way of stacking the deck so I've got a fighting chance of being alive when the sun comes up.* Charlie Moon felt his way to the coat rack by the kitchen door, where he donned a long, black raincoat and a floppy old cowboy hat, also black. *Well, I hope I think of something.* He unlocked the kitchen door and backed away to take cover behind the headquarters' two-foot-thick log walls.

Creeeeak. Squeeeeak.

(These were the sounds the hinges produced as Moon used the toe of his black cowboy boot to push the oak door open.)

Pistol in hand, he waited for slugs to come flying into the kitchen. After a few dozen heartbeats, the Ute slipped silently onto the south porch.

Somewhere out yonder in the outer darkness, several bad actors waited. Eager to play their supporting roles in the unfolding drama, the hopeful performers watched for their cue—which would be the appearance of the leading man.

Mr. Moon was already at center stage.

But it would not be strictly accurate to assert that the quasi-invisible man-in-black had *put in an appearance*.

CHAPTER FORTY-SIX

ASOK, GARFIELD, HERMAN, AND MARMADUKE

These were the nicknames of the four new-hire cowboys who comprised the B Team, the Family's postgraduate felons.

When Charlie Moon opened the headquarters kitchen door, locked it behind him, and stepped stealthily across the porch floor without making a board creak, the bloodthirsty foursome could neither hear nor see the man they were so eager to meet.

When a crooked finger of white-hot lightning reached out to touch an already-dead ponderosa atop Pine Knob, Garfield did catch a shadowy glimpse of something that might have been the stealthy Ute—or some nameless phantom who traveled by night. By the time another flash occurred, the ghostly figure was nowhere to be seen.

Following the maybe-sighting, the armed hooligans heard someone open the machine-shop door. And close it.

At a low, piggish grunt from the team leader (Asok), his comrades emerged one by one from a collection of willows clustered on the bank of Too Late Creek. All in a line they marched, like the trained soldiers they were. Garfield followed Asok by the prescribed three paces. Garfield was likewise followed by Herman. Marmaduke tagged along behind.

The sinister quartet approached the machine-shop shed with keen anticipation.

Asok was carrying his propane-fueled, push-button-activated weed burner.

The long, lean Mr. Moon was the designated dandelion.

After conferring in muffled mutters, Asok extended a leather-gloved hand and turned the doorknob. He opened it a crack and listened intently. The team leader heard only the breeze whispering in the willows, the rattling of cottonwood leaves. The thick gloom inside the cinder-block structure seemed to flow outward, making the dismal night even blacker, bleaker.

Without hesitating or hurrying, the four thugs stepped inside.

Asok aimed his weed burner in the general direction of the diesel generator, where they expected the Indian would be.

Garfield and Herman raised their carbines.

At a whispered command from Asok, Marmaduke switched on his flashlight.

Four sets of eyes goggled at the empty space.

There was no sign of their intended victim.

Charlie Moon, who had not entered the machine shop, closed the door, latched it, and for good measure jammed a hefty two-by-six under the doorknob.

Herman had a tendency to state the obvious. "The sneaky tommy-hawk tosser has locked us in!"

Not realizing that their intended victim was *outside*, Marmaduke instinctively switched off his flashlight. He yelped when Herman turned and accidentally nuzzled the carbine muzzle into his groin.

Startled by this unseemly commotion, Garfield fired three quick shots. The first round struck Herman in the left temple, the second and third drilled neat little holes through a two-gallon gasoline can.

Presumably in the hope of casting some much-needed illumination on a murky situation (but this is mere speculation), Asok thumbed the button on his weed burner. Whatever

the team leader's intent might have been, it was surely not for
the three-meter-long dagger of flame to ignite the spilled
gasoline. But it did.

While the aforesaid sneaky tomahawk tosser (who had
taken note of the carbine shots) was putting some comforting
distance between himself and the machine shop, the gasoline fire ignited other fuels stored in the shed. The surging
pressure of the overheated atmosphere blasted the door off its
hinges as the roof was likewise blown asunder, with flaming
fragments hurled upward until gravity would summon them
back to earth.

The Ute was (as they say in these parts) "a good fifty
yards" from the fiery explosion. One hundred mediocre
yards would have been better than a good fifty. The sprinter
barely escaped serious injury by falling facedown and rolling under a flatbed truck.

CHAPTER FORTY-SEVEN

PRAYER

As burning debris rained down around him, Charlie Moon lay flat on his back under the flatbed. The Catholic Christian closed his eyes and addressed his Best Friend.

"I'd appreciate it if you don't let my house burn down." He thanked the Almighty for the steel roof on the headquarters, which would help prevent such a calamity. "And we sure do need the new horse barn." That structure, still under construction and surrounded by wood chips and sawdust, was an iffy proposition, and even the faithful are sometimes fearful of asking too much of the One whose Word called the limitless universe into being. The new barn would survive. Moon heard his stock milling around in the corral, where glowing coals of fire were falling like hail from hell. "And even if the old barn burns to the ground, I'd be much obliged if you'd look after my horses."

Piece of cake. The animals would not be harmed. Even as Moon was making his heartfelt request, a big dappled stallion panicked and jumped the corral fence, knocking off the top rail. The other horses immediately followed and headed for the river.

Encouraged by these hopeful developments, Moon offered an observation. "We've had lots of thunder and lightning this evening." He followed this with a suggestion. "A little rain would help put out the fire."

No sooner said than done.

Plop. Plop-plop. Ploppity-plop-plop.

A *little* rain was what he got.

Big, fat drops, falling about one or two to a square foot. *Well, that's better than none.* "Thank you, sir."

Moon's momma had taught her bright-eyed little boy that it always helps to say "thank you." The plump raindrops began to fall more frequently.

Within a few minutes, the dusty headquarters yard was transformed into mud. But, as local weatherman Pete Bushman had prognosticated, this was only the preliminary sprinkle. When an earsplitting bolt of lightning busted a big hole in the bottom of the sky, the deluge began. Hunkered under the truck, Moon whispered, "This is mighty helpful." *But I hope you're not thinking forty days and forty nights.*

Despite the cloudburst, gasoline- and diesel-fueled flames continued to roar in the machine shop's blackened cinder-block shell, but all of the secondary fires had been put out.

Hellish cinders ceased to fall from the sky.

Moreover, there was a lull in the rainfall.

I might as well head back to the house.

The rancher got a grip on the truck's rear bumper, pulled himself from under the GMC vehicle, and got to his feet. On the off chance that a rifleman had the crosshairs of a night-vision sniper scope centered on his back, Moon made a run for the headquarters, zigging and zagging as he went. The instant his boots hit the porch steps, the rainstorm revved up again. As he entered the headquarters by the kitchen entrance, Charlie Moon's nostrils picked up alluring scents.

He followed his nose to a half pot of cold coffee. While he was gulping the brackish brew directly from the percolator, Moon searched the dark space for a suitable snack. What he came up with were two pieces of leftover pie. An appreciative sniff identified one slab as apple, the other as cherry. Which confronted Moon with something he did not need at the moment—a decision to be made. His taste buds expressed a definite leaning toward the apple, but that wedge was a smaller portion than the cherry, which was a full quarter section.

Irritated by the delay, his stomach suggested a sensible solution.

Between swallows of stale coffee, Moon chomped his way through *both* chunks of pie. This combination of high-calorie pastry and high-octane beverage was stimulating. Intensely so. Indeed, describing the net effect as *inspiring* would not be going too far. Which is undoubtedly why the sleep-deprived diner came up with a couple of ideas that (at the time) seemed pretty doggoned clever.

CHAPTER FORTY-EIGHT

COLUMBINE HOSPITALITY

Earlier in the day, the rancher had watched his hired hands leave the Columbine for the Big Hat. When the exodus appeared to be complete, he had telephoned Jerome Kydmann at the ranch on the far side of the Buckhorns to verify his list of partygoers. Charlie Moon was certain that six persons had remained behind on the Columbine.

All new hires.

Moon figured that the four greenhorns Bushman had hired on could be safely presumed dead in the charred remains of the machine-shop shed. That left Bill Smith, the admitted felon who claimed to have been a buddy of Loyola Montoya's grandson—and Miss Annie Rose, who had expertly nursed Dolly Bushman back to health. If these two had remained in the vicinity, one might reasonably expect them to show up at the headquarters and inquire about the cause of all the excitement.

When company (invited or otherwise) shows up on the doorstep, western hospitality obliges the host to attend to such preparations as are necessary for their comfort, and despite those recent events that had momentarily distracted his attention, Mr. Moon was not one to ignore his obligations. And so he attended to a few essential domestic duties.

Such as:

Making sure all the downstairs curtains were tightly closed.

Striking a kitchen match under a double handful of pine

splinters in the parlor fireplace and, after the tinder was aflame, adding several resinous chunks of split piñon.

Placing the most comfortable armchair in the parlor in front of the hearth. Close enough so a chilled guest could singe his knees if he pleased.

Lighting a ninety-year-old kerosene lamp in the kitchen, and its twin in the dining room.

Loading the blue enamel percolator with fresh grounds and cold well-water, putting it on the propane range, turning on a blue ring of flame.

Clearing the dining table of breakfast dishes and making sure the chairs were dusted of crumbs and otherwise ready for guests.

Checking the .357 Magnum holstered on his belt.

Thus prepared, all he had to do was step outside and wait for his guests to arrive.

Which he did.

JOB ONE

Still outfitted head-to-toe in black, Moon was one of a thousand shadows.

Not so the pale fellow crossing the yard.

The heel of the Ute's right hand rested on the butt of his sidearm. Smith, he figured, would either be straightforward or subtle. Moon hoped for straightforward. *I'd as soon finish our business here and now.*

He was to be disappointed.

Bill Smith stopped at the west porch steps, called out in a booming baritone, "Hey, boss—you in there?"

The man shrouded in blackness waited.

The hired hand yelled again, "Anybody home?"

"I'm here," Moon said.

Smith squinted at the spot on the porch where the voice had originated. "Mr. Moon—is that you?"

The disembodied voice spoke again: "The parlor door's unlocked, Smith. Go on in."

"Okay." The middle-aged male employee stepped onto the porch and entered the headquarters.

Moon followed, closing the door behind them.

"What a helluva night!" Smith removed his wide-brimmed hat and slapped it on his thigh, wetting the oak floor with a spray of water. "First, the electricity craps out, then I hear gunshots, then there's a big explosion and a hell-for-breakfast fire. What's going on around here, boss?"

"I'll be glad to tell you what little I know." Moon pointed at the snap-crackling piñon. "Let's go over to the fireplace."

"Don't mind if I do—that cold rain has given me a case of the shivers."

Moon followed his employee across the parlor.

At the hearth, Smith turned to address the Indian. "What in hell caused that concrete block building to blow sky-high?"

"Wasn't a lightning strike."

"What was it, then?"

"Some outlaws touched off a fire."

Smith stared at the Ute's dark face, now semivisible in the flickering firelight. "You mean on purpose—like arson?"

"It's more complicated than that." Moon watched the man stiffen. "Sometime during the last day or two, one of those guys planted a couple of booby traps on my porch swing."

Smith's mouth gaped. "You've gotta be kidding me."

"I've never been more serious in my life." Moon pointed at the chair by the hearth. "Take a load off, and I'll tell you all about it."

"Gunshots, biggest explosion I ever saw blows the roof off the machine shop—and now *booby traps.*" Smith was easing his bulk into the armchair. "This has been one of the damnedest nights I can ever remem—" *Oh, Lordy.*

Moon cocked his head. "What is it, Bill?"

Smith's hard, gray face resembled chiseled limestone. He stared at the flickering fire. Without blinking.

His employer persisted. "You feeling all right?"

The stone man opened his mouth. Shut it.

"Well, I guess you just need to sit a spell." Moon continued in a monotone: "But one of the rules of the house is that none of my employees brings loaded firearms inside, so I'll relieve you of that iron." The enforcer of rules reached under Smith's faded denim jacket and pulled a snub-nosed, ivory-gripped .44 Magnum revolver from a fringed leather holster.

There was no protest from the owner of the weapon, but beads of perspiration were forming on Bill Smith's forehead. His heart hammered hard under his ribs.

As Moon got a closer look at the pistol, flickering firelight danced on the stainless steel. "Your friends in ABC Hardware carried fancy sidearms exactly like this." He aimed the lethal weapon at Smith's left ear. "You might've had this cannon when you showed up on the Columbine, but I don't think so. And I'm dead certain you didn't bring those explosive contraptions I found under the blanket on my porch swing. So somebody brought 'em to you. Who was it?" He tapped the pistol barrel on Smith's head. "One of those fellas who planned to bushwhack me tonight?" *Or was it someone else?*

"Okay—you got me cold." Bill Smith turned his head just enough to blink at the Indian's dark profile. "Let's make a deal."

"I'm listening."

"I know how to safe the detonator on this gadget."

"After I back off a few paces, go right ahead."

"I can't. Not without the right kind of tool." Smith tried to smile. Couldn't quite pull it off. "I'll need some help."

"Tell me why I'd want to do a thing like that."

"Help get me offa this damned thing and I'll answer your questions. All of 'em!"

"That's not the way the game is played, Mr. Smith. You tell me what I want to know right up front. If I'm satisfied that you're not lying through your teeth—I might help you get off the hot seat."

Smith set his jaw, turned to glare at the fireplace.

"Okay. But I wouldn't want you to get too comfortable,

maybe drift off to sleep and fall off the cushion and onto the floor." Moon pressed the pistol barrel against the spiny ridge on Smith's neck. "Slow and easy, now—put your hands behind the chair, about waist-high." The seated man followed these instructions. "Now clasp your fingers around your forearms." Stuffing Smith's .44 Magnum revolver into his pocket, Moon used a pair of nylon tie-wraps to strap the assassin's wrists together, then to the back of the chair. "Normally, I'd hang around and shoot the breeze with you, but under the circumstances I'll feel better when I put a little bit of distance between me and what you're sitting on."

"Listen, Moon—this is crazy. You leave me here like this, we both lose. You help me, I'll show you where there's more cash money than you ever dreamed—"

"If there's anything you need, don't expect me to bring it to you. Get up off your butt and go get it yourself." With this, the tribal investigator departed.

FIVE DOWN, ONE TO GO

Charlie Moon had barely gotten outside when he saw Number Six high-stepping it across the Too Late Creek bridge.

Annie Rose was almost to the headquarters porch when she felt a man's big hand on her right shoulder. Suppressing the instinctive scream, the lady bit her tongue. Very painful.

"It's me."

"Oh—Mr. Moon?" She ignored the salty taste of blood in her mouth.

"The very same." *Now ask me what's been going on.*

"What on earth has been happening here tonight?"

"I expect you refer to the shooting. And the explosion and fire."

Resisting the urge to make a sarcastic reply, Annie satisfied herself with a simple, "Yes."

"Some unsavory characters have created considerable mischief here tonight."

"I'm sorry—I don't understand. Are you telling me that someone deliberately—"

"Several of 'em are dead, but there might be more where they come from." Moon's grip on her shoulder tightened. "Let's go inside, where we'll be safer."

Annie's back stiffened. "But—"

"Shhhh." Gently but firmly, the unseen hand moved her to the south side of the headquarters. Up the porch steps. Inside the kitchen door.

CHAPTER FORTY-NINE

JOB TWO

As Charlie Moon closed and latched the kitchen door, he got a good look at new hire Number Six in the yellowish light from the kerosene lamp. Like himself, Annie was dressed for night work. Gray woolen jacket with deep pockets. Matching knee-length woolen skirt. Her outfit was topped off with a gray felt fedora, underpinned with gray cowgirl boots.

The little gray lady turned to shoot a look at the Ute. "Okay, we're behind the log walls. So tell me what's—"

"Looks like the coffee's ready." The percolator on the propane range was popping merrily.

"I'll pour." She twisted a knob to turn off the flame. "From what Dolly Bushman tells me, you take yours black. With honey."

"That I do." *This one don't miss a trick.*

An accurate appraisal. The lady was a pro.

Annie's gaze scanned a dozen cabinets mounted on three walls.

Moon pointed his chin. "Cups are over the sink."

She opened a maple door, selected a china cup for herself and a sturdy crockery mug for the man. "Tell me about the gunshots." She poured the coffee. "And the explosion."

"That'd take a lot of telling."

She found a small pitcher of cream in the refrigerator. "So give me a thumbnail sketch."

"It started a while back, when I had a run-in with some bad guys."

"If you refer to those robbers at the hardware store, you needn't fill me in." Annie dribbled cream into her cup. "I watch the evening news on the tube." The cool-as-ice lady stirred honey into his steaming coffee. "Tell me something I *don't* know."

That might be a tall order. "About a day or so ago, somebody planted a couple of IEDs under the blanket Aunt Daisy put on my porch swing."

Annie presented a puzzled expression that was patently phony. "Planted *what*?"

She'd never make a poker player. "Improvised explosive devices."

"You're *kidding.*"

Moon's smile reflected a deep weariness with deception. "That's what Bill Smith said."

"Well don't keep me in suspense—tell me all about it."

"Not till I've enjoyed some liquid refreshment."

Moon took the cup and the mug into the dining room and placed them on the table. The gentleman pulled out a chair for the lady.

"Thank you, sir." Annie gathered her skirt and seated herself on the cushioned chair. Froze. *Oh my God.*

"I figured you'd know right away what you'd sat down on." Moon, who had remained behind her, removed a couple of interesting items from her coat pockets. "Well—look at that—a 9-millimeter Glock." He aimed it at his coffee mug. "Guess those big pistols the bad boys carry are a mite too heavy for a dainty little lady like yourself." He slipped the automatic into his hip pocket and placed her satellite telephone on the table. "And that's a nice touch, Annie. After your buddies take out the phone lines and the cell tower, you folks are able to communicate. Who had the other sat phone? One of the back shooters that figured they had me cornered in the machine shop?"

Her tongue still aching, Annie bit her lower lip.

The tribal cop seated himself across the table from his

guest and took a sip of the sweetish brew. "When I found a couple of your pie-pan IEDs under that blanket on the swing, I don't need to tell you that I wasn't overly pleased. Sometimes—especially when I'm surprised—I tend to be a little slow on the uptake. But it didn't take me long to understand that those explosives weren't meant for me. Daisy and Sarah were your intended victims—anybody who's spent even a few days on the Columbine knows that hardly anyone else ever sits there." He leaned forward to fix a flinty look on the woman. "Now that was a game changer. I made up my mind right on the spot—not one of you outlaws would leave the Columbine alive."

Annie Rose was as pale as new-fallen snow at twilight. The terrified woman parted her lips to protest. "If you would just listen—"

"Hush."

She hushed.

Moon downed what was left of his coffee and pushed the mug aside. "Ever since I found those explosives, all I've had on my mind is killing *every last one of you*. And I don't mind telling you that I've been making some fair progress." He jerked his thumb in the general direction of the machine shop. "Four of your friends are already buzzard bait." He aimed a finger at the parlor. "And Mr. Smith has his butt planted on the same item that's under your chair cushion."

"Mr. Smith?"

"Go ahead. Tell me you never heard of him."

The woman set her jaw. "May I *please* say something?"

"No." Moon got up from his chair. "And don't ask me to bring you any cookies or cake to go with your coffee." An enigmatic grin curled the Ute's lips. "Like I told Mr. Smith—if you need something, get up and get it for yourself."

Mr. Moon was extremely angry, angry men make mistakes, and our subject had made several. Some of them dandies. Consider this for instance.

REGARDING THE BUZZARD BAIT

Stressed as he was, Charlie Moon could still count up to four, and he was correct in believing that was the number of bloodthirsty assassins he had locked inside the Columbine machine-shop shed.

His error?

Assuming that all four were dead.

Three of the brutal criminals had gone on to their reward.

The exception was the leader of the B Team. Approximately 0.42 seconds after he had ignited the gasoline with his nifty propane weed burner, Asok had been blown through the roof. As a physicist who delights in describing ballistic flight might put it, his body had ". . . followed an approximately parabolic trajectory, rising to an apex of almost forty-two feet, where the relentless tug of gravity overcame the upward component of Asok's velocity and began pulling him back to earth." Delightful chaps, these egghead scientists, but they have a tendency to ignore those pesky anomalies. Such as—the thug's 180-some-odd pounds did not come all the way down—*it never hit the ground.*

Really.

Asok, his hateful heart still throbbing, is still *up there somewhere.*

Sad to say, the troublesome fellow will not remain in his suspended state.

CHAPTER FIFTY

HELP IS ON THE WAY

Scott Parris slowed just enough to make a gut-knotting, tire-squealing turn into the Columbine gate; he barely managed to keep his supercharged black-and-white on the muddy lane. The tough ex-Chicago cop grinned and gritted his teeth at the same time. *I'll be there in ten minutes!*

About nine minutes later: "Oh, dammit!"

About a country mile from the Columbine headquarters, the reckless Granite Creek chief of police rounded a curve on the muddy ranch lane, skidded sideways for about thirty yards before sliding into a ditch full of muddy water, and rammed his unit into a sturdy pine fence post hard enough to flip the sleek Chevy a full 360 degrees so that it landed wheels-down. During this lively process, the driver's head got banged against the steering wheel five or maybe six times; he wasn't counting.

Goodbye, fence post.

Goodbye, Parris?

Not quite. Not yet.

But the lawman had—in a manner of speaking—*given up the ghost.*

EPISODE SIX

Nightmare Finale

U.S. Marshal Scott Parris stood atop Pine Knob, staring at the windswept spot where the Ute had buried his body. From the weedy hump of earth heaped over the grave, and the rotting wooden marker, it was apparent that quite some years had passed.

I wonder if ol' Charlie Moon's still alive.

As if in response, a chill breeze whispered over the Knob.

No, I guess he's most likely gone now. But I don't see another grave here, so I guess Charlie got planted some-wheres else. Some of his relatives probably folded his carcass chin-to-knees and stashed it in one of them little crevices in *Cañón del Espíritu.*

The phantom leaned close to the lichen-encrusted wooden plank and was able to read the whole thing. Name. Title. Date of birth and death. And . . . the epitaph the Indian had burned into the wood. Well I'll be rode hard and put away wet!

The U.S. marshal scowled at the grave marker. I hope that Indian rascal's still alive—so I can hunt him down and haunt the dickens out of him!

A dandy plan, but somewhat premature.

About six miles from the Knob, in the wrecked GCPD unit, Scott Parris's stunned brain was beginning to stir—and like a shiny spinning lure fastened to the end of a long fishing line, the wandering spirit was reeled in. The first thought that came to him was: *I must've been asleep and dreaming.* He could vaguely recall being on a forlorn, windy hilltop where someone was buried. But the stunned man remembered nothing about what he'd read on the wooden marker. Parris was jarred to complete consciousness by a sharp pain in his head, a dull ache in his chest. *I feel like five or six big guys beat me up and pitched me into an alley.* No, that couldn't be right. *It wasn't a fight—I'm strapped into my black-and-white.* The lawman strained to remember. *I was driving. But what happened?* He blinked at the darkness. *And where am I?*

Under the singular circumstances, reasonable questions.

Within a few irregular heartbeats, it all came back to him.

I ran my unit off the road. I'm on the Columbine, probably not more than a mile or two from the ranch headquarters. I hope the car's not bunged up too bad. That hope was overly optimistic, but the left headlight was working and the Chevrolet engine idled along without missing a lick.

I got to get outta here and go see if Charlie's all right.

Parris jerked the gearshift into Reverse and stepped on the gas.

Brrrmmmmm! (The sound of rubber tires spinning impotently in slimy slush.)

#&$%#! (A heartfelt expletive.)

Another *brrrmmmmm!*

And another.

All to no effect, as was Expletive Number Two—an unseemly utterance for a man of his respected position in the community.

The frustrated cop's vehicle was there to stay until the break of a fairer day. Which dawning, regardless of whatever catastrophes might occur in the meantime, would be dished up shortly.

CHAPTER FIFTY-ONE

ANTICIPATING

It would be an unwarranted exaggeration to suggest that Charlie Moon was worried about the potential for still more trouble on the Columbine. But he was moderately concerned, and more than a little suspicious. *Bill Smith seems to be waiting for something to happen.*

And though it was probably merely a reflection from the flickering kerosene lamp, the tribal investigator thought he detected a confident sparkle in Annie Rose's dark eyes.

The combination of Smith's waiting and Annie's sparkling was bound to cause a man to wonder. *Maybe those two know that a backup team of Family bad guys are outside, getting ready to break into the headquarters and pull off a rescue.* That was what had happened at Snyder Memorial Hospital when two other members of the Family had been housed under the watchful eye of the state police. *If they can, the Family'll pull off another snatch.*

Mr. Moon knew just what to do about that.

BAITING THE TRAP

Charlie Moon figured he'd already accomplished most of that task. Like alluring chunks of savory cheese, Bill Smith and Annie Rose were firmly seated—and waiting for their rescue. To make sure this enticement would be seen by the

Family's rats, he opened a pair of curtains in the parlor about two inches, and repeated the operation in the dining room on a south-facing window. Thus prepared, the rancher withdrew into the kitchen, where he snuffed out the kerosene lamp. When the rescuer rodents came sniffing around, they would be bound to spot the captives, and if they decided to break down the parlor door or bust in through any of a half-dozen windows, the Ute would do his level best to make things hot for them. But he had a hunch that before launching a noisy, frontal attack, in which the Family was likely to lose another soldier or two, they would try to find a way to slip in quietly.

Which was why he unlocked the kitchen door.

IN THE PARLOR BY THE FIRE

While Bill Smith knew that a rescue was possible, he did not intend to wait—truckloads of cops might show up any minute now. After agonizing over his limited options, the desperate man settled on a plan. *It's a long ways from being a sure thing.* His tongue was dry as a pine chip; his head ached behind his eyes. *But it might work.* Perspiration beaded up on his face. *It's the only decent chance I got.* Thunder rumbled in the distance. *And with a little bit of luck . . .*

The plan?

Mr. Smith had a very thin, single-blade folding knife concealed in his wallet, which was in his hip pocket, which was not far from his hands, which Mr. Moon had secured behind the straight-back chair. What did he hope to accomplish with the miniature piece of cutlery? It was a simple two-step procedure. The first task involved freeing his hands— But wait.

He is about to explain.

If I could get at my knife without setting this damned explosive off, I might be able to cut through these plastic cuffs. Then, if I poked the blade through the pie pan in just the right spot, maybe I could short out the detonator capacitor.

If. Might. If. Maybe.

Four long shots, and every one had to hit the bull's-eye dead center.

Damn, what a fix I'm in!

Sweat dripped from his nose and chin.

Maybe one of the guys is still alive. And if he is, maybe he'll look through a window and spot me and . . . Bill Smith groaned. *If maybes was silver dollars, I could buy me a shiny little airplane and fly outta here.*

IN THE DINING ROOM

Sitting stiffly in the booby-trapped chair, Annie Rose seethed with fury. *I'm sure my signal was picked up.* The storm had probably slowed things down, but it would just be a matter of time before . . . *the guys show up and take care of things and* then *we'll see what kind of tune Mr. Moon sings!* The feisty little woman smiled.

IN THE KITCHEN

The tribal investigator's musings about how he might react to a sudden attack were interrupted by two occurrences, whose uncanny congruence galvanized his attention.

A sudden, absolute dead silence as the rain stopped on a dime.

One of those creepy, hair-raising noises that is *not* an old house settling.

Cree . . . eak.

Somebody's sneaking up on the porch. Charlie Moon unburdened his holster of the heavy revolver.

Sque . . . eeak.

He cocked his pistol.

Creak-squeak.

Sounds like just one man. The Ute moved across the kitchen floor ever so softly. Imagine a ghost's filmy shadow flitting over a moonlit graveyard.

Not so the heavy-footed trespasser.

Squeak-creak.

Two hundred pounds. Maybe more. Moon aimed his .357 Mag at a void that would soon be occupied.

Creak-squeak-creak.

The last *creak* was just outside the kitchen door.

The Ute's lips moved: *Go on—try the doorknob.*

That shiny brass orb turned.

That's the way. Now give it a push . . .

The door opened, but just a crack.

Don't be nervous, night crawler. Moon's mouth twisted into a hopeful grin. *Slither right on in.*

The door opened wider. About waist-high, something resembling a cobra's head thrust itself through the opening. A big fist, grasping a pistol.

So far, so good. Moon pointed his revolver at an empty space. *Now show your ugly face.*

A man's head poked in.

The intruder immediately felt the cold steel of a pistol muzzle on his temple, a twisting pain in his chest. "Charlie—*please* say that's you."

Charlie Moon lowered his sidearm. "Scott, you never came so close to getting your head blown off."

CHAPTER FIFTY-TWO

THE REVELATION

Pocketing his sidearm, the chief of police turned his head to squint at the spot where he'd heard the Ute's voice. "I took a look through the windows and saw some guy sitting by the parlor fire, and a woman at the dining-room table—both of 'em still as yesterday's corpses. And you—you're holed up in a dark kitchen waiting to poke a pistol into my ear. What in hell's going on here, Charlie?"

"Everybody keeps asking me that."

Parris glared at his unseen friend. "I've had a bad evening and I'm in a nasty mood, so don't mess with me!"

"Shhh. Keep your voice down."

Looking this way and that in the blackness, Parris whispered, "Those murderous Family buzzards skulking about somewheres?"

Moon took his friend by the elbow. "Let's go out onto the porch."

"I don't want to go outside." Parris's boots might've been nailed to the floor. "I been there already and it don't appeal to me."

The Ute insisted.

Parris grumbled as he stumbled onto the porch, "My unit's mired up in a ditch about nine hundred miles down the lane, which is how far I walked in this damned ice-cold rain."

Moon closed the door behind them. "You must be a little bit damp."

"Damp?" Waving his arms, the heavyset cop growled. "Listen, Charlie—*damp* is what a bottom-eating catfish is. Me, I'm soaked to the bone and freezing my butt off." *And my head aches like a boil.* "So be snappy about what you've got to say, then let's go into the parlor so I can pull up a chair beside that other guy and get warmed up." This plea was punctuated by a sudden, violent assault on the porch roof. The brief lull in the storm was over.

To Moon's ear, the racket suggested a humungous dump truck spilling a full load of pea gravel on the Columbine headquarters.

Tugging sullenly at his sodden felt hat, Parris raised his voice just loud enough for the Ute to hear: "Good Lord, Charlie—it's raining daggers, pitchforks, and triple-ought buckshot!"

His internal metaphor outdone, the Ute resorted to a literal interpretation: "Sounds like hail."

"I don't care what it sounds like." Parris shivered. "Let's go get our knees snugged up to the fireplace." As the final syllable slipped passed his lips, the hailstorm ceased as abruptly as it had begun; the sudden silence hinted of worse to come.

"Before we go inside, pard, you need to know what's going on in the house."

"Okay, Chucky." The hypothermic town cop stopped shivering just long enough to get in a bone-rattling shudder. "But keep it sh-short and to the puh-puh-point."

"There's been some troubles."

Parris understood. "What's the body count?"

"When the sun comes up, we'll find four charred corpses in the machine-shop shed, which is pretty much burned to the ground."

"Anybody I know?"

"Only if you're on a first-name basis with members of the Family."

Parris caught another fit of the shivers. *This sounds too*

easy. "You absolutely sure that all of 'em are stone-cold dead?"

"Like they'd been buried for a hundred years."

The Ute's response summoned up a snatch of Parris's dream-memory. The chief of police suppressed a fuzzy image of the 1870s Pine Knob cemetery. *So my buddy's already taken care of business.* Despite his discomfort, the lawman grinned. *A fella could know ol' Charlie for a lifetime and never cease to be surprised.* "Sounds like you've done a pretty fair night's work."

"The night's not over." Moon's voice was hollow. "And neither's the work."

Parris stared into the darkness beyond the porch. "You figure there's more of 'em out there somewhere?"

The Ute gazed in the direction of Black Frog Butte. "Whoever took out the cell phone tower hasn't been accounted for." He pointed his elbow at the log wall. "And I've got two inside the headquarters—the ones you saw in the parlor and the kitchen."

His surprise meter registering off the scale, Parris gawked at the Ute's dim outline. "Are them two dead too?"

"Not yet. But I expect they're thinking a lot about it."

Why can't Charlie talk plain American like everybody else. "What in hell does *that* mean?"

"It's a little complicated, pardner. My guests would rather be anyplace than here. But they're determined to stay right where they are."

After a difficult evening, Parris was dithering right on the edge of testy. "Explain so I can understand."

The tribal investigator was pleased to acquiesce to this reasonable request, and after Moon had had his say, Parris stared at his friend through a pair of blue, squinty eyes. "You're not putting me on—you actually *did* that?"

The dead-serious Ute nodded.

The Granite Creek chief of police was silent for a string of middle-aged heartbeats, the thumpity-thumps arriving at odd intervals. He began by heaving a heavy sigh. "Let me make sure I got this straight. After killing off four of your employees, you've got two more with their butts resting on high-explosive gadgets you found under the blanket on your porch swing?"

"That's a pretty fair summary, except for some minor details."

Parris's tone was distinctly suspicious. "Define minor."

"Well, for one thing—I haven't killed anybody tonight. Those four that thought they had me cornered in the machine shop did the job for me."

The town cop frowned. "You saying they killed *themselves*?"

"More or less."

"Pardon me, Charlie—maybe my brain is cold as my feet—but that don't make any sense."

"Once things are sorted out by the FBI and the fire inspector, I expect the medical examiner will find that their deaths—having occurred during an attempt to commit murder—to be accidental."

"All right. I can't hardly wait to hear the other minor details."

"None of these yahoos are what you'd call regular employees—they're all new hires. Temporaries." Moon took a look through the parlor window; Annie was sitting like a china doll in her chair. "And unless I'm badly mistaken, all six of 'em are from out of state."

Parris snorted. "Well, that puts the whole thing in a different light. Practically makes it all right." But a lawman's work was not all fun. There would be dozens of forms to fill out. "I'll need their names, which'll be about as genuine as nine-dollar bills."

"I was never formally introduced to the four that're dead, but they'll be listed on Pete Bushman's roster." Moon gestured again with his elbow. "But the pair of bad apples in the house call themselves Bill Smith and Annie Rose. Now that you've got the lowdown, we can go inside, and you can place both of 'em under arrest. Which reminds me—Smith was packing some heavy artillery." He passed the confiscated .44 Magnum to the chief of police. "This one's a dead ringer for those the hardware-store banditos were using."

As Parris pushed Smith's big pistol into his coat pocket, the angina stabbed him hard enough to take his breath away. When he eased himself over to a sturdy redwood chair, the sting branched out from his trunk to twist its malignant way along his left arm.

Moon frowned. "You okay?"

"No." Parris's grimace was concealed by the darkness. "I'm not."

The Ute's slender form moved closer to loom over him. "What's wrong?"

"Nothing that a long vacation in a Tahiti beach hut wouldn't fix." *Or sudden death—whichever comes first.* As the pain eased, he inhaled a deep, grateful breath. "Tell me what you've got on this Smith character."

"Aside from some circumstantial evidence, only a couple of things. When he sat down in the parlor and heard that pie-pan crunch underneath him, Smith turned green as pea soup. For a while, he didn't say a solitary word. But when he did open his mouth, Smith offered me a deal if I'd turn him loose."

Parris bit his lip as something like a red-hot poker stabbed him in the chest. The stricken man held his breath until the threat of imminent death had subsided. The best way to ignore the likely prognosis was to keep on talking to Charlie Moon. "So what's the second thing?"

"Those prints on Butch Cassidy's cell phone that the FBI ID'd as a member of the Family—they belong to Bill Smith."

"Then he's a sure-enough bad one." The chief of police waited for the next pain. "What've you got on the woman?"

"For starters, Dolly Bushman's nurse was packing a 9-millimeter Glock automatic."

Parris's jaw dropped. "Dolly Bushman's *nurse*?"

"Sure. And five'll get you twenty she's the nurse that killed all those folks in the Snyder Memorial ICU. On top of that, Annie Rose knew what was going to happen here tonight—like the telephone landline and cell-phone tower going down—she'd prepared herself." Moon patted the automatic in his hip pocket. "When the Family's nurse showed up here a few minutes ago, she wasn't just packing a pistol. She also had a *satellite telephone* in her coat pocket. And here's the nail that puts the lid on her coffin—just like Smith, Miss Rose knew exactly what she'd sat down on."

"The second pie-pan gadget."

"That's right." *Scott seems kinda peculiar. Like he's sick.* "There's no other way to account for all this accumulation of evidence. Annie is definitely Bill Smith's partner in crime. And I'll bet you a shiny Morgan silver dollar that Smith will turn out to be Trout."

Damn! The latest pain seared Parris's chest like a white-hot flame. The pasty-faced cop closed his eyes. *Well, if it's time to cash in my chips, I can't think of anybody I'd rather be with than Charlie Moon. Or anyplace I'd rather be than sitting on the porch here at the Columbine. Well . . . maybe inside by the fire.* Cold as he was, Parris found the quiet to be utterly peaceful. Comforting. Like a warm quilt on a chill night. Or . . . *Like settling down into a grave on Pine Knob.*

The Ute's deep voice broke the stillness. "So d'you want to arrest them?"

Parris managed a shrug.

"What does that mean?"

"Oh, nothing much." The next pain in his chest was not quite as sharp as the previous one, and it was already fading to a dull ache. "Except in the lady's case there might be another way to account for these so-called facts you've been telling me about."

"Name one."

The hurt was saying Goodbye for Now. Parris's left arm began to feel tolerably better. "Give me some time to think about it."

Moon allowed him a full six seconds. "Time's up."

"Okay, how about this. The lady—what was her name again?"

"Annie Rose."

"Okay. Let's say Miss Rose's vocation requires her to carry a satellite phone and a pistol."

"Sure it does." Moon glanced at the woman seated in the dining room. "Her job description included staying in close communication with Bill Smith and those four thugs after the regular phone system was dead, and then helping them massacre every living soul on the Columbine."

"Well . . . not necessarily."

"Then besides being a homegrown terrorist, what is her vocation? And keep in mind that the woman *knew* she'd sat down on one of the Family's pie-pan explosives."

I do believe I'm going to live to see another sunrise. Parris helped himself to a double lungful of the chill, damp, ozone-charged high-country air. *Thank you, Lord.* "Well—and I know this'll sound like a real long shot—but what if the lady was a cop?"

"A cop?"

"Sure. Why not?"

"Well . . ." Moon was beginning to feel a bit uneasy. He was right at the edge of *queasy.*

Parris flexed his left arm. "Let's say, just for the sake of argument, that this Annie Rose is a law-enforcement officer. Like, say—a state cop." A snatch of his nightmare bubbled up from somewhere down there. "Or a U.S. marshal." He effected a thoughtful pause. "She might even be an FBI agent."

Moon blinked. "Annie Rose—a *fed*?"

"It ain't so silly as it sounds, Charlie. Let's assume—again, just for the sake of a heated discussion—that the lady sitting in your dining room is Special Agent Rose. Then—not only would it make perfect sense for her to be packing a government-issue Glock and a satellite phone—she would've been briefed by Bureau explosives experts on the Family's bomb-making techniques."

"That bucket's got a big hole in it." Moon shook his head. "If the woman was a federal agent, she'd have told me tonight."

"Not if she was working undercover."

Moon was experiencing a peculiar, floating sensation of weightlessness. Like an astronaut whose tether to the mother ship has snapped, or a mountaineer who has slipped on ice and is falling from a great height. "Aside from tending to Dolly Bushman, what would an undercover FBI agent be doing here on the Columbine?" *Like I don't know.* But he needed to hear Parris say it.

His friend was happy to accommodate. "Well, Special Agent Rose—if that's who she is—could've been sent here by the FBI to sound an alarm if members of the Family showed up on your ranch. The general notion would be to make sure nothing bad happened to you, or Daisy, or Sarah. Or any of your employees."

"Scott . . ."

"Yeah?"

"How long have you known that Annie Rose was with the Bureau?"

"What are you talking about?" He turned his head to avoid the Ute's flinty gaze, which he could *feel* in the darkness. "Before you mentioned the lady's name, I'd never even heard of any Annie Rose."

"Okay. Let's put it another way. How long have you known that Dolly Bushman's hired lady companion was an undercover agent placed here by the Bureau?"

"Since Day One."

"And you didn't even drop me the least hint because you'd crossed all of your fingers and toes and swore to keep the secret?"

"That's about the size of it. I gave the Bureau my solemn word I wouldn't tell you. And you know well as I do that out here, a man's solemn word is—"

"You're a regular Boy Scout."

"Thanks, Charlie." Parris wriggled his cold toes. "I knew you'd understand."

"What I understand is that I've gotten myself into a bit of difficulty."

"I bet that's what General Custer said when he found out he was surrounded by about ten thousand Indians—all of 'em painted up for war and armed to the teeth." The chief of police pushed himself up from the redwood chair. "Setting this Bill Smith character on an explosive device was shaky enough. But fixing things so a federal agent can get blown apart if she wiggles her . . . uh . . . posterior—that's going a bit over the top, Charlie. Even for a reckless, irresponsible fella like yourself."

"I have kinda put myself on the spot."

Now more or less pain-free, Parris was beginning to enjoy this tasty little slice of life. "One I'm real anxious to see how you'll . . . uh . . . what's the dang word? Sounds like *implicate.*"

Compared to Moon's scowl, the night's inky darkness might have been twilight. "Extricate."

"Right. This is a spot I'm real anxious to see how you'll *extricate* yourself from."

The Ute sounded a hopeful note: "There is an extenuating circumstance that I haven't mentioned."

"Which is?"

As the landscape was illuminated by a white-hot flash of lightning, Moon opened his mouth. *"Kaboom! Barroooom!"*

No. The Southern Ute tribal investigator is not the sort of oddball who goes around yelling, "Kaboom! Barroooom!" The dramatic sound-effects were earsplitting peals of thunder, which made it impossible for anyone who was not (like the chief of police) standing within a yard of the Ute to hear what Moon said.

"You did, did you?" Scott Parris slapped his thigh and chuckled. "Well that's about the damnedest thing I ever heard of." *Ol' Charlie Moon sure takes the cake.*

The man credited with taking cakes squinted his eyes at the still-grumbling sky. "I hope the lady has a sense of humor."

"An FBI agent? Hah! You might as well hope it'll start raining two-ounce gold nuggets and lemon drops." The balding man removed his felt fedora, twisted it to squeeze out about a half pint of rainwater. "So how're you gonna wiggle your way out of this mess?"

"I'll need a while to think about it."

"Well soon as you know, take me along for the show." Parris pulled the soggy imitation of a hat onto his head. "I wouldn't miss it for all the beer in . . . in . . ."

"Milwaukee."

"Right."

"But I'm not taking you along to grin like an ape while I explain myself to the fed."

"Hey—I've had a tough day. Don't spoil my chance to have a little fun."

"Forget about fun until this business is finished." Moon aimed a finger at his friend's chest. "You're a cop and you've got a job to do."

"And I bet you're going to tell me how to do it."

"Since you asked, I'm happy to oblige." Moon seated himself on the redwood chair that Parris had vacated. "While I'm coming up with a rock-solid solution to the Annie Rose problem, you go into the parlor and keep an eye on Bill Smith."

"How about I read the bastard his rights and place him under arrest." *Then shoot him down like a mad dog when he does the least little thing I don't like. Such as looking at me cross-eyed or saying "you know" three times in the same breath.*

"Read him *War and Peace* if you have a hankering," Moon said. "But I'd appreciate it if you'd let Special Agent Rose make the arrest."

"Yeah, I guess you're gonna need to make all the points you can with her." Parris hitched his wet khaki britches up a notch and glanced at the unlocked kitchen door. "On my way, I'll stop in the parlor and say howdy to your female prisoner. I'll also explain how you're not exactly the brightest bulb in Granite Creek County, and ask her to go easy on you on account of your mentally challenged condition." The lawman grinned like a Tennessee possum. "After I'm through sweet-talking the lady, you shouldn't get more than five years behind the walls, which oughta be enough to straighten you out."

"Don't even so much as think about speaking to Special Agent Rose." Moon pointed toward the west porch. "You'll enter the parlor through the front door. Smith'll be right where he was when you looked in the window—sitting by the fireplace."

Fireplace sounds good. But there was a minor complication. "The front door's locked."

"Hold out your mitt."

"What for?"

"I've got a present for you."

Present sounds good, too. Parris extended his hand for the gift.

Moon slapped a brass door key on his palm.

CHAPTER FIFTY-THREE

SINNER MAN

Bill Smith had aged decades since the cunning Ute had maneuvered him to that singular seat by the Columbine parlor fireplace; the villain's vain attempt to get his fingers on the concealed pocketknife had been the last straw. His gallows eyes stared unseeing at the waning flames; his chin dripped sweat on a shirt already soaked with odorous perspiration. Smith's face was twisted in that hellish, soul-warping anxiety reserved for those who are truly condemned and *know it*.

The criminal's decline was not merely a matter of outward appearance. Deep inside, where his soul lived, an essential essence had withered and died. The once-brash man was almost without hope. Almost.

Despite everything, a trace of stubborn, mannish pride survived.

THE SETUP

The metallic rattle of hard rain on the porch roof was drowning out all the ordinary sounds. What Smith *did not hear* was of some significance:

The chief of police turning a key in the well-oiled latch.

The west porch door gently opening.

And closing.

The creak of Scott Parris's wet boots as the heavy man slowly made his way across the parlor.

The murderer-torturer-cannibal was intensely aware of only one aspect of the lawman's entrance—the transient draft from the briefly opened door, which swept across the parlor to swirl up the chimney and blow a puff of gray ashes onto the hearth.

In his rapidly deteriorating state of mind, Smith imagined this *visitation* to be the vengeful spirit of one of his dozens of victims. *It must be somebody who can't wait until my ghost crosses over.* He sweated harder. *I bet it's that young woman whose two children we roasted right in front of her.* Or—and this chilled him to the marrow—*It could be that old blind man in Texas we poured gasoline on and set afire.* The superstitious criminal blinked at the flames and wondered what eye-for-eye, tooth-for-tooth justice would be meted out on his wretched soul. *Maybe I should've been more careful about what I did to folks.* But such moments of reflection pass all too quickly for those of Smith's ilk, and the porch door had closed behind him. *I don't feel any coldness now.* Indeed, his place by the fireplace was absolutely cozy. *And I don't see nothing.* He hoped that the ghost had departed. But he realized that the hateful spirit was probably lurking somewhere close-by . . . *just waiting to get its clammy hands on me.*

Parris was now close enough to reach out and touch the back of the man's head. *I bet he'd jump out of his skin!* The lawman resisted the temptation.

The assassin went tense as a drawn bow when, by some means, he sensed the presence behind his chair. "Who's there?"

A gruff voice growled back at him, "Who wants to know?" *That don't sound like a ghost.* "Uh . . . the name's Smith."

"Well get your lazy butt outta the chair, Smith, and pitch some wood on the fire." Parris shuddered. "I'm wet as fresh seaweed and cold as a Yukon whore's heart and you're sittin' in my favorite spot!"

"Well I'd sure do that if I could." Smith's hope surged. "Thing is—I can't get up."

"Why not—you *glued* to the damn seat?"

"Uh—no." *Not exactly.*

"Well what's this—why, somebody's strapped your wrists behind the chair."

"That's why I can't get up. And because . . ." Smith drew in a long breath, "because I'm sitting on an explosive device that'll detonate if I get off it."

Parris gave his victim the gimlet eye. "Don't you mess with me, boy—I don't like to be played for a fool."

"No, it's the honest truth. That crazy Indian put me in this chair." Smith pointed with his nose. "The explosive's under the cushion."

"That's about the damnedest thing I ever heard." The lawman paused as if considering the likelihood of such a thing. "Ol' Charlie Moon may have a screw or two loose, but I never heard of him making anybody sit down on a bomb."

"Well, maybe he never did before, but he sure did to-night!"

"If Charlie did a thing like that, you must've done something to deserve it." Parris snickered at the chair-bound man. "What'd you do—rustle some of his prize stock? Try to cheat him at poker? Use his personal toothbrush?"

"I didn't do *nothing*." Smith groaned. "About an hour or so ago, there was gunshots down by the machine shop and then it caught on fire and the roof blew off. I came over to the headquarters to see what was goin' on, and the boss invited me in nice as you please. He brought me over here by the fire and said, 'Bill, have a seat and warm yourself.' And I said, 'I don't mind if I do,' and when I sat down I heard this peculiar noise under the cushion and asked him what it was. That treetop-tall Indian says, 'Bill, you've just set down on a gadget that'll blow your butt off if you move it so much as a quarter inch.'"

"That don't sound like Charlie." Parris put on a worried expression. "Unless he's on one of his drunks."

"Well, maybe he is."

In the faint firelight, Parris could see that the whites of Smith's eyes were yellow. He backed two paces away. "Maybe I ought to go look for Charlie and ask him about—"

"Don't go anywhere—you've got to help me!"

"I don't know." Parris backed up another step. "I wouldn't want to get blown to kingdom come."

"Please. I know how to . . . uh . . . what I mean to say is—I *think* I might be able to disarm this damned thing."

"No kidding." Parris gave him a wide-eyed look. "How'd you do that?"

"Well, I figure all I need is a slender blade."

What a sneaky bastard. "Let me get this straight—you want me to give you a knife?"

"Not just any knife—the blade shouldn't be sharp, or too wide." *I might cut one of the wires.* Smith made a slight movement, cringed when the aluminum pie pan crunched again. "I need something dull. Like a butter knife. Or better still, a letter opener."

Parris took his time thinking about this. "Charlie has an office upstairs. I think I might've seen a letter opener on his desk."

"Then go get it for me."

"This better be on the level." The chief of police reached out with a clenched hand. "If this is some kinda sicko joke, I'll wring your neck like you was a fat chicken for Sunday dinner."

"I swear on a stack of Bibles—I'm telling you the honest truth."

"Be careful now. You know what happens to folks that play fast and loose with the Scriptures. 'Their eyeballs fall out and their socks catch on fire.' Second Deuteronomy, Chapter Eleven."

"Uh . . . right. But if I'm lying, I hope I get struck by a lightning bolt!"

"Well all right then." Parris marched across the parlor to the stairs. "I'll see if I can find you a letter opener."

Up the stairway he went. Down the second-floor hallway. Into Charlie Moon's office, where the desk was barely visible in a soft glow of moonlight. *Looks like the storm's over.* Parris used a small penlight to illuminate the desk. Nothing on top except for the brass gooseneck lamp, the cranberry-glass vase containing a yellow No. 2 pencil, a ballpoint, and an old-fashioned fountain pen. *My buddy's a regular neat freak.* He opened a drawer, then another, and spotted Moon's fancy ivory-handled letter opener. And something else.

An envelope labeled:

> TO BE OPENED IN THE EVENT OF MY DEATH
> C MOON

CHAPTER FIFTY-FOUR

A DELICATE SITUATION

Charlie Moon's objective was clear enough; what he needed was to get on the right side of Special Agent Annie Rose. How to accomplish this taxed his gray matter. After considering one or two complex plots and not a few subtle ploys, he came to a firm conclusion: *I'll just play it by ear.*

Armed with manly determination, he entered the darkened kitchen with the firm gait of a man who owns the premises. After touching a lighted match to the kerosene lamp's curled wick, the rancher removed his John B. Stetson hat and headed for the dining room. Mr. Moon approached the table where the lady was seated, her back straight and stiff, her upper lip stiffer.

If Special Agent Rose's eyeballs had been equipped with high-power lasers, the beams would have burned holes all the way through Moon's face and out the back of his skull. And Annie would have enjoyed the process. She glared at her persecutor. "Well, where have you been?"

"Outside." Moon placed his hat on the table brim up, like any sensible cowboy. (So all his luck wouldn't spill out.)

"Doing what—looking for additional victims?"

He gazed at the angry little woman. Thoughtfully. To enhance the impression of a man who has been engaged in deep meditation, even transcendent contemplation, he said, "I've been thinking."

"Fancy that." About to toss her head in derisive fashion,

she remembered her precarious situation and raised an impudent chin instead. "And what did you think about?"

"Oh, this and that." He seated himself at the dining table. "Like how this has been a stressful evening for everybody concerned."

"Tell me about it," she snapped.

"There've been gunshots. A fire in the machine shop, and an explosion that blew the roof off. I've had to make some snap decisions."

Annie Rose sniffed. "What is this I smell—the sickening odor of a feeble excuse?"

She does have a sense of humor. "Now that things have calmed down, I've had time to reflect upon my actions."

"And what have you concluded?"

"That even though there's plenty of evidence to tie you in with Bill Smith and the Family, I realized there's just the slightest chance you might be what's called . . . a victim of circumstance."

Special Agent Rose arched an artfully plucked brow. "Really?"

"Yes ma'am." *She sure is pretty when she's mad.* "And that being the case, I mean to give you the benefit of the doubt."

"How very generous of you."

Seemingly impervious to caustic sarcasm, the lanky man leaned back in his chair. "While I was outside thinking things over, it occurred to me that there might be some other plausible explanation for you packing a concealed weapon— and being the only soul on the Columbine with a satellite telephone when the landlines and cell-phone tower was taken out, and knowing *what* you'd sat down on when you heard the pie-pan crunch."

The lady seriously considered spitting in his eye. "I'm sure you're just dying to tell me—so don't hold back on account of my not having the least interest in a single word you're saying."

"Thank you kindly." Recalling a trick Aunt Daisy had taught him when he was a twelve-year-old, Moon picked up a pepper shaker. He passed it from one hand to the other until it *vanished*.

Annie's eyes popped. *How did he do that?*

The Ute conjurer continued as if nothing remarkable had occurred. "Way I figure it, there's about one chance in a hundred thousand that you're some kind of undercover cop." He closed his empty left hand to make a fist. Opened it to show her the pepper shaker. "You could be a state-police officer." He made the fist again. "Or a U.S. marshal." The sly man opened the sly hand to show her an empty palm. "You might even be an FBI agent."

Where did the pepper shaker go? "What a preposterous idea."

"When the notion first came to mind, that's what I thought." He flipped *nothing at all* from his left hand.

Annie's gaze could not help following Moon's as he watched an invisible something rise almost to the beamed ceiling and hang there for an instant before falling.

The performer caught a solid-as-rock pepper shaker in his right hand, and pointed the object at his audience. "I asked myself—why would an undercover cop be plying her spooky craft out here, of all places?" He placed the pepper dispenser on the dining table. "Then it occurred to me that your assignment might be to stake out the Columbine. Just in case some bad guys from the Family showed up to create some mischief." He flashed the thousand-watt smile. "What do you think about that?"

A prickly silence preceded the lady's tart reply. "I am surprised that you were capable of coming up with such an original and complex theory." Annie raised her chin, which had advanced from impudent to downright insolent. "Are you sure you didn't have some assistance from an adult?"

"Now that's an unkind thing to say."

"Compared to what's coming, you will consider it a compliment."

"All I wanted to do was let you know that on the off chance that I've made a mistake, I'm sorry as all get-out."

"I do not doubt it for a second. But being *sorry* is not sufficient to atone for your crimes, Mr. Moon—and I use that word in a quite literal sense. It is a serious federal offense to . . . to . . ."

"To interfere with an FBI agent while she's pursuing her official duties?"

"Yes it is! And it is far worse to deliberately put her life in jeopardy. And I could go on. But your being sorry—even being bone-headed stupid—does not alter the fact that you have committed several felonies." She made her hands into tight little fists and leaned just slightly forward, as if pouncing on her victim and punching his face black-and-blue was at the very top of the list of things she most yearned to do. "Almost two hours ago, I called for a helicopter and six armed agents. They have apparently been delayed by the storm, but as soon they discover what you have done, an explosives expert will be dispatched from Denver to get me out of this predicament. And make no mistake, Mr. Moon—I will relish filing charges against you. I shall clap my hands when you are indicted. I will stand up and cheer when you are found guilty of all charges. And when you are put behind bars for the rest of your unnatural life, I will celebrate with expensive fireworks and pink champagne!"

"Yes ma'am."

"And don't 'yes ma'am' me—I hate and despise that!"

"Sorry." He raised both palms to placate the lady. "I know I've messed up. And you've got every reason to be mad at me." Moon inhaled. "But before you get your hands all primed for clapping and order a case of champagne, there is what my defense attorney would call a 'mitigating circumstance.'"

"That your IQ is comparable to room temperature in an Inuit's igloo?"

"Uh—that might help sway a jury, but it's not what I had in mind."

"It is unkind of you to keep me in suspense. After all, I am a captive audience."

"Well, actually that's the point—you're nothing of the sort."

Her eyebrow arched again. "What do you mean by that opaque remark?"

"Just what I said. You're not a captive of any kind. Anytime you want to, you can get up from that chair."

Her brow furrowed. "You don't mean . . ."

"Yes I do." Moon cocked his head and this is what he said: "Never, in a billion-million years, would I trick a pretty lady like yourself into sitting down on an explosive device."

Pretty? "You . . . you wouldn't?"

The sweet-talker sensed a glimmer of light at the end of the tunnel. "Not if you buried me up to my neck in a hill of red killer ants and poured a gallon of honey over my head." He explained, "Cowboys don't do bad things like that to sweet young ladies."

Sweet? "They don't?"

Moon shook his head. "Code of the West."

She stared at the enigmatic westerner for quite some time. Long enough for a man who'd just shaved his chin to grow a noticeable beard. Or so it seemed to the Ute, who had never had to remove whiskers from his face. "Please tell me—if I am not sitting on one of the Family's notorious explosive contraptions, precisely what *is* under this cushion?"

He was pleased to tell her. "Nothing the least bit dangerous. Just an aluminum pie pan I found here in the kitchen when I was looking for a snack."

This revelation was not easy to come to grips with. "For all this time, I've been sitting on an ordinary pie pan—there's no explosive under the seat cushion?"

"That's right." Charlie Moon took this opportunity to remind his guest of a significant factoid: "I never actually said there was."

CHAPTER FIFTY-FIVE

HIGH ANXIETY

While Scott Parris was upstairs in Charlie Moon's office, and the repentant Ute was doing his level best to charm Special Agent Annie Rose into forgiving his understandable error, the murderous man sitting in front of the parlor fireplace had some time to kill. Not one to waste his thoughts on trivia, Bill Smith had been occupying his gray matter by pondering various and sundry issues that were of considerable and immediate importance. As is so often the case, this intense mental activity neither provided a solution to his problems nor calmed his troubled psyche. Two examples of this fruitless pondering come to mind.

First (following an urgent high-pressure signal from his bladder):

What'll I do if I have to take a leak? His concern was that if he lost control of his sphincter valve, would the release of an electrically conductive fluid onto the explosive booby trap set off the detonator? Unsure of the answer to this timely and pertinent question, Smith made up his mind to refuse any offer of refreshment that included a beverage. He was also determined to continue to sweat away as much of his internal body fluids as possible.

Second (with a brow-furrowing scowl):

I wonder if they have capital punishment in Colorado? If so, he concluded that his execution was more likely to be by injection of a deadly toxin into his veins than such arcane practices as sentencing a citizen to hang by his neck until he was thoroughly deceased, or by a firing squad (his choice). *But what if they still use an electric chair?* The very thought of being connected to high-voltage electricity made the felon shudder.

THE DEAL GOES DOWN

When Scott Parris left Moon's office, the normally uncomplicated fellow found himself in one of those thoughtful, brooding moods that a more philosophical type would have described as reflective. Or, if the philosopher wore horn-rimmed spectacles and smoked a curly-stemmed brier pipe—*pensive*. Not even halfway to pensive, the Granite Creek chief of police descended the carpeted stairway into the parlor without making a sound, approached the seated man from behind, and—put his hand on the assassin's shoulder.

An already tense Smith jerked like he had been electrocuted. He also swore under his breath.

Parris pretended not to notice the electrifying effect of his arrival. "How you doin', sport?"

"Uh—okay I guess." Smith stared straight ahead, squinting at the sooty fireplace. "You find me a letter opener?"

"Sure did."

"Then cut my hands loose and give it to me."

"Not so fast, Dog Face. While I was upstairs, I had some time to cogitate about your unlikely tale—and I don't believe Charlie Moon would do a mean thing like sitting a nice fella like you onto an explosive gadget." Parris patted Smith on the shoulder. "Way I figure it—ol' Charlie was just joshin' you."

"No—he—*wasn't*." This earnest assertion was punctuated by a vigorous head shake. "That Indian was dead serious. I move my butt offa this pillow, I am *monkey meat!*"

"What makes you so sure Charlie wasn't playing a prank on you?"

Smith hesitated. "Well . . ." Also faltered. "Thing is . . ." And dillydallied. "The guy was acting crazy. Like he thought I was some kinda outlaw."

"For all I know, maybe you are. Maybe that's why Charlie strapped you to this chair. But that don't convince me you're sittin' on some kinda rigged-up bomb. For all I know, all this stuff about dynamite and how you can make it safe with a letter opener is a scam—all you really want is to get cut loose. You figure you'll stick this blade between my ribs and be outta here faster'n a scalded jackrabbit."

"Then hold a gun to my head."

"Well . . . I might just do that."

"Look—I know this damned thing I'm sittin' on ain't no joke, because the Indian told me how the explosive contraption works. And it sounds like the real McCoy to me."

"Sounds like you know a little something about explosives."

"Sure I do. Few years back, I did some hard-rock mining up in Nevada."

"Tell me how Moon rigged this one."

"Uh . . . why's that important?"

"Before I cut the plastic restraints and give you a pointy instrument that you might blow yourself up with—and maybe me to boot—I'd like to know exactly how you intend to disarm whatever it is you're sitting on."

"Uh—it's kinda complicated. With electronic stuff and whatnot."

"Not a problem. In my younger days, I graduated from DeVry Technical Institute in Chicago. You ever hear of it?"

"I don't think so."

"It was on Belmont Avenue, just a few blocks east of Cicero. Great school. I learned how to repair TV sets, built an AM radio from scratch, even got myself a first-class FCC license. And for years after that, I was a ham-radio operator. So tell me about the detonator."

"Well, there's this battery that—"

"What kinda battery?"

"Nothing special—a standard nine-volt transistor. When

somebody sits on this damned thing, the pie pan crunches down on a coiled spring and makes contact with a stainless steel screw head—"

"Did you say *pie pan*?"

"That's what the Indian told me. Anyway, the pie pan makes an electrical connection that charges a capacitor—"

"Years ago, we called 'em condensers." Parris knelt by the remnants of the fire and held his hands out to the embers. "What kind of capacitor?"

"Uh, the Indian didn't say."

"Probably an electrolytic."

"Maybe so. The point is, I can get myself outta this situation if you'll help me."

"Oh, I don't know about *that*." Parris shrugged. "If Charlie Moon wants you dead, he must have his reasons."

"Listen to what I'm telling you—that Indian is *crazy*!"

"Sane or nutty, ol' Charlie's still my buddy."

Smith ground his teeth. "If I get blown to pieces, your buddy'll get charged with murder."

Parris seemed to mull this over. "Well, you've got a good point there. I'd hate to see ol' Charlie do hard time in the slammer." The chief of police got to his feet with a grunt. "Tell me how you'll do the trick with this letter opener."

"The way the Indian explained it to me, the pie pan is insulated from a stainless steel plate." Smith jabbed his finger at the pillow. "If I stick the blade through the explosive assembly, I ought to be able to short the pan to the plate; that'd drain the charge off the capacitor."

"Okay. But don't make your move till I get out of the house."

"I promise."

The cop cut the felon loose.

"Thanks." Smith rubbed his wrists. "You won't regret this."

"You will, if you try to pull a fast one—I'll shoot you deader'n hell." Parris was not kidding. He laid the letter opener on Smith's shoulder. "Count to twenty before you start punching holes in things. By that time, I'll be on the porch."

"You got it." Smith took the lethal-looking instrument in a trembling hand. He listened to Parris's boot heels click away toward the front door. He heard the squeak of the hinges as the door opened. The click of the latch as it closed.

What did the felon *not* hear?

The chief of police removing his Roper boots and returning stealthily to stand behind Smith's chair. But not too close. And not too far away.

CHAPTER FIFTY-SIX

SUSPENSE

Pulled this way and that by conflicting obligations and concerns, Charlie Moon had compromised by taking up a position in the dining-room end of the dark hallway that connected to the headquarters parlor, where a dangerous felon was (he believed) securely fastened to an armchair. That Scott Parris would have cut the man loose had not so much as entered the tribal investigator's mind.

Moon's strategic location served a twofold purpose.

First and foremost, it enabled the Ute to cock his left ear for any suspicious sounds from the parlor. Should Bill Smith get some fool notion and create even the smallest commotion, Mr. Moon would be all over him like Sidewinder on a coyote. The Ute's sensitive ear strained for the least whisper of sinister activity. *It's awfully quiet.* In the absence of any audible evidence, his fertile imagination conjured up ominous scenarios. *Maybe Smith's smarter than he looks.* Also worries. *I hope Scott's keeping a close eye on that sneaky cannibal rascal.* But of course he would be. The chief of police was one of those rare men you could count on to get the job done.

Purpose number two? While Charlie Moon busily listened, imagined, and worried about what Mr. Smith might be up to, the multitasking fellow was also *watching.* His entire visual attention was focused on the tense little woman seated at the Columbine dining table. Since her semi-hypothetical question ("I've been sitting on an ordinary pie pan—there's no explosive under the seat cushion?"), the FBI agent had not uttered a word. Which was not necessarily a good omen. On the contrary, her silence gave Moon another thing to worry about. *The lady's thinking things over.*

Charlie Moon figured this was one of those either/or situations and resorted to an internal assertion that was both inarguably true and entirely lacking in content: *Either she'll file charges or she won't.* Unable to read Annie Rose's expression, he estimated the odds to be about fifty-fifty, which is what poker players do when they don't have a clue. Having no other apparent options, he waited for the outcome. It wasn't easy: passivity was not Moon's long suit.

HER CONUNDRUM

Though enormously relieved to learn that she was in no danger of being mangled by a charge of high explosive, Special Agent Rose was not quite ready to celebrate. Indeed, the lady now found herself entangled in a complex situation that presented a frustrating mixture of opportunity and risk. *I could still think of a few things to charge Moon with.* Then, there was the downside. *But if I reveal how he duped me into sitting on a harmless pie pan for almost an hour, the anecdote would become the talk of the Bureau.* Her face burned. *My career would be toast.* It was all so terribly unfair. *I was sent here to protect this skinny Indian and his friends, and this is what I get.*

Annie hung her head, closed her eyes, and sighed. She would have cried, but FBI agents also have their Code. Weary of sitting, she made an effort to get up. Could not. She cleared her throat. "It seems . . ." *This is so humiliating.* "It seems that my legs have gone to sleep."

Moon helped the lady to her feet.

Unsteady, she had no option but to lean against the tall, lean man.

Which Moon did not mind. Indeed, the tribal investigator

began to think that things might just turn out all right after all, and decided to take the situation firmly into hand. (What a man.) He put his arm around her slender form. "Soon as your legs feel like walking into the parlor, I expect you'll want to arrest Mr. Smith."

Annie Rose looked up at the Ute's craggy face. The question she dared not ask, *could* not ask, was in her eyes. *Will you keep your mouth shut?*

Charlie Moon understood. Perfectly. But the delicate subject had to be approached in a roundabout way, which is to say—a circuitous path. "I might as well admit it, Special Agent Rose. I've made a fool of myself tonight, treating you like I did. I'd sure appreciate it if you wouldn't say anything about it."

The FBI agent also understood. Perfectly. Annie gazed at Moon with an expression that spoke of gratitude. And trust. And also just a touch of . . . No. That shall remain between the man and the woman.

Suffice it to say, he returned the lady's gaze.

The deal was done.

But, as is so often the case, there was One Last Thing.

Special Agent Rose glanced toward the dark hallway that tunneled through the darkness to the headquarters parlor. "There's something I'd like to ask you."

"Ask away." *She sure does have pretty eyes.*

"This Mr. Smith—does the Code of the West apply to him?"

"Yes it does." The Ute's face hardened. *And one way or another, I'll make sure he gets what's coming to him.*

Charlie Moon had no way of knowing that *what was coming* to Mr. Smith was—in a literal sense—just around the corner. And approaching rapidly.

CHAPTER FIFTY-SEVEN

PARLOR GAMES

The gravity of his situation was not lost on the gritty fellow who had gnawed the heads off writhing copperhead snakes, wrestled twelve-foot alligators, and fought men half again his size with his bare hands. The simple act of pressing a letter opener through a chair cushion would be the scariest thing Bill Smith had ever attempted.

As he tried to find the courage to do what was necessary, Smith's hand trembled. *If I don't poke a hole in that pie pan at just the right spot, the damn thing's liable to detonate and blow off both of my legs and mangle my butt and . . .* The full extent of the hideous injuries were too horrible to contemplate. But, try as he might, Smith could not evict the haunting images from his mind. He shuddered at the bloody memory of a terrified victim who had panicked and attempted to jump off the Family's improvised explosive device *before it could detonate.* And, like that terrified unfortunate . . . *I wouldn't die right away.* Thirty seconds of such suffering would seem an eternity. *But if I don't get away from here, I'll be arrested, tried, convicted, and sentenced.* This was a now-or-never situation. *I've got to chance it.* Trying to look on the bright side, Moon's prisoner had to squint to see just a tiny flicker of light. *With a little luck, this'll turn out all right.*

But, unlike courage, luck cannot be summoned up.

And there was another factor that might muddy up the waters. Chief of Police Scott Parris.

If Mr. Smith had been aware of the silent, shadowy form lurking behind his chair, the edgy assassin might have concluded that the Angel of Death had come to snatch his miserable soul.

Parris was no angel. Moreover—and this was perhaps the most unsettling aspect of the situation—the lawman was virtually oblivious to the painful drama being played out within arm's length. Whether his mental state was the result of simple stress or could be attributed to sinister machinations in some murky dimension of Reality that lies beyond mortal understanding, Granite Creek PD's top cop was experiencing the singular sensation of *slipping out of his body*. Whether this condition was actual or imagined is neither here nor there. What matters is that for all practical purposes—his conscious self was *elsewhere*.

More specifically, hovering in the midst of that sparsely populated cemetery atop Pine Knob.

While Smith prepared himself for his dangerous task, the lawman behind him dreamed.

Or so it seemed . . .

EPISODE SEVEN

His Crime Revealed

Scott Parris stood by the mound of earth whereunder his moldering corpse slept that long, dreamless sleep. As before, it was the graying slab of wood at the head of his grave that fascinated the visitor. The self-mourner mouthed the words as he read them:

SCOT PARIS
U.S. MARSHAL
1822–1877

HUNG FOR
BACK-SHOOTING

It was bad enough that the Indian hadn't spelled his name right. But Hung for Back-Shooting—what a helluva thing for Charlie Moon to write on my grave marker. *And not only that*—Who did I back-shoot? *The marshal figured it might've been the judge's favorite brother, who was a notorious horse thief and card cheat.* Or maybe it was that Sandwich Islands ukulele player over at the Tennessee Saloon that I never did like.

But maybes and mights were distinctly unsatisfying— like slurping up muddy ditch water when you craved a mug of cold beer. What Marshal Parris craved right now were answers. And, though they didn't put it this way in 1877—closure. This business of insulting epitaphs and not knowing who he'd back-shot was enough to make a fellow bite tenpenny nails in half and spit 'em in somebody's eye!

As it happened, there was a shortage of both nails and somebodys in the immediate vicinity.

No, that is only half right.

Parris realized that he was no longer alone on the Knob. He glared hatefully at the dark, sinister form of a man. What was so offensive about this uninvited guest? The brazen fellow was sitting on the U.S. marshal's grave maker. And, as if that affront were not sufficiently insulting, the newcomer was showing his backside to the marshal.

A man can take only so much guff before push comes to shove. But that is mere metaphor. Parris was way beyond either pushing or shoving. The marshal pulled his sidearm from a leather holster.

As they are apt to do at such moments, faraway on the prairie, a lonely coyote yip-yipped.

Parris aimed his weapon at the man's back.

In a lightning-scarred ponderosa on Pine Knob, a sooty-black owl hooted.

The lawman's gristly finger tightened on the trigger and—

* * *

Time out.

It is necessary to raise an issue that may prove to be pertinent.

As he is subjected to his unsettling out-of-body experience, Parris's finger tightens on the trigger of *what* firearm?

An imaginary 1870s-era six-shooter? No.

The marshal's finger is tightening on the actual trigger of an *ivory-gripped .44 caliber Magnum revolver.* Right. The sidearm that Charlie Moon confiscated from Bill Smith, and subsequently passed to Chief of Police Scott Parris on the Columbine headquarters porch. The deadly weapon is aimed directly at Mr. Smith's spine.

Unaware of the full extent of the trouble he was in, Bill Smith made up his mind to get on with the job. His teeth literally *on edge*, the felon placed the slender letter-opener blade at his crotch and began the nerve-jangling task of pressing it oh so gingerly through the cushion. The process was exquisitely agonizing. No one could see the assassin's pained grimace when the tip of the blade suddenly completed its path through the innards of the pillow and touched the pie pan. *Okay.* Sweat dripped from his nose. *So far, so good.* Also from his chin. *All I got to do now is pierce the thin aluminum pan, and drive the letter opener through the IED—without hitting anything that'll trigger the detonator—and short the pie pan to the steel plate.* He grinned. *Then I'm outta here.*

The hardened criminal set his jaw.

Clenched his yellowed teeth.

Ditto for an unmentionable orifice situated very near the cushion.

Well, here goes nothin'.

Bill Smith held his breath, made the fateful plunge, and—

CHAPTER FIFTY-EIGHT

BOOM!

—A deafening explosion jarred the Columbine parlor.

Annie Rose gasped, and clutched at her companion. *The IED has exploded!*

Charlie Moon held her close for a little longer than the situation called for. "I guess we'd better go see what happened." But he knew well enough. *Scott has shot him dead.*

Moon assisted the lady, whose sleeping legs were still dozing, into the parlor to see—

A punctured aluminum pie pan rolling merrily along the parlor floor.

Scott Parris standing behind Smith's overturned chair. In his hand, nothing less than the proverbial *smoking gun*. Bill Smith's .44 Magnum.

The victim?

Mr. Smith was facedown on the hearth. Silent as Death itself.

Annie shook her head in stunned disbelief. "He's *shot* the suspect!"

Scott Parris is no longer evening-dreaming about his grave marker atop 1870s Pine Knob, or that ill-mannered stranger sitting on his grave marker who needed shooting. The chief of police is wide awake, cold sober, and well aware of where he is and what he's done and would not have denied that the act was wholly intentional and had been carried out with considerable malice aforethought. Moreover (as can be seen by the satisfied grin on his face), the GCPD chief of police is quite pleased with himself.

Scott Parris has not shot Bill Smith in the back, or in any other part of his anatomy. Here's what happened: At that instant when the letter opener in Smith's hand had penetrated the pie pan, which event had been signaled by a nervous "eeep!" from the chair-bound assassin, the chief of police (who has a mischievous streak) had fired the thunderous shot into the *floor beneath Smith's chair.*

Moon and Annie Rose? The Ute and the FBI agent have noticed the bullet hole in the oak boards.

The victim? Mr. Smith is firmly convinced that the IED detonated when probed, that both his legs (along with other essential parts) have been blown off, and that the residue of his body shall expire shortly. This, despite the fact that he feels no pain? Most certainly. Smith has concluded that he is in a state of shock and (if he survives long enough) will eventually feel some considerable discomfort at those locations where said anatomical parts were severed by the explosion. In light of this unhappy expectation, he hopes to expire quickly, forthwith, and without undue delay.

Scott Parris continues to grin like a half-wit chimpanzee. His belly shakes with laughter. Indeed, the chief of police has not enjoyed himself so much in years.

CHAPTER FIFTY-NINE

IT AIN'T OVER TILL IT'S OVER

Loud enough to wake the dead? no.

But, like that fateful "Shot Heard Around the World" on April 19, 1775, at Old North Bridge in Concord, Massachusetts, the resounding boom of the .44 Magnum cartridge fired through the parlor floor by Chief of Police Scott Parris would lead to alarming consequences.

ASOK

His hateful heart still throbs; he is still *up there somewhere*. But the troublesome fellow will not remain there.

When the sole survivor of the B Team was jarred all the way back to full consciousness by the Granite Creek cop's thunderous gunshot, he was startled to find himself rather—sorry, there is no better way to put it—*out on a limb*. More to the point, the felon was faceup, spread-eagled on a sturdy cottonwood branch where his body had rested since being vigorously expelled from the Columbine machine-shop shed when his weed burner ignited the inferno, which incident caused so much commotion and subsequent comment.

The stunned man opened his eyes to the moonlit sky. *Where the hell am I?* A pertinent question for one of his religious persuasion. The avowed Satanist blinked several times. Asok's left eye was out of commission. His left ear picked up a few night-sounds, but on account of a ruptured drum his right one did not function.

Damn. I'm half blind and half deaf.

Not only that . . .

I'm freezing to death.

Ever so gradually, Asok realized why.

I'm naked as a Tennessee jaybird!

The latter assertion was an exaggeration.

True, his scuffed leather jacket, blue work shirt, smelly undershirt, faded jeans, over-the-calf socks, and boots had all been blown off by the violent force of his explosive expulsion from the shed. The single scrap of clothing left on his body was a pair of boxer shorts that were neither white, gray, nor navy. Brace yourself. Asok preferred red Valentine hearts on a pink background, and as if this fashion statement were not sufficient, a multitude of plump, naked infants armed with bows were aiming arrows at the hearts. And though a man who willfully wears such an appalling undergarment deserves not a speck or smidgen of pity, it must be admitted that the felon had awakened to find himself in difficult circumstances. Even so, for a laborer about to begin collecting the Wages of Sin, these misfortunes were merely the loose change in Lucifer's deep pockets.

As a chill breeze blew some of the soot off Asok's face, the B Team leader began to get annoyed. Then angry. Finally, downright chagrined. His dander all up, the fellow had one thing on his mind—revenge on that Indian who was responsible for turning a straightforward task into a fiasco. Figuring the best way to get even was to finish the job, he rolled over on the branch and fell about thirteen feet to the ground. A long way down. He moaned softly and ground his teeth. *I think I cracked my collarbone.*

Couldn't be helped.

The malefactor had some dirty work to do, so as soon as he got his wind back the game fellow crawled around, searching with his good eye and grubby hands for something that might come in handy. For the longest time, all Asok found were bits of smoldering rubbish. Broken bits of tree branches.

A tattered leather vest. Marmaduke's bloody left hand. Did this macabre discovery discourage our searcher? Not a chance. He tossed the dismembered appendage aside and kept right on mucking about.

Perseverance is a sterling quality, and one that is often rewarded. Which is why we should not be surprised that Asok eventually found what he was looking for.

A functional Winchester carbine.

CHAPTER SIXTY

IT'S ALMOST OVER

It was not an easy choice for a girl to make, but Sarah Frank did what is widely regarded hereabouts as the Right Thing. After murmuring a shy "maybe later" to the Wyoming Kyd's request for a dance, Sarah had followed Daisy Perika into the Big Hat kitchen, leaving Mr. Jerome Kydmann in the parlor with a hopeful, boyish smile pasted firmly on his face. Then (when no one was paying them any attention) the Ute-Papago orphan snatched up Mr. Zig-Zag and slipped out the kitchen door with the tribal elder. They met an expectant Sidewinder on the back porch. After installing the Columbine hound in the F-150 bed, the pair boarded the trusty pickup and headed lickety-split toward the big ranch on the west side of the Buckhorns, where, Daisy was convinced, her nephew was in some kind of serious trouble.

Twenty-nine minutes later, they were bouncing along the twisty-turny miles-long dirt lane that connects the ranch headquarters to the paved highway. The girl stretched her neck to look over the steering wheel. "What's that in the ditch?"

This was a purely rhetorical question. What *that* was, was perfectly obvious.

Daisy did not appreciate wasteful nuances of speech, or those who resorted to such pointless affectations. "It's a cop car." Recalling her recent telephone conversation with a particular cop, she added, "Looks like the one Scott Parris drives."

Sarah braked to a skidding stop and got out to shine a
flashlight into the black-and-white's open door. She hurried
back to her pickup. "There's nobody in it."

"You mark my words—those witches are behind whatever's going on here tonight." The shaman wagged a finger at
her wide-eyed apprentice. "They've run Scott off the road,
then carried his body off." *Most likely, to soak it in barbecue
sauce and roast it over a fire.* The morbid old woman shuddered.

Cringing at the thought of witches with enough gumption
to attack the tough-as-boot-leather chief of police, the girl
closed the pickup door, locked it, and got the truck moving
again.

The tribal elder shook her old gray head. "I told you
something was wrong here." *We'd better not go barging in
like a couple of idiots.* This business needed some serious
thinking over. "Switch your headlights off and drive slow."
Sarah did as ordered.

As they approached the foreman's residence, Daisy felt a
sudden prickling on the back of her neck, a thumping in her
temple that drummed, *Danger Ahead.* "Pull over and stop."

The obedient seventeen-year-old parked her truck at the
foreman's house.

Daisy looked up to see a lone raven gliding under the
stars. Beyond all probability, the aged shaman believed this
night visitor to be her special friend from *Cañón del Espíritu.*
The winged creature circled a scraggly elm in the Bushmans'
yard before settling lightly on a twisted branch. The shiny
black bird cocked its head, eyeballed the elder—and croaked
twice as if to say . . . *They're waiting.*

They were. Just on the other side of the Too Late Creek
bridge.

Lowering her gaze, Daisy saw a sight in the glimmering
moonlight that almost stopped her heart.

Three horses. Two riders.

Seemingly eager to get on with the night's grim work, the
pale, unmounted horse pawed at the muddy earth and snorted.

The riders on the pintos exchanged somber stares with the tribal elder.

Recognizing the orphan's parents astride the spotted ponies, Daisy felt a thrilling chill. *They've come for their daughter—the white pony is for Sarah.* The girl was destined to die tonight. *And there's not a thing I can do about it.*

Before Daisy had time for another thought, she was stunned to witness the descent from the dark heavens of an immense, glistening screen. It was (she thought) as if some unseen hand had pulled down a rolled-up white window shade. Whether this experience was merely her overstressed mind's hallucination or a genuine revelation, the effect was perfect. As she stared at the multidimensional projection on the silvery screen, the aged woman's vision was flawless. Daisy could see everything in all directions, be it the Columbine headquarters, the new horse barn, a hollow old pink-barked ponderosa housing a variety of rodents, a towering blue-granite mountain veined with gold and silver—and she could see all these marvels inside and out in the most minute detail. Moreover, the privileged old woman could hear every sound, and delighted in the soft murmuring of the creek, the joyous rippling of the rocky river, the gentle whispering of a damp breeze in the willows, and every single syllable that anyone might utter and—*what they were thinking*.

The shaman could even see and hear *herself*, urging Sarah to stay in the pickup.

Strangely, none of this frightened Daisy Perika.

CHAPTER SIXTY-ONE

THE SCROLL UNROLLED

Sarah Frank did not see her parents waiting patiently with the painted and plumed white pony for her to mount and ride, but she did share Daisy Perika's conviction that Charlie Moon was in some kind of trouble. And . . . *I can't just sit here in the pickup and wait to see what happens.* Ignoring the old woman's urgent pleadings to stay put, the teenager (accompanied by her aged tomcat) got out of the vehicle and strode down the lane toward the Columbine headquarters. The farther Sarah went, the faster her gait, the more hopeful her thoughts. The storm was certainly responsible for the slippery roads that had caused Mr. Parris's accident, and lightning striking a pole had probably knocked out the Columbine phones. *Charlie will be okay.*

But in spite of this effort to convince herself otherwise, Sarah *knew* that all was not well.

With a disgruntled Sidewinder locked in the back of the pickup, a grumbling Daisy in the cab, and Mr. Zig-Zag padding along at her heels, Sarah fairly trotted across the Too Late Creek bridge, her path illuminated by the glow of moonlight. Nearing the headquarters, she was pleased to see Charlie Moon's big automobile and a glimmer of firelight between the curtains in a parlor window. The scent of a few smoldering embers from the tool shed suggested a cheerful domestic scene that brought a smile to her lips. *I bet Charlie's sitting in front of the fireplace with a mug of coffee and—* Sarah saw something that stopped her in her tracks.

An almost-naked figure of a man was limping crossing the yard in the shadows. She watched him mount the head-quarters porch, one stealthy step at a time. *What's going on?* Sarah's blood ran cold as the sinister stranger peeked into the parlor window. She heard herself whisper, "What's that in his hand—a walking stick?"

Even in his present, somewhat addled state, Asok recognized a golden opportunity when he encountered one. This would be almost too easy for a fellow who enjoyed his work more when there was some measure of challenge in it. But, as Trout was apt to remind him, the bottom line was to get the job done. *I'll shoot the skinny Indian first, then the other guy, then the woman.*

He raised the carbine, took aim at the taller of the two men. . . .

Certain that Moon was in the parlor and about to be murdered, Sarah Frank shouted as loud as she could, "Charlie—he's going to shoot you!"

Everything happened within three heartbeats.

The startled B Team leader turned, instinctively fired the carbine at the slender, moonlit figure.

Sidearm drawn, Charlie Moon sprinted across the parlor to the porch door.

Special Agent Rose was right behind him, her 9-mm Glock ready for action.

Smith's .44 Magnum in his hand, Scott Parris got a glimpse of the seminaked man at the window. He shot through the glass. Three times.

Call it overkill. The first of the plump slugs severed Asok's spine at the base of his neck, the second took his left arm off at the shoulder, and number three punctured a lung and knocked him off the porch, facedown into the mud.

Call it coincidence. Chief of Police Scott Parris, aka *Marshal Scot Paris*, had shot his man . . . *in the back.*

IT'S OVER

Charlie Moon was kneeling beside Sarah.

The girl's pretty party dress was soaked in blood that gleamed black in the silver moonlight.

Moon caressed her pinched face with his fingertips. "Hang on, now. Everything's going to be . . ." The lie stuck in his throat. Everything was *not* going to be all right. Not tonight. Not tomorrow. Not *ever.*

Blood gurgled in the girl's throat, trickled from the corner of her mouth. Sarah had no breath left for final words.

Never mind.

The Ute read her lips in the moonlight.

I love you, Charlie Moon.

"I know." He felt her slipping away. "I love you too."

Did the seventeen-year-old hear these words she had yearned for for so long?

Only God and Sarah know.

He is silent.

She is gone.

Charlie Moon embraced the limp, frail corpse against his chest. The husk she had left behind was like a bag of brittle sticks.

The stricken man was unable to move. Or to make a sound.

Not so Mr. Zig-Zag. Sarah's spotted cat *screamed.*

The hound locked in Sarah's pickup *howled.*

Scott Parris threw his head back and roared like a wounded cougar.

Stunned by this night's final act of violence, Special Agent Rose stood as still as the trees, where there was not the least breath of breeze to stir a leaf. The woman listened. What did she hear?

The Columbine is not entirely silent.

Under the porch step, a fat black cricket chirps.

In the ruins of the burned-out machine-shop shed, a few embers snap and crackle.

Farther away, the rolling of the river can be heard.

But what is that faint throbbing, rhythmic whump-whump?

It is not the B Team leader's blood pump. Asok's spirit has also departed, but to a different destination than Sarah's.

The whump-whumping is generated by the whirling rotors of an incoming FBI helicopter. Finally, the cavalry Special Agent Rose summoned is arriving.

Daisy Perika? She remains in the parked pickup truck.

CHAPTER SIXTY-TWO

LEFT BEHIND

Oh god! Daisy Perika moaned in impotent fury. *Why couldn't it have been me instead of that poor little girl whose life had barely got started?* All alone in the pickup cab, the tribal elder hung her head and wept.

But wait. Is Daisy alone?

No. It would appear that someone is sitting beside her.

A gentle hand touched her shoulder. "Why're you crying, Aunt Daisy?"

The weeping woman turned to stare at the girl. *She's alive.*

Very much so. And Sarah's spotted cat was on the seat between them.

And then . . . *and then . . .*

Daisy looked up to see a lone raven gliding under the stars. Beyond all probability, the aged shaman believed this night visitor to be her special friend from *Cañón del Espíritu*. The winged creature circled a scraggly elm in the Bushmans' yard before settling lightly on a twisted branch. The shiny black bird cocked its head, eyeballed the elder—and croaked twice as if to say, *They're waiting.*

They were, of course.

Three ponies. Two riders. Just on the other side of the Too Late Creek bridge.

Like a cloud-shrouded sunrise, the truth dawned slowly on Daisy Perika. *It hasn't happened yet.*

But it would.

That white horse intends to carry someone away. The stubborn old woman shook her head. *But it won't be this little girl.* Daisy's dark face resembled chiseled obsidian. *Not if I have anything to say about it.* Seldom right, but never in doubt—Daisy knew exactly what to do. "Listen to what I tell you, Sarah. I want you to go into Pete Bushman's house and find the rusty old Colt pistol he keeps underneath that ugly little lamp stand beside his bed. It's in a Redwing shoebox, and there's a box of cartridges there too. Bring both of 'em to me."

"But—"

"No back talk. Just go do it!"

Small details tend to give credence to a carefully constructed lie, and are especially enhancing to a hastily contrived falsehood. But we must not be quick to censure others who commit such offenses. The way Daisy Perika saw it, her story about Pete Bushman keeping a *rusty old Colt* pistol in a *Redwing* shoe box underneath the *ugly* little lamp stand by his bed was not an outright, deliberate, one-hundred-percent, barefaced fabrication. For all she knew, the Columbine foreman probably did have an unsightly lamp stand by his bedstead, and it would be just like Pete to stash a six-shooter and some cartridges in a shoe box, and put the shoe box underneath the lamp stand, and the shoe box might have once contained a Redwing product. Not that the practical old soul tended to give much thought to such ephemeral issues as truth and falsehood, particularly when there was urgent business to attend to.

TAKING CHARGE

Even before the girl was out of sight, Daisy had pushed the cat off the seat and positioned herself behind the steering wheel. The instant her fingers found the ignition switch, she twisted the key and held her breath. The warm engine stuttered, grumbled, then settled down to a reassuring rumble.

So far, so good. But . . . *Now I've got to remember how to drive one of these things.* Searching her memory of past escapades in motor vehicles, Daisy took hold of the gearshift. *It must be in Park.* This wasn't so hard. *It's all coming back to me now.* She pulled the lever as far down as it would go.

The pickup lurched forward like the favorite at Churchill Downs exploding from the gate.

Having been unable to find a shoe box anywhere in the Bushmans' dark bedroom, Sarah Frank heard the sound of her F-150 roaring away and realized that once again—she'd been *had*. The girl emerged from the foreman's residence just in time to see her treasured pickup go careening across the Too Late Creek bridge, watch it bounce off the left railing, swerve to bump into the right one. *Oh, no!*

Wringing her hands in dismay, the girl (as old-timers like to say) *took off after it.*

SAINT DAISY THE SELFLESS

Barreling along like the Night Train from Memphis, Daisy Perika was pleased to see the three spirit-ponies and two riders move aside at her approach. *That's right, get outta my way before I run you down!* The tribal elder was absolutely delighted to spot the seminaked man with the carbine—who had not yet taken up his firing position at the parlor window. *Wa-hoo—I'm just in time!*

ASOK THE REPROBATE

As he crossed the headquarters yard, the half-deaf Asok did not hear the approach of the pickup truck. He did hear Daisy toot the horn, and would have seen the headlights come on if the flustered driver had managed to find the appropriate switch. Diverted from his primary objective, which was to take a gander into the parted curtain on the headquarters porch, the man who had already survived several ordeals this evening turned to deal with his current problem. Seeing a vehicle without lights bearing down on him, it took no great stretch of Asok's meager intellect to conclude that the driver (whom he assumed was a man) was not kindly disposed toward him. *He's gonna run me down!*

Prepared to die in Sarah's place, Daisy muttered, "Go ahead, you two-bit half-wit—shoot me dead."

Asok did his level best, but the urgency of his situation called for a shooting that was more or less "from the hip." No matter what we may've heard about the legendary accomplishments of Old West gunslingers, shooting a firearm without looking down the barrel tends to degrade a fellow's marksmanship.

Bam! The first slug penetrated the F-150's radiator.

Bam! Number two clipped off the radio antenna.

Bam! The third lead projectile passed through the windshield to whistle past the driver's right ear and spray her face with tiny shards of sharp glass.

HER BEATIFICATION IS PUT ON HOLD

This unpleasant experience did nothing to endear the shooter to the cantankerous old woman. Indeed, the sting of a sliver of glass in her eye tended to distract our heroine from her sacrificial mission. Daisy's natural instincts (anger and aggression) took over. All the furious woman could think about was *getting even*. "Oh, I wish I had me a loaded pistol so I could shoot back!" The vengeful wish reminded the bloodthirsty woman that she did have a lethal weapon in her possession.

A model F, 150-caliber, V-8 projectile.

Mrs. Perika was no shooter-from-the-hip. Dead-eye Daisy got her target lined up with the chrome-cougar ornament Sarah had installed on the hood, and *stepped on the gas.*

Unnerved by this bold frontal attack, the terrified terrorist dropped his weapon and made a run for it.

DAISY'S REVENGE

About a half second after the firing of the third shot from Asok's carbine, Charlie Moon burst through the west-porch door, pistol in hand.

Armed with the .44 Magnum he'd fired into the floor under Bill Smith's chair, Scott Parris almost knocked his Ute friend over in his attempt to get out and get in on the action.

Special Agent Annie Rose was close behind, her recovered Glock 9-mm automatic at the ready.

Despite uncharitable rumors to the contrary, and that occasional exception that serves to prove the rule: Sworn officers of the law do not use their deadly weapons lightly. By training and temperament, these trusted guardians of our lives and property prefer to find out a little something about what's going on before contributing to the carnage.

What the tribal, town, and federal cop witnessed in the moonlight did little to clarify the situation.

A white man—apparently of the semi-nudist persuasion—was being pursued by a pickup truck whose punctured radiator was spewing steam in great, gray puffs. The chase-ee was sprinting toward the river as rapidly as his spindly legs would carry him, which was not quite fast enough.

With every stride of its intended victim, Mr. Pickup was gaining ground.

Asok made a hard left behind the new horse barn and disappeared from sight. So did the truck.

It was much like one of those tense periods at NASA's Houston Control, where edgy technicians watch yard-wide computer terminals as a tiny spaceship passes behind the moon. While the capsule is on the far side, there is no way of knowing whether the astronauts are safe or have perished in some unforeseen disaster. One can only wait and drum one's fingers on the console in front of the flat-panel display.

Having nothing handy to drum fingers on, Tribal Investigator Moon, Chief of Police Parris, and Special Agent Rose held on to their sidearms and waited for the situation to clarify itself.

From somewhere on the yonder side of the barn, there was a sound of wood splintering as the pickup smashed something or other to flinders. Almost simultaneously, a heart-rending shriek from Asok, who imagined himself being flindered.

Moon leaned, mumbled to his buddy, "Twenty bucks on the truck."

"You're on." Parris grinned. What a dandy night this had been.

The running man reappeared first, skinny legs and arms pumping like pistons.

"Here he comes." Parris raised his fist. "Go for it!"

After losing some ground in a wide turn, the F-150 also completed the orbit—now spewing searing vapors like an enraged dragon.

Catching a glimpse of the driver, the Ute groaned. *I should've known.*

Sarah Frank showed up at about this time, to witness the wacky chase. It did not even occur to her to wonder, *What's Aunt Daisy up to now?* Though the tribal elder's behavior might seem somewhat peculiar to a person who was sane, Daisy always had her reasons—which she never bothered to explain.

Encouraged by putting a few additional yards between himself and his single-minded pursuer, Asok apparently intended to make another circle around the horse barn—perhaps in hope that the truck would run out of gas (or steam) before he did. The outcome of his intended strategy will never be known, because in the murky moonlight the sprinter did not see the horse trough. He stumbled over it, tumbled facedown in the mud.

"Hah!" (Daisy.) "I've got you now!"

Despite the many dark sins that had brought Asok to the predicament he found himself in, one feels compelled to give the man credit for having a measure of grit. The plucky fellow got to his feet like a bunged-up rodeo cowboy that'd been bucked off a fire-eyed bronco, and clearly meant to make another go at it, but—

What happened next is entirely too grisly to merit a detailed description.

Suffice it to say that Daisy ran the pickup over Asok. And that after doing so, she braked it to a stop—possibly to determine whether she had hit the runner or the horse trough—and backed up to find out. While chugging along in Reverse, she rolled the F-150's knobby tires over the unfortunate terrorist for a second time.

Enormously satisfied with her night's work, Daisy shut off the ignition and took a deep breath. *I feel twenty years younger.*

Her long-suffering nephew sighed and holstered his pistol.

Sarah stood speechless. *She's killed that man!*

Mr. Zig-Zag puttered a satisfied purr.

Still locked in the back of Daisy's assault vehicle, Sidewinder barked just to let folks know he was there.

Scowling at the felon who'd been smashed like roadkill, Scott Parris pocketed the confiscated .44 Magnum. *Looks like I owe Charlie twenty dollars.*

Annie Rose put away her Glock automatic. *Everybody on the place is insane.* A harsh judgment, but the federal undercover cop has had a difficult evening.

White Shell Woman brushed aside a cloud to beam on the gathering. A measure of peace and quiet returned to the Columbine.

The edgy FBI agent listened.

Charlie Moon had also cocked his ear.

What did they hear?

The whump-whumping of an incoming helicopter. FBI.

The cavalry Special Agent Rose had summoned was finally arriving. Which was what she'd been expecting, but the no-nonsense fed had the eeriest sensation that . . . *This is the* second *time tonight I've stood out here and heard the Bureau copter coming in.*

But that was absurd, so she filed it in a dusty folder marked DÉJÀ VU and forgot about it.

CHAPTER SIXTY-THREE

TYING UP A FEW LOOSE ENDS

Asok did not perish under the pickup's tires. It may have been because the muck in the rain-soaked barn lot was about a foot deep, or because he was the luckiest man in the county named after Granite Creek. Whatever the reason, Daisy's victim survived with approximately two dozen fractured bones, a ruptured spleen, and a mind that would never quite recover from the violent evening's final ordeal. Mr. A. was destined to spend his remaining years in a twelve-by-ten-foot room with padded walls and steel bars on the single window that overlooked a verdant valley watered by a fine river.

Without delving into tedious legal technicalities, it shall be reported that no charges were filed against Daisy Perika. The Family felon, who would be indicted and tried on several murder counts, had, after all—taken three shots at the tribal elder. Asok insisted that he had fired in self-defense, and those familiar with the Ute elder's hair-trigger temper did not doubt the injured man's testimony. And though additional mitigating circumstances would never be admitted by District Attorney Pug Bullet as influencing his decision to overlook Daisy's "potential technical infraction of the law," they did play a prominent role. Three examples are herewith provided.

The woman who had deliberately assaulted the semi-nude, unarmed-at-the-moment citizen with malice aforethought was Charlie Moon's aunt.

Daisy was a member in good standing (more or less) of the Southern Ute tribe.

Also a lifelong citizen of Colorado.

By contrast, Asok wasn't anybody's aunt, and belonging to a tribe of insatiable cannibals did not help. Most damning of all, he was from *out of state.*

The three ponies and two riders?

By the time she completed her madcap race with Asok, Daisy had almost forgotten about these sinister apparitions. And when they did come to mind, the shaman did not see them loitering about the Columbine. She had no doubt that sooner or later they would return and that . . . *Somebody will have to ride that white pony.*

Possibly.

But in the meantime, in between golden dawns and soul-renewing dreamtimes, the feisty old woman still has a few precious hours to burn.

Daisy Perika will not waste one of them fretting about the future.

CHAPTER SIXTY-FOUR

THREE WEEKS AFTER DAISY'S
PICKUP-TRUCK ASSAULT

On those still nights when a full-faced white shell woman illuminated his Columbine bedroom with silvery moonshine, Charlie Moon would occasionally lie awake.

And think.

Oh, about various matters. Such as—

Maybe I'll put a hundred head of Texas longhorns over on the north range.

My foreman won't retire till he's six feet under, but it's high time I eased the Bushmans over to the Big Hat, where Pete and Dolly wouldn't have to do any real work.

Jerome Kydmann would make a dandy foreman for the Columbine.

And—

FBI Intel is dead certain that Bill Smith isn't Trout, and they're just as sure that the hardware-store robbers were the Family's C Team, and that the bad apples who showed up on the Columbine was the B Team.

Which conclusions by the feds raised unsettling questions.

If Smith isn't Trout, who is?

Where's the Family's A Team?

And . . .

What's their next move?

Such prickly issues tended to keep Charlie Moon awake well into the wee hours. On this particular night, the memory of a seemingly insignificant encounter bubbled up from the bottom of his subconscious. As is so often the case with the sons of Adam, his recollection involved a woman—but in this instance, not a particularly appealing female. As his mind reconstructed the embarrassing encounter with the pushy tourist who had asked for his autograph, Moon recalled something the woman had said. Something that made him get out of bed and pace the floor.

It's probably a distorted memory.

He knew it wasn't. And Moon knew something else.

If I don't do something about it, I won't get a wink of sleep all night.

But what could he do?

Pass the buck, that's what.

THOUSAND OAKS, CALIFORNIA

FBI Special Agent Lila Mae McTeague was deep in a restful sleep when her telephone jangled. The lady groaned, grabbed the instrument, and blinked at the caller ID. *What's he doing calling me in the middle of the night?* A silly question, she realized. Back when they were an *item*, Charlie had developed an annoying habit of calling at the most indecent hours. This barely warm ember of an Old Flame had just about decided to let her ex-boyfriend have a conversation with her voice mail when she reminded herself that the Southern Ute tribal investigator had not telephoned her at home in almost two years. And that she had urged Charlie to contact her *at any hour* if he thought of anything that might assist the Bureau's search for the still-at-large members of the Cannibal Family. She pressed the Talk button and tried to sound civil. "What's up, Charlie?"

His deep voice boomed in her ear. "Sorry to call at this time of night, but I just thought of something."

The federal cop plopped her bare feet onto the carpeted

floor and reached for the yellow pad and ballpoint on her bedside table. "Tell me about it."

"Wind your memory back to that fine morning when I met you and Scott for lunch. You were waiting for me in the private dining room in the Silver Mountain Hotel."

"Okay. I'm there."

"About a minute before I showed up, I met this woman in the hallway." Moon cleared his throat. "She'd seen that stuff on the TV about the ABC Hardware robbery and wanted to talk to me about it."

Lila Mae smirked as she made hurried shorthand notes. "Another of your devoted fans?"

"I don't think so." The business about an autograph was too embarrassing to think about, much less to mention to Lila Mae.

She felt the warmth of Charlie Moon's blush. "Then she must have been a card-carrying member of the ACLU who objected to your use of excessive violence in subduing the alleged felons."

"You might be about half right." Moon's tone was flat. "She wasn't the sort that cares much about other folks' civil liberties. But it'd be another matter if the armed robbers were her friends . . . or relatives."

The FBI agent's pen stopped dead on the pad. *Charlie's onto something.* "You think this tourist was a member of the Family?"

"That and more. I'll wager you a brand-new fifty-dollar bill that I was talking to Trout."

"I'll pass." She had learned the hard way never to bet against Charlie Moon. "Tell me how you reached this conclusion."

"The woman in the Silver Mountain Hotel introduced herself as one Daphne *Donner.*"

McTeague frowned at her oak-paneled bedroom wall. "As in the Donner party—those snowbound California settlers who resorted to cannibalism?"

"That's right." *I'll have to start paying closer attention to what people say.*

The FBI agent frowned. "That's an interesting coincidence, Charlie—but a little thin, don't you think?"

"There's more. This self-proclaimed Daphne Donner mentioned being from Alder Creek."

McTeague searched her encyclopedic memory. Came up with a zero. "Okay, I give up."

"While they were trying to keep from starving, the Donner family camped at Alder Creek."

McTeague sprang off her bed. "It must have been Trout. And she was *teasing* you!"

The mortified tribal investigator sighed. "That's what it looks like."

When confronted with a conundrum, McTeague tended to mumble to herself. "But why would she take a chance like that?"

Moon grunted. "Because she figured me for a dope."

"No." The fed shook her head. "I don't think so." *Maybe she's a danger freak who gets her kicks from adrenaline rushes.* But that didn't fit the Bureau's profile of the individual who planned the Family's crimes with such meticulous attention to detail. And Trout was particularly careful about concealing her identity. *So why did she bait Charlie with a reference to the tragic experiences of the Donner party?*

In her entire life, Ms. Lila Mae McTeague· had never posed a more relevant question, and the truth would have stunned her. Trout had not cared whether Charlie Moon caught the Donner hint or not, because the Family's chief assassin planned to— Hold on. McTeague is about to butt in.

"Was our Ms. Donner a guest of the Silver Mountain?"

"Most likely. Aside from a few private dining rooms, there wasn't anything but first-floor guest rooms in the direction she was coming from."

Lila Mae jotted that down, then poised her pen for some furious scribbling. "Give me a physical description of the suspect."

Moon did the best he could, capped it off with, "And she was just a tad cross-eyed."

Miss Know-It-All assumed a crisply pedantic tone. "I

believe you mean that the lady was afflicted with strabismus."

"Tropia."

McTeague frowned. "What?"

Moon grinned. "It's a synonym for stabismus—but you'd
know that."

"Oh, right. Tropia." *Big smart Aleck.* "So what did Trout
have on her mind?"

"Women's minds have always been a mystery to me."

The pretty woman in Thousand Oaks rolled her big eyes.
"Why would the head of the Family want to chat with you
about the hardware-store shoot-out?"

"I figure she was sizing me up."

"For what?"

"Her roasting spit."

"I doubt it." McTeague doodled a stick man with a cowboy hat. "You're too skinny for a Family barbecue."

"Come to think of it, she did say something about me not
having much meat on my bones."

"Were there any witnesses to this encounter?"

"Hobart Watkins showed up while me'n the woman were
talking, so he must've gotten a look at her." Anticipating her
next question, Moon added, "Hobart's a stockman with a
twenty-section spread he calls the Little Texas. It's about
twenty miles south of Granite Creek."

"That's enough for now; I need to jump right on this.
Good night, Charlie."

"Good"—sharp click in his ear—"night, Lila Mae." *Just
like old time*s.

His duty duly discharged, Citizen Moon was sound asleep a
few heartbeats after his head hit the pillow. By and by, the
hardworking man was rewarded by a pleasant dream.

*Light as a ghost-eagle's feather, Charlie Moon drifted
over Ignacio Creek, under the heavy branches of a fine apple orchard where honey-bees buzzed, over a grassy yard
and toward Loyola Montoya's fine farmhouse, which was
painted a dazzling white with blue trim around the doors*

and windows. Passing over the back porch and through the closed kitchen door, the dreamer was pleased to see everything from the maple dining table to the iron cookstove looking so shiny and new, just like they had been in 1935, when Loyola Montoya was a starry-eyed bride. And despite the fact that the woman bustling around the kitchen was also young—and remarkably pretty—the Ute recognized his old friend as if he'd known the Apache maiden way back when. Other than that . . .

Other than that, Moon's night-vision was much like those not-so-old times of a mere decade or so ago, when the uniformed SUPD cop would respond to a 911 call from the agitated widow, and calm Loyola's fears about the latest outrage to visit her ten-acre farm.

Accepting the lady's invitation to "belly up to the table," the guest hung his black John B. Stetson on the back of one sturdy chair and seated himself in another. The modest fellow shrugged off Loyola's "Thank you so much!" for an unspecified favor that she was "so grateful" for. It is true that women know the way to a man's heart and also a fact that Mr. Moon knows how to express his appreciation—he let out a great big wa-hoo! when Loyola pulled a pan of hot cookies from the oven.

Those happy souls who expect blessings are seldom disappointed. Charlie Moon found the hot pastries to be very tasty. Without batting an eye, he'd have bet you ten to one that Loyola's recipe for oatmeal, piñon-nut, red chili pepper, and pimento cookies was a sure thing for a blue ribbon in next year's La Plata County Fair.

CHAPTER SIXTY-FIVE

GOVERNMENT WORK

Charlie Moon's strictly-business ex-girlfriend had no time for dreaming.

Special Agent L. M. McTeague and eighteen of her colleagues who were working the Cannibal Family case would be wide awake for thirty-six hours after the lady hung up on Charlie Moon. The Tiger Team would inspect the booking records for Granite Creek's Silver Mountain Hotel and every other hostelry within fifty miles for the period when the potential Trout was spotted by Charlie Moon. Rancher Hobart Watkins would be grilled about a woman he could barely remember until he finally lost his temper and ordered the relentless federal cops off the Little Texas.

The tireless FBI agents would also examine every available database to identify potential suspects.

The criteria for phase one of TROUT-Donner search were:

- *Female Caucasian (or Caucasoid), Age > Fifty-five.*

- *A criminal record involving felony offenses.*

The search produced 15,802 hits, which caused considerable moaning and groaning among the feds clustered about the computer terminal.

McTeague reminded her colleagues about the Snyder

Memorial Hospital massacre. Perhaps Trout had been the stand-in nurse. Team consensus was that it was worth a shot.

Specifying that the suspect should have sufficient training and/or experience to pass herself off as a qualified nurse reduced the population to a mere 18. After the backslapping and cheering were over, a sad-eyed statistician informed the Tiger Team that this result was "of limited utility." Why so? Because—for 12,044 subjects of the 15,802, the database listed "No Information" on medical qualifications. One way or another, the population must be narrowed down to a manageable number *based upon data actually available*.

The clever fellow behind the bifocals knew everything worth knowing about frequency, binomial and chi-squared distributions, not to mention standard deviations, inferences from sample means, and the like. Everyone knew he was right, but at that moment the statistician was the least popular member of the team.

Other approaches were tried, with no more success and no less "nit-picking" from the finicky academic. Somewhat subdued by meaningful glares from several armed colleagues, he decided to hold his tongue. But the man was not made of stone. When no one was looking, the critic would shake his head. Roll his eyes.

McTeague, who had been holding something back from her associates, decided it was high time to play her hole card. Not in the mood for advice from the learned opposition, she shot a warning glance at the human number cruncher who dreamed nightly about subtle implications of the Central Limit Theorem, potential forensic applications of the Leptokurtic Curve, and that gorgeous redheaded waitress at the Five-Spot Diner whom he lusted after and intended to woo and wed.

Well. Talk about your long shot.

No, not the statistician's aspirations regarding the shapely waitress. (She was eagerly awaiting the shy man's first "hello.") The long-shot reference was to the playing of the ace of clubs that Miss McTeague had up her sleeve.

Charlie Moon's former main squeeze mentioned her ex's

remark about Trout's opthalmological impairment. It was (McTeague suggested) just barely possible that sometime during her disreputable career, Trout, aka Daphne Donner, had sought medical treatment for strabismus. Or tropia. Or crossed eyes.

This was greeted with everything from "go for it!" to languid "why not?" shrugs.

A graduate of Harvard Law School advised her that a warrant would be required to search confidential medical databases.

As it happened, McTeague had already secured the necessary permissions from a federal judge, which foresight on her part enabled FBI computer specialists to immediately initiate searches of a multitude of medical databases. With a little luck, there would be a few cross-eyed females in the base list of 15,802 potential suspects. With a lot of luck, fewer than ten.

Six floors beneath them, in a subbasement, a Cray CX1 mainframe munched on bits and bytes of its digital lunch.

Crunchity-crunch.

The tension afflicting the FBI Tiger Team? Thick enough to slice with a Bowie knife and spread on sourdough bread.

A half-dozen slightly superstitious Tigers crossed their fingers.

Four team members prayed. (Three believers and an agnostic who habitually hedged her bets.)

A special agent from Reno (who talked to roulette wheels and dice) stared pleadingly at the computer terminal and whispered, "C'mon, baby—cough up Momma Cannibal's name!"

They waited for hours while thirty-six seconds passed into the past.

Beep! The result flashed on the Sony display.

"Well, bless my sweet soul!" The delighted lady at the keyboard turned to smile at her colleagues. "We got *one* hit, and it's from that group of eighteen that has enough medical training to pass as a nurse." Which (bless her sweet soul again) included an address.

The potential Trout had served as a U.S. Navy nurse until

she received a dishonorable discharge for purloining cocaine from the base pharmacy. And just last year, she had consulted a specialist in Detroit about her strabismus.

The Tiger Team let loose with lusty hurrahs, happy back-slappings, even an impromptu tap-dancing display by a limber young fellow from Kansas City, MO.

The ecstatic statistician? He treated himself to a hint of a smile.

At precisely 3 A.M. the following morning, seven armed-for-bear Bureau agents approached a remote farmhouse in North Dakota's Sheridan County. Excepting the raspy death rattle of a rusty windmill, there was not a sound on the moonlit prairie. Aside from a sizable family of hungry, beady-eyed rodents, no one was inside to resent their presence.

Some six months earlier, a Minneapolis bank (since failed) had foreclosed on the abandoned property.

Disappointed but not discouraged, the Bureau began a detailed search of the premises and grounds for any clue to the identity of the former inhabitants of the site aptly dubbed "Cannibal Farm." They would vacuum up every scrap of dusty debris in the house and outbuildings for detailed analysis, lift partial fingerprints from window glass and doorknobs, and examine every scrap of trash to determine preferences in such products as cigarettes, canned foods, toothpaste, and toilet tissue. The dogged special agents would also interrogate every neighbor within ten miles, and . . . No. Enough already.

Let it merely be said—for the benefit of any misguided citizen who might be considering a fling at counterfeiting, kidnaping, or bank robbery—federal cops are a tenacious lot.

EPILOGUE

On the Lakeshore

No, not the lovely lake set like a glistening jewel in the Columbine's alpine pasture. This body of water is considerably larger than the bijou Lake Jesse, and is located about 1,250 miles east of Charlie Moon's ranch. The reference is to Barkley Lake, which adorns the lush green hills of western Kentucky.

The character who has recently arrived at the lakeshore to close a deal on the rental of a seven-bedroom, three-bath log "cabin" is the same person who had forwarded the improvised explosive devices (detonators disabled) via FedEx to one Bill Smith, c/o Columbine Ranch, Granite Creek County, Colorado. (The Columbine has its own Zip Code, but in respect for Mr. Moon's privacy that information shall not be revealed.)

CONDUCTING FAMILY BUSINESS

The seventy-six-year-old woman (who prefers to think of herself as late-middle-aged) had an understandable distaste for credit cards and checking accounts. Such conveniences made it relatively easy for the legally constituted authorities to snoop about in one's private enterprises. Which was why she made the entire prepayment in cash.

"Well, well." The overweight real estate agent rubbed his palms together, eyed the neat stack of crispy greenbacks the lady had placed on his desk—and the purse she had taken it from. "That's a fair-size pile of money."

The client, who was "Mrs. Yolanda Hepplewhite" this month, snapped her oversized leather purse shut as a precaution. It would complicate matters if the nosy stranger got a look at the silenced .32-caliber automatic that she'd come *this close* to using during her fortuitous hotel encounter with the skinny Ute Indian whose continued presence among the living remained a festering thorn in her flesh. (For the record, she would as soon have collected samples of belly-button fuzz from so-called celebrities as their autographs.) "I'll move into the cabin immediately. The rest of my party will be arriving within the hour."

"Well, I hope y'all have a fine old time." The courteous businessman pretended not to notice how, when this client looked at him with her right eye—her left one seemed to be gazing at something behind him.

Her crooked smile betrayed a hint of amusement at his discomfort. "I'm sure that we shall."

The avaricious fellow pulled the currency close to his belly. "So what's the big event—a get-together of some sort?"

"A family reunion." She was reading the fine print in the rental agreement with her right eye. "But sad to say, it will not be all that large." Her tinted lips went thin. "What with one thing and another, there are less of us every year."

"I know what you mean." He breathed a heavy sigh. "All of my family's either moved away or in the cemetery."

Looking up from the contract, she blinked behind her trifocals. "You're all by yourself, then?"

He nodded. "Ever since my dear wife passed last September."

"I'm so sorry." She wasn't. "I just had a thought." She had. "We're planning a barbecue tomorrow night. Nothing fancy, mind you—but I would be so pleased if you would join us at the feast."

"Well, that's mighty nice of you." He put on a doubtful

look that was as artificial as her sorrow at his bereavement. "But I don't know that I should barge in, being an outsider and all."

"Nonsense. We will be delighted to have the pleasure of your company."

"D'you really mean that?"

"I certainly do." Her smile was sweet and charming. "And I will simply *refuse* to sign this contract unless you agree to be our guest of honor."

The real estate agent's good-natured chuckle shook his ample stomach. "Well, since you put it like that, I'll be much obliged to accept your invitation."

"Very well, then—it's settled." The so-called Mrs. Hepplewhite signed on the dotted line.

The rental agent slipped the signed contract into a desk drawer. "I sure do appreciate your invitation to supper tomorrow night. On the way, I'll stop by the deli and pick up some potato salad—"

"Don't bother." The gourmand licked her lips. "Just bring yourself."

THE EN—

No. Not to worry.

The plump Kentuckian did not end up as the main course at a Family picnic. Our amiable rental agent was spared that ignominious end.

Though the FBI's farmhouse raid in North Dakota was not a spectacular success, every run of bad luck has to end someday, and the Bureau finally got a break when a sleepy member of the cannibal clan carelessly stuck the *wrong* plastic rectangle into a slot on a gas pump in Cadiz, Kentucky. The VISA card, which had been stolen three days earlier in Chillicothe, Ohio, should have been discarded within twelve hours. That was one of Trout's Rules. Not caring to confess his blunder to the woman whom he regarded with justifiable terror, the fellow who committed the inexcusable error tossed the rejected card into a trash can already half filled with wadded blue paper towels and . . . hoped for the best.

Before the guest of honor showed up for the feast, Special Agent McTeague and sixteen male FBI comrades were joined by enough Kentucky state troopers to mount a successful assault on a medium-size Caribbean island. The rental cabin was surrounded; there would be no escape for "Yolanda Hepplewhite," who was busy preparing her mother's special secret-recipe BBQ sauce. They would also put an end to the vaunted A Team, which was comprised of the cross-eyed woman's three extremely mean brothers and a second cousin whose hobby was suffocating infant—

But that sadistic business is too horrific to mention.

What can be mentioned is that the FBI and state cops *did not take a single member of the Family alive.* Not because the felons were determined to fight it out until the bitter end. And it would be uncharitable to suggest that the mainly circumstantial evidence against the cannibal-murderers (which made a jury trial problematical) figured in the outcome. Nor was the bloody battle that ensued due to a miscalculation, or some kind of mix-up in signals.

It happened like this:

Just minutes before the suspects inside the cabin were to be notified that they were surrounded and had no sensible course but to surrender to the authorities—some person among those sworn officers of the law—whilst aiming a rifle equipped with a telescopic site at the cabin window for the worthy purpose of determining what was going on inside— apparently squeezed the trigger an ounce or so past its specified five-pound limit, thereby drilling a high-velocity, copper-jacketed bullet into the sadistic second cousin's left auditory canal, which projectile promptly exited his right ear.

The pulling of the trigger was, almost without a doubt, merely an unfortunate reflex action. It was most certainly an event that led to several wild shots being fired by "Yolanda Hepplewhite" and her brothers, which resulted in sufficient return fire from the cops to create general pandemonium and considerable loss of life inside the outlaw's rented cabin.

By one means or another, the structure caught fire and burned to the ground. Not a single member of the Family's ruling hierarchy survived.

The investigation conducted by the Department of Justice was complicated by the fact that several lawmen insisted that he (or she) had fired that first shot. It would have been helpful to have a bullet with rifling marks that could be matched to a weapon, and the slug was probably among those recovered from the burned rubble—but all were shapeless blobs of melted lead. Even if a pristine specimen had been recovered, there was no way of knowing which bullet among tens of dozens had passed through the alleged felon's head. The inevitable conclusion of the investigation was that during the "heat of the moment" and "general confusion," an "unfortunate mishap" had occurred.

As might be expected, there were persistent rumors of a conspiracy.

Those who were wont to repeat unsupported allegations asserted that "more than a dozen FBI employees" and "not a few uniformed troopers" knew who had fired the initial shot that had started the firefight.

Perhaps.

But if they did, not one of these upstanding lawmen was inclined to identify the pretty lady—or, for that matter, the steely-eyed state trooper who set fire to the cabin.

Here endeth the lurid account.

Read on for an excerpt from

A Dead Man's Tale

James D. Doss's new Charlie Moon mystery, available in
hardcover from Minotaur Books!

PROLOGUE

ELSEWHEN IN A FUZZY CHRONOLOGY

When times get hard, most of us manage to cinch our belts
up a notch or two and tough it out until the dawn of a brighter
day. But on those moonless nights when chill winds moan and
groan under the eaves and starving rats gnaw in the walls,
keeping body and soul together is easier for some than for
others. While our hardest-hit neighbors face home foreclo-
sures, extended layoffs, and diets heavy on macaroni, beans,
and rice, better-off citizens cut back on steak-and-lobster din-
ners, sunny Caribbean cruises, and other benefits that fall
into the category of sugar and spice and everything nice.

Then, there are the high-end outliers—those fortunates
who thrive in good times and bad.

Among that envied latter category, one such privileged
soul is Samuel Reed, PhD. The former professor of physics,
apparently sound of mind and limb, is happily optimistic
about his future. And why shouldn't he be? This prime-of-
life alpha male has a top-of-the-line trophy wife who is
about to celebrate her thirtieth birthday. Is the fellow well
heeled? Very much so and then some. The scientist-turned-
entrepreneur has sizable accounts squirreled away in several dozen banks and credit unions, and every dollar and
dime is federally insured. Floating atop that radiant lake of
liquidity is a fleet of lucrative investments. The remarkably
successful financier owns more prime real estate than a Wall
Street shyster could shake a crooked stick at—including that

upscale habitat where Sam Reed hangs his hat in Granite Creek, Colorado. As a sideline, he also turns a nice profit by placing wagers on major sporting events.

When envious friends inquire about the secret of his success, a cold-sober Sam Reed will assert that the process required years of detailed study of the ins and outs of investing, and recommend patience to those who aspire to accumulate an unseemly share of earthly treasures. After a double shot of rye whiskey, he might admit (with a sly wink) that he has benefited from "two or three lucky streaks," the first of which transformed him from Chevrolet to Mercedes within a few weeks. Neither explanation is wholly satisfying.

So what is the truth of the matter—how did a university professor with no prior record of accumulating filthy lucre manage to acquire a massive fortune? Therein lies the kernel of a sinister mystery, which has to do with the subject of Sam Reed's remarkable *memory*. It's not just that the gifted man can recall detailed market data for stocks and commodities and recollect practically everything there is to know about high-strung jockeys, wild-eyed quarter horses, and cool-as-ice NFL quarterbacks—plenty of aspiring millionaires have excellent memories and end up flat broke. If Reed is to be believed, he has the uncanny ability to remember—

But we get ahead of ourselves.

Perhaps it will be better to let Professor Reed describe what it is that he does. As it happens, the obstinate fellow won't do that until he is so disposed, and at present he is not. In a little while, as his options become limited, he might be. We shall see.

In the meantime, let us reconsider our earlier query: "And why shouldn't he be?" (happily optimistic about his future).

Because the fourth of June has arrived, that's why. This is the day when Samuel Reed's coconut-cream pie in the sky is destined to turn decidedly sour. As it happens, he has an appointment with that gloomy, cloaked personage who totes an oversized scythe on his bony shoulder.

Blissfully ignorant of his looming misfortune, the wealthy man is in for a big, bad surprise. At this very moment, Irene

Reed's faithful husband is homeward bound with an eighty-dollar box of birthday chocolates for his comely spouse. We find him in a gay, almost whimsical mood. We know this because Dr. Reed is crooning a happy tune. ("Lida Rose.")

Look out, Sam. Mr. D is about to enter, stage left.

Being something of a showman, the hollow-eyed performer appeared with a touch of fanfare—right on cue, a massive bronze bell dolefully began to toll the eleventh hour.

Samuel Reed's lighthearted crooning was not dampened by this discordant downbeat. Oblivious to the timely omen that was booming off his final seconds, the victim stepped into the abyss. It was not to be a peaceful, painless passing, as when a saintly aunt falls asleep to awaken in another, brighter world.

As a plump lump of spinning lead drilled its way through his chest, Sam's happy life was terminated in a searing agony—his heart and spine mangled beyond any hope of repair. About one and a half missing heartbeats later, another heavy projectile exploded from its brass casing to enter his left eye, and—there is no delicate way to put this—his cerebellum was transformed into a substance resembling lumpy oatmeal.

A classic instance of overkill.

Citizen Reed had kicked the proverbial bucket.

His chips were cashed in.

Curtains for certain.

End of the trail.

Why this seemingly excessive emphasis on the permanence of Samuel Reed's condition? Because—if one accepts the victim's testimony—his absence will prove transitory.

Seems unlikely in the extreme? Agreed. But in the interest of clarification and fair play, we shall allow the dead man to have his say. For which purpose, we must turn the clock back some thirty-two days.

CHAPTER ONE

10:54 p.m., May 3
Play it Again, Sam

Samuel Reed is every bit as cheerful as he had been (and would be again) on the evening of his untimely demise. As the jolly fellow slips along Shadowlane Avenue in his sleek gray Mercedes, he sings at the top of his fine tenor voice. ("Sweet Adeline.")

Without missing a beat, our happy crooner turns into a graveled driveway that snakes its way through a small forest of spruce and aspen before looping around his two-story, nine-bedroom, twelve-bath brick residence.

SOME STRANGE GOINGS-ON

Having activated a radio-frequency device on his key chain to open a twenty-foot-wide door, Sam Reed pulled into the spacious garage under his so-called guest house. Because Mr. and Mrs. R. rarely entertained overnight visitors, the upstairs apartment served as the businessman's at-home office. But even that designation was not entirely accurate; in actual practice, the quarters over the detached garage provided a quiet sanctuary upon those occasions when Irene was in one of her snarling-snapping moods. As it happened (and not by accident), Sam's spouse did not have a key to the guest house, nor did she have need of one. His better half kept her pink Cadillac in the attached six-car garage, where that symbol of GM's pre-Chapter 11 days was alone except for the lady's shiny new ten-speed bicycle.

Sam Reed parked his superb German motorcar beside his buff black Hummer and closed the garage door with his remote. Before getting out of his automobile, he reached across the seat to pick up the—

Pick up the *what*?

There was nothing on the passenger seat for his gloved fingers to grasp.

The driver blinked at the empty space. *Now what did I expect to find there?*

This reasonable question triggered the recollection of a chain of seemingly mundane events, which began with Reed's usual routine after a long, tiring day of turning tidy profits. He remembered locking the door of his downtown office over the Cattleman's Bank and clearly recollected walking down the stairway to emerge onto the parking lot.

So far, nothing remarkable.

Then . . . *The moment the cold air hit me in the face, I remembered that I had something important to do before driving home. Something to pick up for Irene . . . but what was it—something from the supermarket? No. I don't think so.* Like a big-mouth bass breaking water to gulp up a plump insect, the memory surfaced abruptly: *Oh, of course— I walked a few blocks down to the Copper Street Candy Shop and arrived just minutes before their ten thirty P.M. closing time.* Reed could still taste the delicious double espresso he'd tossed back while the proprietor was wrapping a box of gourmet chocolates in shiny silver foil. This latter recollection was particularly significant: the purchase of absurdly expensive sweets for the lady of the house occurred only once each year. *And then I walked back to the parking lot, got into my car and placed the box of chocolates on the passenger seat.*

This explained his reaching for a box of chocolates. Sort

of. His brow furrowed into a puzzled frown. *But the choco-lates are not there.* And Reed knew why: *Because I did not stop at the candy shop this evening.* Why? *Because Irene's birthday is a month away.* Which raised a relevant ques-tion: *What the hell is going on?* As trained scientists are wont to do at the drop of a beaker, he postulated a plausible theory: *I've been working too hard; my mind is playing tricks on me.* Even when endowed with a superior intellect (he reasoned), a minor malfunction was bound to occur from time to time.

Shrugging it off, Reed emerged from the Mercedes with his ivory-knobbed cane in hand and exited the garage by a side door facing the rear of his residence. He paused for a sweet moment to inhale a breath of the invigorating night air and treat his eyes to the silvery aspect of a half inch of late-spring snowfall. *What I need is a glass of wine and a good night's sleep.*

Alas, the prescription for what ailed him was to be found in neither bottle nor bed.

As he trod along, tugging a foreshortened moon shadow toward his home, a chill breeze wafted by to cool his face. Endowed with an exquisitely sensitive imagination that could be triggered into delightfully whimsical visions by the slight-est suggestion, the closet romantic was instantly transformed into a lean, hard-eyed mountain man—leaning into a blind-ing blizzard. To enhance the dandy fantasy, Sam Reed com-menced to croon a few lines of "Bury Me Not on the Lone Prairie," adjusting his pace so that the crunch-crunch of his pricey Florsheim Kenmoor shoes in the snow provided a synchronized rhythm to the melancholy old cowboy song. He was just about to bellow out the good part about *where coyotes howl and the wind blows free* when his shoe crunch-ing was accompanied by a distant downbeat.

From somewhere miles and weeks away, a half-ton bronze bell began to count off the eleventh hour.

Uh-oh?

No. Not tonight. This was not that dreaded End of the Trail.

But the dreadful tolling (which not another mortal soul could hear!) was suddenly accompanied by an extremely unpleasant phenomenon.

Samuel Reed's initial sensation was that a white-hot poker had been thrust through his chest. This assault was instantly followed by an agonizing pain behind his forehead. Believing that he was suffering a heart attack or a stroke or both, the stricken man staggered and almost fell. *This is it—poor Irene will find my frozen body here in the snow.*

Not so.

At the seventh peal of the imaginary bell, his pains began to diminish. At the eleventh and final gong, after a half-dozen rib-thumping heartbeats and half as many gasping breaths, they were gone. Professor Reed was fully recovered. A most welcome development, indeed—and one that should have been entirely gratifying.

But, by some means or other, he had become aware of a stark new reality: *Before much time has passed, I am destined to reside among the deceased.* And not due to natural causes.

Enough to make a man stop and think. Which he did.

I'm a goner unless I do something about it. Which he would.

In the meantime . . . *I'm glad this creepy experience is over.* It was not.

The first indication of *more to come* was a slight buzzing at the base of his skull. This was followed by a giddy sensation of weightlessness . . . as if the slightest breeze might blow him away like a dead cottonwood leaf.

What's this? The expectant fellow cocked his ear as if listening for something. Or perhaps *to* something.

Then . . . *Oh my goodness!*

Samuel Reed was suddenly bedazzled by a stunning jolt of mental clarity that would have felled a lesser man. As he looked up to see the moon's pockmarked face staring blankly back at him, his mouth curled into a grin that was a notch or two beyond silly. An uncharitable observer might have described the expression as teetering right on the ragged edge of *idiotic,* and concluded that the unfortunate fellow was suffering from an attack of lunacy.

Sam would have disagreed with that diagnosis, and asserted that he was experiencing a wonderful epiphany. But it is worth noting that the fellow is an authentic specimen of that gender whose members are frequently mistaken—but rarely in doubt.

What is the truth of the matter? We do not know. The jury is still out.

But right or wrong, the man grinning at the earth's silvery satellite was convinced that he understood precisely what had occurred. He threw back his head and enjoyed a hearty laugh.

This was—in a very real sense—a new beginning.